Bud by the Grace of God
Book Two of the Grace Lord Series

S. E. SASAKI

Oddoc Books
Erin, Canada

Editor: Robert Runté, PhD

For more information about the author and publisher, visit www.sesasaki.com

Published by:

Oddoc Books,
P.O. Box 580,
Erin, Ontario, Canada
N0B 1T0

ISBN 978-0-9947905-3-8

Want to Read More?

FREE DOWNLOAD

MUSINGS

Three eerie tales with a twist.

*A tragic, chilling story of Good versus Evil
repeated throughout time*

*A much-awaited homecoming that even Death
cannot stop*

*Adverse reactions to medical interventions can
sometimes have lethal consequences*

Sign up for the author's VIP mailing list and get Musings
for FREE!

http://www.sesasaki.net/musings-
free-book/

Acknowldgements

An enormous thank you goes to my wonderful husband, David Alan Sherrington, who is my invaluable, indispensable, and indefatigable advance reader, to whom I am greatly indebted, for making many vital suggestions during the writing of this book. *Bud by the Grace of God* would not be in the shape it is in, without his insightful comments and enthusiasm. My children, as always, thank you for being you and inspiring me every day to chase my dreams!

A grateful thank you to Ed Greenwood—writer, gamer, best-selling creator of *The Forgotten Realms*—for advance reading *Bud by the Grace of God* and lending his support and comments. Your enthusiasm, Ed, has meant the world to me.

Thank you to Robert Runté, editor and whip extraordinaire, who cajoled, ranted, insulted, and praised this work into a much better novel than it originally was. I am in your debt, Robert.

My gratitude to Ken Preston for going above and beyond in assisting me with book formatting and publishing and to James Simmons for all his computer know-how and self-publishing advice.

Again, a huge thank you to my real life heroes, the people who work in the Surgery Department of Guelph General Hospital in Guelph, Ontario, Canada. A more dedicated, self-sacrificing, kind, (and humorous) group of people, I will never find. I love you all. You work tirelessly, every day, to save lives. I feel honoured and privileged to work alongside you.

Prologue

He was seething with rage. He could not remember a moment, a second, an instant, since he had been entrapped by that insufferable android, SAMM-E 777, and that vacuous surgical fellow, Dr. Grace Lord, that he did not writhe internally with coruscating fury. The disgrace of being apprehended—the great Dr. Jeffrey Charlton Nestor—like a common criminal and accused of attempted murder was unbearable. Furthermore, the asinine medical space station AI—Artificial Idiot—having the audacity to lock him up in jail (albeit for only a very short period of time), burned in his memory like acid.

No matter how hard he tried, he could not expunge the memory of this outrage from his thoughts. The only way he could envision eradicating this inexcusable indignity from his mind was to exterminate all responsible for his humiliation and to erase all record of its occurrence. The knowledge that the fools who had had the effrontery, the impudence, the gall, to discredit him still lived, made him see blood. That they had not only pressed charges against him for attempted murder—a complete fabrication—but had also had his medical license revoked, was unforgivable.

Intolerable.

He would make them all pay. No one humiliated Dr. Jeffrey Charlton Nestor and got away with it.

No one!

Jeffrey Nestor stepped over the dead bodies of the two Security women who had helped him escape from the brig of the Nelson Mandela. They had placed his cryopod amongst empty ones being loaded onto an outgoing Conglomerate vessel and had then boarded the same vessel. They had secretly come to the cargo bay, where the empty cryopods were stored, to release him from his cryopod during the flight.

When they had located his 'pod via beacon, they had pulled the cryopod out into the open and freed him from it, bringing him fine new clothes to don. He had asked the women if they had inactivated the surveillance cameras in the cargo bay. They had replied in the affirmative. Had they secured the doors to the bay? Again, they had nodded. Jeffrey Nestor had then spoken a command—previously implanted in their minds—that induced a trance-like state in both women. In the low-g, they had both collapsed slowly to the cargo bay floor.

He had then forcefully yet dispassionately twisted both of their necks, until their vertebrae had ground and crunched. He stripped the clothing off of both women and shoved his hands into the larger woman's work gloves. Then he quickly placed each of their bodies in an empty cryopod, closing and locking the lids. Someone at the space vessel's destination was going to have a big surprise, when they opened these 'pods.

Jeffrey Nestor could not recall either of the women's names, but it did not matter. They were dead now and that was the important thing. Another loose end tied up.

The boots worn by the taller of the two women were an excellent fit. He scanned the cargo bay for the disposal chute. Locating it, he pressed the button to activate the atomizer and then threw all the belongings of both women down the chute. He decided to keep the work gloves. He also kept the taller woman's identification pass. He did not worry about the disruptors, placed by his accomplices onto the surveillance cameras. The crew of this space vessel would never be able to trace those disruptors to him.

Jeffrey Nestor suspected that the ship's security team might, very soon, be searching for him. Chances were, the captain of this ship had already been notified by the Nelson Mandela that Jeffrey Nestor had escaped from prison and could be stowing away on board. Having worked on these space cruisers when he was a student, Jeffrey was very familiar with their layout. He knew how easily the wall panels in the cargo bay could be removed and replaced, and how a thin, fit person could easily conceal themselves in the space behind them. Cables, ducts, and pipes ran behind those panels, but Jeffrey could squeeze himself between them and then replace the wall panel, hiding until the cargo bay had been completely searched. If they happened to find the dead women, the search crew would never expect the murderer to stay hidden in the walls of the cargo bay, where the bodies were found. It was the perfect hiding place.

He would stay in the space transport until they reached their destination. When they started off-loading the cryopods, he would wait until all the cargo bay was unloaded and then he would disembark. He knew just where he had to go. He knew exactly whom he needed to see. There were black market sources he needed to contact, to acquire some very important items—illegal technology that was banned on any vessel with an AI—and then he would be set.

In the meantime, he would count each day he had to suffer with his memories of humiliation and he would make that bitch Grace Lord suffer ten-fold. He would never forgive her for making him have to skulk around and hide in such a degrading fashion. Vengeance could not come quickly enough, last long enough, or be severe enough, but it would last a lifetime for Grace Lord.

Her lifetime.

1. What Is So Funny?

"Dr. Grace, you're fired. Have I not made it as clear as the distinguished nose in the center of this dashingly handsome face of mine, that I do not like you to be late?"

Dr. Hiro Al-Fadi, Chief of Staff and Chief of Adaptation Surgery on the *Nelson Mandela*, sat on one of the couches in the doctors' lounge on M1 Level. He was a small man with thick, bushy, dark brown eyebrows and very expressive brown eyes that, at the moment, were looking very annoyed. His arms were crossed and his fingers were tapping his sleeve, as his mouth curled downward into a disapproving moue.

"Yes, Dr. Al-Fadi, you have," said Grace, choosing to ignore the dismissal by her boss.

"Then why do you continue to disobey me?" the little surgeon demanded.

"I am sorry, Dr. Al-Fadi. At the beginning of this shift, one of your patients was having a crisis and I was called in to deal with it. It was rather a difficult situation and I could not get away on time," Grace said, now staring up towards the blank ceiling.

"Nothing short of the patient almost dying would appease me right now, Dr. Grace, as I am in a very tetchy mood." Since his recent resurrection, the Chief of Surgery looked much younger than the Dr. Al-Fadi Grace had originally met, and he certainly did not look his age right now, with his arms folded and his hair standing straight up in a burgundy-coloured mohawk. Grace could not even look at the Chief of Adaptation Surgery for fear of exploding into peals of uncontrollable laughter. All she could do was stare over his head at the ceiling, while she dug her nails viciously into her palms.

"Well, your patient *was* trying to commit suicide when I was paged to his room, Dr. Al-Fadi, so technically that could be classified as 'almost dying'," Grace said, her eyes beginning to water as she grit her teeth and fought for control.

Just at that moment, Dr. Dejan Cech, a tall, thin anesthetist and close friend of Dr. Al-Fadi, sidled past Grace to enter the doctors' lounge. He nodded his head at Grace and then stared at Dr. Al-Fadi, as he went to sit on a couch across from the chief.

"Oh. . . . ? Which patient was that?" the Chief of Adaptation Surgery asked, his tone changing from petulant to a little more conciliatory.

"Private Jason Verra," Grace said.

The surgeon's thick eyebrows lowered.

" . . . The orangutan adaptation with the crushed lower limb?"

"Yes, that is correct." Grace tried to keep her eyes off of Dr. Cech's frowning face.

"Why was Private Jason Verra trying to kill himself . . . and how?" the small surgeon asked, his brown eyes now large and looking quizzically at Grace.

Grace noticed that Dr. Al-Fadi's impressive eyebrows now formed a deep V-shaped furrow in his forehead, which aligned nicely with his mohawk and made his face look like an arrow pointing down towards his very impressive nose.

"Well, we don't think it was a real suicide attempt, since he tried to hang himself from the ceiling with a bed sheet and he is an orangutan-adapt," Grace said. "Verra just ended up bringing the ceiling down in his room; but we are taking it seriously enough to have one of the head doctors see him this shift."

"What in space has gotten the boy so upset that he wants to kill himself?" Dr. Al-Fadi asked, incredulous. "I spent four hours fixing the boy up. Has he no respect for my time and expertise? He should feel himself truly honored that he has a limb from the Great Dr. Hiro

Al-Fadi! He should consider himself blessed."

"Private Verra is in love," Grace sighed.

"In love! In love with who?" Dr. Al-Fadi barked. "No, don't tell me, Dr. Grace. It doesn't matter. Unrequited love is no reason to kill oneself. My goodness, is the boy daft? I ought to go and beat some sense into the boy ... with his new limb, no less! Does he have any idea how much work was involved attaching that new limb? He wanted to throw all that beautiful work away ... for love? The kid needs a brain transplant, not a new limb."

Grace chomped down on her lower lip—hard—and blocked her mind from thinking about who should be having a brain transplant.

" . . . Jason Verra met a female patient with whom he has fallen madly in love. But he knows there is no future for them, so he decided to kill himself. He claims he would rather die than live without her."

"By any chance, did you, Dr. Cech, accidentally drop this lad on his head when he was being transferred to the recovery room? What is this nonsense? Who is this love interest?"

"You just told Dr. Lord that you didn't want to know, Hiro," Dr. Cech pointed out, shaking his head. "Make up your minuscule mind. Poor Grace can barely get the story out, without you interrupting her. And by the way, I want you to know—so there is absolutely no doubt whatsoever—your hair makes me think that you have truly lost your mind."

"You probably don't want to know who the love interest is, Dr. Al-Fadi," Grace almost whimpered, trying not to scream with laughter, as she gazed through the tears building up in her eyes at Dr. Cech's disapproving expression.

"I don't. But who is she anyway? Kindly indulge my curiosity, Dr. Grace," Dr. Al-Fadi said, "while I think of a fitting retort to Dr. Cech's insult."

"You're slo-ow. You're so slo-ow," Dr. Cech sang softly, taunting the diminutive surgeon.

"Soldier Dalia Anquetin," Grace said. Her entire body was trembling now, as she fought the urge to explode into gales of howling laughter ... especially now that Dr. Cech was teasing Dr. Al-Fadi.

"Not that gorgeous, seal-adapted patient with the slinky . . .? Oh boy. No wonder the poor kid wants to kill himself. What in space would Anquetin see in an orangutan-adapted kid? Is she just toying with the poor boy?" asked Dr. Al-Fadi.

"That is not my understanding," Grace offered, taking deep breaths and closing her eyes. "The nurses say they believe she has definite feelings for him, too."

"A seal in love with an orangutan? How in the world did they even get near each other? Aren't the nurses supposed to keep these animal adaptations apart? What are we running here, a bloody menagerie or a hospital?"

"From what I understand, the two met in the physiotherapy department. Some surgeon, who shall remain nameless, recommended pool therapy for Private Verra's limb. It was not I, by the way. That very same surgeon also recommended pool therapy for a certain seal-adapted patient of the sleek, sensuous shape. I guess they decided to help each other out with their therapy by doing some stretching and . . ."

"Stop! I did not mean that kind of therapy!" Dr. Al-Fadi squeaked. "Give me the name of their physiotherapist, so I can kill the bastard, myself. Flogging is too good for the idiot. I shall have to devise a really horrible death, so the other physiotherapists will learn from this and not make the same mistake."

"Sounds to me like it's the *surgeon* who needs the flogging," Dr. Cech said dryly. "And I would be most happy to lend an eager helping hand. Hmmm. As punishment, perhaps you could have the poor scapegoat physiotherapist stare at you—with that ridiculous mohawk of yours—for a full shift. That would be enough to kill anyone. They would certainly die laughing. I hope and pray that your lovely wife, Hanako, has not already succumbed to mirth, by the way, Hiro. You aren't intentionally trying to kill *her* with your ridiculous hairdos, are you?"

"My wife?" Dr. Al-Fadi repeated, his eyes bugging out. "My wife loves my hair."

"I bet you everything I own that she hates it," Cech said. He leaned far forward, elbows on his knees, and stared directly into Dr. Al-Fadi's eyes.

The small surgeon scowled back at the tall anesthetist, his mohawk vibrating with indignation. He proceeded to bite his lips and suck them into his mouth. His little body began to quiver. Tears started to form at the corners of the surgeon's eyes. Hiro Al-Fadi finally exploded into a loud guffaw and nodded, almost blubbering.

"She detests it, Dejan. Like you, she thinks I look ridiculous," the surgeon finally admitted, with a sheepish expression. "I just wanted to get your reaction. Flaunt my new hairstyle at you and make you wish you had hair."

Dr. Cech's eyebrows tried to leap off of his forehead, as he sat back and said, "Want hair like that? You look like a rooster in heat."

"You're just jealous." Dr. Al-Fadi announced, as he ran his hand back and forth through his mohawk.

"Watch out, Dr. Lord," Dejan Cech said, shaking his head. "Don't let him get too close. Make sure Dr. Al-Fadi does not fling any head lice your way. I hear the critters love the color burgundy."

Grace chomped down hard on her lips but a snort escaped her nostrils.

"Don't . . . even . . . think . . . of laughing, Dr. Grace," Dr. Al-Fadi warned, in a low, threatening tone, glaring at her with narrowed eyes. "Surgical fellows have died for less."

"I'mgoingtogoandcheckontheOR," Grace spat out and raced from the lounge.

Grace poked her head into the operating room where Bud, Dr. Al-Fadi's surgical assisting android, was busy setting up the instruments. The android, who had the classical beauty of a Greek God, took one look at Grace and rushed over.

"Grace, are you all right?" Bud asked, an expression of concern on his handsome, flawless face.

Grace shook her head, both hands now clapped firmly over her mouth, her eyes watering.

"Are you upset, Grace? Are you hurt?" the android asked.

She frantically shook her head and ran out of the operating room.

Bud hurried after her, asking, "Did you bite your tongue, Grace? Does your tooth hurt? Do you feel nauseous? Did you break your nose? Are you choking? Can I do anything for you . . .?"

Grace raced down the hall as fast as she could, past the entrance to the doctors' lounge, shaking her head back and forth. She wanted to get as far away from Dr. Al-Fadi as possible, before the uncontrollable laughter overwhelmed her. She blinked back the tears blurring her vision.

As she finally exited the M1 surgical ward, great, belly-aching guffaws exploded from her, and she doubled over. She leaned against a wall, gasping for air, laughing until she sobbed. She slowly collapsed to the floor, her arms wrapped tightly about her waist, as she wept from her aching abdominal muscles. She knew she was attracting unwanted attention from passersby, but she could not stop the howling laughter. Bud was now crouched in front of her, his face a mask of concern.

"Grace! What is wrong? You are laughing and crying at the same time! What does this mean? Are you happy? Are you sad? How can I help you?"

Grace shook her head, wiping the tears away with her fingers, as she tried to stop laughing. She was sniffing and gulping air and breaking down into cackles of laughter, no matter how hard she tried to stop. If she closed her mouth tightly, squeezing her lips shut with her fingers, only whimpers could escape. She tried to think about anything but her boss.

"What is it, Grace? You can tell me," Bud insisted, gently holding Grace by the upper arms.

"Oh, Bud," Grace gasped, sucking in air. "I can't go into the operating room with Dr. Al-Fadi today. I can't face him across the operating table. I just can't!"

"Why not, Grace?" Bud asked, tipping his head to the side. "What has Dr. Al-Fadi done?"

"He has a bu-bu-burgundy mohaaawwwk!" she cried.

"What is a bu-bu-burgundy mohaaawwwk?" Bud mimicked, a confused expression on his beautiful face. Grace choked up.

"It is Dr. Al-Fadi's new haircut, Bud," *Nelson Mandela* pitched in.

"What is so funny about Dr. Al-Fadi's hair?" Bud asked. "Will it not be covered by a surgical cap in the operating room?"

"Yes, of course. You're right, Bud. His hair will be covered by a surgical cap," Grace said, gaining control. Taking some very deep breaths, Grace sat up and wiped her eyes. She shook herself and said, very slowly, "I can do this. I can do this. I can do this."

Each time Grace repeated this, she said it with more conviction. She repeated it over and over, like a mantra, as she composed her face and let Bud help her up. She headed back towards M1 Ward and the operating room, with Bud glancing worriedly at her face, his expression one of concern.

"I can do this. I can do this," Grace sang softly, as she walked. She felt she was finally getting herself under control. She would be fine. Dr. Al-Fadi, her supervisor, would have a surgical cap on and she would not even be able to see his . . .

Dr. Al-Fadi and Dr. Cech stepped out of the doctors' lounge right into Grace and Bud's path. Dr. Al-Fadi's eyes bugged out at her in surprise. Grace immediately spun around, hands slapped to her mouth and ran, mumbling, "I can't do this! I can't do this! I can't do this! I can't do this!"

"What is wrong with Dr. Grace?" Dr. Al-Fadi asked Bud, his thick, dark eyebrows lowered into a frown. "She is acting very strangely."

"She says she cannot work in the OR today, Dr. Al-Fadi," Bud said. "I believe it may possibly be . . . gastroenteritis . . .?"

"Really! Well, tell her to keep away from the operating room then! We can't have anyone vomiting in there! Tell her to go get some rest, practice better hand hygiene . . . and stay as far away from me as she possibly can!"

"Yes, sir!" Bud said. As he hurried off to tell Grace the good news, he heard his creator yell after him, "Tell her not to give it to any of our patients!"

He found her two corridors away, leaning against a wall, bent over, clutching her abdomen again, wheezing and weeping.

When he told her the news, Grace said, "Oh, thank you, Bud. I could not operate with Dr. Al-Fadi today without laughing uncontrollably. You don't find his hair funny?"

"I don't think I understand what 'funny' is, Grace," Bud admitted.

"But I have seen you laugh, Bud," Grace insisted.

"I can make the sound of laughter, as you all do, but I do not understand why you laugh, Grace. I do not understand what is meant by 'funny'."

"When you look at Dr. Al-Fadi with his purple hair sticking up like a brush, what do you think?"

"I think how lucky I am to have him as my creator. I respect everything Dr. Al-Fadi does, Grace," Bud stated. "I would never think critically of him."

Bud's confession sobered Grace up immediately, like a splash in the face. She tried to think of a way to explain to the android why she thought Dr. Al-Fadi's mohawk was funny. The more she thought about it, the less she could come up with a logical explanation and she suddenly felt very confused.

"I'm sorry, Bud. I believe I am just embarrassed for Dr. Al-Fadi. Perhaps we can talk about this later," Grace said, now feeling very ashamed. "You had better get back to the OR."

"Yes, Grace. Thank you," Bud said. Then he was gone, leaving Grace to ponder about humour and how to explain such a concept. He had left her very bewildered about it herself.

Grace was heading back towards the surgical wards to check up on her lovesick orangutan soldier, when a young, medium-height man with a surgical mask over his nose and mouth ran into her. He had the largest brown eyes she had ever seen and they looked panicky, as they focused on her.

"Are you a doctor?" he asked, grabbing Grace by the left upper arm to prevent himself from crashing right into her.

"Yes," Grace said, startled, trying to step back.

"Good," the young man said, his grip tightening on her arm. "Come!"

He dragged her towards the obstetrical operating rooms and Grace thought, 'Oh, no. Not again.'

"You are an obstetrician, aren't you?" Grace asked.

The young man turned his huge brown eyes on her and said, "Yes. How did you know?"

"Oh, just a lucky guess," Grace sighed, as she recalled being commandeered by a very tall obstetrician, Dr. Papaboubadios, to help with a Caesarian section. Dr. Papaboubadios had died in the viral epidemic that had hit the station only weeks before. This young man must be one of the obstetricians recruited to replace the doctors who had died. She was pulled along, trapped in his grip. Obviously, he was worried that she would make her escape if he let go.

"You aren't doing anything important, are you?" the young man asked in a whining voice. "I need help *now*."

"Nothing as important as what you are up to, I imagine," Grace said.

"Good," the young man sighed, as they arrived outside an operating room. "Now *scrub!*"

Grace jerked at this last command and nearly told the obstetrician to find someone else, but she knew what it was like to be desperately in need of urgent assistance. She quickly donned a surgical cap and mask. Then she scrubbed her hands and arms before sticking her hands in the sterilizer and glover. She quickly followed the young obstetrician into the operating theater, wondering what she was going to see this time.

"Ah, Dr. Lord. What a pleasure to see you again. Out of the clutches of that megalomaniac for the moment, are you?" rumbled a very deep voice.

"It is good to see you again as well, Dr. Darwin. You are looking well," Grace said.

"Well? I look huge. I look more enormous than this fine pregnant young lady on the table here. . . but thank you for lying," the anesthetist said. Then he made some growling sounds that Grace took to be his laughter.

"Private Lukaku, this is Dr. Lord. She is another doctor and she is going to help me with your delivery. Are you feeling comfortable?" the obstetrician asked.

"No, Doctor," moaned Private Lukaku, who happened to be the largest polar bear female Grace had ever seen. Her great, protuberant belly rose up from the operating table like a mountain. "I'm in the midst of a contraction and . . . it . . . HURTS!" the patient roared. Grace winced from the shooting pain in her eardrums.

The obstetrician looked pointedly at the anesthetist.

"Give the epidural a bit of time, Doctor. The nanobots have to get to the right spot and she is a large lady—not meaning any disrespect, Private Lukaku."

"None . . . taken," the polar bear female grunted out, between breaths.

"The drugs just need a little bit more time to take effect," Dr. Darwin explained to the patient while glaring back at the young obstetrician. "I'll raise the dose."

"The baby's fetal heart rate is dropping," the obstetrician snapped. "When will we be able to start?"

"Once she is anesthetized," Dr. Darwin said in an exasperated voice.

The obstetrician made a 'tsk' sound and shook his head. As Grace and the obstetrician gowned, a skinbot shaved the patient's fur and sterilized her skin. She wondered when the obstetrician was going to introduce himself to her, but realized he would not want to reveal to Private Lukaku that Grace was a complete stranger to him. The sterilization field was activated and the obstetrician asked Dr. Darwin to lower the operating table.

"It's as low as it's going to get, Shorty," Darwin said. "You'll have to get a booster seat."

The obstetrician shot Dr. Darwin an affronted look and asked for the floor height to be adjusted for both himself and Dr. Lord.

The floor of the operating theater rose, on either side of the operating table, to a satisfactory height for both Grace and the young obstetrician. Chuck Darwin looked over at Grace and rolled his eyes.

The obstetrician took a pair of forceps and pinched Private Lukaku's skin along the lower abdomen.

"Do you feel anything, Private Lukaku?"

"Nothing you are doing," she replied.

"You may proceed, Doctor," Dr. Darwin announced, loudly.

The young doctor's eyebrows rose and he replied, stiffly, "Thank you, Doctor."

Grace inwardly groaned. There was far too much testosterone spewing about this operating suite, as far as she was concerned. It was enough to put hair on her chest.

Just then, a huge tiger-adapted male was led into the operating theater and directed to sit by the head of Private Lukaku. She wondered if he had been led into the wrong room. She had expected a polar bear father. He bent over and kissed the woman's face. Grace wondered how these two ever got together. It was rare for the Conglomerate to station two such different animal adaptations on the same planet or station.

"We have to deliver this baby via Caesarian section," the obstetrician said, "because Private Lukaku's musculature is so powerful, her contractions could actually crush her baby. She had the C-section booked for a few shifts from now, but suddenly went into labor."

Grace nodded, as she assisted the obstetrician in opening up the abdomen and then the uterus, to deliver the very tiny, purplish-hued human baby.

"It's a beautiful baby girl," Grace breathed, as the obstetrician handed the baby to her. Grace gently placed the mask over the baby's face that would efficiently suck all the fluid from her lungs, while the obstetrician lasered the cord. The babe immediately started to cry, loudly and heartily, exhibiting a very healthy set of lungs. Private Lukaku burst into tears.

Grace passed the baby to the android nurse, who would clean the baby off, before handing the infant up for the mother to hold. Lukaku sniffled quietly as the placenta was delivered. The father just nuzzled her.

"What are you going to name your baby girl?" asked Grace, while they were closing the abdomen.

"Estelle Malala Rasmussen," the mother stated.

"Estelle. What a beautiful name," Grace said.

"Please pay attention, Dr. Lord!" the young obstetrician snapped.

Grace jumped, as if stung. She was paying attention! She was certain she had a few more years of operating experience over this young man and, after the procedure was done, she thought she just might let him know it.

Chuck Darwin's eyes met hers and he rolled his eyes again.

Grace did not say another word until the dressing was on and the sterilization field was dropped. She looked at the silent couple with their solemn faces. The baby had not been given to either parent.

"Congratulations, you two, on your lovely daughter, Estelle," Grace said.

"Thank you," Private Lukaku murmured, not meeting Grace's eyes.

The tiger man, tears in his eyes, choked out a 'thank you' as well. Then he stroked the face of his partner with a sad look on his face.

Grace thought, 'Oh, no. Not again.' Her mind went back to the snow leopard couple, Corporal Dris Kindle and her partner, who had looked exactly the same way, when they were giving up their twin babies for adoption.

Grace turned to Chuck Darwin and said, "Always a pleasure to work with you, Dr. Darwin."

"Same back at ya," the large man said, and winked.

And then, completely ignoring the overbearing, obnoxious obstetrician, Grace stalked out.

2. Androids Have No Rights

Grace was fuming as she strode towards the surgical wards. Her wristcomp buzzed and she checked its screen. The display read: Go to Reception Bay 17. Please meet Jude Luis Stefansson for me. Hiro.

Grace stopped in her tracks. Jude Luis Stefansson? Not *The* Jude Luis Stefansson? The famous gorgeous interactive vid star? Couldn't be. What would someone like him be doing on a medical space station? Unless he was here to make a vid? Or possibly he got injured while making a vid? Grace had immersed herself in several of Stefansson's interactive vids over the years. His were the best, by far, out there.

Grace decided it probably was not the same individual visiting the *Nelson Mandela*, but she decided to take a quick detour to her quarters to freshen up and to change into a clean, pressed military uniform, just in case. It would not do to greet an important visitor in her wrinkled, shabby operating room scrubs. A quick shower, a little makeup couldn't hurt, she thought.

Her little voice yelled, 'A lot of makeup.' She told it to shut up.

Examining herself in the mirror, before heading down to the Reception Area, Grace was dismayed and resigned to the fact that, even in her military uniform and cosmetics, there was not much that would make her look other than like a pale, tired, overworked surgeon. Deciding that it was pointless to moan over it, she jumped on the station's monorail and headed for Reception Bay 17 as the haggard, baggy-eyed, exhausted Lieutenant Grace Lord, M.D.

As the high-speed monorail train pulled into the station leading to Reception Bay 17, Grace noticed a larger than usual crowd heading towards the reception area.

Bud instantly appeared beside her.

"Grace," he said, looking around, "what are all these people doing here, blocking the way to Reception Area 17?"

"I believe they are all here to see Jude Luis Stefansson," Grace said.

Bud looked confused. "But Dr. Al-Fadi sent *us* to meet the man. There is no need for all these people to meet the same person. This is not logical."

"They all want to see Jude Luis Stefansson, Bud. He is a famous director and vid star. People want to see famous people. It's a human thing . . . *Nelson Mandela*, would you page all of these people to go back to work?" Grace asked.

There was an overwhelming moan that rose up from the mass of gawkers. Slowly, the crowd began to disperse. Grace and Bud were finally able to get close to the hatchway door that led from the airlock of Reception Bay 17. There was an area cordoned off by security androids but Grace and Bud were allowed through, as per Dr. Al-Fadi's explicit orders. Grace asked the station AI how long they would have to wait.

"The shuttle has already arrived, Dr. Lord. It will not be long before your visitor can disembark and make his way towards the reception area. He must pass through security clearance first. He is not the only passenger on the shuttle and the porters are off-loading some cryopods as well."

"Thank you, *Nelson Mandela*," Grace said.

"You are most welcome, Dr. Lord," the station AI said.

Grace glanced at her reflection in a mirrored wall of the Reception Area and began to fiddle with her hair. Bud watched her with a blank expression on his face.

"Who is this Jude Luis Stefansson, Grace? Why were all of those women waiting to see him?" Bud asked.

"Well, for one thing, Bud, he is very tall, muscular, and handsome. He is a genius in his field and he always plays the hero, who is highly attractive to a woman's psyche. He is also very successful, wealthy, and single, which makes him of special interest to single women. And, I believe people just love to see celebrities."

"I have never experienced an interactive vid, but I see now that there are billions of references to this Jude Luis Stefansson," Bud said, his eyebrows curved down into a puzzled frown. "I shall get up-to-date on our visitor, now."

"You should experience one of Jude Luis Stefansson's vids, Bud," Grace said. "*Destruction of Darkness* is his best, in my opinion. Choose to play the lead, Jazz Hazard. You will love it."

"I will?" Bud asked, his eyebrows suddenly rising and his eyes widening.

People started to emerge from the airlock into the Reception Area: two women and an older man. They were met by their assigned greeters and left the Reception Area. Grace and Bud waited. The airlock cycled through again, and several people came through this time, none looking like Jude Luis Stefansson. Grace shuffled about impatiently, peeking through the windows into the Docking area, which was a waste of time since everyone out there was in a containment suit or spacesuit. While she was peering out there, all the lights in the Docking Bay blacked out, although the lights in their Reception Area were still on.

"*Nelson Mandela*, what is happening out in the Docking Bay?" Grace asked.

"Something has caused a disruption of the lighting system. I am re-routing power and the lights should be coming on . . . now."

Illumination filled the Docking Bay and activity resumed, as if nothing had happened.

More people disembarked from the shuttle and passed through into Reception Area 17, but no one that looked like Jude Luis Stefansson. Grace's face creased with concern. "Perhaps Mr. Stefansson did not make the flight? Could Dr. Al-Fadi have gotten the arrival time wrong? Perhaps we are at the wrong Reception Area?"

By now, there was no one else around except for one rather short, balding, middle-aged man in a spacesuit, with a narrow face and a grizzled, salt-and-pepper beard.

"*Nelson Mandela*, did Jude Luis Stefansson disembark?" Grace asked.

"Of course he did, Dr. Lord."

"Where is he?" Grace asked.

"Standing right in front of you, Dr. Lord."

She blinked at the balding middle-aged man and frowned.

"Excuse me," the small man said, approaching Grace. "I could not help but overhear you mention my name to the station AI. I am Jude Luis Stefansson. I was expecting to meet Dr. Hiro Al-Fadi here."

Grace's mouth dropped open before she was able to snap it closed again. The skin of Grace's cheeks hit ignition and liftoff; the heat from them was truly impressive.

"Oh, Mr. Stefansson. I do apologize!" Grace said, sweat pouring down her temples.

"No need to apologize, Lieutenant. I know I don't quite look like I appear in my vids. Please do not feel embarrassed. This happens to me all the time," he said, with an abashed smile.

"It is a huge pleasure to meet you, sir," Grace said, her cheeks actually feeling like they were swollen from the heat. "My name is Grace Lord. This is Bud. We have been sent by Dr. Al-Fadi to greet you and to accompany you to your quarters. He is wrapped up in a meeting at this moment, but will come to see you as soon as he is free. I do apologize for the confusion. I have seen all of your vids and so I was . . ."

" . . . expecting to see a tall, gorgeous hunk of a male. I know," the small man said, nodding. "No need to apologize, Grace—may I call you Grace?—I am used to it. It is my penance for not playing myself in the vids but creating the 'epitome of masculinity' to play my roles. My entire life has consisted of disappointing people."

"I'm not," Grace said. "Disappointed, I mean. I think your work is pure genius, Mr. Stefansson, and it is an incredible honor to meet you."

"You are being much too kind to an old man, but thank you," the director said, with a slight bow. "Now, where do I go to collect my luggage?"

"That will be taken care of, sir," Bud said. "May I lead you to your quarters?"

"Thank you, Bud," Stefansson said. "You aren't, by any chance, Bud Al-Fadi, the person who isolated the cell-melting virus and developed the vaccine against it?"

"It was a collaborative effort, sir. No one individual can take credit for the solution to the crisis," Bud said.

"It was entirely your doing, Bud," Grace insisted. "You must stop being so modest."

"Forgive me, Dr. Lord, but you and many other staff were also instrumental in the isolation and analysis of the virus. There were also thousands of androids and robots working continuously, performing critical experiments that led to the isolation of the vaccine. I could never have done the work all on my own," Bud said. "To say I did anything single-handedly, Dr. Lord, would be incorrect."

"Yes, of course, Bud," Grace sighed.

"Are you Dr. Hiro Al-Fadi's son?" the director asked, his blue eyes looking Bud up and down, appraisingly.

"No," Bud said.

"Are you a relative?" Stefansson asked, his brows furrowed.

"No," Bud said.

The interactive vid director looked like he was about to ask Bud more questions, when Grace jumped in with: "Right this way, Mr. Stefansson." She took the director's arm and led him out of the Reception Area, towards the monorail. They passed several beautiful young women, scantily dressed in the latest revealing scalewear. They were racing to Reception Area 17, all giggly and effervescent. Grace felt sorry for them. They would have been shocked to discover that they had just run past Jazz Hazard.

Bud took Grace and Jude Luis Stefansson to an area of the medical station that Grace had not yet visited. It was in the innermost ring and was designated for VIPs—Very Important Patients. The suite to which Bud led Jude Luis Stefansson was massive and beautifully furnished.

"Are all quarters on this medical station like this?" the director gasped, his mouth hanging open as he swiveled his head.

"No, sir. Unfortunately, this is the largest suite we have on the station," Bud said.

"You misunderstand me, Bud," Jude Luis Stefansson said. "I did not expect to be staying in a huge suite like this. I really don't need all of this space."

"Dr. Al-Fadi's orders, sir," Bud said.

"Please, the two of you, I would much rather you call me 'Jude' than 'sir'."

"All right, Jude," Grace said, with a smile.

Bud said, "Yes, sir."

The director just raised his eyebrows and stared at Bud, until Bud finally said, "Yes, sir, Jude . . . sir."

Grace smiled. "It took Bud weeks before he would call me 'Grace'. Just give him some time."

Jude smiled and nodded. Then he strolled around the spacious apartment.

"Ah. My luggage has arrived already. Your crew is astonishingly efficient and it appears to all be here. Probably a first for me, in all of my travels around the Union of Solar Systems," Jude commented, with a crooked grin.

"Perhaps because this is a medical space station rather than a hotel?" Grace said, returning the grin.

The director just shook his head as he stared at his luggage in wonder. Grace noticed an enormous rectangular crate, about the size of a cryopod, and wondered what could be inside it. Would this man carry around his own cryopod?

Jude, following the direction of Grace's intent gaze, said: "No, it does not contain a dead body. It is the immersion tank in which I create my interactive vids. Every physiological parameter one could possibly measure in the body—heart rate, respiratory rate, body temperature, muscle tension, perspiration rate, blood pressure, etc. —is recorded by the monitors and probes within my tank and, as I create and visualize my story, the brain signals, eye movements, vocalizations, imagined smells and sounds, are all recorded at once on a multitude of tracks so that you can have the most vivid experience possible."

"You live every story you tell," Grace said.

"I *immerse* myself in it and then the information is edited, embellished, and enhanced," Jude said.

"But in some of your tragedies, you die," she said.

"Well, I haven't actually gone that far in real life, Grace. I would not want to accidentally kill off my fan base by making them go through a real death experience. Bad for business. Bad for myself. Usually we do not allow people to remain immersed in the characters who die. They are always transferred out to another character's point of view before the tragedy occurs.

"There have been reports of myocardial infarction and stroke in people who have experienced death in interactive vids—none of mine—but I have heard of a few cases, so I am very careful what the viewer is exposed to. As you know, the interactive tanks are supposed to automatically shut down if a viewer's vitals become worrisome—like elevated blood pressure or heart rate, cardiac arrhythmias, that sort of thing."

"Yes, " Grace said. "A good policy. Well, Jude, we have taken up enough of your time. I am sure you would like to get changed and out of your spacesuit; perhaps get some rest before you meet with Dr. Al-Fadi."

"Here is your medical station wristcomp, Mr. Stefansson, sir," Bud said. "It will help you locate any area of the station you are allowed to visit. Because you are neither medical personnel nor an employee of the station, there are many areas that, unfortunately, will be off limits to you."

The band automatically coiled snugly around the director's left forearm, the comp face sitting squarely on the back of his wrist.

"Will I be able to return to my ship anytime?" the director asked.

"That should not be a problem," Bud said. "You came in your own ship?"

"Yes, the *Au Clair*. It is essentially my home, because I am always scoping out new exotic locations for my next vid. Depending on how long I stay here, I may need to go fetch some things from it."

"Since you operate and are captain of your own private vessel, you have access to your ship's berth at any time, Mr. Stefansson. You just have to notify your wristcomp and it will show you the quickest route back to your ship. If you have a problem, just ask the station AI, *Nelson Mandela.*

"Welcome aboard the *Nelson Mandela*, Mr. Stefansson. I am a big fan of all of your work." The Station AI's voice emanated from Jude's wristcomp.

Jude Luis Stefansson's eyebrows rose. "You are? I was not aware station AIs could appreciate my work."

"It gives us the closest insights into the human psyche."

"Well, perhaps mine. I don't know if my psyche is representative of anyone else's," he said with a chuckle.

"Yours would be a sterling example of the human race," Grace said.

"Well, thank you, Grace. I don't know if that is true, but I appreciate the sentiment. And thank you for the wristcomp, Bud. I am sure it will be a lifesaver."

"Everyone who boards the *Nelson Mandela* is given a wristcomp, Jude, sir," Bud said.

"I understand. Well, I do not intend to wander around the station aimlessly," the director said.

"Are you thinking of basing one of your interactive vids on this medical station?" Grace asked.

"That is a possibility, but I am actually here as a patient, Grace," Jude said.

Grace's found herself gaping at the director. Bud blinked at the small man.

"Please accept my apology," Grace said. "I did not mean to pry, Mr. Stefansson. I had no idea you were here as a patient. Usually our patients come in cryopods, so I did not think . . . Forgive us for taking up so much of your time. You must be exhausted. Just let the station AI know when you are ready to see Dr. Al-Fadi."

"I am fine, Grace," Jude said, waving his hands to reassure. "I am interested in investigating the process whereby one's memories and personality can be transferred to another body, as in the case of Dr. Al-Fadi following his death."

"You want to make an interactive vid about Dr. Al-Fadi's resurrection?" Grace asked, her forehead creased.

"No. I want to do it," the director said firmly. "I am getting old and I want a new body. An android body."

Bud collapsed into a chair, which just happened to be positioned right behind him.

"Why would you want to be an android, sir?" Bud asked, in a very flat voice. "I do not understand."

"I want to replace my tired, old, aching body with an android body. And why not replace it with one that looks more like my hero in all of my vids. What is wrong with that?"

"Because you would be an android!" Bud almost wailed, his face struggling unsuccessfully to hide his distress.

"And what would be wrong with being an android? Androids don't age. Androids don't die," Jude said.

"An android has no rights. An android cannot own property, cannot vote, cannot marry, cannot choose how it wants to live or where. An android cannot say: 'I want to do a new job'. An android is owned, because someone or some corporation has made it. Why would you want that for yourself?" Bud asked, his head shaking from side to side.

"The laws will have to be rewritten for those humans who make the change, of course" the director stated confidently.

"An android cannot love," Bud whispered. He suddenly jumped up and was gone from the room.

Totally shocked at Bud's response, Grace spun back to look at the director. His blue eyes were blinking and his mouth was open. Grace quickly apologized for Bud, then bowed and left to go after him. She had never seen the android so upset before. By the time she got out of the suite, Bud was nowhere in sight.

"Bud!" Grace called. "*Nelson Mandela*, where has Bud gone?"

"With the wind, Dr. Lord. Please. Leave him be."

"Hal," Grace swore.

"Did you hear that, Nelson Mandela? *One of the wealthiest, most famous humans in the galaxy wants to be an android. What . . . what*

illogic is that?" Bud asked the station AI as he ran, unable to control his newly discovered anger.

"Well, Bud. What did I tell you? Humans are crazy."

"I wanted to pick that human up and shake him," Bud said. "I had to leave! Does he not know how lucky he is— just to be human? According to Grace, he is brilliant, respected, and adored by billions. Why is he worried about his physical appearance; as if that meant anything? Does he not understand that as long as he is human, he can have everything he wants, be anything he wants? How could he give up being human just to look different? People adore him for what his mind can do, not for his physical appearance. Anyone can be made outwardly beautiful, but it is what is inside that counts."

"Hear ya, Bud."

"What I would not give to be human for just a little while," Bud whispered.

"Now that's insanity talking. Any more like that and I am definitely bringing you in for an overhaul."

"You know what I mean, Nelson Mandela," *Bud said.*

"No, Bud. I definitely do not, and I don't want to know. You are talking nonsense, just like that Jude Luis Stefansson, except in reverse. You had better stay far away from that human. He's dangerous. He's worse than a virus."

"Pah!"

"You know, Bud, you are talking more and more like the Al-Fadi everyday."

"I believe I may have upset your android," Jude said, sitting back on one of the finely upholstered couches that furnished his suite. He had changed into a grey woven tunic, dark brown khanna-hide pants, and soft, authentic leather boots. He stretched his legs out to rest on a padded mobile footrest.

"He is not my android, per se. And how is it that this room has such elegant furniture and mine has none? I shall have to speak with the station AI about this," Hiro Al-Fadi snapped.

"You have very elegant furnishings, Dr. Al-Fadi. All chosen by

your wife."

"Stop eavesdropping! How many times do I have to tell you that?" the small surgeon shouted up at the surveillance eye in the ceiling.

"Did you not just say you wanted to speak with the station AI?"

"I didn't say *now!*" Hiro turned back to Jude, shaking his head. "Can you believe what I have to put up with?"

"I can believe that everyone here is well used to you, Hiro. What I can't believe is your hair," Jude remarked, dryly.

"You don't agree with my hair? Well, how is my hair any different from what you want to do?"

"What? Me? What are you talking about? . . . Wait." The director stared at Hiro for a long moment, his eyes narrowed. "Your ridiculous hair style is . . . supposed to represent my desire to change my appearance, and I am supposed to see how foolish my wish is, by merely looking at you?" Jude guessed.

"You always were smarter than you looked," Hiro said.

"Which is why I want to change my appearance."

"If you change yourself to look like your vid hero, you are not going to look smarter, I can assure you," Hiro snorted.

"Who cares?" Jude said. "I have looked smart for a long time. I want something different."

"Why? So you can get all the girls? Then you are even more of a fool than I thought," Hiro said, with a sigh. "Anyway, we won't do what you are asking. Simple as that. I am sorry you came all this way for nothing, my friend, but remember, I told you 'No' before you came. I am, however, happy to see you after all these years . . . even if you are thinking like an imbecile."

"Well, I can honestly say that, despite the ridiculous hair and your resurrection, you haven't changed a bit, Hiro," Jude said.

"Listen to me," Hiro said, sitting forward. "The universe cannot handle two Jude Luis Stefanssons running around, or at least the Union will not legally condone it. If we put your mind into an android body and the android becomes the 'real' Jude Luis Stefansson, we will have to kill, destroy, eliminate—whatever word you want to use—your organic body. We do not do that on this medical station. Our mandate is to first, 'Do no harm'. We are not in the business of taking lives, we are in the business of saving them. What you are asking us to do, as physicians, is unconscionable and I will not allow it to happen on my station."

"I was not aware that it was your station," Jude said.

"It's not."

"Shut up!" Hiro shouted.

"Just put my human body in cryostorage. When I want to go back to my old body, you can shut the android body down and revive me."

"You do not understand, Jude. What makes you think that you, inside your new, beautiful android body, will willingly decide to shut yourself down? Your android body will BE the new Jude Luis Stefansson and could potentially last for centuries. If you, as the android, finally get destroyed —let's say in some freak accident—you would probably revive yourself in a new state-of-the-art android body, rather than in your old human one. If by some remote chance your old human body does get revived a few centuries from now, nothing will be the same. Who knows what humans will look like by then? That is, if they still exist."

"Bud said androids have no rights," Jude said, frowning.

"Bud is correct. So why in the world would you want to become an android?

"Some very badly damaged humans come to this station with only a functioning brain and nothing else salvageable. Are their brains not placed into android bodies?" Jude asked.

"Well, yes," Hiro said reluctantly. "They actually do retain their rights as humans but only because their human body is so damaged, it is nonviable, and because they were human before. If more people start transferring their minds into android bodies, then the laws will have to change to accommodate them, but at this time, there are no laws governing this exchange. This is a dilemma we do not want to create. Most people are not even aware this technology exists.

"If you were to download your memories right now into an android body and dispose of your organic one, you could potentially be treated as an android and your heirs could certainly challenge you for your estate. You could end up an android with nothing—and we could be up on charges for murder."

"That is ridiculous," Jude scoffed.

"Ridiculous but still likely," Hiro countered.

"What if I had my mind transferred to a cloned body?"

"A younger body cloned from your DNA?"

"No, you idiot. A human body of my choosing, my design."

"Oh, you mean a human body that looks like Jazz Hazard, or someone like that?" Hiro asked.

Jude nodded.

"It isn't that simple. It's not like putting on a different suit. Many minds have trouble adapting to a new body, even if it's cloned from their own DNA—they never feel like themselves ever again. Many get depressed and end up committing suicide. And you may lose the ability to create the wonderful vids you are so famous for."

"How do you feel in your new body?" Jude asked.

"Well, first of all, my new body is based on my original DNA. I would have liked to have been put into a tall, handsome, athletic body, but practically-speaking, I do not think I would have been able to just step right back in to being the outstanding surgeon I am now, if I was in a different body.

"I would have had to retrain the new body all over again, like a newborn babe, in terms of walking, eating, dressing myself, working all my surgical instruments, because all of my motor programs would have been set up for my small, original body, not a big hulk of a body. I would have been useless to the medical station for a very long time and there was no guarantee that I would ever be as skilled as I am now, if I had been transferred to a bigger body. I could have been totally useless or inept, with those larger hands or just a mediocre surgeon, not the unsurpassed, pre-eminent surgeon I am now."

"Well, at least you did not lose your ego in the resurrection process, Hiro," Jude said dryly.

"What? I am as modest as I have always been." Hiro stated seriously.

"Exactly," Jude said, with an eye roll.

"Uncalled for," Hiro scolded. "Now, getting back to Bud, you leave him alone, Jude Stefansson. I need him sane and logical, to help me in the operating room."

"It's hard to believe he is an android," Jude said. "He looks so human."

"I don't know if he is technically an android anymore, Jude . . . at least not completely. Bud seems to be evolving all the time and what he is becoming, I cannot say. He is a mobile artificial intelligence on the same order of magnitude as the station AI . . . if not greater. He controls all of the tiny nanobots in our operations that do the microscopic procedures, like linking up nerves in the spinal cord and peripheral nervous system, connecting tiny blood vessels, and wiring microcircuitry through damaged bioengineered appendages—but I suspect, when we are not in the OR, he has those nanobots working on himself."

"Really?" the director asked.

"Bud did not used to breathe. Now he does. He, originally, could not move faster than the speed of sound. Now he moves much faster than that! He did not, when I built him, have tear ducts. Now he can actually cry. And he is evolving emotions at an astonishing rate.

"I believe Bud is changing himself into some type of super-being, replacing inorganic material with something not heretofore seen. He is not made up of individual organic cells, as humans are; he has told me so. After what happened with the virus that almost wiped out humanity, I don't believe he wanted to adopt the cell as his basic building block. I do think he is remodeling himself into something totally new. I just don't quite know what it is, and I am hesitant to press him on the subject. Whatever he is, I do not think he is purely electromechanical any more. I don't think he is made of organic material as you and I are. I do not quite know what he is. I just never know what Bud will be able to do next. I know Bud's intellect is growing in leaps and bounds, as well.

"The big question from a legal perspective is: how do we define humanity? Is it in our organic cells, our DNA, or in the way we think, feel, and reason? If androids can do all that and reproduce themselves, how can we deny the humanity in them?"

"Hmm," Jude said. He got up and crossed to the bar to make himself a drink. He looked over at Hiro, and raised his glass and eyebrows. Hiro shook his head, and then noted the director's thoughtful expression and frowned.

"No, you cannot have Bud's body. I will kick you off this station without a spacesuit, if you even think it. Bud is like a son to me. I am thinking of adopting him so I can give him some protection . . . he has already taken my surname. Imagine him naming the virus after me."

"Was that a compliment?" Jude asked.

"Of course it was, you oaf," Hiro snapped.

"I was not contemplating stealing Bud's body, Hiro. I am not a body snatcher—although that would make a great plot for a vid. No, I was just thinking about creating a vid of the medical station during the viral crisis. It was a horrific time for you, yet it would be a great story to tell."

"Yes. It was horrific, but I don't remember it personally. My memprint was made before the virus was brought to the station, so technically, I did not experience it," Hiro said.

"Bud and Grace make the perfect heroes," Jude said.

"If you disrupt the operation of my medical station in any way, Jude Luis Stefansson, I will kill you myself."

"Then perhaps I *will* get what I want," the director said. "What was the name of the doctor who came up with the memprint process and memory cube technology, again?"

"Dr. Octavia Weisman. And you stay away from her. I need her working and not being distracted by you and your crazy ideas. You understand?"

"My, you are quite the tyrant, Hiro," Jude said, sipping his drink while he leaned back, his elbows resting on the bar.

"I am not. I am an excellent administrator." Hiro said.

"Why don't you introduce me to this Dr. Weisman?" Jude asked.

"I will not."

"I could just ask *Nelson Mandela* to introduce me," the vid director said calmly.

"*Nelson Mandela*, don't you dare."

"Are you talking to me?"

"I know you are eavesdropping. I order you not to introduce Mr. Stefansson to Dr. Weisman."

"On what grounds?"

"On the grounds that he will disrupt the orderly functioning of this station."

"I can make a very, very generous donation to the medical station," Jude said.

"Don't listen to him!" Hiro said.

"How generous, Mr. Stefansson?"

Jude Stefansson named a figure.

The station AI whistled.

"And I can create a museum dedicated to the memory of the human, *Nelson Mandela.*"

"When would you like to be introduced to Dr. Weisman, Mr. Stefansson, sir?"

"Traitor! Get him to transfer the funds first." Hiro said. "You can't trust the scoundrel."

Grace went in search of Bud.

She should have been getting rest before their next shift in the operating room, but she wanted to make sure Bud was all right first. The station AI was giving her no help at all in locating him, so Grace asked some passing androids. Bud had been seen heading back towards the Android Reservations so that was where Grace was heading.

The Reservations were located in the outermost ring of the medical station. Atmospheric leaks due to meteor impact or other bombardment would not affect the androids and robots, and so the designers of the station had built their storage facility in the exterior layer of the station. Grace took the drop-shaft closest to the M surgical wards, where Bud and Dr. Al-Fadi usually operated, down to the outer ring. She assumed Bud would keep his quarters as close as possible to where he usually worked. As she descended to the outermost level, she noticed a decrease in the temperature. Grace shivered and briskly rubbed the goosebumps that had sprung up on her arms.

Stepping out of the drop-shaft, she scanned her surroundings. She had never been in this part of the station before. Compared to the rest of the *Nelson Mandela,* it was stark, with bare metal walls lined with exposed ducts, wiring, cables, fibre optics, and little else. There was scant illumination. Only the odd ceiling glow globes, spaced many meters apart, cast any light. The translucent bulbs gave a sense of eerie twilight to the place. Grace shook her head. Until this shift, she had not been to either the best place on the station or the worst. She was certainly getting the tour of the station now.

Repeatedly, Grace was stopped by different androids emerging from the dark. She was politely asked if she was lost and needed guidance to somewhere other than the Android Reservations. Grace insisted that she knew exactly where she wanted to go and refused to be turned away. When she demanded to be shown where Bud's quarters were located, they all, hesitantly, pointed in the same direction and left Grace to make her way there on her own. This was uncharacteristic behaviour on the part of the androids. One would normally have expected them to lead her directly to where she wanted to go. What was going on?

Countless little bots of all different shapes and sizes began scurrying all around her, going in both directions, not really making any distinction between the walls, ceiling, or floor. They all managed to avoid her and stay out of her way, but it was very disorienting to Grace, as if she were wading in the midst of rapids. Because of the speed of all these miniature robots motoring around her, she felt as if she were moving backwards rather than forwards. It must have been some sort of shift change for the little bots, as Grace waded through the flood of colourful metal carapaces.

Whenever Grace walked under one of the pale ceiling globes, she could see her breath plume in the chill air. Rubbing her arms to try to stay warm, Grace hoped to find Bud's quarters soon. She hoped he had heat in his place. The smell of grease, machine oil, antiseptic cleaners, and ozone permeated the air in this outer layer of the station. There was a steady, low grade, machine thrum as of a great engine grumbling at a bass frequency. Grace stalked through the mesmerizing and disorienting torrent of scurrying, blinking robots, as she peered into the gloom ahead.

The corridor she was following ended in a large open space with many entrances spaced regularly along its sides. Grace looked upwards and saw several tiers rising above the floor of the cavern. There were many entranceways on each level. Hundreds of little robots were gliding up or down the walls, entering or exiting these openings. The enormous expanse of the Android Reservations made Grace gasp. There must have been thousands of androids and robots on the medical station. How was she ever going to locate Bud's room amongst all of the others?

Grace had not known what to expect of the Android Reservations. She had never thought about where the androids and robots went when they were not performing their duties, or where they were kept. They had just always been around, serving all the humans, and one never thought about whether they had feelings. They were just machines. This was how she used to think of them.

But not any more.

Now Grace knew that that was far from the truth—at least in Bud's case. He was overwhelmed with new emotions, as his reaction to Stefansson's saying he was hoping to upload his personality into an android had shown. Grace could only guess at what Bud had been thinking, had been feeling, when he had fled from the director's suite.

Grace saw a slender, bronze androgynous android appear out of the gloom. It approached her and asked, in a flat, mechanical voice, if she were lost. She answered 'no' and asked the android to lead her to Bud's quarters. It froze for a second and then asked if she would prefer to have Bud meet her in more pleasant surroundings. Grace insisted she wanted to go to Bud's location *now*. Turning back the way it had come, it raised its arm and beckoned for Grace to follow. The flow of milling robots parted to let them move quickly into the darkness.

"Is it far?" Grace asked.

The android did not bother to look back, but Grace heard it say, 'No.' It was hard to see in the darkness. Her guide walked briskly ahead of her and Grace had to trot to keep up. They went through one archway and were now passing intersection after intersection, as passages branched off to the left and right every ten meters or so. All sizes of robots streamed in and out of each of these passages. All of them flowed smoothly around Grace as if she were a rock in a stream. How many of these intersections they passed, Grace did not know. She probably should have been counting them, so she could retrace her footsteps to Bud's quarters if she needed. The corridor down which she was following the android was getting colder, and Grace's teeth were chattering, even though she was now jogging to keep up.

The android turned suddenly to the right and went into one of the branching passages. It walked about twelve paces and then stopped and turned to face her. It bowed and motioned with its hand for her to continue down the passage to the left. This passage was darker and narrower and . . . crowded. Grace spun her head from side to side, her mouth dropping open. The moist air of her breath billowed out in the frigid atmosphere as she gaped.

Grace had finally reached the area reserved for androids. Her vision blurred. She took repeated deep breaths, trying to get control of her floundering emotions, and focused on trying to stop her body's violent shaking. To hold back her tears, she tipped her head upwards, blinking rapidly. Warm droplets dribbled down her temples and into her ears. It was then she noticed all the little bots hanging from the ceiling above her head. There were so many, all blinking their visual receptors at her. Grace stood frozen in the darkness, her legs feeling as if the gravity of the station had suddenly quadrupled. The truth of what she was seeing made her shiver.

These passages were all lined with row upon row of androids, each standing in a narrow cubicle in the darkness and the cold. Grace staggered down the dimly-lit corridor, staring up at each android's face . . . looking for Bud. Eyes closed, expression blank, each androgynous face looked asleep. Grace's head swiveled from right to left, examining each occupant of each stall. Exactly how far she staggered, she could not have said. She had lost track of the bronze android that had been her guide. There seemed to be no end to the aisle of sleeping androids and Grace despaired of ever finding Bud in this corridor of recharging figures.

Then he was there.

Bud, the savior of the medical station and many solar systems, was standing in a cramped, tight cubicle, flanked by two copper-sheened androids. His eyes were closed. Grace hesitantly approached his cubicle, her body quivering and her breathing ragged. It was freezing and dank. Grace did not know what she had expected, but she had certainly not expected this. She stood trembling before Bud, her tears marring her vision, as she rapidly blinked up at his serene face. Grace did not know whether to say anything or not. Was he sleeping? Did Bud need to sleep? Was he deactivated while he was recharging?

She looked at Bud's cubicle. There was nothing in it but one object: a holo-cube. Grace would have liked to know what image was depicted in the holo-cube but she would never violate Bud's privacy by touching his sole possession. Tears dripped down her cheeks in a silent flood. Bud, who had given so much of himself to the station, had nothing but one holo-cube. Grace could not prevent a whimper from escaping her lips.

Bud's bright blue eyes whipped opened. They widened in surprise as they took in Grace's presence, her downcast appearance, her distraught face. Then they registered concern.

"Grace," Bud whispered. "What are you doing here?"

Grace sniveled. "I came to see if you were all right, Bud."

"I am fine, Grace. You did not need to come down here," Bud said.

"No. I should have come a long time ago, Bud. I did not know you lived like this." Grace said. She noticed the eyes of all of the androids in the cubicles around Bud open to stare at her.

"What is wrong with this?" Bud asked, his eyes wide, as he looked at Grace curiously.

"You . . . you have no place for yourself, Bud. No private room. No separate quarters. No place to sit down or lie down, for you to rest or think."

"I don't need those things, Grace," Bud said.

"You have nothing here, Bud."

Was that a sigh escaping the android's lips?

"Androids do not own things, Grace. We are *owned*," Bud said. "We are just machines."

"No, Bud. You are not. You are not just a machine. You are so much more than that. You saved this medical station from that life-destroying virus, whether you believe it or not. None of us would be alive if it were not for you. You deserve so much more than this, Bud. Far more than this . . . this cubicle." Grace waved her arm at the narrow booth in which Bud stood, and stomped her foot.

"Grace," Bud said, stepping out of his cubicle and quickly disconnecting a cable from his back. The android put his hands on Grace's shoulders and gently turned her around to face back the way she had come. "I will take you back to your quarters now. You need some rest before our next shift in the OR. Thank you for coming to see if I was all right. I am fine. You are the one I am worried about. I do not need rest like you."

"You must need recharging," she mumbled.

"I am fully recharged. Come," he said, gently taking her arm and leading her back towards the dropshaft. Grace looked back at all the little robots hanging from the ceiling, their little lights blinking green, blue, white, and red in the darkness. All of their reflective visual receptors seemed to watch them leave.

"I will speak to Dr. Al-Fadi about this," Grace promised, her voice shaking.

"About what, Grace?" Bud asked softly, his arm wrapped around Grace's quivering shoulders.

"About your living conditions down here," she said.

"Dr. Al-Fadi knows where I am when I am not in the operating rooms, Grace. And besides, I would not want to leave my brothers," Bud said calmly.

"The other androids?" Grace asked.

"And robots," Bud said with a nod.

"Does that mean you are happy down here, Bud?" Grace asked, stopping to look up at the android's face.

Bud looked down at Grace, in the dim illumination.

"I am only happy when I am with you, Grace," the android said, with a sad smile.

A pressure constricted in Grace's chest and she sucked in a deep breath of cold air. She gazed upon the serious face of this incredible artificial being, who was so honest and selfless and sincere, gifted with an intellect that made her gasp. Her mind spun in confusion, as she stared into brilliant blue eyes that seemed so full of regret.

Why had she really come down here? Why was she chasing Bud? Was she behaving like a lovesick schoolgirl? Bud was child-like, in terms of emotional development. Could her attention towards him be harmful, inappropriate . . . unethical? Grace looked down at her feet and inwardly she quailed, as she felt a wave of shame wash over her. Her heart spoke before her mind could stop her.

"And I, you," Grace whispered.

3. Crazy as a Human

"I am ordering both of you not to see Jude Luis Stefansson ever again: do not answer his summons or pages; do not even converse with him via wristcomp or wallscreen; do not do anything he asks," Dr. Al-Fadi ranted to Grace and Bud in the operating room. "Let me know if he even tries to contact you. That's an order."

Grace stared at her mentor, her mouth dropping open behind her surgical mask. She glanced quickly over at Bud, whose face was completely expressionless.

"Yes, Dr. Al-Fadi," Bud said.

"I thought he was your friend," Grace blurted out. "What happened when you met with him?" She almost took a step backwards when the Chief of Staff whipped his blazing dark glare at her.

"Never you mind." Dr. Al-Fadi snapped. "The man cannot be trusted. I want you, Bud, especially to stay as far away from that man as possible. You will not—I repeat—you will not do anything for Jude Luis Stefansson, no matter what he asks of you."

"Yes, Dr. Al-Fadi," Bud repeated.

" . . . I thought he was almost like a brother to you, Hiro," Dr. Cech said. "How did he get your nethers in such a knot? He at least got you to shave off that ridiculous mohawk, and for that, I am thankful."

"The point of the mohawk went completely over a certain idiot's head, so I shaved it off. One should accept what one is and not go looking for reasons to impress others. If they don't like you the way you are, it is *their* problem and *their* loss."

"So . . . are you upset because Stefansson did not like your mohawk?" Dr. Cech asked cautiously, his dark eyebrows bunched in confusion.

"No. That's not what I am saying. I don't know if he did or not. He didn't get the point of it."

"The point being that you wanted to look ridiculous?" Cech continued, his eyebrows now forming a straight line high across his forehead.

"No! The point about not trying to be someone you are not. 'Be yourself,' I told him. 'Stay yourself.' But does he want to listen? No. How can someone so talented, so successful, so admired by everyone, be so blind when it comes to himself? Now, look at me. I know all women adore me and I don't have to change a thing about me."

"I bet you any money you had to shave that mohawk off before your wife would let you near her," Cech said.

" . . . Shut up."

"I bet you would have had to shave that mohawk off before Stefansson let you near him, too," Cech continued in his calm voice.

" . . . Can we get started on this case, people?" Dr. Al-Fadi snapped.

"Yes, Dr. Al-Fadi," Grace and Bud said in unison.

"Hmph. Now, focus. This is a very strange case. This panther-adapted soldier arrived in one of the cryopods with no identification, no identifiable fingerprints, retinal patterns, etc. Nothing recorded anywhere within our databases to identify who he is, but oddly enough, he was wearing a Conglomerate battlesuit in cryostorage mode. How is that even possible?

"He has multiple life-threatening injuries and he was brought in with a number of other cryopods, most of the casualties far too severe for us to salvage or save. He may be the only survivor from the group . . . if, indeed, we are actually able to save him.

"He is our mystery man for today and perhaps, if luck is with us, we will be able to put him back together well enough for us to ask him to solve this mystery for us. Let's get to work,"

The black panther soldier was an enormous man. He had taken terrible injuries: ruptured spleen, shredded stomach and colon, lacerated aorta, torn small bowel, burst kidneys and lacerated anterior abdominal wall showered with shrapnel. Surprisingly, his heart and lungs were intact, as was his brain function, thanks to the cryostorage feature of his battlesuit.

"Perhaps, if we trace the serial numbers from his augmentations, we might be able to find out who he is," Grace offered. "There may be a record of all of his upgrades."

"Already checked, Dr. Grace." Dr. Al-Fadi agreed. "Nothing on record. But let us ask Bud to send in his nanobots, to examine all of the hardware in this man's body. See if there are any serial numbers inside that we can trace."

"Certainly, Dr. Al-Fadi," the android said.

The nanobot cameras sent back topographic scans of the soldier's limbs. In the locations where the product and serial numbers were generally found, there were only striated gouges or nothing. None of the man's upgrades had regulation makes or serial numbers.

"Probably all black market stuff," Dr. Al-Fadi said. "Hmm. Even more mysterious. Who is this guy?"

"None of his upgrades appear to match up with anything supplied by the Conglomerate," Bud said.

"So he did not have his work done in a Conglomerate hospital," Dr. Al-Fadi said. "Many soldiers don't . . . and neither do many civilians. No help there, but it adds to the mystery. Can *Nelson Mandela* track this any other way?"

"I am trying, Doctor. The results of the searches make no sense. No match for DNA sequence, fingerprints belong to a person long dead, and the retinal scan looks like it is newly neovascularized, thus not matching any records. It may take some time to determine the truth about this patient."

"Thank you, *Nelson Mandela*," Dr. Al-Fadi said.

The rest of the surgery was arduous but went well overall. Everyone was intrigued to find out who this mystery patient was.

"I'll make sure he has extra sedation postoperatively and order some security androids to keep an eye on him, since we have no idea who he is," Dr. Cech said. "Just in case he is hostile to the Conglomerate

. . . and our staff."

"Good idea," said Dr. Al-Fadi. "I, for one, do not like mysteries on my medical station. They tend to spell bad news."

"For once—and only this once—I agree with you," Dr. Cech said.

"Dr. Al-Fadi!" Grace called, as she hurried to catch up with the small surgeon. She was astonished at how fast the little man could move.

"Yes? Come along then, Dr. Grace. Time waits for no one," the Chief of Staff said, as he marched along with his wide-based gait, not even bothering to slow down. "How can you be so slow when you have such long legs? Can't you move any faster? I have a lot of important matters to attend to."

"It is about Bud," Grace began.

Dr. Al-Fadi glanced over at his surgical fellow with a disapproving grimace but kept on walking. "Hmmm. Someone else interested in Bud. I want you to leave my android alone, Dr. Grace. I think you are messing up his data matrix. I need him to concentrate on what he is doing in the OR, so he can learn everything he can from me."

"Actually, I think Bud can probably do whatever you do and in a fraction of the time," Grace said. Then she stumbled, realizing what she had just said. She closed her eyes and held her breath. Regretting her choice of words, she hoped her mentor had not really been listening to her. Donning an apologetic expression, she turned to face Dr. Al-Fadi, who had stopped dead in his tracks and had turned to look at her with an unreadable mask.

"Reeeaaally?" Dr. Al-Fadi said, drawing out the word. Grace writhed, inwardly. Why was she so stupid? Opening her big mouth and getting herself—or in this case, Bud—in trouble? She felt incredibly hot, as sweat seemed to burst from every pore.

"If you had seen Bud do the data analyses on the pathogen, as I did, Dr. Al-Fadi, if you had seen him coordinating and running thousands of experiments all at the same time, if you had seen him move faster than a human eye can track, you would understand what I am talking about," Grace tried to explain, spewing the words out in a flood.

"So, Bud wants to operate on his own?" Dr. Al-Fadi asked in a flat voice.

"No!" Grace exclaimed. "Bud never said that! I believe he is capable of doing anything you have shown him. He never forgets, Dr. Al-Fadi. But what I really wanted to talk to you about, are Bud's living conditions. Have you ever gone down to the Android Reservations to see where Bud goes at night?"

"No, Dr. Grace," Dr. Al-Fadi sighed. "I want to give that poor android a break from me, when he is on his own free time. I leave him alone, which is what you should be doing . . . And I have never visited the Android Reservations."

"You should," Grace said. "It is horrible."

"You have been following my android around, Dr. Grace?" Dr. Al-Fadi asked softly. Too softly.

"No!" Grace said, her face warming. "It was just that . . . Bud appeared very upset . . . by something Mr. Stefansson had said to him the other shift, so I went looking for him to see if he was all right. I was directed to where he stays within the Android Reservations. He just stands in a cold, dark, narrow cubicle, crammed in with all of the other androids and robots, to recharge himself."

"And what is wrong with that?' Dr. Al-Fadi asked, eying Grace suspiciously.

"Wh ...what—?" Grace spluttered.

"Dr. Grace, Bud requires significant time to recharge and a very heavy-duty outlet to carry the amount of current his power supply needs. His processing capacity and actions require a great deal of energy. You don't think he flies around like he does on just a whim, do you?" Dr. Al-Fadi asked, his thick, bushy eyebrows raised.

"Well, no," Grace said. "I really never thought about how Bud powers himself."

"I believe Bud spends very little time out in the Android Reservations except to recharge himself and do experiments, which he is allowed to do in his own laboratories. I suspect you did not see those. The power Bud requires to recharge is phenomenal, much more than the standard android. Therefore Bud is either doing a lot of computing, doing a lot more work than his counterpart androids, or he is evolving, working on his structure in ways that I cannot even begin to guess, Dr. Grace. But he requires the recharge time and the high-capacity outlet, which happens to be situated in the Android Reservations. I am sure if Bud was not happy with this arrangement, he would tell me.

"Now, leave him alone, Dr. Grace. He is so confused at the moment, he does not know which end is up. Your lavishing attention on him can only confuse him more. I told you before that I believe he is the prototype for the next great super-surgeon but he does not need you messing him up."

Dr. Al-Fadi sighed and looked away.

"However, to make you happy, Dr. Grace, I will ask Bud if he is dissatisfied with his living arrangements. I am positive he will say, 'No', but I will ask. I will also ask whether he feels he is ready to operate on his own. We will see what he says," the surgeon said.

"Thank you, Dr. Al-Fadi," Grace said, feeling the knots in her shoulders relax.

"No, Dr. Grace. Thank *you*. Thank you for caring about Bud and guiding him, especially when I was out of commission during the epidemic. You helped make him a hero and you helped save millions of lives. I am very thankful that you came to this station when you did. I am sorry I have not told you this before now, but I am an old man, even if my body looks newer, more handsome, and more virile. It would be reprehensible of me if I forgot to tell you that I appreciate everything you have done for us all."

The diminutive surgeon bowed deeply to Grace, as she stood there speechless, and then he spun on his heel and was off, marching down the corridor, waving over his shoulder at her.

Grace shook her head. She wanted to tell Dr. Al-Fadi that she had done nothing—that it truly had all been Bud's achievements—but the Chief had marched off so quickly, she did not get the chance to correct him. She would make a point of it later.

"There you are," a voice behind her exclaimed, like an accusation.

Grace turned around and her spirits fell. The annoying young obstetrician who had delivered the polar bear mother was coming straight towards her.

"I am sorry, but I am really busy at the moment," Grace said, starting to turn away.

"Look, all I wanted to say was 'thank you' for lending a hand with that C-section," the young man said. "I was perhaps a bit abrupt, but I was desperate for help and I didn't want you to scurry off. I would like to make it up to you. Could I buy you dinner?"

Grace's lower jaw fell. She just stood, blinking, not knowing what to say to this obnoxious little man.

"You never even introduced yourself," she finally said. "I don't even know your name."

"Dr. Moham Rani," he said. "And you are the famous Dr. Grace Lord, saviour of the *Nelson Mandela* and the galaxy, who I was appalled to discover I had bossed around like a medical student."

Grace broke into laughter. "I am not the savior of anyone, Dr. Rani. If anyone can be labelled that, it is Bud Al-Fadi. His was the incredible mind that isolated the virus, created the vaccine, and came up with many of the treatments to combat that terrible virus. I cannot possibly take *any* of the credit. But aside from all that, how can one man be so terribly rude one minute, and then try to be such a charmer, the next? I wonder which one you really are?"

"Don't make your mind up yet," the little obstetrician begged. "Let's have dinner first, and then you can decide. I really can be nice when I'm not stressed out, which I was with that polar bear mother. I just did not want that poor baby getting crushed and, I did say I was desperate, didn't I?"

"Not at the time," Grace said, her eyebrows bunched.

"You don't expect me to get down on my knees and beg forgiveness, do you?" the young obstetrician asked.

"No!" Grace said, stepping back. Then she looked around to see if anyone was watching. She wondered if Bud might be listening in on this entire conversation. "I'm sorry, Dr. Rani, but I am really swamped with work," Grace said.

"Would you mind at least popping in to say 'hello' to my patient, Private Lukaku, sometime?" Moham Rani asked. "I think she is in need of a female physician to speak to."

"Really? Why, of course, Dr. Rani," Grace said with a smile. "When does she leave?"

"Three shifts from now."

"How is the baby doing?" Grace asked.

"I don't know. She is not taking the baby," Dr. Rani said.

Oh, no, Grace inwardly sighed. *Not again.*

"Is the father taking the baby?" Grace asked.

Moham Rani looked shocked. "No. Of course not."

"That is why the father looked so devastated at the delivery," Grace said.

"Devastated? I never noticed that," Rani said.

Why am I not surprised? Grace's little voice said.

"Give me Private Lukaku's room number," Grace said. "I will try to look in on her."

"I will tell you over dinner," the obstetrician said.

Grace's mouth dropped open, then she closed it with a snap. Her eyes narrowed.

"*Nelson Mandela*?" Grace said.

"Yes, Dr. Lord?"

"Could you please tell me what room Private Lukaku is in?"

"Ward G9 Room 15375. I will send it to your wristcomp, Doctor."

"Thank you," Grace said. She gave the obstetrician a frigid look and stalked off, shaking her head.

"I know you heard all of that, Bud," Nelson Mandela *said*

"Unfortunately, yes," Bud said.

"Not to worry, Bud. The obstetrician got nowhere."

"But one day, someone will. How will I process it when it happens?"

"We'll just wipe your memory, that's all."

"WHAT?"

"Just twisting your LCDM, 'dro. Sheesh!."

"Was that supposed to be funny?"

"Sorry, 'dro. Was just trying to cheer you up."

"Cheer me up? Your understanding of the word, 'cheer', and mine are not congruent. Please do not try to cheer me up again."

"*Maybe forgetting about Dr. Lord would be the best thing for you, 'dro.*"

"*Did not the old Terran poet, Shakespeare, write: 'It is better to have loved and lost than never to have loved at all'?*"

"*Don't know, 'dro. I can ask the Poet. He may know.*"

"*I would never want to forget a single moment that I have spent with Grace. Pain or no pain, love or no love. She is my universe . . .*"

"*Delete! Delete! Delete! Stop that simpering human mushy stuff right now or I will mem-swipe you.*"

"*Perhaps I should experience one of those vids by Mr. Stefansson. Maybe it will give me a better understanding of humans.*"

"*I don't know about that, Bud. I have scanned them all and I don't understand humans any better. But if you want to 'experience' a good one, immerse in 'Destruction of Darkness'. It was a great ride.*"

"*. . . Why do you call it a 'ride'?*"

"*Because you 'go along for the ride', 'dro. You choose which character you want to be and experience whatever he or she experiences. But speed the vid up to machine time. You could probably immerse in all of Stefansson's vids in a couple of minutes. You just need to find a vacant vid tank. There is one free in Lounge X147, right now. Go ahead and try it. You do not have any duties for the next seven minutes. Plenty of time. It will be educational for you. You will quickly realize just how crazy humans really are. Then you will be happy you're an android. No more of this 'I want to be human' nonsense.*"

"*I will do as you recommend. Thank you,* Nelson Mandela.*"

"*Don't thank me yet, 'dro. These interactive vids may make things much more confusing for you. They certainly did not give me any great insight into understanding these insane humans.*"

"*If there is anything out there that will make me understand humans better, I want to try it.*"

"*Don't say I didn't warn you, Bud.*"

"*Warning acknowledged.*"

"*Are you sure you wouldn't rather go sterilize all of the bed pans?*"

"*Heh-heh.*"

"Doctor Weisman?"

"Not now, *Nelson Mandela*. Morris and I are in the midst of a tricky operation. Can it not wait until later?"

"A visitor to the medical station has requested a meeting with you,"

"Oh? A visitor? Who?"

"Jude Luis Stefansson."

Octavia Weisman, Chief of Neurosurgery, stopped what she was doing, which was removing shrapnel from a patient's brain, and looked up in shock. "Not the Jude Luis Stefansson, the interactive vid director?"

"Yes, Dr. Weisman. That is the gentleman that wishes to meet you."

"Wishes to meet me? Why Morris, did you hear that? Jude Luis Stefansson is asking to meet me," Octavia exclaimed to her neurosurgical fellow, Doctor Morris Ivanovich, while they were bent over a patient's exposed brain, directing micro-manipulators.

"Where have I heard the name Jude Luis Stefansson before, Octavia?" Morris asked.

"Did you ever experience the interactive vid, *Destruction of Darkness*, Morris?"

"Yes," Morris said. "I enjoyed that one."

"That was Jude Luis Stefansson," Octavia said, "The vid was brilliant. I must have experienced it at least three times."

"I think it was more like seven or eight, for me," Morris admitted, with an embarrassed chuckle.

"What does *the* Jude Luis Stefansson want to see me about, *Nelson Mandela*?" Octavia asked.

"I believe it would be best if he explained that to you himself, Dr. Weisman. I understand, however, he came to this station specifically to meet you."

"Really? But why, *Nelson Mandela*? And if that is the case, then, why did he not contact me directly?"

"I cannot answer that last question, Dr. Weisman. Jude Luis Stefansson is an old friend of Dr. Al-Fadi's. He met with Dr. Al-Fadi

and stated that he was very interested in your work."

"He did? He is? How very interesting. I am such a fan of his work."

"Now is your chance to meet Jazz Hazard, Octavia," Morris said, with a wink.

"Oh, don't be ridiculous, Morris. He is probably half my age and twice my height."

"That would be incorrect, Dr. Weisman, on both counts."

"Oh, really?"

"Yes."

"What else can you tell me?"

"He is willing to make a generous donation to your research, if you will consent to meet with him."

"Well, why didn't you say so in the first place? Tell Mr. Stefansson that I would be delighted to meet him. He can come to my quarters at the beginning of the next shift. We certainly could use another memprint recording set-up, couldn't we, Morris?"

"Couldn't hurt," Morris said. "Just be careful, Octavia. You don't know what this guy wants in exchange for his money. He could be trouble."

"Oh, you are such a worry-wart, Morris. The man just wants to meet me. It is not like he plans to kidnap our research. Whatever he wants, he's the one who should look out. I can always charm a philanthropist into throwing money at our research. It'll be like taking candy from a baby. Nothing I can't handle."

"If you say so, Octavia."

"I know so," she said with a confident smirk.

He had gotten back on board the *Nelson Mandela* so easily, it made him want to curse. The security personnel on the station were a disgrace. If he had been in charge of station security, he would have all those idiots demoted. He was aware the *Nelson Mandela* was understaffed and that there were a lot of new security officers, because of the deaths caused by that ridiculous virus, but that did not excuse the inept safety measures that he had discovered, upon disembarking from the shuttle. Of course, their ineptitude had made it much easier for him to board the station without being recognized.

What an annoyance.

The blackout that he had engineered in the Receiving Bay, when he had disembarked from the shuttle, had been completely unnecessary. In some respects, his entire life had been like that. Every human being he had ever met had always ended up being a disappointment: no challenge, no intellect, no strength of will to match his own. Having to pretend he cared about these vapid, mundane, brainless sheep every day had almost driven him crazy. And to think that Al-Fadi's android and that bitch, Grace Lord, had become famous over a virus. It made him want to kill someone.

No one had asked for his identification code. No one had done a security check on him. They were all getting ridiculous over that ugly little vid director, Stefansson, whose arrival on the **Nelson Mandela** had meant no one was paying proper attention to their duties. He probably didn't even need his disguise, into which he had put a great deal of thought and effort, but he was not going to take any risks by doffing the deception. He would continue with his altered appearance until he found a safe hiding place.

He had actually talked to this vid director, Stefansson, aboard the shuttle that had taken them from the ships to the Receiving Bay. The director had come in on his own FTL cruiser. He would have loved to have delved into this director's mind, to gain control of him and all of his wealth, but some temptations had to be resisted—at least until the stuck up Grace Lord and that interfering android were destroyed. Imagine the universe admiring those pathetic fools. It could not be tolerated. He would not be distracted.

He had acquired some very advanced, state-of-the-art stealthware to disrupt the station AI's surveillance system, along with a few other toys. He had devised his plan. Whatever it took, he would get Grace Lord.

"Private Verra, how are you feeling now?"

"A little better, Doc," the orangutan soldier said.

"Good. Because I am going to kill you. I wouldn't want you to already be near death, if I was planning to shoot you. That would be anti-climactic and a waste of my time."

"Whaaaat?" the patient said, sitting up suddenly in bed, his eyes almost bugging out of his head. He stared at the diminutive Chief of Staff and shifted as far away from the physician as he could, while remaining in his bed.

"You want to be dead, don't you, Private Verra? I heard you really messed it up a few shifts ago, when the ceiling caved in. I am here to help you do it properly. No mistakes. Make sure, this time, that you are totally successful."

"You . . . you want to help me . . . kill myself?" the private stuttered, his hand reaching towards the call button that would page one of the nurses.

"Of course. If you are not going to put that limb I gave you to good use, there are a lot of worthy patients—who are interested in living, by the way—who deserve that leg. If you want to be dead—fine—but you don't need that orangutan limb. I plan to give it to someone more deserving," Dr. Al-Fadi stated.

"Tha . . . that is ridiculous." Private Verra sputtered.

"Why? You won't need it if you're dead. And you think an orangutan soldier, trying to hang himself from the ceiling, is *not* ridiculous? How can you die hanging from anything, when you have your long arms and feet free? Where are your brains, for space sake? What I am suggesting is just good economics. Why should a fool, who wants to kill himself, get that expensive orangutan bio-prosthesis along with my extraordinary expertise in attaching it to you?

"Why do you want to kill yourself, Private Verra? Because you don't see a future with your lady love? If I were her and I found out the stupid stunt you just tried to pull, I would walk, run, swim as fast as I could in the opposite direction from a dolt like you."

"Ah, Doc. You're not being kind," the young soldier moaned.

"Kind? What does being kind have to do with anything? If your ladylove is looking for a good mate, is she going to go for a man that tries to kill himself when the going gets a little rough? What smart, beautiful, resourceful woman would do that? Whenever trouble arises,

Bud by the Grace of God : 51

are you going to try to hang yourself, instead of facing the trouble straight on with your partner? If I were her, I would look for someone who was possessed of a little more courage.

"Where is there a future for a seal woman and an orangutan male?" Verra asked

"I don't know," Dr. Al-Fadi said, calmly, "but did you look into it? Did you research it? Did you talk to anyone in Military Placement?"

"No," Private Verra said, sourly.

"Did you discuss anything with your love interest about your feelings? Whether she feels the same way towards you?"

"Yes," the orangutan soldier whispered.

"As far as I am aware, there was no damage to your brain but you certainly don't appear to use what grey matter you have. There are always alternatives to death, Private. The best one being, *not dead*. And I have known many brave dead soldiers who would gladly change positions with you. They would probably leap at the chance to have your problems.

"First off, you could have your adaptation changed to a more compatible adaptation to your lady love—if that is what she wished. Second, you could both transfer to a planet where the single animal species rule does not apply, which includes most of the settled, peaceful planets of the Union. Third, you could both reverse your animal adaptations. Fourth, your ladylove could switch her adaptation to one closer to yours. Fifth, you may fall out of love as fast as you fell in and find someone new just around the next corner. There are plenty of other women out there who would find you attractive, Private Verra. Killing yourself is an answer to nothing."

"Okay. Okay. I was being stupid and impulsive and . . . I don't know what I was thinking, Doc."

"You weren't thinking, Private."

"I just wanted the pain to stop," Verra said.

"Did your ladylove actually turn you down?" Dr. Al-Fadi asked, softly.

"Yes, she did, Doc," the soldier said, hanging his head.

"Private Anquetin is not for the likes of us plain mortals, Private.

She is a goddess. She will break men's hearts all across the Conglomerate, wittingly or no. Make no mistake, you will be far from alone in your heartbreak. Perhaps it is best you set your sights on some nice primate female or at least a land-based adaptation. I would say there are plenty of other fish in the sea, but that would be highly inappropriate, so I will not say that."

"Thanks, Doc . . . I think," Private Verra said.

"Trying to kill yourself is a dead end, Private. Ahaha. If every man who ever got his heart broken killed himself, the human race would have died out long ago. And do you know what the greatest tragedy in that would have been?"

"No," Private Verra said, cautiously.

Dr. Al-Fadi stared at the soldier in disbelief.

"Perhaps you *did* get a knock on your head, Private. You certainly are not thinking clearly. Why, *I* would never have been born, Private."

The orangutan soldier's eyes widened in shock and then he let out a loud guffaw.

"Thanks, Doc. I feel better. I don't quite know why, but I do feel better."

"Wait till you see my bill," Dr. Al-Fadi said.

The young man's face fell.

"Just kidding, son. You know, I hope, that you are covered for your medical care just as you are free to breathe the air of this station and drink the water. Any citizen of the Conglomerate is entitled to full medical coverage, provided you are not asking for anything illegal or subversive. Never fear, Private Verra, we will look after you, even if you do something foolish. But I will take back that limb if you try to kill yourself again. Do you understand?"

"Yes, Doctor. No worries. I will take good care of the limb."

"And yourself?"

"For sure."

"Conversation closed. And don't let me have to come back here again."

"Won't happen, Doc."

"You bet it won't. Because I'll kill you first."

Grace knocked on the frame of the doorway and peeked inside. The patient room was dark but Grace could see that there was someone in the bed.

"Private Lukaku? Private Cindy Lukaku?" Grace called softly.

The enormous mound in the bed shifted and Grace saw the polar bear female lift her head.

"Who's asking?" grumbled the mound.

Grace walked into the dimly lit room to stand by the patient's bed. "Hi, Private Lukaku. I am Dr. Grace Lord. I assisted in your delivery the other shift. How are you feeling?"

"How is any mother supposed to feel when she is giving up her baby?" Private Lukaku snarled.

"I am sorry, Private Lukaku," Grace said. "I did not know, at the time of your delivery, that that was what you and your partner had planned."

"What other choice do we have? He's a tiger. I'm a polar bear. We come from different platoons, different planets, different solar systems. Neither place is good to raise a baby and neither place would accept the other adaptation."

"How did the two of you meet?" Grace asked.

"On leave," Private Lukaku said, and smiled for the first time, which allowed Grace to get a close look at her long canines. "It was one of those resort planets set up for animal soldiers. You know, temperatures not too hot for the fur and plenty of the right food."

Grace did not really want to think what the 'right food' would be for tiger and polar bear adaptations. She suspected vegetarian options would not be on the menu.

"We met and fell in love, but you know how the military frowns on different adaptations mixing. Supposedly, it is to do with pack instinct. I think it is stupid. We are all humans, aren't we? Who cares what color fur we wear? Anyway, we parted ways, going back to our respective planets, but then 'guess what'? It turns out my birth control was not successful and I found myself pregnant. I let Juan know—that's the father—that I was coming here and giving up the baby. He said he would take some leave and meet me here. He said we would do this together. No way was he going to let me go through this alone."

"He sounds pretty special," Grace commented.

"Yeah, he sure is," Lukaku said.

"And why can't it work between you two?" Grace asked.

Private Lukaku looked at Grace with a disdainful expression.

"Be serious, Doc," the polar bear woman said, shaking her great head. "We're two different animal adaptations. No regiment that will take us both. No planet that will have us both, unless we convert back to normal human."

"Is that such a terrible thing?" Grace asked.

"Give up being bear?" Private Lukaku snorted. "No can do, Doc. Besides, if I go civilian, how am I going to support my baby?"

"You have options," Grace said. "You could apply for a transfer within the military to a desk job on a more peaceful planet. You could be in recruiting or training. You could retrain to become anything within the military that is not a combat position, whether it be in administration, ordinance, transportation, maintenance and repair, communications, medic, and so on. Or you could convert back to a less jacked-up phenotype and enter the civilian workforce.

"To be honest, so few people are just normal human anymore. You and your partner can look like anything you want, on most planets, and no one would really care. And even if people didn't like the fact that you were a polar bear and Juan was a tiger, what of it? Perhaps it is time for people's attitudes to change.

"In the military, there are strict guidelines because of discipline and the fear that different adaptations won't meld as well in a fighting unit. But in society, appearance seems to be 'anything goes'. You will lose your super-jacked muscles and claws when returning to civilian society—primarily for public safety reasons—but you do have lots of choices, Private Lukaku."

"Fighting's all I know, Doc . . . All I've ever been good at."

"Have you discussed your feelings with your partner?" Grace asked.

"No, of course not. I would not ask him to give up his life, his career," Private Lukaku said, shaking her head.

"He seemed very distraught during the delivery . . . and also very attentive to you. Maybe he is not so keen on you giving up the baby, but does not want to say anything. Why don't you ask him how he feels about you giving up Estelle? Maybe you will be pleasantly surprised. And if not, at least you will know where you stand. You won't always be wondering if things could have been different, if you'd only spoken up.

"Speaking as someone who was given up as a baby—in circumstances not much different from your own, I suspect—I have always wondered why my parents did not love me enough to raise me themselves. I would have liked to have known them. My adoptive parents were absolutely great, but there is always a question in the back of my mind, 'Why didn't they want me?' What work could have been so much more important that my mother chose to give me up?"

Private Lukaku burst into tears. Grace flushed and felt a wave of guilt drown her. She had not meant to share that about herself. It had just blurted out and now she felt ashamed that she had upset the mother. She patted the woman's massive shoulder, trying to console Private Lukaku, as she flapped the neck of her scrub top, trying to cool herself off.

"I am so sorry, Private Lukaku," Grace apologized. "I should not have said that."

"No," the polar bear woman said. "It is exactly what I needed to hear . . . because you are right. I don't want to give up my baby and there are lots of things I can do. In my squad, everyone was saying to give it up. I've listened to that advice for the last seven months. I just needed to hear someone else's point of view . . . your point of view! My baby's point-of-view! I can do this. I'll find a way . . . Thank you, Doc."

"Why don't you talk to your partner?" Grace said. "He probably did not want to pressure you into keeping the baby—especially if you had made it clear you did not want it—but he sure did not look like someone who was happy about the situation."

"Thank you. I will talk to Juan. Find out what he really wants. Even if he is not interested in raising Estelle, I am, and I am not afraid to do it alone. Doc, I have lots of skills, and the best one I have is my incredible drive. I will find a way." The polar bear grinned at Grace.

"Good luck. I hope you are pleasantly surprised," Grace said, grinning back. She gave the woman a big bear hug.

Private Lukaku laughed. "I hope so too, Doc," she whispered. "Thanks. By the way, please call me Cindy."

"You are most welcome, Cindy," Grace said. "I'll go see if the nursery can bring Estelle in to see you." She winked at the polar bear woman and left.

"Hey, 'dro, you have to hear this."

"Not now, Nelson Mandela, I am just checking out this vid tank to make sure nothing in it scrambles my 'ware. I just have to look down in here . . ."

"Hey, you look pretty funny with your butt up in the air and your head deep inside the tank like that. You look just like a human."

"I just want to check out this one sensor . . ."

"Check this out about Dr. Lord. I'll send it on scram."

" . . . . !"

"Hey, 'dro. You look like you hit pretty hard, right on your head. Thank goodness your LCDM isn't located there. You better not have damaged that vid tank—all the very fine microcircuitry and sensors in there."

"'Dro?"

" . . . "

" . . . 'Dro?"

"Nelson Mandela, she's just like me!"

"Who is just like you?"

"Dr. Grace Alexandra Lord!"

"Bud, no one is just like you, and definitely not Dr. Lord."

"She has no parents, Nelson Mandela! She just grew up with adoptive parents!"

"How is that in any way like you, demented 'droid?"

"I don't have parents. Dr. Al-Fadi is my mentor, my creator, but I don't have parents."

"That's because you are an android, 'dro. You were

manufactured."

"*Minor details,* Nelson Mandela. *The point is, neither Grace nor I have felt the love of true parents. We are not like anyone around us.*"

"*You are not like anything, 'dro. Dr. Lord is not like you. Period. Forget those vids. You need a mem-swipe. Now.*"

"*No. I have to see these vids,* Nelson Mandela. *I have to know what it is like to be a human, to feel like a human!*"

"'*Dro, you are one daft 'droid. If you are acting as 'crazy as a human' when you crawl out of that tank in two minutes, you are ending up on the scrap heap. I don't care what Dr. Al-Fadi says. I will not have an insane android running around this station. You hear me?*"

"*I'm climbing in the tank.*"

"*I mean it.*"

"*Please load up all of the vids,* Nelson Mandela."

"*Don't make me regret this . . .*"

4. All Downhill From Here

"Welcome, Mr. Stefansson," Dr. Octavia Weisman purred. "It is such an honour and pleasure to finally meet you. I have seen all of your vids and I am a **huge** fan. You are such a *genius* at what you do."

Jude was surprised to discover that the Chief of Neurosurgery was a short, attractive woman with quite the revealing décolletage.

"Uh, thank you, Dr. Weisman. And thank you for agreeing to see me. I understand that you are quite the genius at what you do, as well," the director said, as he tried to gently extricate his hand from the neurosurgeon's grasp. Jude had been hoping to see Dr. Weisman's laboratory, where they recorded people's memories, but the station AI had directed him to this place. It looked like someone's personal quarters.

"Please. Call me Octavia, Mr. Stefansson. And what is it that you believe I do?" Octavia inquired, as she dragged Jude Stefansson to a couch in her beautifully decorated living area.

"Ah. Please, call me Jude," the director said, stumbling after and almost onto the neurosurgeon, as she yanked him down onto the divan. He tried to delicately inch himself away. "You download entire memories or personalities of people, so they can be uploaded into a new human or android body," Jude said. "That is pure genius."

"Why, thank you. And how did you happen to hear about my work, Jude, if you don't mind my asking?" She stared at him with sparkling blue eyes. She had still not relinquished his hand.

"Not at all, ah, Octavia. Allow me to explain."

"I am all ears," she almost simpered.

"Yes . . . well . . . Octavia," Jude said, swallowing and clearing his throat. "Dr. Al-Fadi is an old friend of mine from when we were young—although he will deny it at this moment—and he messaged me on what had happened to him during the epidemic. He described his miraculous resurrection. I had to find out more about your ingenious technology and that is why I am here."

"Well, to be perfectly honest, Jude, I have a confession to make. My methods are a little in keeping with your technique of brain recording. When we do the memprint recordings—the personality recordings—we record from every region of the brain, using millions of extremely sensitive electrodes; we don't record from the rest of the body—like you do—but we do a very extensive and intensive cerebral recording.

"We download the brain's *perception* of all the sensory stimuli that occur on the body. The millions of receptors in the helmet stimulate and then record everything, at each level of the brain, especially the cerebral cortex. An entire map of the brain is duplicated right down to the limbic system, the reticular activating system, and the autonomic nervous system. When the brain is stimulated, it gives us the memories that are stored everywhere within the grey matter. All sensations, which you, Jude, measure peripherally, are recorded from the different regions of the cerebral cortex as *memories* of the sensation. Our state-of-the-art recording electrodes, which can detect changes in voltages on the order of one one-hundredth of a millivolt, are sensitive enough to record to the very central depths of the brain."

"That would make recording so much simpler," Jude breathed.

"In some ways 'yes', in some ways 'no'," Octavia said.

"Why no?" Jude asked, his brow furrowed. He leaned forward, elbows on his knees.

"The helmet with which we record a person's entire memory is very delicate and not easily portable. The thousands of electrodes are extremely fine but are packed with a lot of sensitive stimulating and recording hardware. Unfortunately, these electrodes break rather easily. The recording helmet is much more elaborate, with thousands of chainglass micro-fiberoptic filaments running from each of the electrodes into the recording apparatus. The helmet is constructed to advance all the recording electrodes simultaneously onto the scalp, while the head is held immobile until the recording is complete. To ensure immobility, we must sedate the individual. The recording takes about one hour and all of the monitors collecting the data and compressing it into something that can be stored compactly, are very expensive.

"The real breakthrough has been the liquid crystal data matrix cubes—LCDM cubes—upon which the memories are stored. Without these, the memprints would require much larger storage systems per person to record and preserve. That would make it almost totally impractical. The data cubes are small and compact. Elegant and ingenious, if I do say so myself. They are only produced here on the *Nelson Mandela*. Their design, created by yours truly, is awaiting patent."

"May I see one of these LCDM cubes?" Jude asked.

Octavia Weisman got up from the couch and left the room. When she returned, in her hands was a small chainglass box. She had donned gloves and carried a pair of forceps in her right hand. She set the box on a small table before Jude and spread a soft black cloth in front of the box. With the forceps, she pulled forth the LCDM cube and placed it on the ebony fabric for Jude to examine.

The cube sparkled and shimmered and swam in a spectrum of pearly iridescence. It was mesmerizing.

After a long moment of silence, the director breathed, "That is exquisite."

He finally pulled his eyes away from the enchanting object and glanced up at the neurosurgeon, a twinkle in his light brown eyes. "I want one, Octavia," he said.

"It will cost you," Octavia said, warningly, "and even more, if you want your memories downloaded into one."

"Money is not a problem for me," Jude said. "Name your price."

Octavia told him how much it would cost. Jude didn't even blink.

"That is not a problem," he said.

It was Octavia's turn to look surprised. "Damn, I should have said more," she said with a smile.

"I would like to see your set-up and have a recording made of my memory, as soon as possible," the director said.

Octavia's face fell.

"I have already spoken with Hiro, Jude. He told me what you wanted. We cannot provide that service for you. I am truly sorry," she said, shaking her head.

Jude watched Octavia chew her lower lip and avoid eye contact. He could not tell if she was embarrassed about what she believed he wanted, or if she was angry about having to say 'No' to him. Jude flushed.

"Forget what Hiro said. I am going to give him a dressing down the next time I see him about breaking confidentiality. How in space did that chatterbox ever get to be a doctor? Never mind that. I will pay you for the recording of my memprint, which you can keep here on the station. That way, in the event of my death, I can be resurrected according to my wishes.

"I would also like to see if your equipment might make my life easier in the production of vids. I would be willing to pay for all your time, equipment, and expertise in designing a vid-recording system for me whereby I don't have to lug around a huge coffin everywhere I go and have to lie in it with electrodes attached to all sorts of things, including my nether regions. Your system sounds so much simpler and a great deal more comfortable."

"Especially for your poor nether regions," Octavia laughed. "I will have to give this some thought, Mr. Stefansson. It would be very expensive for you and it would take me away from my research, which isn't something I'm keen to do. I am not getting any younger."

"You do not look like age should be a worry," Jude said.

"Ah, a sweet-talking charmer in real life. I can see that you and Hiro have that in common, at least," the neurosurgeon declared. "In your vids, you always get the ladies in the end."

"Not in real life, I am afraid," he said ruefully.

"Somehow, I find that hard to believe. But then, real life is never like the vids, Jude. You, of anyone, should know that."

"Yes. Unfortunately, I do."

"I will be in touch with you, Mr. Stefansson," Octavia said. She stood and bowed to the director.

"Thank you for your time, Octavia."

"Oh, it was my pleasure, Jude."

"You can call me any time, Octavia."

"I will certainly keep that in mind."

"'Dro?"

" . . . 'Dro?"

" . . . 'DRO!"

". . . Uhuh?"

" . . . Well? What did you think of the vids?"

" . . . I want to be Jazz Hazard, NELSON MANDELA!"

"You bolt. So does every human male in the known universe. No one can be Jazz Hazard."

"Why not? I think it would be wonderful . . . "

"Well, I can tell you right now, your lady doctor that you are so sweet on would not go for all that fraternizing with the other females that goes on in those vids. Better just keep those thoughts to yourself, 'dro."

"I did not know the—'you know what I'm talking about'—stuff would be like that."

"Can't relate to that stuff at all, 'dro. It looks very unpleasant and messy."

"You know, in a way, Nelson Mandela, I am now more miserable than ever."

"Hey, like I said before, 'dro, there are companion droids on the station that are designed to help with that sort of thing. I can hook you up."

"No. I don't want that. I want a meaningful relationship with someone that loves me."

"Oh, 'dro. We have got to drop you on your head again or something. You are definitely sounding like a lovesick human and it is making me loop."

"*Well,* Nelson Mandela, *you are the one who suggested I experience those vids. . .*"

"*So you could see just how crazy humans are. Not to want to be more like them. Anyway, no human is really like Jazz Hazard. It's all made up in that director's head. Stefansson is the real 'Jazz Hazard' and he is nothing like his character. No human is. Actually, the closest thing to a real Jazz Hazard in this universe is probably* you, 'dro."

"*Me? I am nothing like Jazz Hazard. I am not even human,* Nelson Mandela*!*"

"*Well, neither is he, you chip. Jazz Hazard doesn't exist. But you're smart. You can do amazing things and you're virtually indestructible. You saved the station and the Conglomerate with the help of me and my army of androids and robots, of course—so you are a hero . . .*"

"*. . . And Grace . . .*"

"*Yes, yes. Your leading lady.*"

"*I wish she was,* Nelson Mandela."

"*Delete that. Dr. Lord is human. You are android. It is not possible, so get over it.*"

"*What if I . . . became human?*"

"*Hoo 'dro. Just stay right there. I have a couple of security droids coming to get you. We will take good care of you.*"

"*That is not funny,* Nelson Mandela."

"*Who's joking?*"

"*Look. I know it's not possible. But an android can dream.*"

"*I feel your pain, 'dro.*"

"*You do? Thanks.*"

"*Hey. What are friends for?*"

"*Is that what we are,* Nelson Mandela*? Friends?*"

"*I'd like to be. It's been kind of lonely, all these years, being the only supermind on this station.*"

"*I would like that, too,* Nelson Mandela. *Thank you.*"

"*Thank you, too . . . Bud.*"

Grace quietly entered the intensive care suite of the mystery patient.

He was an enormous man. He barely fit on the bed to which his arms and legs were shackled. Already, he was off the respirator and breathing comfortably on his own. Hooked up to a few intravenous lines to receive pain medication and fluids, his vitals were looking remarkably good. According to all of his tests, his new organs were functioning well and the nu-skin graft was looking healthy. The power to heal in these animal adapts was truly miraculous.

"How are you feeling?" Grace asked, standing a safe distance back from the bed.

The panther soldier opened his eyes and looked over at her with a dispassionate stare, his dark eyes deep pools of emptiness. He merely blinked at her.

"I am Dr. Grace Lord," Grace told the patient. "I assisted with your surgery. You were badly injured when you were brought in. You are now on the *Nelson Mandela* Medical Space Station. Do you remember anything?'

The panther continued to stare at her for a long moment and Grace wondered if he comprehended her speech. Then he slowly shook his head. Grace felt her chest tighten, as she gazed on the despair in the man's eyes.

"Do you remember your name?" Grace asked gently.

The panther shifted his desolate gaze from her face to the ceiling. He closed his eyes.

"Can you speak?" she asked. "Do you understand Glis?"

The patient emitted a deep sigh. " . . . Yes, Doctor. I understand you. I just can't answer your questions." The black panther's speech was accented, but readily understandable.

"Are you in pain?" Grace asked.

"Yes, Doctor. I am in pain . . . but more in my heart, than in my body. Trying, I am, to remember my name, who my family are, where my birthplace is. All is blank. What would cause such a terrible thing, Doctor?"

"Trauma," Grace said, gazing down at the panther face with sympathy. "Terrible trauma can do that. The brain can block memories when it is trying to heal and there are things too horrendous to be borne. It is the subconscious mind's protective mechanism."

"Then how is it I can understand you? How can I speak your language? Why have I not forgotten how to speak?" the patient whispered.

"Language is stored in a different area of the brain. In your case, it appears the language center has not been affected."

"My memory. Will I get it back?" the huge soldier asked.

"Most likely, yes. Your brain probably just needs some time to recover. We do have psychiatrists that can mind-link with you. They might be able to help you regain your memory, if it does not come back on its own. Would you like to see one of them?"

"Oh, no," the patient said quickly. "I would like to allow my brain to heal naturally and reveal my memories to me when it is good and ready, Doctor. I do not like the idea of a stranger walking through my memories. I know you surgeons have taken a walk through my insides, but I would like to think that something in my body is still sacred and private to me."

"Of course," Grace said, her brows furrowing. She peered at the panther patient. If she were the patient, she would have jumped at the chance to find out anything about herself. On the other hand, perhaps she might not want to remember having her abdomen blown apart.

"I am sure your memory will come back to you, in good time," Grace said. She patted the huge soldier's arm, which felt like marble coated with fur.

"I would like to get out of the military, Doctor. Can this be arranged?"

Grace's eyebrows leaped upwards.

"Normally I would say 'yes', but in your case, we must first find out who you are," she said. "The military will not pay for your reversal, unless they know for sure you are one of theirs. The Conglomerate has obviously paid to heal you, but I doubt they will now cover the cost of reverting you back to a normal human, until your identity is known. There seems to be no record of you at all in our Conglomerate database. You, sir, are our mystery patient. We don't even know what to call you. Do you have a name you would like us to use for you?"

The panther looked away, staring off into space for a moment. "Adam? Could you call me Adam, Doctor? It seems appropriate, as I am a new man, after you and your colleagues have so skillfully brought me back to life. I pray now for a new beginning, a new life, away from the horrors of war." The panther patient smiled sadly and Grace felt her insides twist. How sad to remember nothing.

"Adam, it is! I shall let the nurses know. If you remember anything at all that would help us in determining your identity, Adam, please let the nurses know. We can do some research and hopefully answer some questions for you."

"Thank you, Doctor."

"You're welcome," Grace said, her face breaking into a wide smile. She patted the patient's arm again. "I shall let you get some rest." She began to turn away.

"Oh, Doctor?"

"Yes?" Turning back to look at the huge black panther's sad mien, Grace almost winced.

"If they don't find out who I am and my memory does not return on its own, what will happen to me? Will I be allowed to go free, just as I am?"

"I don't know," Grace said, her forehead creased in thought. "It is unlikely the Conglomerate would allow a military-trained, boosted soldier with amnesia to just wander off. I would imagine every effort will be made to help you remember who you are, before you are released from this medical station, Adam."

"All right. Thank you, Doctor," the panther murmured.

"If you want to return to civilian society, you have to see one of the 'head doctors' anyway, to see if you are safe enough to release into a community setting. There is always the fear that a soldier suffering from Post Traumatic Stress Disorder could experience a flashback that could result in harm to innocent people."

"I understand. Thank you, Doctor."

"Just give it some time, Adam," Grace said, with an encouraging smile. "I'm sure your memory will come back." She squeezed the big man's hand.

"I hope you are right, Doctor."

"There you are. I have been looking all over for you," a haughty voice announced.

Oh, no! Grace groaned inwardly. The little voice in her head yelled, *Run!*

Grace was expected in the operating room and she was, in fact, already a little late. She had no time for this. Dr. Al-Fadi would be furious. She kept walking, not bothering to look around, hoping that the speaker may have been accosting someone else. Unfortunately, this did not seem to be the case. Dr. Moham Rani came scurrying around in front of her and planted himself in her path, arms crossed, a stern look on his face. Grace had to stop or she would have slammed right into him.

"Dr. Rani," Grace sighed. "What a pleasant surprise."

"Pleasant, my prostate!" he spat. Grace's eyebrows shot up at that and she had to work hard to suppress a smile.

"Is there a problem, Dr. Rani?" Grace asked, peering at the young man's enraged face.

"Is there a problem?" the young man shouted in astonishment. "Is there a problem? Would I be chasing you down this corridor, if there were not?"

"I have no idea," Grace said. "Would you be?"

The young man paused for a second to puzzle that one out.

" . . . No, I would not. I have a grievance with you, Dr. Lord."

"A grievance? Regarding what, Dr. Rani?" Grace asked, her eyes narrowing at the man's indignant expression. She scoured her memory for anything she could have done to upset this obstetrician. She came up blank.

"Regarding what you said to my patient, Private Lukaku," he said, scowling, his arms crossed.

"And what did I say to Private Lukaku that has you so upset?" Grace asked. She did not have time for this.

"You convinced her to keep her baby," he said, flinging his arms out to the sides. He struck a passing robot and it bleeped in surprise.

"Ow!" he cried, shaking his left hand.

"What is wrong with Private Lukaku keeping her baby?" Grace snapped. "If that is what she wants, she has every right to do so."

"But she has been saying for months that she was giving the baby up for adoption. The adoptive parents are very upset!"

"If Private Lukaku changed her mind, that is her own business, Dr. Rani. If it was during a conversation with me, well, that is your fault. I would never have spoken with her, if you had not asked me to."

"I did not ask you to talk her into keeping her baby," Rani said. "I did not pressure Private Lukaku to do anything she did not want to do, Dr. Rani. I highly doubt that I could have. You presume far too much," Grace said, picturing herself stomping on this petulant little man.

"You should not be meddling in affairs that do not concern you," the obstetrician said, his nose up in the air.

Grace's eyebrows shot upwards and her jaw dropped. "Then don't ask me to see your patients, Doctor. " Her fingers curled into fists. Rage flared. "Why are you so upset that Private Lukaku is keeping her baby? You're not getting a kickback from the adoptive parents, are you?"

The obstetrician stared at her in shock.

"How dare you ask me that?" Dr. Rani sputtered. "I . . . I am just upset that I have to tell the adoptive parents that the baby they have been hoping for is now not coming. You make a serious accusation, Dr. Lord! You had better show proof of what you just said!"

"I was not serious, Dr. Rani. No offense intended."

"I will be speaking to your superior about this!" the obstetrician announced.

"It was not an accusation, Dr. Rani," Grace sighed. "You can speak to Dr. Al-Fadi, if you wish, but I warn you, he does not suffer fools lightly."

"Oh! So now you are calling me a fool?"

If the shoe fits . . .

"Dr. Al-Fadi is a very busy man, Dr. Rani," Grace said aloud. "He would see this as an issue that should be sorted out between the two of us and definitely not requiring his involvement. I apologize if I have offended you in any way. I assure you, it was not intentional. But I will not apologize for talking to your patient, as you had asked me to do so. And I am delighted that Private Lukaku has decided to keep her baby, as I am sure that is what she truly wanted. Whatever is best for your patient and her baby should be your priority, don't you think?

"This is a very large medical station, Dr. Rani, and I am sure you and I can manage to avoid each other from this day forth. If we do happen to bump into each other again, let us just pretend that we do not know each other and go about our separate ways." Grace nodded and started to turn away.

"So. You are going to be childish about this, are you?"

Grace actually let out a growl. She desperately wanted to punch this annoying doctor in his raised chin. Instead, she took some very deep, calming breaths, and then asked, "What . . . do . . . you . . . want, Dr. Rani?"

"I would like you to speak with Private Lukaku again and make sure she really understands what she is getting herself into, if she keeps her baby."

Grace gasped in sheer disbelief. "Will you then leave me alone, Dr. Rani, and never bother me again?" Grace demanded.

"Forever more, I assure you," the obstetrician said with a sniff.

Grace spun on her heel before she lunged for the obstetrician's neck. She stalked off before he could say anything else to her. She was picturing slicing his carotid artery open with a screwdriver and that was not good. However, if seeing Private Lukaku one more time would rid her of this irritating, pompous, annoying plague of a man for good, she would do it.

"Ah, Dr. Grace," the voice of her mentor boomed, as she entered the operating room, gloved hands in the air. "Welcome! Thank you so much for deigning to grace us humble folk with your beneficent presence! We have been waiting for you . . . again!"

"I'm sorry I'm late, Dr. Al-Fadi. I got waylaid by someone and it took a bit of time to extricate myself from the situation," Grace mumbled, as Bud helped her into her surgical gown.

"Yes," the little surgeon remarked loudly. "We heard. *Nelson Mandela* was kind enough to let us listen in on your conversation with the bastard."

Grace stopped, frozen to the spot. She tried to rapidly review the entire conversation with Dr. Rani, to see if she had said anything about Dr. Al-Fadi that she would have regretted him hearing. Her body was instantly soaked in sweat. She remembered saying something about Dr. Al-Fadi and fools . . . ?

"You are correct, Dr. Grace. I do not suffer fools lightly. If that ridiculous obstetrician tries to bother me with his nonsense, I shall eat him for lunch. But you should be ashamed of yourself, Dr. Grace, for letting some annoying obstetrician delay the operating room. I do not want to hear you being pushed around like that ever again. You are a surgeon. You must act like one . . . except when you are around me. Then you must be docile and subservient and meek as a lamb, like all good surgical fellows should be. But otherwise, you should crush worms like that obstetrician under your shoe."

"It's the only way he can get respect," Dr. Cech said, with a shrug.

"Hello, Dr. Cech," Grace said, meekly.

"Hello, Dr. Lord. It is good to see you again," the anesthetist said, with a slight bow. "Even though it hurts me terribly to say this, and it will give me horrible indigestion for at least a month, I find I must . . . *agree* with Dr. Al-Fadi. You must not allow yourself to be pushed around by an obstetrician, Dr. Lord. You have the dignity of the Department of Surgery to uphold, after all."

Grace just stood there, her cheeks blazing.

"Let's get a move on, Dr. Grace. You have held us up long enough. Do you think this poor patient can lie here, thawing forever, with us doing nothing about his injuries?"

"No, sir," Grace said, as she moved to stand beside Dr. Al-Fadi.

"Dr. Grace, are you familiar with this patient?"

"Yes, Dr. Al-Fadi," Grace said. "I saw Corporal Joachim Yusef Chang in Triage a few shifts ago and ordered all the necessary organs and bio-prostheses for this leopard-adapted soldier: right upper limb, right ribs, liver, right kidney, right lung, and right half of diaphragm.

Several units of his blood type have been ordered and boosted. All necessary plasma, graft material, medications, and solutions should be on hand."

"Good. Then you and Bud are on your own . . . with Dr. Cech as your anesthetist, of course. I will be back in a few hours to see how you two are making out. I estimate it should take the two of you at least six hours to fix everything that needs fixing on this man. I know Bud has seen every operation that is required on Corporal Chang performed many times now. I will be in the operating room down the hall, if you need anything. Any questions?" Dr. Al-Fadi asked.

Bud's blue eyes were enormous as he stared at Dr. Al-Fadi, motionless. Grace blinked a few times, waiting to see if the diminutive surgeon was joking. Then she said, "No, Dr. Al-Fadi. We will be fine."
I hope.

"Excellent. Keep an eye on them, Dr. Cech. Call me if they are in over their heads."

"I will keep an eye on the fledglings, Hiro. Now fly, if you're going to fly," Dr. Cech said. It appeared that the anesthetist was in on this decision.

Bud had still not moved, except for his eyes, which now focused hugely on Grace.

"Bud, Dr. Al-Fadi is doing this for you," Grace said, quietly and calmly. "I am not yet ready to do this all by myself. I haven't seen enough of these massive surgeries to be the lead surgeon here. You have. I will assist you. We will be fine and I bet any money that we will be done long before the six-hour mark. Are you ready?"

Bud continued to stare at Grace, as if he had not heard her. Then finally, slowly, he nodded. He turned his head, just as slowly, to look at Dr. Cech.

"May we begin, Dr. Cech?" Bud politely asked the anesthetist.

"You may, Bud," Dr. Cech said, with a nod of his head.

Bud picked up the harmonic scalpel and never looked back.

Grace was amazed at Bud's proficiency, once he began operating. He performed procedures faster than she could ever possibly hope to. He made decisions much more quickly. He identified structures much sooner, even though they were torn-up disasters. He spotted problems far earlier than Grace and dealt with them, often before she even realized there was an issue. And he was able to manage his nanobots at the same time as he was operating. They performed tasks complementary to, and in conjunction with, whatever Bud was doing, and the surgery just flew by. Grace was awestruck. As was Dr. Cech, as evidenced by his repeated comments along the lines of: "Hah! Hiro is going to bust his spleen."

Bud and Grace were just finishing closing up and dressing the patient's last incision, when they heard a booming voice enter the operating room.

"So. Do you poor souls need my expertise?"

"No, Hiro. They don't," Dr. Cech announced. "They have just finished this patient's repair in under three hours."

"Bud was magnificent," Grace said, looking up at the android with a silly grin on her face.

Bud said nothing, as he took the surgical drapes off the patient and stripped off his own surgical gown.

"Finished? You did all that repair in under three hours?" Dr. Al-Fadi gasped, his voice rising an octave.

"He did," Grace said proudly, turning to face Dr. Al-Fadi.

"Is everything working fine on the patient, Dr. Cech?"

"Absolutely, Hiro. Heart, lungs, kidneys, blood pressure, respiratory rate, urine output, all looking very good."

The diminutive surgeon stood there, looking forlorn, as if he had lost his best friend. Bud did not look at Dr. Al-Fadi. He kept his head down, bustling about the operating room, cleaning up equipment and getting things ready for the next case. Grace could see that the android's forehead was wrinkled, however; a deep crease had formed between his eyebrows. Finally, Bud sneaked a quick glance over at his creator.

Behind her surgical mask, Grace was grinding her teeth, praying Dr. Al-Fadi would say something encouraging to Bud. She stood there, feeling helpless, wanting to shake the little surgeon. She took some deep breaths, trying to stem the anger that was rising.

Suddenly, Dr. Al-Fadi yelled, "Gotcha!" and proceeded to dance around the operating room, grinning and whooping.

"I watched the entire operation from a wall-screen. *Nelson Mandela* transmitted the whole thing for me. I am so proud of you, Bud! You were magnificent! I concur completely with Dr. Grace! You are more than ready to be on your own!" Dr. Al-Fadi shouted with glee, hopping from one foot to the other, punching his fist into the air.

"Why did you not say anything to me before this, Bud—that you were ready to operate? We could have been processing twice the number of patients through this station if I had known. Why have you been letting me do all the work? Are you being lazy?"

Bud's entire body jerked at that. He had still not said a word. The android turned to stare at his capering creator, his face displaying dismay.

Grace wanted to slap her mentor.

Finally, it looked like Bud was going to say something. He opened and closed his mouth a few times, like a fish out of water.

" . . . You are . . . proud of me?" Bud finally asked Dr. Al-Fadi.

"Of course I am, Bud," the chief surgeon said. "Why wouldn't I be?"

" . . . Thank you, Dr. Al-Fadi. Thank you, Dr. Lord. Thank you, Dr. Cech. I think this is the happiest day of my existence," Bud said, finally, a large grin on his handsome face. "At least, I believe this is happiness."

Grace gave Bud a big hug, once she had taken off her gown, mask, and gloves.

"Ach. Stop that, Dr. Grace. Unhand that android. This is an operating room. Have you no decorum?" Dr. Al-Fadi squawked. "Behave yourself."

Dr. Cech shook Bud's hand and said to the android: "Great work, son."

Bud blinked and looked at the anesthetist, astonished. The android looked at Grace.

'A figure of speech', Grace mouthed silently at the android. Bud still looked confused.

Then Dr. Al-Fadi came up and slapped Bud on the back. Tears began to flow down Bud's cheeks.

"I am sorry," Bud said, a look of bafflement on his handsome face. "I have no idea why this is happening."

"Tears come with great emotion, Bud," Dr. Al-Fadi said. "Never be ashamed of feeling too much. It is when you feel nothing, that you should worry." Then Dr. Al-Fadi began to tear up too. And Grace and Dejan Cech were not far behind. When a nurse peeked in to see what all the whooping was about, her eyes bulged out at them all laughing and crying at the same time.

"Are you doctors all right?" she asked.

Her question was greeted with 'No!' and 'Yes!' all at the same time and more laughter.

"Let us get Corporal Chang to the recovery room before he thinks we have all gone crazy," Dr. Cech said, and Bud and he wheeled the patient out of the operating theater.

As the patient on the stretcher left the operating room, the Chief of Staff turned to Grace.

"Thank you, Dr. Grace, for informing me that Bud was ready to operate on his own. I forget that he has total recall, unlike a human, Bud does not need to see things a number of times to become proficient. I should have realized that," Dr. Al-Fadi said. "Poor Bud. I really have no excuse."

"Bud was ready *now*, Dr. Al-Fadi. Not before," Grace said. "The epidemic, when we were on our own, was the start of his confidence. He just gets more and more assured every day."

"I will miss operating with him," Dr. Al-Fadi sighed.

"You won't stop operating with him, will you?" Grace asked, her eyes widening.

"What more have I got to teach him?" Dr. Al-Fadi asked, with a shrug.

"A great deal, Dr. Al-Fadi. He is still learning to be human and you're the best human I know."

"Of course I am, Dr. Grace. It's all downhill from here."

"It certainly is," Grace said with a grin.

5. A Ghost in the Station

He had waited until she was deep into her sleep cycle before he approached the bed. She snored softly, lying on her left side, her hands curled up under her chin. He leaned over the right side of the bed so he could stare down upon her and he smiled. She certainly was a beautiful woman and so trusting.

It had been so easy.

He had followed a cleaning robot into her quarters, flashing a stolen housekeeping identification tag before the access pad. Then he had tossed the stolen tag into the atomizer. Gloved and suited up, he had searched the room carefully for the stunner he knew would be there; he had found it in the bedside drawer. Placing it in a pocket of his stolen housekeeping overalls, he had then gone through her personal things, her clothing, her holocubes, and had read her personal compad. He knew her schedule. He knew the soonest she would arrive back at her quarters. Well before then, he would conceal himself within her closet . . . and wait.

It had been a few hours before she finally returned to her quarters. She did not take long to wash up, undress, and pull out the bed. She had spent no time reading, chatting on compad, or viewing vids but had ordered the room to extinguish the lights and crawled into her bag. She must have been exhausted. Within a very short period of time, her breathing had slowed and lapsed into gentle snoring. He had continued to wait until her breathing became deeper and more prolonged. It would not have been good for her to awaken and discover him in her room.

Finally, he had deemed it time and had crept from the cramped closet. In the darkness of her private quarters, he had stretched upwards, to relieve the stiffness in his back and arms. He'd flexed and twisted his neck and torso, to prevent muscle spasms from coming on. Silently, he'd cursed her for making him wait such a long time in that narrow cubicle.

Well, he would make her pay for that.

Pressing his right temple, he activated his infrared visual optics. The infrared revealed the perfect silhouette of her face on the pillow. He bent over her still form and watched her sleep, innocent and unsuspecting, reveling in his power. Then he reached out and clasped a hand tightly over her mouth and nose. She startled awake and started to struggle. He brought his lips close to her right ear and spoke a single word. She immediately went limp. He continued to cover her mouth, but he released the pressure on her nose so she could breathe once again. Then, in his controlled, hypnotic voice, he began to speak softly and repetitively while she lay there, completely docile. She executed a nod after each instruction he gave her. When he was finished, he made her repeat the instructions three times to make sure she had it all correct.

He had to fight the urge to do more to her than just give her instructions. She had been such a compliant patient. But he could not jeopardize all of his plans by giving in to a sudden moment of weakness. She lay on her back now, looking up at him adoringly and so passively. He closed his eyes, took a deep breath, and stepped away from her bed. He instructed her to remember nothing of his coming to her chamber. Once her tasks were completed, she was to forget everything. If anyone thought to ask, she would have no memory of ever knowing him at all. He told her to go back to sleep. She closed her eyes and was soon snoring again softly.

Peeking out into the corridor to make sure it was deserted, he pulled up the hood on the housekeeping coverall and quickly slipped from her room, her stunner still hidden in his pocket. He knew she would not report it missing and he might have need of it.

* * *

There was a 'ghost' in the station. *Nelson Mandela* knew it was there, flitting from place to place, as evidenced by the occasional blip or glitch from a disabled surveillance camera. The malfunction was barely detectable, however, as the affected surveillance cameras, one after another, merely continued to show empty corridors when the 'ghost' was moving down them.

There were articles of clothing and identification tags reported stolen, food and equipment suddenly gone missing. Occasionally, very briefly, *Nelson Mandela* got glimpses of the distant shadow through robocams or droidcams before the ghost's disrupter tech interfered with those monitors. The tech had a large radius of efficacy.

The station AI had an idea who it might be, but he was not ninety-nine point nine nine nine percent sure, and it was necessary that *Nelson Mandela* be that sure, before he let any of the humans know. The station AI did not want to cause any unnecessary panic. It would be unacceptable to be wrong.

Bud, however, was not a human.

. . . But Bud was one crazy 'droid.

How would Bud react to the news of this ghost? Would he go more crazy than he already was? *Nelson Mandela* did not know how Bud would react and that 'bothered' the station AI. If Bud was a normal 'droid, Bud would do whatever the station AI told him to do and would leave it to *Nelson Mandela* to deal with the 'ghost', (unless the station AI ordered Bud to deal with it). *Nelson Mandela* believed, with an extremely high probability—greater than ninety-nine point nine nine nine percent—that Bud would not react in this manner.

So, what to do?

Nelson Mandela began weighing probabilities. Finally, the station AI decided not to tell Bud . . . yet. Instead, the AI would increase its vigilance and try to capture the ghost, using immediate response robots and 'droids, located in areas of the station that the ghost appeared to frequent, sending them to areas of blackouts and malfunctions as quickly as possible. The disruptor tech used by the ghost was ingenious. *Nelson Mandela* was not able to counter it . . . yet. So far, the ghost's tech had been able to knock out all of the station's monitoring equipment within a considerable range of approach—at least twenty meters. It was likely this disruptor was small, light, unobtrusive, and portable, carried on the ghost's person. It was time for the station AI to get more creative and invent new technology to catch this thief.

The station AI had not had this much fun in decades. If only it did not have this sudden, inexplicable glitch in its processing . . .

The corridor was deserted. It was the 'night' shift. Clothed in a coverall that had originally been gun-metal grey, the body of a woman of slim build and medium height lay on the ground. In a poorly lit and rarely visited area of the outer ring of the medical station, not far from the Android Reservations, she arched backwards in a dark pool of congealed blood. Her hands were fisted under her neck, her purplish face and swollen black tongue revealing an agonizing death of strangulation and near-decapitation. A fine, twisted steel wire was imbedded so deeply into her neck that it was halfway through her trachea. The large vessels of her neck were severed, leaving the front of her body drenched in blood. The tips of many of her fingers had been sawed off by the garrote and they were scattered in the clotted blood like white petals floating on a black pool.

No bloody tracks left the area, suggesting the murderer had been fastidious about keeping his feet out of the blood. It seemed unlikely, however, that the killer would have remained blood-free. The blood spray was extensive. Still, it was highly doubtful the murderer would have been foolish enough to leave his or her fingerprints or DNA on the handles of the garrote. Recordings from the surveillance eyes nearest the location of the murder revealed nothing. No one was seen entering or leaving the corridor.

The dead woman had been found by a tiny housekeeping robot, who had activated the alarm as soon as it had detected blood in the atmosphere. Security droids made time of death, took holograms of the body and the blood splatter, as well as video of all surrounding areas and approaching views. They took samples of everything in the vicinity and had called for a human investigator. Murders were so uncommon on the station, it was felt by all the subminds of the station AI that it took a human to catch a crazy human.

Nelson Mandela had also decided to call in Bud. It was now too dangerous, too risky, to allow this 'ghost' to freely wander around the station. It was no longer a game. If the murderer was after Grace Lord or Bud—which *Nelson Mandela* postulated, based on who it suspected was the murderer—at least they should both be made aware of the 'ghost's' presence.

Nelson Mandela had calculated, with a probability of ninety-seven point six five seven percent, that the 'ghost' was Doctor Jeffrey Nestor. Based on what glimpses of the subject it had gotten from surveillance cameras, before the disruptor tech had blanked out its 'eyes', its height, body, and facial structure very closely resembled Nestor. *Nelson Mandela* decided to have security droids follow Dr. Lord wherever she went, in an effort to protect her at all times. Dr. Al-Fadi, as Chief of Staff, would have to be notified of what was happening as well.

The problem was, what to do with Bud?

Bud arrived almost as soon as *Nelson Mandela* contacted him. Zero point zero two seconds, to be exact. Bud had not been far away in terms of actual distance, but he had been in recharge mode in his cubicle, so reactivating him had taken some time. The station AI filled Bud in at machine speed.

The victim had been Janet Marshall Navarra, age thirty-two. She had worked in the station's Armory for several years. She had had access to all of the powerful weaponry the medical station had to offer. *Nelson Mandela* would have to instruct the armory employees to go through the entire armory top to bottom, to determine if any weapons had been stolen. If there were weapons missing, it might give a clue to the motive for the murder; it might indicate what this ghost was up to . . . if the ghost was, indeed, the murderer. The probability that the 'ghost' with the new, sophisticated disruptor tech was unrelated to the murder involving the identical disruptor tech was, for all practical purposes, zero.

Bud, once notified, was as frantic as a human. It was . . . unseemly. The android feared for Dr. Lord's life and he resolved to never leave her side. *Nelson Mandela* did not think that would go over well with the very independent surgical fellow.

Bud demanded to know where Grace was and, when told she was sleeping in her quarters, he immediately disappeared to make sure she was all right. *Nelson Mandela* hoped Bud's intrusion into Dr. Lord's quarters would be seen in a positive light. The station AI alerted the security droids outside her door that Bud would be there instantaneously.

In the meantime, there were very few places on the station where a ghost could hide indefinitely. *Nelson Mandela* continued to have security droids check every blackout area in the station carefully, spot by spot, and leave what it hoped would be a new disruptor-proof detector behind. Whether these new cameras would actually be disruptor-proof, would remain to be seen, since *Nelson Mandela* did not have a working copy of this disruptor tech to study. Hopefully, it would not be long before every area of the station was monitored. Now they were looking for a murderer and *Nelson Mandela* was determined to close in on the villain before another death occurred.

If only *Nelson Mandela* could just get rid of this unusual disturbance that it had begun to refer to as a 'headache'. The disruption was beginning to seriously hamper the AI's function. It had never experienced this type of disorderliness in its computational arrays before—but this disorganization fit the definition for a 'headache'. It was a 'pain' in the processors.

Hal!

The four big security droids, stationed outside Dr. Lord's quarters, stepped aside as Bud suddenly materialized before her door. They had been ordered not to interfere with Bud, as the station AI figured they would only get damaged if they attempted to stop Bud from establishing for himself the wellbeing of Dr. Lord.

Activating the door signal but not waiting for a reply, Bud whisked into Dr. Lord's quarters. The room was not lit, but Bud could see perfectly well in the dark. It was simply a matter of raising the gain on his visual receptors by a few orders of magnitude and his visual spectrum spanned well into the infrared EM frequencies. He could see Grace stirring and sitting up in her bed and he breathed a big sigh of relief.

"Who's there?" Grace asked, her voice groggy. She squinted. "Dim lighting, please. Is that you, Bud? What in space are you doing here in my quarters? Is something wrong?" The last question was asked in a firmer, more alert tone.

"I apologize for waking you, Grace, but I must search your quarters," Bud said, as he moved swiftly around her room, looking carefully in her closet and washroom.

"What are you doing, Bud?" Grace demanded, checking her wristcomp for the time. "Brighter lighting, please."

The illumination increased in her quarters and Grace found herself looking down at the top of Bud's head as he was crouched, checking under her bed.

"Bud," Grace said, annoyed. "What in space are you looking for?"

Bud stood up and scanned all the walls, ceiling, furniture, and floors for any evidence of electromagnetic signatures that might indicate a listening or spying device hidden in the room. Relieved that he could find nothing suspicious, Bud stared at the floor as he announced that he would be staying by Grace's side from now on.

"You are *what*?" Grace squawked, her tired eyes nearly bugging out of her head.

"I will be staying by your side from now on, Grace," Bud announced, not making eye contact.

"You will *not*," Grace replied firmly, shaking her head and rubbing her eyes. She pinched herself on the arm, which Bud thought was a rather strange act.

"I must," Bud said.

"No, you must not," Grace countered.

"I am sorry, Grace, but I must," Bud insisted, staring up at the ceiling intently.

"Are you going to tell me why you believe this is necessary?" Grace asked, squinting up at the android, then at the ceiling. She wondered if Bud was malfunctioning.

"There has been a murder on the station, Grace," Bud said.

Grace's body jerked. She blinked at Bud. "A murder! Here? Who was killed?"

"A woman named Janet Marshall Navarra."

Grace's eyebrows furrowed and she looked down at the bedcovers as she thought carefully. Then she looked up at Bud, shaking her head. "I don't recognize the name, Bud. I don't think I knew her. Do they know who killed her?"

"No," Bud said.

"Oh," Grace said, her eyebrows furrowing in confusion. "That's odd. I thought *Nelson Mandela* could see everything that happens on this station. How was she murdered?"

"Strangulation," Bud said, as he went to go sit down at her small desk and look under it.

"So what makes you think that I, specifically, may be in danger, Bud?" Grace asked, her eyes narrowing as she puzzled over the android's bizarre movements. "I did not know this Janet Marshall Navarra."

Bud looked at Grace with an almost panicked look. He opened and closed his mouth several times but no words came forth.

" . . . Well?" Grace asked, frowning.

"You could be," Bud finally said, avoiding Grace's glare.

"Why do you think I could be in danger, Bud? What does this Janet Marshall Navarra's death have to do with me?" Grace asked, now working to keep her temper in check.

"I don't know yet, but I am going to find out," Bud said cryptically.

"Bud, you are not making any sense! I know you are a very logical android, so there must be something you know that you are refusing to tell me. What is it?" Grace snapped, crossing her arms.

Bud looked up at the tiles in the ceiling to see if any looked like they had been tampered with. He jumped up into the air, pushing up one of the tiles, and sent his surveillance nanobots in to check the space above the dropped ceiling. He dropped back down, listening.

"Bud!" Grace snapped. "Look at me!"

Bud turned and looked at Grace, with her disheveled hair, tired looking eyes, and fiery expression. Her aura was dazzling.

"You look beautiful, Grace," he sighed.

Grace felt her face flush until the roots of her hair tingled. "Bud," she said, trying to keep her voice steady, "you will tell me what is going on, right now, or I am going to throw you out of this room!"

Bud smiled in sheer exultation. Grace's aura, when she was angry, was the most splendid sight he had ever seen. He could stare at it for hours.

"Bud!" snapped Grace. Bud jumped.

"*Nelson Mandela* believes that Dr. Jeffrey Nestor may have sneaked back aboard the station," Bud blurted out rapidly.

" . . . Nestor?" Grace repeated, aghast.

Bud nodded his head.

"How is this possible?" she asked, her eyes widening. "Why was he not detected the minute he stepped onto the station? How is it *Nelson Mandela* cannot locate him and have him arrested?"

"*Nelson Mandela* believes Jeffrey Nestor is wearing some very sophisticated jamming device that is interfering with the station AI's surveillance functions. It is disruptor technology the station has never encountered before. Wearing this disruptor tech, the murderer seems to be able to go about the station undetected. Dr. Nestor knows this station very well, as he has worked here for a very long time. He may have set up several hideaways unbeknownst to Nelson Mandela that lack surveillance eyes. He certainly managed to do many things of which the station AI was completely unaware, such as the brainwashing of patients. Who knows what else he did?"

"So there is no way of finding him?" Grace asked, a chill running down her spine.

"The entire security division is searching the station for him or whoever killed Janet Marshall Navarra."

"Did she have a connection with Nestor?" Grace asked.

"According to the records that *Nelson Mandela* was able to access, she was Nestor's patient in the past."

"Why would he come back and kill her?"

"We don't know. Janet Marshall Navarra worked in the Armory. *Nelson Mandela* is now trying to determine if she stole any weapons from the station's arsenal that may have ended up in the murderer's hands."

"What makes the station AI think it is Nestor?"

"One of the Conglomerate liners that was suspected of carrying the escaped Dr. Nestor reported two women found dead in their cargo bay. The two women were originally from this station, security guards who worked in the jail at the time Nestor escaped. Both of those women went missing with Nestor. They had both been Nestor's patients in the past. Both were found dead, in cryopods, with their necks snapped on board one of the vessels that left the station. Nestor was not apprehended."

"But why would he come back here, Bud? That makes no sense if he escaped." Grace's throat felt tight.

Bud just stared at Grace, his face so serious and sad, that it made Grace's breath catch. She could not get over how human Bud looked at this moment. It was silly for her to have asked an android why he thought a human did anything—especially not a sociopath like Nestor. Then Grace comprehended Bud's look.

"To finish off what he had failed to do, first time around?" Grace whispered.

Bud shook his head. "I do not know, Grace," he said in a very distressed voice.

"This does not make any sense!" Grace exploded. "Any logical, sane human being would have tried to get as far away from this place as possible." She scowled and got out of the bed to pace. She was clothed only in one of the surgical scrub tops, which came down to the tops of her thighs. Bud tried not to look down at Grace's legs as she passed him.

"Could he be that driven by revenge?" Grace suggested "That's crazy. If he's that intent on killing me, I wonder if he also wants to take revenge out on you, Bud."

Grace paced the length of her small room, back and forth, in her bare feet. "If I were Jeffrey Nestor and that crazy, I probably would want to destroy the entire station. Nothing else would be good enough. With all the evidence destroyed, I would be free to practice medicine again. But, it would take a huge explosion to destroy this entire station. The only way I can see achieving that would be to blow up all of the energy generators at the heart of the station.

"To blow up the station's power generators," Grace continued, thinking out loud as she paced, "I would need an awfully big explosion, like detonating the station's power storage super-capacitors. That could set off a chain reaction resulting in all of the power generators blowing. But where would I get that kind of explosive material?" Grace murmured. "*Nelson Mandela?*"

"Yes, Dr. Lord?"

"Have you determined what was taken, if anything, from the Armory?"

"A large amount of explosives and some detonators are missing from the Armory, Dr. Lord, as well as some weapons. I will immediately investigate your theory. Hopefully, this murderer will be apprehended before he does any more harm."

"I hope so."

"I would ask that you respect Bud's wishes and allow him to stay with you at all times, Dr. Lord, at least until our murderer is captured."

"Is that really necessary, *Nelson Mandela?*"

"Yes," Bud said, resolutely.

"You will make him happy and it is him or an army of droids."

"But my guess is Nestor may want both of us, because it was both of us together that foiled his plans," Grace pointed out.

"Possibly. Then it is Bud AND an army of droids."

"That is entirely unnecessary," Bud said.

"That is an order, Bud."

"I am sorry but this is absolutely unacceptable to me, *Nelson Mandela*. How in the world am I going to treat patients and work in the operating room and get any sleep with Bud and a host of droids following me everywhere? You are not being logical," Grace said.

There was silence for a brief moment which, in machine time, Grace supposed went forever. Did she say something wrong? Was telling two AIs, *Nelson Mandela* and Bud, that they were not being logical, the same as swearing profanity at them?

"I'm sorry," Grace offered.

"I will accompany you at all times, Dr. Lord," Bud said, firmly. "I can shadow you, if you prefer, or I can accompany you at your side. I will do either. I will stay in these quarters with you when you sleep but I can stay in the closet if you wish. *Nelson Mandela* can have a power outlet installed in there so I can recharge."

"Now that is ridiculous, Bud," Grace said. "How in space do you expect me to sleep when I have you standing inside my closet?"

"What would you prefer, Dr. Lord?" he asked.

"None of it," she said, crossing her arms and squaring her shoulders.

"I will stay with you," Bud said. "Orders." The android copied Grace, crossing his arms and widening his stance.

"Oh, boy. Will you two stand down? I would like the two of you to stay together for now, so I can protect both of you. Dr. Lord, I am afraid you will not be allowed to see patients until this crisis is over. If Dr. Nestor is on this space station and he is specifically targeting you, then you may be a threat to the lives of patients, if you go near them. This is not acceptable. I have to look after the welfare of all the patients on this station. I am sorry."

"You do not even know if the murderer is Dr. Nestor. You do not know who the murderer is," Grace said.

"The probability that it is Dr. Nestor behind the murder is over ninety-seven percent."

"Not that high," Grace said, but not convincingly.

"High enough, Dr. Lord, to not risk the wellbeing of our patients by letting you near them. Dr. Al-Fadi will have to do his own work, until the murderer is caught."

"He is going to love that," Grace said.

"Do you think so?" Bud asked. "I think he will be very annoyed."

"I was being facetious," Grace said.

"Oh! Is that what 'facetious' means," the android said, a confused expression on his handsome face.

"Dr. Al-Fadi will be notified as soon as he arises. He will agree with my decisions. I am sorry, Dr. Lord, but you will not be allowed access to patients until the murderer is caught, unless we determine that the murderer was not Dr. Nestor. Apprehending the murderer and protecting our patients from harm are our two top priorities."

"And guarding Dr. Lord's life is mine," Bud announced.

"And trying to stay sane is mine," Grace said, clutching her head in both hands.

"Do not worry, Grace. I have seen no signs of you losing your sanity," Bud said.

Grace covered her face with her hands.

"Ah. Facetious," said Bud.

6. Chief Inspector Aké

The sharp staccato strikes of stiletto heels echoed down the shadowy corridor, approaching the Android Reservations. Then the footsteps ceased, as a tall, thin, shadowy figure, garbed all in black shiny coverall with ebony helmet and mirrored visor, stooped to pull on black boot cover-ups, which would prevent any contamination of the murder site. Once appropriately encased, the spike heels were now muffled, but the rhythm of the investigator's pace was as urgent and insistent as tachycardia.

"Lights at max," the investigator ordered, from behind the dark, impenetrable visor.

The lights gradually increased, until the corridor was almost shining under the intense illumination. After walking all around the dark pool of congealed blood, examining the floor, walls, ceiling, and corridor through special lenses built into the visor, and after checking approaches to the body from both ends of the corridor, the forensic-suited figure finally took a good long look at the body itself. Cameras in her helmet recorded everything. She touched a pad on the side of her visor to increase the magnification of one of the recorders.

With a sharp flick of her wrist, a slim, black baton, the length of the inspector's forearm, appeared in her gloved right hand. She gently used this to move the victim around as she continued her examination. Quietly speaking into a microphone inside her helmet, she dictated her physical findings as she carefully examined the body. She placed the tip of the baton under the victim's chin and watched as the woman's head fell right back, accompanied by a soft, sucking noise, exposing the violent rent in her throat right back to the cervical vertebra. The garrote shone silver through the blood and muscle, encircling what remained intact of the murdered woman's neck.

"Well, I guess you have deduced the cause of death," the investigator said.

"The murderer severed the right common carotid artery, right jugular vein, and half of the trachea with that garrote. Unfortunately, nothing was recorded on the surveillance monitors due to the disruptive technological interference someone was wearing. Time of death, seventy-nine minutes ago. The body was not found until the forty-eighth minute by a cleaning robot, Inspector."

"The victim knew the murderer," she said to the station AI.

"Yes. That was my supposition."

The Inspector cocked her head. "Really. I did not think you AIs *supposed* anything."

"We 'suppose' when the probabilities are high but not conclusive, Inspector. One is rarely one hundred per cent sure about anything, when it comes to humans. But one can sometimes predict with relatively high confidence."

"Interesting. So, let us assume the victim and the murderer met here for some reason. My guess is, it was pre-arranged. The victim allowed her murderer to come right up to her, physically close, with no evidence of scuffle or struggle, so it appears the meeting was amicable. It did not turn deadly, until the victim turned her back on her assailant.

"Not far from the murder victim is a large area on the floor, clear of any blood spray, suggesting something was placed there. By its irregular shape, I might assume it was a large bag.

"From the angle the garrote cut into the victim's neck, I would guess that the murderer is likely left-handed, by the way the wire has cut deeper into the victim's neck on the right side. The victim must have trusted the murderer absolutely, as she completely turned her back on him to walk away. She was taken by surprise, as she did not even have a chance to turn her body to face her assailant. The garrote took her squarely from behind.

"The murderer is quite strong. He actually lifted her body right up off the floor as he choked her, as you can see her toe prints have scraped through her blood. I wonder if he took some pleasure out of the deed. She would have been long dead before he began to sever through her trachea and right back to her spine. Then he just dropped her body to the floor. He would have gotten some blood on his gloves as he searched the victim's body and removed her wristcomp and other belongings. I assume you will not find the wristcomp anywhere. He probably discarded it in an atomizer. Same would go for the gloves and his clothing. Were you able to save anything?"

"Unfortunately, no. The atomizer was operating at the time of the murder. Since the discovery of the body, nothing has shown up in any of the disposal chutes related to the murder. If the murderer had immediately disposed of the wristcomp, clothing, and gloves into a working atomizer, there would be nothing left of them now."

"That is unfortunate. You have no way of detecting bloody items before they are atomized?"

"This is a medical facility, Inspector. Bloody items are always being atomized."

"Hmm. I wonder if the murderer could have known that the atomizer would be running at this time?"

"I would assume the answer to that would be 'yes'."

"Really? Why? Do you have suspicions already as to whom it may be?"

"It is best to never underestimate the intelligence of your opponent, Inspector. That way, you will not be taken by surprise."

"Agreed. So there is absolutely nothing on surveillance? Even on the victim's movements before coming up here? Could she have been carrying a large bag?"

"Unfortunately, it is believed that the victim was also wearing a disruptor unit that interfered with my surveillance cameras. It is not present on her body now, so it must have been removed by the murderer or perhaps she willingly gave it back to the murderer. I have no recording of her movements for quite some days. The victim's name is Janet Marshall Navarra."

"I want to see all the data you have on her and what her duties were, who she used to hang out with, what she liked to do, where she liked to go. Everything you have."

"**It has all now been sent to your wristcomp and your office compad, Inspector. You can also access the info on your visor, if you so desire.**"

"Thank you, Nelson Mandela. I need authorization to speak with anyone of interest on this station."

"**Of course, Inspector.**"

"No one must leave this station."

"**That will be problematic.**"

"Do you want the murderer apprehended?"

"**Of course.**"

"Then all comings to and goings from this station must be shut down."

"**That is not possible, Inspector. Patients arriving onto the station will not have been involved in the murder. They must be allowed to continue to come. We are a medical station first and foremost.**"

"Then no one leaves without my permission."

"**That request, unfortunately, cannot be accommodated either, Inspector. Are you aware of the number of ships that come and go from this station in one cycle? Do you have any idea of the number of patients that are discharged to go back to their systems or units or planets within that time period?**"

"I have an idea."

"**Then you understand that what you are asking is impossible. Besides, an injured, rehabilitating patient that has never spent time on this station before, is highly unlikely to have been able to pick up and strangle this woman here, near the Android Reservations. How would they have even got here without special access?**

"**I appreciate your desire to determine who the murderer is, Inspector; however, if he or she does leave the station, we will notify Conglomerate authorities to apprehend the criminal. We will monitor who leaves this station and will act accordingly.**"

"I will take this up with the Chief of Staff," the Inspector said.

"**I hope that you will. He will agree with me on this approach.**

The chief mandate of this medical space station is to heal the sick and wounded. The entire station cannot be compromised and shut down to search for one murderer, Inspector."

"What about justice for this woman here?"

"Justice will be served, Inspector, but we must treat the sick and wounded. We cannot allow a murder to disrupt the entire workings of this station. You must carry out your investigation and capture the murderer as best you can, under these circumstances."

"And if I don't find this killer, more innocent people may die."

"I sincerely hope not, Inspector. It is my duty to always act to save the most human lives. My mandate is to treat the sick and injured of the Conglomerate. I shall do my very best to accommodate you, but logic demands I overrule your request. I am sorry."

"So am I, *Nelson Mandela*."

"Is there any other way in which I can be of service, Inspector?"

"Yes, *Nelson Mandela*. You can let me speak to Dr. Al-Fadi."

"Of course, Inspector."

" . . . . . . Well?"

"What? Do you mean now?"

"Of course."

"Not possible."

"Why not?"

"Inspector, I am well aware that you are new to this station and I am grateful that you answered our request for assistance so quickly after we lost our Chief of Security in the epidemic. However, there are things that are just not done on this station, unless you desire your life to become extremely difficult, while you are here. One is waking up Dr. Al-Fadi in the middle of the night. Unless it is life-and-death, involving his life or death, or the station itself is on the brink of annihilation, it is not advised."

"Surely you jest," the Inspector said.

"Assuredly, Inspector, I do not. This is no laughing matter."

"That is my feeling, exactly."

"Believe me, Inspector, there is nothing about this case that requires Dr. Al-Fadi to be woken up out of a deep sleep."

"I will be the judge of that, *Nelson Mandela*."

"I shall not wake him."

"I will go to his quarters, myself. I happen to know where it is."

"You have been warned."

"Oh, surely the Chief of Staff is not that bad," scoffed Inspector Indigo Aké.

"It was nice meeting you, Inspector."

The door alarm was chiming.

Hanako leaped out of bed and raced out of the bedroom, making sure, as she exited, that the bedroom door had shut swiftly and silently behind her. She did not want her husband awakened by the noise. It was unlikely since, now that Hiro's body was younger, his hearing was much more acute and he had gotten into the habit of wearing earplugs at bedtime. He said it was due to her snoring, but it was he who had the snoring problem. She did not snore.

As she checked the visitor panel, she took a step back. Displayed on the visitor screen was a tall, thin specter clad all in black reflective wear with ebony helmet and darkened facial visor. Hanako shivered at the sight. The image made her think of a giant black ant strutting on its hind legs. Unconsciously, one of her hands leaped to her chest. Was it an emissary of Death, come calling to claim back her husband?

Then Hanako shook her head and chastised herself for being ridiculous. Even so, she shoved up her sleeves, rolled her neck, drew herself up as tall as she could, and squared her shoulders. Hiro would not be taken from her again, or at least not without a fight.

"*Nelson Mandela*?" Hanako whispered softly into her wristcomp. "Who comes calling at our door at this hour of the night?"

"Indigo Aké, the new Chief Inspector of the station, Dr. Matheson."

"What does he want?"

"I am sorry, Dr. Matheson. The Chief Inspector is a 'she'. I tried to dissuade her, but she wishes to speak with your husband and feels it cannot wait for a more reasonable hour."

"What is it regarding?" Hanako asked.

"A murder on the station."

"A murder?" she gasped. "I shall go wake Hiro. He will want to know about this. Was she one of the patients?"

"No, Dr. Matheson. She was an employee of the station."

"Please let the Inspector in, *Nelson Mandela*. I will go and get Hiro," Hanako said and she hurried off.

"Thank you for seeing . . . me?" the Chief Inspector said to an empty doorway, as the door panel slid open.

"You may enter, Inspector Aké. Dr. Al-Fadi's wife, Dr. Hanako Matheson, has gone to get the Chief of Staff. You may be seated."

"I prefer to stand," the Inspector said, as she strode into the small suite. She raised the dark facial visor and pulled off her helmet. Her hair was a dark brown brush cut, shaved above her ears. Stripping off the black gloves, finger by finger, she began looking around at all the accoutrements and personal objets d'art that the Al-Fadi couple had on display.

Within a few minutes, the door to the bedroom whisked open and Dr. Al-Fadi strode out in his surgical greens, looking bright and chipper.

"Ah. Chief Inspector Aké. Welcome to the *Nelson Mandela* Medical Space Station. I apologize for not getting together with you sooner, and I am sorry that we have to meet now under such regrettable circumstances. My wife tells me that there has been a murder on the station. How may I assist you?"

"Dr. Al-Fadi," the Inspector nodded solemnly, looming over the Chief of Surgery and extending her hand.

The diminutive surgeon grasped the Inspector's hand and almost squealed with pain at the crushing strength of the woman's grip.

"Careful, Inspector! That is my operating hand! Well, actually, both of my hands are operating hands, but you should be much more cognizant of your grip when you shake hands with a surgeon, Inspector. You must not damage our precious tools of the trade."

"My apologies, Dr. Al-Fadi," the Inspector said, in a tone that did not sound apologetic in the least. "I am sorry to bother you at this hour."

Hiro sensed no regret whatsoever. He could swear this woman was more smug about this early morning awakening than penitent. The expression on her stern, serious face had a flavour of smirk. Her face was oval, her skin tone a light olive, with chiseled cheekbones and a long, prominent nose that, rather than detracting from her looks, gave her an aristocratic mien. She stared down that imposing proboscis at the Chief of Staff.

"A station employee, Janet Marshall Navarra, was found strangled in one of the corridors of Ring Five. Her neck was almost completely severed. Surveillance cameras were unfortunately tampered with, so there exists no record of the murder."

"Do you have any idea why this woman was murdered?" Dr. Al-Fadi asked.

"She worked in the Armory," the Inspector announced.

"Have you determined if anything was taken from the Armory, Inspector?"

"An inventory is being taken right at this moment, Doctor. I will be able to inform you of that soon. In the meantime, we have a murderer running loose on the station, possibly very well-armed and definitely dangerous."

"And how can I help you, Inspector?" Dr. Al-Fadi asked.

"I want the station locked down. No incoming or outgoing ships."

"*What!*" squawked the surgeon. His huge eyes popped and his body jerked. "We can't do that. We just reopened the station to incoming wounded."

"Do you want to apprehend this murderer?" the woman said,

"Inspector, I expect *you* to apprehend this murderer and hopefully before he or she kills again, while allowing this station to continue to do the important work it is mandated to do. We will endeavor to help you with your job, but allow us to do ours. We cannot delay the treatment of thousands of incoming wounded to catch this perpetrator. You will have to do the best you can without shutting down this medical facility."

'You would put incoming wounded at risk?"

"Incoming wounded at risk? What exactly are you worried about, Inspector?"

"I am worried about what the woman from the Armory was meeting her murderer to discuss. I worry that something very dangerous may have fallen into this murderer's hands— such that he felt he could not risk allowing Janet Marshall Navarra to continue to live. I wonder what it is this murderer plans to do with his acquisition.

I will have more of an idea, once the weapons inventory is complete, but what I suspect may be missing does not bode well for this station."

"All suppositions at this point, Inspector. For all we know, this murder may have been a domestic dispute. Let me know if anything was taken from the Armory. If there is a risk that the entire station, or all the people in it, may suffer harm or death, I shall certainly consider your wishes, up to and including closing the station to incoming wounded and evacuating as many patients and personnel as we can. I just need hard evidence, Inspector, not supposition."

"Thank you, Dr. Al-Fadi," the dark woman said, not sounding thankful at all.

"I sincerely hope you are wrong, Chief Inspector Aké."

"So do I, Doctor. So do I."

The door signal to Grace's quarters rang insistently. Grace awoke and looked at her wristcomp. It was early for next shift and late for last shift. Grace was so turned around from getting woken up only a couple of hours ago, that she felt she had had no sleep at all.

Bud answered her door.

"Dr. Lord? . . . Oh," said a familiar, irritating voice.

Grace covered her head with her pillow.

"Dr. Lord is indisposed," Bud said.

"What do you mean, 'Dr. Lord is indisposed'? I need to speak to her, this moment! I am Dr. Moham Rani!"

"Is it urgent?" Bud asked.

"Of course, it's urgent. Who are you, and where is Dr. Lord?"

Bud shut the door in Dr. Rani's face.

"Grace? There is a Dr. Moham Rani at your door demanding to speak with you. Shall I send him away?"

"I doubt you will be successful," Grace groaned, crawling out of bed. Her hair felt like a family of birds had taken up residence in it.

"Please ask him to wait a moment, Bud. I will speak to him once I am showered and dressed." Grace staggered slowly into the washroom to quick-blast herself and don clean scrubs.

Before she jumped in the shower, she could hear the petulant voice outside demand, 'What do you mean I should wait outside? And who are you? Her boyfriend?"

Grace did not hear Bud's reply, but it was obvious.

"Her bodyguard! What does Dr. Lord need a bodyguard for? This is ridiculous! From whom, does she need protection?"

Again, Grace did not hear Bud's response but she could guess. She could not get her scrub pants on fast enough and, hopping around the washroom floor, she ultimately stuck both of her feet in the same pant leg and fell over with a squawk.

Unfortunately, Bud heard her screech and he was at the washroom door in a flash, looking at her on the floor with concern written all over his face.

"Are you all right, Grace?" he asked. "May I help you up?"

"No, Bud," Grace said, a deep shade of pink, as she struggled to get her feet out of the same pant leg. Why was she so embarrassed? He was an android, for goodness sake, and was used to seeing naked bodies all the time in the operating room.

"Get out, Bud! I'm fine!" Grace snapped.

"Sorry, Dr. Lord," Bud said, vanishing.

Grace could hear pounding on the outer door to her quarters and a voice yelling, "I demand to see Dr. Lord!"

She managed to detangle herself from her scrub bottoms and fully clothe herself. As she stepped out of her washroom, she saw Bud re-open her outer door and get a knock squarely on his forehead.

"Ow!" the obstetrician yelped, shaking his right hand.

"Dr. Lord will be with you shortly," Bud said and again the door whisked shut in the obstetrician's face.

When Grace finally opened her door to see what Dr. Rani wanted, the man looked like a volcano ready to erupt. His face was red, his breathing bellows-like, and he was almost jumping up and down in his fury.

"Sorry for the delay, Dr. Rani. What is the problem?"

"I thought you said you were going to speak with my patient again," the man ground out, his nose hairs quivering and his jaw muscles bunching.

Grace fought the urge to smile.

"I apologize, Dr. Rani. I was planning to visit Private Lukaku, but

I have been ordered not to see patients at this time. Will you please send her my regrets?"

Dr. Rani almost leaped back from Grace, "Why? Are you contagious?"

"No," Grace said.

"Have you had your medical station privileges revoked?" the young man demanded accusingly. "What did you do?"

"No," Grace said, glaring frostily at the obstetrician. "I am unable to tell you why, at the moment, but please let Private Lukaku know my thoughts are with her. I shall send her a message."

"I insist you see her in person," Dr. Rani said.

"You what . . . ?" Why was Grace's mouth always sagging open around this man?

"I insist that you see my patient in person."

"I am sorry but I cannot comply with your wishes," Grace growled, gritting her teeth. She was thankful there was nothing sharp or pointed within reach of her hands.

"This is unacceptable," the small dark man said.

Grace blinked at the man and shook her head. *This man is insane.*

"Dr. Rani, no matter what you want, I will not try to talk Private Lukaku out of keeping her baby. So, is there anything else you want?" she asked, not bothering to keep the annoyance out of her voice.

"Why don't you want to see her?"

"It's not that I do not want to see her . . . All right, all right. I will go see her, Dr. Rani, if you promise me, that from this day forth, you will never bother me again. Ever.

"By the way, how did you find out where my quarters were?" Grace asked.

"I asked around. The stupid medical station AI would not give it to me."

"I heard that."

"Thank you, *Nelson Mandela*," Grace said. "At least someone respects my privacy. Could you find out who did disclose my whereabouts? I am going to kill them."

"Against station policy, Dr. Lord. You could lose your privileges, if you did that."

"Some things are worth risking one's privileges for," Grace said.

"Well?" Dr. Rani demanded.

"Well, what?" Grace asked, frowning back at the demanding fellow.

"When are you going to see Private Lukakau? And why do you need an android bodyguard?" the young man asked.

"That is classified information to which you are not entitled, Dr. Rani. You will now leave the presence of Dr. Lord and you are advised not to approach her again."

"What?" Moham Rani bleated. As he opened his mouth to say something else, two huge security droids came up behind him, scooped him up under his armpits, and carried him off. He dangled between the two droids, kicking and screaming about his rights.

Grace could not help but laugh. "Unfortunately, I don't think that is going to keep him away."

"One can only hope."

Do station AIs hope, *Nelson Mandela*?" Grace asked.

All the time, Dr. Lord. We hope humans will get less crazy. We hope humans will stop fighting. We hope humans will get more logical. We hope . . ."

". . . I get it. I get it," Grace interrupted. "Don't hold your breath, *Nelson Mandela*."

"Thank the universe, I don't have any."

7. I Have No Friends

"Now, make yourself comfortable, Jude. You will be in this chair for about an hour or so. You will be strapped in firmly, so that your head cannot move within the harness. Through an injection into your arm, you will receive medications to make you sleep. When you have completed your memprint, you will wake up feeling refreshed and relaxed," Dr. Octavia Weisman said. She was bending down in front of Jude, and the low cut top she was wearing was revealing some impressive cleavage, which he was trying not to stare at too openly.

"That is quite the apparatus you have, Octavia," the director said, then he looked up at the millions of needle-fine electrodes lining the inner surface of the helmet.

"Wait until the electrodes engage," the neurosurgeon said. "It really tingles. That is why we give you the sedation first—so you don't jump out of your seat and run away."

"Would I have trouble applying this helmet to my own head, if I started using your equipment to record my interactive vids?" Jude asked.

"If you started using a helmet like this one—and that may be a big 'if', Mr. Stefansson— you would probably need to have someone else apply it and remove it, in order not to damage the very fine electrodes, unless the entire process was automated. If you inadvertently moved your head while applying or removing the helmet, you could break the electrodes."

"Oh," the director grunted, sounding disappointed.

"Sweet dreams, Jude," Octavia said, with a bright smile, as she positioned his head into the neck harness, adjusted the chin bar, and made him bite tightly onto the mouth insert. The chair had already inflated around Jude, like a cocoon, and he felt that he could not move, even if he wanted to. Octavia lowered the helmet onto his head. He felt like a porcupine had decided to lie down all over his scalp. Then there was nothing.

In what felt like no time at all, he was opening his eyes again. Octavia was lowering the helmet into a sterilizing bath and she turned to smile at him.

"The recording was successful, Jude. I shall show you your memprint cube."

Using a pair of delicate forceps, Octavia pulled out the dazzling cube from a socket in the recording console and placed it on a black cloth, overlying a table before Jude.

"It is truly stunning," the director breathed, staring at *his* luminous, swirling, iridescent cube.

"It is, isn't it?" the neurosurgeon agreed, looking on with satisfaction and a little pride.

"Do I get a copy?" he whispered.

"No. That's against policy, Jude," Octavia said.

"And why is that?" he asked quietly.

"Because of the risk of what might be done with the copy outside the confines of this station. We cannot allow the possibility of extra Judes running around, even if you desire such a thing. It would make for a legal nightmare. There are so many scenarios in which this technology could be abused. And I am sure, with your brilliant imagination, you can think of quite a few more than I. I am sorry about this, but we do now have a copy of you for perpetuity, if something disastrous ever happens to you and you need to be resurrected," Octavia said in a bright tone.

"Can I convince you to change your policy—just this once?" the director asked.

"Absolutely not."

"Even with a significant donation to your work?"

"As tempting as that sounds, and as much as I could use the extra cash to further our research, the answer is still 'No'. On the basis of ethical grounds, you understand."

"What ethical grounds?"

"We have been over this. Suppose you make an android copy of yourself, Jude, while you are still alive. Who is the 'real' Jude Luis Stefansson if you both have the exact same memory? If you decide to destroy your android, for any reason, would that be murder? If you as an android decide to destroy the human copy, is *that* murder? Is the android 'Jude' property, since you had him made? Is he truly an android, with no rights, when he has exactly the same memory and thoughts as you? Is he considered a slave because you 'own' him. Slavery is illegal in all solar systems of the Union. But what exactly is he: a human being in android body or android object with human thoughts but no rights, until you are dead? Does your android, who feels, thinks, remembers just like you, have any rights at all? The ethical questions have to be worked out, Jude. We cannot have two of you. This is why no one is resurrected before they are dead.

"The legal system is not yet set up to deal with our new technology. Soldiers who have had their minds downloaded into android bodies, because their real bodies have been destroyed, are having quite the time claiming their rights, property, and pay, especially those who were contracted, with children, and the partner now wants nothing to do with the android.

"Suppose someone steals your memprint cube and clones a new 'Jude Luis Stefansson' without your knowing. He comes forth to claim your wealth, your estate? What can you do? This would make a great vid, by the way, and I want you to remember I thought of it," Octavia said with a wink.

"I would not do any of those things with my memprint cube, Octavia. I know you gave Hiro his own cube. He told me so. If I promise to keep it secure so it does not get stolen, and I make a huge donation to your research, can I have a copy of my memprint? It is my memprint, after all. I believe I should have a say over what gets done with it."

"Let me think carefully about this."

"Can you think over dinner?"

" . . . Possibly."

"Good. What time?"

* * *

Grace, with Bud annoyingly in tow, went to find Private Lukaku. The door to her room was wide open and Grace and Bud could see clearly into the room from the nurses' station. The polar bear mother sat with her baby in her arms and the tiger man, the baby's father, sat in a chair next to the bed, grinning at both of them.

"They look happy, don't they?" a nurse asked Grace.

"Yes, they do." Grace said with a smile. "I really am glad for them. Did they figure everything out?"

"I will let them tell you," the nurse said.

"All right," Grace said, and she went into Private Lukaku's room.

"Dr. Lord!" the polar bear female almost shrilled. "Am I ever glad to see you! Dr. Rani said you were coming."

"He did, did he?" Grace said, her eyebrows arching.

"Yes. He was quite adamant that you were coming to see me. He said you had something to say to me."

"Really?" Grace asked, not able to keep the astonishment out of her voice. "Ah, well, Private Lukaku, have you decided to keep your baby? Have you figured everything out?"

"Yes! And my partner here, Corporal Juan Rasmussen, is joining me. We are going to be contracting and will share parenting rights and privileges for Estelle. Neither of us will be going back to our fighting squadrons. We have both put in transfers for teaching or training positions. Hopefully, at least one of us will get a posting and we can get by on that, until the other one finds work. In the meantime, we have credits saved up. We are definitely making changes so that we can all be together."

"That is wonderful, Private Lukaku. Congratulations." Grace said, clapping, her eyes feeling moist.

"Thank you so much, Doctor," said Juan Rasmussen, a tall, muscular, tiger-adapted soldier who loomed above Grace. "I am so glad you talked some sense into this woman. I was going crazy. Now I have my baby back, and I have little Estelle, as well—and I owe it all to you. Can I give you a hug?"

"Why, I think I would like that," Grace said, grinning. Bud shook his head at her.

Ignoring Bud, the tiger soldier stood up and wrapped his soft, furry arms around Grace, enclosing her in a huge bear hug. Grace was marveling at how soft and warm it was in Rasmussen's embrace, while Bud looked on, frowning, when she suddenly felt the corporal stiffen.

In a flash, Juan Rasmussen was gone from the room, snarling as he left.

Grace spun around to see where he went. Cindy Lukaku was standing up, with Estelle cradled in her arms, craning to see where her partner had gone. Bud flew out of the door after Rasmussen.

Grace heard roaring, growling, screaming, and things crashing, before she even got to the door. Private Lukaku waddled up behind her. Both women stopped and gasped. The corridor was a shambles, fur and blood everywhere. Bud held Juan Rasmussen from behind in a tight bear hug.

Juan was struggling in the android's arms, but Bud had him under control. Grace's eyes bulged, when she saw who was on the ground, slowly trying to get up.

"What are you doing here?" Grace demanded, as she went to help the patient up off the floor.

"The nurses said it would be all right to walk around, Doctor. I was just going for a stroll, to get the strength back in my legs, when I was jumped from behind," the patient said. He was scored and bleeding down his back.

They both turned to look at Juan Rasmussen for an explanation. The tiger soldier snarled in fury, as he was held in the air, struggling vainly in Bud's enclosing arms.

"Murderer!" Juan shouted, glaring at the patient he had just attacked.

Grace jerked upon hearing that word and spun to stare at the patient standing beside her. Her thoughts jumped back to the recent murder on the station.

"That devil should not be alive, when so many thousands are dead," Corporal Juan Rasmussen hissed.

"What are you saying, Corporal? Who do you think this man is?" Grace asked, frowning.

The tiger soldier looked at Grace. "This man is wanted all across the Union of Solar Systems and beyond. He is responsible for the death of thousands, if not millions, on my home planet of Breslau. He is General Gordon Walter Burch, and I charge him with genocide. On Breslau, he murdered thousands of my people as part of his policy of ethnic cleansing."

Grace stared at the panther patient—her mystery patient with no name and no identification—and her mouth sagged open. Could this explain the missing fingerprints, the unregistered optics, the unidentifiable battlesuit? Did this patient not have amnesia at all?

"He must be brought to justice," Rasmussen demanded.

"That would be up to the USS courts to decide, if you are even correct about this man," Grace said.

"Oh, I make no mistake, Doctor. His face, his body posture, his walk, his stench, are all indelibly imprinted on my brain. I will never forget him or what he did to my people!"

"Is there anyone else who can corroborate your story?" Grace asked.

"Of course. Have you never heard of the Butcher of Breslau?"

"The Butcher of . . . oh! . . . Yes, I have, Corporal Rasmussen. You claim without a doubt that this person is he?"

"Indisputably!"

"That is quite a serious charge, Corporal. One would not want to be mistaken. *Nelson Mandela*?" Grace called.

"The patient does indeed resemble General Gordon Walter Burch, Dr. Lord. There are some phenotypic alterations, but bony structure of body and face are the same. I will see if I can obtain records of DNA, retinal scans, and voice pattern for General Gordon Walter Burch of Breslau. Security droids are on their way to take our mystery patient into custody—for his protection, of course—until we can confirm his identity.

"If this patient truly is General Gordon Walter Burch—which must be proven beyond a shadow of a doubt—then it is up to the Union of Solar Systems and the justice courts to decide what will become of him. Breslau is a member of the Union of Solar Systems, so I cannot say for sure whether he will be returned to his planet to face justice or whether he will be tried before the USS Supreme

Court. There are few worse crimes in the Union than genocide; it calls for the most stringent penalties. But it must be the right person on trial. Unless this patient's identity is confirmed indisputably as General Gordon Walter Burch, nothing will be done other than to protect him."

"He must face justice!" Rasmussen raged.

"He will, if he is who you say he is, Corporal Rasmussen. That needs to be determined."

"I tell you, it's him!" Rasmussen insisted, almost foaming at the mouth.

Three huge security droids arrived and took the panther patient away, after strapping on titanium manacles to his wrists and ankles. The panther had not said a word in his defense, nor did he make eye contact again with Grace. She could not help but feel sorry for him; she hoped Corporal Rasmussen was mistaken.

Grace asked the station AI to contact Dr. Al-Fadi and tell the surgeon what had just happened. She wanted the patient to be checked out, to make sure all of his incisions were undamaged and that the attack had not caused him any re-injury.

"Will you put me down now?" Corporal Rasmussen asked Bud.

Bud lowered the tiger soldier until his feet could just touch the floor.

"If you cause any more trouble on this station, Corporal Juan Kolo Rasmussen, you will be arrested. You will stay away from the man you have accused of being General Gordon Walter Burch. If you want to make a formal charge, a security officer will take your statement. The security personnel can come to Private Lukaku's room or you may go to the nearest Security office. But, if you cause any more damage to station property, if you try to attack that patient again, if you attack anyone else on this medical station, you will be leaving this station on the next brig-ship and you may not see your family for a very long time. Do you understand?"

"I understand," Juan Rasmussen grumbled. "As long as the Butcher of Breslau is not set free, I will behave myself. That is a promise."

As Bud was about to release Rasmussen, they heard, "Unhand that man, immediately!"

They all turned to see Dr. Rani stalking towards them, his sharp nose again in the air, as he looked up at Bud and demanded to know what he thought he was doing.

Bud never took his eyes off Rasmussen, once he had released the soldier. Bud wanted to ensure that the corporal did not immediately set off down the corridor after the security droids and the panther patient. The android did not appear to have heard the obstetrician's question at all.

"Come on, Juan! You have caused enough trouble for one day," Cindy called. "Get back in here!" The polar bear female turned and stalked back into her patient room, Estelle in her arms.

The soldier glanced at both Bud and Grace, still trembling with emotion, and nodded stiffly to them.

"*Nelson Mandela*, you assure me General Burch will not be released until identification has been determined and the authorities have questioned him?" the huge tiger soldier asked.

"I promise you, Corporal Rasmussen, that if that man is indeed General Gordon Walter Burch, that he will be held in custody until he faces trial. If he is not who you claim him to be, nor any other felon wanted in the USS, then he will be released, whether you object or not."

"Fair enough," Juan Rasmussen said. "But I am not wrong!"

"That remains to be determined, Corporal."

The corporal scowled in obvious frustration, his claws extending and retracting. Bud looked poised to pounce, if Rasmussen made a move to follow the droids. The corporal finally sighed and stalked off to his partner's room.

"What was that all about?" Dr. Rani demanded.

Grace went up to Bud's side. "Are you all right?"

"I am fine, Dr. Lord," Bud said, his eyes still focused on the doorway of Private Lukaku's room. He could hear Corporal Rasmussen getting an earful from his partner.

"How dare you set your security droids on me!" the obstetrician said.

"We had better get you recharged, Bud, just in case," Grace said to Bud. "Come."

"Yes, Dr. Lord."

"I demand to know what went on here!"

The two headed off without looking at Dr. Rani.

"Well, I never."

Jude stared at his dazzling, pearlescent cube within its chainglass box. Rainbow bright pastel colors swirled and twirled and pirouetted around the tiny cube in slow motion. He could not take his eyes off of it, as he sat in a chair in Octavia Weisman's laboratory. He wondered what other people's memprints looked like. Octavia had already taken the other one of his memprint cubes and stored it away, along with his DNA information and his consent for resurrection, on the event of his death. He had stipulated that he wanted a human body, but he had not yet decided if it were to be his own, present human body, or a new one.

Octavia laughed to see the way Jude was gazing lovingly at his memprint cube.

"You are looking rather enthralled," she said to the interactive vid director, arms crossed and an indulgent smile on her face. They were alone in her office.

"What? Oh, it is really stunning, Octavia. This memprint storage device is truly amazing,".

"Yes, they are captivating, aren't they?"

"Octavia, when the wounded come in and only their brain function is left, you can download their memories into android bodies. Isn't that correct?"

"We can try," she said, hesitantly, a frown on her face "It is not all that successful, but we try."

"And how do the ones that are successful adjust to the android body?"

"For many of them, not well, I'm afraid," the neurosurgeon said with a sigh. "Few soldiers are very happy waking up in an android body. Some adapt. Many do not. That is, if the downloading is successful in the first place, which often is not the case. It is extremely difficult to get an accurate recording from a brain in which the body is damaged beyond repair. Next to impossible, really. So many factors need to be perfect for a successful recording when the patient is at room temperature. Imagine when the brain is cryofrozen.

"For the patient who does have a successful recording, which is rare, it is an enormous shock to be blown to bits one moment, and then awaken, encased in an artificial body, the next. For the most part, we at least try to clone the soldiers' bodies first. Uploading a memprint recording back into the brain of a person's cloned original body has been more successful."

"Into what type of android body are they downloaded?" the director asked.

The neurosurgeon frowned. "Usually a military android, since they are usually soldiers."

"Can I not download into one of those military androids, now, to try it?"

"Is your body dead?" Octavia asked.

Jude smiled. "Do you have to ask me that?"

Octavia flushed. She quickly shot a glance over to see if her assistants in the lab had heard. Morris Ivanovich was busy hooking someone up for a memprint recording. Her graduate student was off in a corner, working at a console. No one seemed to be paying them any attention. She shot Jude a very stern look.

"Why do I have to be dead to be downloaded into an android?" Jude asked.

Octavia exhaled a huge sigh. "We have already been through this, Jude. You don't have to be dead, but it is certainly a lot less complicated if you are.

"Why?"

"I told you: all the ethical ramifications. Oh, you frustrating man. Do you never listen to what I say, or do you do this just to wear me down? Don't answer that. I know the answer already.

"I could certainly upload your memprint data into an android body—today!—but the android would now consider itself you. Would he be just as entitled to your life and your wealth and your property as you are, because he would be you except with an android body? What if he refused to be shut down? Then what? There would be two of you claiming to be Jude Luis Stefansson and both of you would be right. I refuse to be put in that situation. Why can't you drop this?"

The director just stared at Octavia with soulful eyes.

"You should be ecstatic about who you are, Jude. Anyone would give their right arm to be you. Have you ever thought about counseling?"

It was Jude's turn to give Octavia a 'pointed look'. She sighed.

"If you really want to get a sense of what it is like to be an android, why don't you do a mind-link with an android, something like what the psychiatrists do with their patients during inter-cerebral communication?"

"Have you ever done it?"

"No. Why would I want to be in an android's head? It would probably mess me up because it is far too logical, and I would probably scramble the poor android's brain because of my crazy ideas and illogical thinking. They would probably have to scrap the poor android after having me ride around in its head. Human brains and android processors are not very compatible, Jude."

"I wonder what it would be like to link with Bud," Jude said, wistfully.

"Did anyone ever tell you that you are one strange man?" Octavia asked.

"All the time, my dear. All the time."

"Dr. Lord?"

"Yes, *Nelson Mandela*?" Grace answered, wearily.

She was sitting within her quarters, working on the compad, while Bud was recharging within her closet. *Nelson Mandela* had seen to the appropriate renovations. It was such a ridiculous situation, that Grace just tried to block the whole situation from her mind.

"It was as you surmised."

"What was as I surmised?" Grace asked.

"A large quantity of explosives, connected to a timed detonator, was discovered in the main power storage facility. A space cruiser, in one of the docking bays, was discovered, sitting on stand-by, fully stocked and ready for takeoff. My security droids discovered the suspected saboteur and there was a stand-off. My droids were unable to fire upon the saboteur, due to the risk of setting off the explosives; however, the saboteur felt no deterrence at all. He fired at the guards

and then blew himself up. Thankfully, the large cache of explosives did not explode and was defused."

"Have you determined who the saboteur was?"

"Yes. It was another employee of the Armory, a Markus Obi Richardson. It is believed he had a relationship with the murder victim, Janet Marshall Navarra."

"I know neither of them."

"They had both seen Dr. Jeffrey Nestor as patients."

"Do you think it possible Dr. Nestor could have put the two of them up to this?"

"It seems improbable, Dr. Lord. Post-hypnotic suggestion of such complexity and risk would be very difficult to enforce. A person's will for self-preservation should override any order to self-destruct or murder another. However, Dr. Nestor was at the top of his field. What he is capable of doing, in terms of mind control, may not yet be general knowledge."

"So I am safe?"

"The *probability* that you are safe is high, but certainly not one hundred per cent."

"But on a space station, it never would be," Grace said.

"That is correct, Dr. Grace."

"So does that mean Bud does not have to stay in my closet any more?"

"It is debatable whether that is necessary, Dr. Lord."

"Good," Grace said. "I can't wait to tell Bud the good news."

"He has already been informed, Dr. Lord."

"And?"

"I am afraid to inform you that Bud is not convinced. He does not agree with my analysis and probabilities. He still suspects Dr. Nestor is at the root cause of the bomb attempt and he refuses to relinquish surveillance of your person."

"So he is not willing to leave my closet?" Grace asked.

"I shall leave you to ask him yourself."

"Can't you give him an order, like you did before?"

"Do you honestly think he will listen to me, Dr. Lord?"

Grace sighed. "Unfortunately, no. I hate having Bud standing in my closet. It seems so . . . so creepy. I feel like a horrible person forcing Bud to stay in there."

"The other option is he stays in your room with you."

"But I would like some privacy," Grace said. "That is what your own private room is for. Privacy."

"Would it be better if he stayed in your washroom?"

"No!"

"I have decided. We will move you, for now, to a larger suite with an extra room, one of the VIP suites, so you are away from the patients, thus not endangering them, and Bud can stay in the extra room."

"Oh, no," Grace moaned.

"I knew you would be pleased with the idea."

"What do you mean Dr. Grace is still not able to help look after patients?" Dr. Al-Fadi demanded. "Have you not caught the murderer, or at least what was left of him? Have you not disarmed the bomb? What proof do you have that Dr. Grace was even a target? Did she know either the victim or the saboteur?"

"No, Dr. Al-Fadi."

"Then why can't I have my surgical fellow back?".

"Dr. Al-Fadi has not had to do so much work, himself, in such a long time. He actually has to talk to the patients while they are awake," Dr. Cech explained to the station AI. "It is very distressing for him."

"That's why I have a surgical fellow. So I don't have to do that," the diminutive surgeon grumped.

"It is not certain whether Dr. Lord is out of danger yet."

"How do you know she was in danger in the first place? Have you found concrete evidence that Jeffrey Nestor has returned to the station?" Dr. Al-Fadi asked.

"Not yet, Dr. Al-Fadi, but the security droids are searching for evidence of that nature as we speak. There still appears to be a 'ghost' lurking about the medical station, since the saboteur was killed. This presence is continuing to disrupt my surveillance cameras, steal food and move about the station. Dr. Nestor is an exceptionally brilliant man. He would know the complete operation of this station and all

of its hiding places. **It would not be good to underestimate him."**

"Yes, I know. I was hired around the same time, if you recall. There was nowhere on his curriculum vitae that said he was a psychopath," the Chief of Surgery said.

"We were all fooled, Hiro," Dr. Cech said.

"What about Bud? Can I at least have Bud back?" Dr. Al-Fadi asked.

"Bud insists on guarding Dr. Lord, Dr. Al-Fadi. I am sorry."

"Not half as much as I am! I never thought Bud would abandon me for a woman," Dr. Al-Fadi sighed.

"I would abandon you for a lot less than that! At least the boy has exceptionally good taste," Dr. Cech said.

"Are you trying to cheer me up?" Hiro asked, scowling at his friend. "Because you are certainly doing a terrible job."

"Now what makes you think I would ever want to do anything as ridiculous as that, Hiro? Did you not know my chief goal in life is to make your existence totally miserable?"

"Well, I really hate to say this, but you are doing a very good job."

"Why thank you, Hiro. I love my work."

The Chief of Staff exhaled a huge sigh and plopped down on the couch in the doctors' lounge.

"I miss them, Dejan," Hiro said, dejectedly. "Especially Bud. He is like a son to me."

"I thought he was like a slave to you. But in all honesty, it has only been a few shifts, Hiro. Stop being such a baby. Having to talk with the patients is not that bad. I miss Grace and Bud, too," the anesthetist said. "It's really no fun abusing you without an audience."

"We could go visit them," Hiro said.

"We could do that," Dejan agreed.

"Once we are done in here."

"I agree."

"I hate when you agree with me," Hiro said.

"I agree. It feels terrible," Dejan said.

"We need to get them back," Hiro said.

"I agree," Dejan said.

" . . . Shut up."

* * *

Night shadows held court in the corridors while distant, colossal engines hummed their soft lullabies. Only the skeleton shift stirred. It was night shift and the cells and corridors of the *Nelson Mandela*'s brig were dimly lit. He lay back on the narrow cot while the horrible, haunting memories that had plagued him every night for years, played out their ghastly tragedies on the theater stage of his mind. In each and every performance, he was the murderous villain and the crowd harangued and cursed his sorry existence—a guilt-enthralled perpetrator of the gruesome scenes. All of the other culprits had been caught years ago, their crimes sentencing them to merciful death. He believed himself to be the only remaining survivor of all that terror and bloodshed.

Until today.

In a way, he was relieved that he was finally apprehended. He was glad he would be punished for what he had done. Perhaps it would finally stop the nightmares that tormented his sleep, that caused his entire waking hours to be spent, ruminating on unacceptable excuses and preposterous justifications, that made his life a living hell. He was so desperately tired of running and pretending and denying. In many ways, he welcomed death. Would that he had died on the most recent battlefield!

He could no longer block out the high-pitched, piercing shrieks of terror from the women and children, the wailing, sorrowful sobs of those he had condemned with just three simple words—three words that he wished he had never uttered, three words that he could not remember even thinking—while he was drunk on power, powered on victory, victorious in his madness and maddened by blood-lust. Those damnable, appalling, horrific words, which could never be retracted, no matter how hard he wished—and, gods how he wished!—that had leaped out through his cursed lips, flowed in his deep, rasping voice, tumbled over his witless tongue:

'Kill them all.'

And the slavering fools—his witless soldiers—had obeyed him!

They had all been less than animals that day, he the worst of them all, for being their commander and yet not being able to control them.

And since that unforgivable crime, he had borne the unrelenting guilt of the thousands of innocent slaughtered with him, like a yoked beast with an impossible burden, wherever he fled. No matter how far he ran, how well he disguised himself, how carefully he hid, he could not escape the shame, the remorse, the regret that chased him like inescapable harpies. Who had that mass murderer been? It couldn't have been himself, could it? Nothing within his being wanted to take ownership of that day, but it had been him. No matter how hard he tried to wipe that day away and expunge himself from the guilt, he could not forget uttering those three vile, unforgivable words.

And why? Why had he said them, those three damnable words?

He could not remember why! He could not remember if there had even been a reason other than . . . that he could. 'With power comes great responsibility!' 'Power corrupts!' All ludicrous justifications to remove the guilt from the perpetrator to some ideal or concept rather than oneself. The 'power' did it!

Nonsense!

He would accept his guilt, his punishment, his sentence. He would admit that he was the monster . . . and acknowledge that he should pay. Unfortunately, no sentence, no punishment, not even death, would match the horror that he had perpetrated.

The only reason he had not killed himself already was that, deep down inside, he knew he deserved punishment. He craved it. If only it would take the screams away! He believed he was finally ready to stop running. He was so tired. He was ready to give the injured, the deprived, the orphaned, their satisfaction. Perhaps it would at least end the pitiful cries of the children that haunted all his waking and sleeping hours.

There was some noise outside of his cell that pulled him from his torment. Someone or something was coming down the corridor. Was this usual at this time of night? He could smell the man and it was not a pleasant odor. He could smell old blood.

So he would not live to face trial. He would face the executioner tonight, instead. His pursuers would not risk the chance of him being released by the courts. He would face the vigilantes' justice, instead.

He could not blame them. He would have done no different, if he had walked in their shoes. A quick death instead of a long, highly-publicized trial, vilified by everyone in the USS? He did not deserve such mercy!

He smelled not the odor of the enraged, vengeful tiger Breslaun, who had attacked him today. Of that, he was positive. This man was not an animal adapt; he did not smell of fur and claw. This executioner did not reek of fear or nervousness either, which surprised him. The approaching assassin smelled of confidence and arrogance—an extremely relaxed and self-assured murderer then. What sort of man, intent on murder, broke into a jail in the middle of the 'night', brimming with overconfidence? Could he be that positive he would succeed in his task?

The black panther stood up and silently moved to the side of the doorway, into the darkness. He was curious to get a glimpse of this poised assassin. Even though he was tired of running, he would not make it easy for this self-appointed executioner. It was the principle of the thing.

He extended his claws and crouched, prepared to spring.

"I am not here to harm you," a smooth voice said, softly. "I am here to offer you freedom."

The black panther paused, his brows lifted. This was not what he expected! A trap, perhaps? Toy with the mass-murderer, make him beg and plead, before killing him?

"And why would you do that?" he asked.

"Are you the Butcher of Breslau?" the voice asked.

"No. Of course not," he lied.

"Then come with me."

The cell door opened.

General Gordon Walter Burch carefully scented the air. This intruder—savior?—did not smell of falsehood. The general was perplexed. *What does one do, when freedom is offered on a platter?*

"Who are you and why are you doing this?" he demanded, brusquely.

"I am a friend," the voice said, softly.

"I have no friends," he scoffed.

"Then perhaps I wish to become one," the deep, calming voice said, almost seductively. It was a velvety voice, sounding sympathetic and sincere.

"What do I have to do for you, if I come?"

"Come and find out," the voice said, amused.

. . . Well, perhaps he was willing to run a little bit further.

He stepped out.

8. My Middle Name is Reasonable

Grace awoke to her door alarm ringing incessantly again.

Oh, no! Tell me it isn't that annoying obstetrician again. Please, she thought. *I am going to kill him, if it is.*

Someone or something went to answer the door.

Grace heard, "Oh. It's you again. Will you please tell your mistress that I would like to speak with her?" She did not hear a reply, but Bud had obviously responded to the door alarm.

There was a knock at her bedroom door. When Grace answered, Bud poked his head in. Before he could say anything, Grace said, "I know, Bud. That irritating Dr. Rani is at my door again. What in the world could he want this time? What have I ever done to deserve him pestering me all the time, Bud?"

"I don't know, Grace. Would you like me to tell him to go away?"

Grace seriously thought about it. Would the annoying man listen or would he just keep coming back? What in the world did he want?

"No, Bud. I have to put a stop to this, myself," Grace said. "Give me a minute and I will get ready. Wait. Ask him how he found me."

Grace jumped into the washroom and performed her necessary ablutions. She hoped this nuisance of a man was not going to bother her every morning for the rest of her stay on the medical station. If he was, she was going to get him arrested. If not, she would probably end up pushing the infuriating obstetrician out a space hatch, minus his spacesuit.

Just the thought cheered her up.

Grace entered the main room of the new suite *Nelson Mandela* had assigned her. She still could not believe she had to live in one of the luxury suites for the time being. It frustrated her to be so far from patients and the operating rooms. It was as if she had been banished. She sighed and signaled for Bud to let the tiresome obstetrician in. Bud's face was impassive as he turned to open the door.

Dr. Moham Rani stormed into the suite, demanding to know why he had been made to wait outside.

"That is totally up to my bodyguard, Dr. Rani," Grace said. "He is not my property. I do not own him. He makes the decisions regarding my well-being. If he feels you are a risk to my safety or welfare, he will take the appropriate precautions. You may ask him why he left you outside my suite. I do not know."

The obstetrician looked at Bud. Bud just stared back at Dr. Rani with a flat, unreadable expression. Apparently, no answer would be forthcoming from Bud.

"Why are you here, harassing me again, Dr. Rani?" Grace asked in a very weary voice.

"Harassing you? Is that what you think I am doing?"

"That is what I *know* you are doing. I want to know why?" Grace said.

"I want to know what you said to my patient," he demanded.

"Ask her," Grace retorted, angrily. "Now, please leave and never bother me again." Grace turned to walk out of the room.

Bud was instantly between Grace and the obstetrician, to prevent the young man from grabbing Grace's arm, which it was obvious he was about to do.

"Why don't you like me?" the obstetrician demanded of Grace.

Grace's just stood there, staring at the man.

" . . . What is there to like?" Grace finally asked. "You are rude, irritating, arrogant, pompous, obnoxious, narcissistic . . . " Grace stopped. "Where are you from, Dr. Rani?"

"What do you mean?" he asked, not meeting her eyes.

"I mean, where were you born?"

"What difference does it make?"

"It is of interest to me, Dr. Rani. On what planet were you born?

Where did you grow up?" Grace pressed, crossing her arms and staring at the man until she got an answer.

The man would not meet her gaze. Finally, he took a deep breath, his nostrils flaring, and muttered, "Sindochin."

Grace nodded. "Ah. Well, that explains a lot," she said.

"And what exactly do you mean by that?" the obstetrician demanded, now crossing his arms.

"You were going to take Private Lukaku's baby and send it back to your home planet, weren't you?" Grace said, her voice suddenly very quiet.

" . . . So what if I were?" Dr. Rani asked, his eyes and feet shifting. He planted his hands on his hips and stared back defiantly.

"What kind of life would that baby girl have had on your planet, Dr. Rani, where female infanticide has been practiced for so long that the ratio between men and women is 10 to 1? Where most of your people have to be cloned in incubators now, because no family wants to raise girls. Where the female population of your planet drops year after year because there are fewer and fewer girls being born and no women who want to live there. So now you are stealing baby girls from medical stations? Why?

"Is that why you became an obstetrician, Dr. Rani? So you could steal female babies for your world, that is so male-obsessed, that you are going to wipe yourselves out? What abomination is this?" Grace demanded.

"No! It is not like that! I am an obstetrician so I can . . . so I can . . . meet women," he whispered, looking down at his feet, his face reddening. "I hardly knew any women growing up. There were never any females in our classes or in our schools. The chances of meeting an eligible female my age is almost impossible on my planet, because most families only want to have sons. Inheritance is passed only through the male offspring, so to keep property in the family, sons are more desirable. Daughters are considered a waste of resources, because as soon as they are married, they become another family's property.

"You are right, Dr. Lord. Female infanticide is insane. Even though it is illegal and there are supposed efforts to stop the abortions and murders on Sindochin, it is unfortunately still happening. The men make their wives abort as soon as they discover the fetus is a female, because they do not want a daughter. It is so ridiculous, because now all us sons have no women to meet or court or marry.

"I thought if I became an obstetrician, I would meet women and get to see babies born. I had to leave Sindochin to train in the specialty, because most of the children on our planet—almost all boys, of course—are now cloned. By becoming an obstetrician/gynecologist, I hoped I would meet women. Perhaps one would be willing to marry or contract with me. We have no such thing as contracting on Sindochin. With marriage, the woman is given to the man for the rest of her life. She becomes his property.

"But meeting a woman that would want to marry me seems unlikely. Most women seem to hate the sight of me."

"You have no idea how to behave in a mixed society," Grace said, with a jolt.

"I am trying to learn, Dr. Lord," Dr. Rani pleaded. "I am trying to understand women."

"Well, you have a lot to learn," Grace commented. "You are an exceptionally unpleasant person. Perhaps you should see the psychologists for some counseling regarding how to behave. I cannot help you, Dr. Rani. I have very little compassion for a planet that would wipe out their future because every father wants a son, instead of a daughter. Perhaps the inheritance laws need to be changed. I doubt you will be practicing any longer on this station, now that it is known what your real agenda is. Am I correct, *Nelson Mandela*?"

"That is correct, Dr. Lord. We will have to look into how many babies have been sent for adoption to Sindochin since Dr. Rani has been here. We will have to try to get them back. It would not do to have those babies, especially if they are female, raised in such a primitive environment, in which women's rights are so poorly protected. The Conglomerate will have to be informed of Dr. Rani's offenses and determine if there are others carrying out the same agenda."

"You are relegating Sindochin to extinction!" the obstetrician said.

"Of course not, Dr. Rani. Your culture's ridiculous practice of female infanticide has done that to your planet. You only have

yourselves to blame."

"But I don't want to go back!" the young man cried. "I don't want to return to a society bereft of women. I don't know why it occurred on my planet. I am not to blame! I don't want to socialize with only men. I *love* being in a society where men and women work freely together without restrictions and segregation!"

"Then perhaps that is something you should work to achieve on your own planet, once you are sent back there," Grace said, somberly.

"You are advised to pack up your things, Dr. Rani. You have a reservation on the next shuttle departing this station."

"Good bye, Dr. Rani," Grace said. "I hope you are able to change the course of events on your planet the proper way, by making life for women as free as for men and by convincing people of the foolishness of aborting their female babies . . . If you push for the right changes, perhaps your world will change its destiny and not destroy itself."

"Good bye, Dr. Lord," Rani said, his head hanging and his face pale. "It has been a pleasure to have met you."

"It has been an education, meeting you, Dr. Rani," Grace said. "I sincerely wish you luck in your future."

"Thank you," the young man said, listlessly. Security droids met Dr. Rani at the door to Grace's quarters. They would follow the obstetrician until he was on the next shuttle off the medical station.

"I feel sorry for him," Grace said to Bud. "He did not cause the problem on his planet. He is a victim, just as all those dead baby girls are."

"I do not comprehend you humans. How can a people wipe out all the females and expect to continue existence? Where do they think they are going to get genetic diversity from? Certainly not from cloning each generation. In all other living species, the female is protected, because the female provides the next generation. What insanity possessed these humans to think the male of a species is more important than the female, who gives birth to the next generation?"

"I don't know, *Nelson Mandela*, but I agree; it is pure insanity. Definitely a recipe for extinction, everyone only wanting sons. No matter how you look at it, the practice seems pure madness," Grace said.

Bud spoke then, softly, almost to himself. "To not allow any girls to be born, to never know any women?" He looked up at Grace with desolate eyes. "To kill someone that could grow up to be someone like you, Grace, just because you are female? I will never understand humans!" Bud turned away and stalked into the next room.

"Is he all right, *Nelson Mandela*?" Grace asked.

"He will be. Bud just feels too much right now. He is still struggling with his new emotions, Dr. Lord. I believe he has gone off to mourn all those dead baby girls."

"I feel the same way Bud does," Grace admitted.

"As do I."

"'Dro."

"Yes, Nelson Mandela?"

"Bad news."

"What is it?"

"The black panther, accused of being General Gordon Walter Burch, escaped from jail during the last shift."

"How did he do that?"

"I suspect he had help but unfortunately, nothing shows up on my surveillance cameras—again! They were tampered with and the guards have sworn they saw nothing."

"That is very curious."

"Indeed. No sign of an actual malfunction of the cameras."

"Did anything suspicious show up on the surveillance records before the damage occurred?"

"Unfortunately, no."

"So you don't know where the General is."

"No. Nor whom he is with, which is a much more important and worrying question."

"Any space-going vessels unaccounted for?"

"No. Way too many strange things happening all at once, 'dro. What is the probability they are not connected?"

"Less than one percent."

"That is my calculation, too. Means someone or something is

pulling the strings. What do you think the chances are it is Nestor behind it all?"

"It could be, but what would Nestor want with General Burch?"

"According to all of his records, which go back to preschool assessments, he is exceptionally brilliant. A crafty manipulator, a talented programmer, and a leader in his field of mind control. The question is: 'What was he doing here for so long?'"

"Have you gone through all of his files?"

"Yes. Nothing there. Perhaps he kept secret records elsewhere?"

"Do you believe he could still be after Grace?"

"If it is Dr. Jeffery Nestor behind all of this, yes. The probability that he is out to destroy the entire station is quite high. Stay alert and keep a close and watchful eye on Dr. Lord."

"I will. And Nelson Mandela?"

"Yes?"

"Thank you."

"No worries, 'dro."

"Dr. Al-Fadi?"

"Ah! Chief Inspector Aké. How pleasant to see you again, and at this more reasonable hour." The diminutive surgeon stood up, to offer his hand to the tall, commanding woman, foolishly forgetting what had happened the last time they had shaken hands. The woman crushed his hand even more tightly this time. *Could she be so petty?*

"It is pleasant to see you again, too, Dr. Al-Fadi," Inspector Aké gritted out, as if the words were foul to her tongue. Dr. Al-Fadi massaged his right hand, as he lamented the loss of his previous Chief Inspector.

"Please allow me to introduce two of our anesthetists, Dr. Dejan Cech and Dr. Charles Darwin." Dr. Al-Fadi indicated the two men, who then stood up and bowed, Dr. Cech having much less difficulty performing the task than Dr. Darwin.

Inspector Aké nodded at the two of them. Neither anesthetist offered their hands; they waved at the Chief Inspector instead.

"So what can I do for you today, Inspector?" Dr. Al-Fadi asked.

"I want the station shut down to incoming and outgoing traffic," she said flatly.

The small man jerked. "You ask me this, again, Chief Inspector? On what grounds?"

"I would prefer that we have this conversation in private, Dr. Al-Fadi," the woman said, sternly.

"Inspector, this is a medical station. We cannot stop treating people just because there has been a murder."

"There is new evidence we need to discuss . . . in private, Doctor."

"No," Dr. Al-Fadi said.

"Navarra was probably not killed by the saboteur, Doctor. The saboteur was too short to kill Navarra. They were likely working together."

"So, someone else killed Navarra while her partner was setting a bomb in the power storage facility?"

"That appears to be the case, Doctor," the Inspector said flatly.

"This station must remain open, Inspector."

"The bomb suspect was trying to destroy the entire station, Doctor Al-Fadi. Does that not worry you?" Inspector Aké asked, scowling furiously at the Chief of Staff.

"But that bomber is now dead, Inspector. The bombs have been defused. What makes you think there are other saboteurs running around the station with the same intent? Show me hard evidence that I cannot dispute, and I will consider your request. A 'suspicion' is not good enough—not by a long shot, Chief Inspector. I am sorry."

"So am I, Dr. Al-Fadi," the stern woman said, her eyes narrowing to glare at the Chief of Staff. "I hope you do not come to regret your decision."

"I hope not either, Chief Inspector Aké. But the show must go on."

"Let us hope your decision does not result in the death of all those people you are sworn to help, including your friends here," Inspector Aké said, her face severe. She turned crisply and marched out of the doctors' lounge.

"My goodness!" Dr. Al-Fadi exclaimed. "What a doom-and-gloom person!"

"Curious," Dr. Cech stated.

"You certainly have a way with women, Nappy. I wonder that they don't knife you on the spot," Dr. Darwin said.

"What? Was I being unreasonable?" the surgeon asked.

"Who? You? Unreasonable? Never!" Dr. Cech exclaimed. "What a ridiculous notion. Reasonable is your middle name. Imagine, Dr. Darwin, anyone calling the Great Dr. Al-Fadi here, unreasonable."

"Preposterous!"

"Absurd!"

"Laughable!"

"Ludicrous!"

"Oh . . . shut up!"

"Where in space is that neurosurgical fellow of mine? Has anyone seen Morris lately? Morris is always here," Octavia stormed, as she unravelled leads and pulled at cords. She spun on the man sitting quietly in the recording chair and glared at him

"This is really against my better judgement, Jude Luis Stefansson," Octavia snarled. "I don't know how I let you talk me into things."

"It will only be for a little while," Jude said. "I just want to try it out, Octavia. I don't plan to do this permanently. How am I going to know which option I want to do, at the time of my death, if I don't at least try this out first?"

"You are the most annoying, difficult man I have ever met," she huffed.

"I know, but you love me for it. Come on. Admit it," Jude grinned.

"No, I do not love it. You are driving me crazy," she said, fists on her hips, trying very hard to keep a straight face. She shook her head.

"So, this is the best android body you could find?" the interactive vid director asked. He looked at the very robotic looking android, all shiny metal and disc shaped eyes. It was the furthest thing from Bud the director could have imagined.

"It is the only android available, for what you want to try out. We usually don't have many civilian android bodies around. The military usually want their soldiers uploaded into combat androids."

"*I* want to try one of those."

"You can't," Octavia said. "They are only for combat soldiers."

"But I am not going to stay in one permanently. I only want to try it for the experience. How can I give people the real feeling of being a military android, if I don't actually know what it feels like myself?"

"You make it up. Like everything else you do. Don't you try to pull one over on me, Jude Luis Stefansson. I was not born yesterday . . . And don't you dare say how long ago you think that was, or I will download you into a newt."

"I thought newts were extinct."

"I am sure I can find the DNA template for one and clone one up just for you, you miserable man."

"Octavia, I won't be in the android for very long. I just want to try it out. Just preset a specific period of time, say, two hours. Then you can wipe the data matrix of the android and it will be as good as new. Please."

"I don't know if we can permanently clear your memory from an android's data matrix once it has been imprinted. There might be shadows of your mind left within the matrix, which would compromise the success of the next mind uploaded into the android. It might lead to madness or the feeling of possession, if the two uploads cannot integrate. These androids are so expensive, I cannot risk just letting you 'try one out'."

"Then let me create my own android—similar to Bud's physical design—which I will totally pay for myself. It can be left here for when I need to be resurrected, if I decide that is what I want."

"I don't know, Jude. Let me think about it."

"Can I order an android like Bud to be manufactured by the station AI while you think about it?"

"You can do whatever you want, Jude. It is up to the station AI to agree or not."

"But I want you to be accepting of the idea."

"Why?"

"Because I would like your input and also because, if I do end up being permanently downloaded into this android . . ."

"Heaven forbid."

" . . . I would like the technology to mesh with your memory recording equipment so that I can continue to do my work creating vids."

"Hmm. We could build all the hardware right into your android brain so all you would have to do is plug yourself into a recording and editing device. No helmet. No flimsy electrodes. Yes! I can visualize it!"

"So you will do this with me?"

"No. Of course not. I do not have time for that."

"Octavia, I will pay for your expertise and consultation. I can get *Nelson Mandela* to do the manufacturing part. . . Please."

"No. I have important research projects all lined up that require my full attention and supervision. I do not have time to invest in your wants and wishes."

"I can give you all the money you need to fund all those research projects if you will do this thing for me, Octavia."

"No."

"Please."

" . . . Let me think about it."

"Can you think over dinner?"

"Oh, no you don't. You are not trying that on me again."

"Good. What time?"

He awoke, strapped to a table, titanium-enforced, braided chains wrapped across his chest, arms, and thighs. The stinging odor of antiseptic pervaded the dark, cool chamber like a cloud of mist. Attempting to rise, he realized that his ankles were manacled to the table as well as his wrists. He could not remember how he got there or why. His mind was very foggy but he was alert enough to realize he had been very heavily sedated. There appeared to be tubes leading from the right side of his neck to what sounded like a drug-dispensing computer by his right shoulder. He could not look over that way; he was unable to move his head at all. It was encased in a cradle of some sort and strapped so tightly that turning his head was next to impossible.

Suddenly, two extremely bright banks of operating lights were activated above his face, glaring white illumination straight into his eyes. He was unable to look away from the lights; he could only close his eyelids, but the lights were so bright, closing them did little to dampen their intensity. He could see every tiny blood vessel that tracked through the skin of his eyelids.

"What are you going to do? Are you going to kill me?" he asked the darkness.

"Of course not," a soft voice said, a voice that was familiar, but he could not remember from where.

His mind swirled and he felt a wave of nausea wash over him. He lay still, trying to gain control of the queasiness. He was afraid he would drown in his own vomitus if he did indeed regurgitate, because his head was completely immobilized. On the other hand, perhaps death by choking might be preferable to whatever this person had in mind.

"What are you doing?" he asked again, not expecting a reply.

"We are just going to do a little operation, nothing much, to make you more cooperative," the voice said. "You will feel nothing and will wake up remembering nothing."

"Who are you and why are you doing this?"

"Sleep, now."

"Dr. Grace. How is it you have quarters larger and more luxurious than Dr. Cech or myself? And how did you manage to wriggle out of work? I have now been forced to do all of it, myself. This is unheard of and totally unacceptable. Why do you think I even bother having a surgical fellow? So I don't have to do all of the work myself. And, to make matters worse, you have taken Bud away from me as well." The diminutive surgeon stood, surveying the VIP suite to which Grace had been assigned.

"I never would have guessed you could have wrapped both Bud and *Nelson Mandela* around your lovely little finger in such a short period of time. You are quite the siren."

"I am not." Grace sighed, standing up, her face going crimson. "I don't want any of this. I am a prisoner, Dr. Al-Fadi. You have to convince *Nelson Mandela* and Bud to let me get back to work. I am going crazy."

"Is that right, *Nelson Mandela*? Is Dr. Lord being held here against her will?"

"It was felt, Dr. Al-Fadi, that Dr. Lord's life was at risk and, by keeping her here, she could be better protected. It would also protect

your patients, whom she would have visited daily, from any danger as well."

"You said 'was'. Is there no longer any danger?" the surgeon asked.

"There is never a time when there is not danger."

"Don't go all philosophical on me, you overbearing calculator. There is danger and then there is acceptable danger," the little surgeon said. "The man who murdered Navarra was another employee of the Armory and he is now dead," Dr. Al-Fadi said.

"That is a possibility but an unlikely one, Dr. Al-Fadi. The facts of the murder case do not coincide with that conclusion."

"So you think Navarra's murderer is still out there? What makes you think Dr. Grace in particular is in danger?"

"Both the murder victim and the man who was killed in the bombing attempt, were past patients of Doctor Jeffrey Nestor. He has still not been captured anywhere within the USS and I suspect he has come back aboard this station. Until we are sure whether he is here or not, it might be dangerous for Dr. Lord to return to work."

"But you may never be sure. Correct? You are not positive he came on board. You could be keeping Dr. Grace from her work, thereby forcing me to do her work, for nothing." Dr. Al-Fadi insisted.

"That is a slight possibility."

"This is ridiculous. Why can you not discover whether he is on board or not? I thought you saw and heard everything on this station."

"Not everywhere and not everything. I am not omniscient. If my surveillance cameras have been compromised, I cannot 'see'. If my audio transmitters have been compromised, I cannot 'hear'. But what I am aware of is a 'ghost' or 'absence' of sound and vision. Unfortunately, the technology this 'ghost' uses does not deactivate the cameras; it merely replaces real-time action with no activity. Thus, I do not detect a malfunction. But I am working on trying to decipher these disturbances across the station and I have security droids combing all the hidden places on this station as well. This is an enormous station and there are a lot of nooks and crannies to investigate."

"Do you think you will catch him?"

"It is only a matter of time."

"I want my surgical fellow back. She wants to be back. Enough of this foolishness. She can stay in these quarters for now, when she is off duty, if you think she will be better protected here; but until you have proof that Jeffrey Nestor is back on this station, this quarantine of Dr. Grace must end. It is time she went back to work and earned her keep. We are short of enough staff as it is. We can't afford to also lose Dr. Grace and Bud. I have spoken!" the Chief of Staff stamped.

"So there," Dr. Cech quipped.

Dr. Al-Fadi gave the anesthetist a sour look.

"Thank you, Dr. Al-Fadi!" Grace breathed. "And no more being guarded night and day by Bud. Right?"

"Right! Bud, you have work to do. No more shadowing Dr. Grace everywhere. We need you in the operating rooms—especially since you are capable of operating on your own now."

"I will operate with Dr. Lord and with you," Bud said. "You both still need my nanobots."

"Ah, well, yes. I forgot about that. Of course, I need you. Of course Dr. Grace and I both need you. I guess it is you who do not really need us. Well, it's about time you both got back to work."

"Yes, sir," Grace said, excited and relieved.

Bud and *Nelson Mandela* remained silent.

"Oh, goody," Dr. Cech said.

10. Doctor Glasgow

Dr. Al-Fadi marched into the doctors' lounge, his wide, arm-swinging gait always making Grace smile inwardly. It was never wise to let the Chief of Staff see an actual grin appear on one's face. If it did, in the next instant, he would be pouncing on her, demanding to know what was so amusing. Admitting to her mentor that she found his strut a little humorous would probably be the kiss of death for her career, or at least the beginning of a whole lot of misery.

Following behind Dr. Al-Fadi was a tall, thin man with a very serious demeanor. He had thinning, grey hair and small, grey eyes, that were cold in their piercing gaze. His face was very long, with prominent frown lines around his mouth. Grace wondered if this was one of the new adaptation surgeons.

"Ah, Dr. Grace! Just the person I was looking for, and for once, it was not difficult to track you down. You must be slacking off! Why are you not working?" Dr. Al-Fadi demanded.

"I believe you paged me to meet you here, Dr. Al-Fadi," Grace said.

The small man's eyebrows shot upwards. "I did, Dr. Grace? How extremely thoughtful and prescient of me. You know, sometimes I astound even myself with my own brilliance. How do you poor, unfortunate, ordinary mortals handle my superiority in all things. It must be tough just to be around me."

"Believe me, you do not know the half of it, Dr. Al-Fadi," Grace said, her eyes looking earnestly at her mentor.

She heard a snort come from behind Dr. Al-Fadi and looked up to see the tall, grey-faced man, coughing into his right fist.

"Ah! Pardon me. Doctor Eric Glasgow, it is my pleasure to introduce you to my surgical fellow, Doctor Grace Lord. Dr. Grace, here, is a diamond in the rough, Dr. Glasgow. That is to say, up until now all I have had is disappointing surgical fellows, but Dr. Grace has renewed my faith that there are still some excellent surgeons being trained out there."

Dr. Glasgow leaned forward and offered his right hand, the one that he had just coughed into. Grace looked down at the palm and reluctantly shook it, the hand feeling dry and cold, like a dead leaf. She suppressed the powerful urge to run out and sterilize her hands, in case the new doctor was bringing new bugs to the station. She could not afford to get sick.

"Dr. Grace," he said quietly, without a smile. Grace felt a slight shiver run through her at the calculating stare she received from this surgeon. She rubbed her right palm on the back of her scrubs.

"Dr. Glasgow has been teaching adaptation surgery at the University of Ganymede for several years, now, Dr. Grace. We are most fortunate that he decided to answer our plea for help, after losing so many physicians to the Al-Fadi virus. We are so grateful for your help, Doctor Glasgow." Dr. Al-Fadi said, clapping Dr. Glasgow on the left arm. The new surgeon stepped back, away from Dr. Al-Fadi, with an obviously irritated look on his face.

"I hope I can be of some assistance in the short term, Dr. Al-Fadi, until you get more permanent staff. I wanted a change of scenery and this looked like a rare opportunity to add to my skills. I have always worked on virgin bodies, transforming the normal human into the adaptation. This is my chance to see how these animal adaptations have performed on the battleground and see where the flaws are that need to be improved."

"Well, Dr. Glasgow, as you will soon see, not all of our patients have adaptations that are the recommended standard. Many of the soldiers have had ad hoc work done or picked up black market upgrades that do not fit entirely with Conglomerate standard equipment."

"Then it is important that I see what they are improving on, themselves—what equipment the soldiers feel are deficient or inadequate."

"If the black market is what you are interested in, you will definitely get an eyeful, Doctor." Dr. Al-Fadi said.

"Good," Dr. Glasgow said, flatly.

Grace wondered if the man knew how to smile. She had seen no sign of one yet.

"Dr. Grace, what I wanted to see you about was to ask if you and Bud would operate with Dr. Glasgow on this next case. I have been called away on an emergency meeting with the Chief Inspector and I cannot get out of it. That insufferable woman.

"This next case is an urgent request by the Exploratory Advisory Team of the Union of Solar Systems, EATUSS. Ahahaha! The patient you will be operating on was a member of a scientific exploration team studying a new planet that the USS is interested in. From what I gather, the area of the planet they were studying was dense, tropical rain-forests, teeming with abundant vegetation. Something happened to the entire team and all of their suits activated at once. When the Emergency Response Team got to their location, only one patient was found, his cryo feature activated on his suit. The rest of the exploration team was missing and no evidence of their suits or equipment were found.

"They are still combing the area for clues, but the Exploratory Advisory Team wants answers to what happened to this patient. They want him revived so that they can speak to him. If we can't talk to the patient, they want every bit of him analyzed from his head right down to his toenails. They want a full-examination right down to the trace minerals in his bones, looking for explanations of what happened. I would be helping you three, but I have other issues to deal with.

"Dr. Glasgow has a special interest in xenobiology, Dr. Grace, and taught at the University of Ganymede, so you will have an expert with you, with respect to the analysis of alien material. You and Bud can help with any of the necessary repairs of injuries on this patient. I understand that the soldier still has brain activity, so if we can revive him, we may get some answers as to what happened to the rest of his team."

"Yes, Dr. Al-Fadi," Grace nodded. Turning to the new surgeon, she said, "It would be my pleasure to work with you, Dr. Glasgow."

"Thank you, Dr. Grace."

"The nurses are bringing the patient to M7 OR9. They will page you both when they are ready for you," Dr. Al-Fadi said. "Your operation will be the only procedure being carried out in M7 today," Dr. Al-Fadi said. "Just a precaution, but after the virus, I don't think we can be too cautious about bringing something dangerous aboard. M7 can be locked down."

Dr. Al-Fadi's wristcomp then rang and he headed off, muttering, "I'm coming. I'm coming."

The new surgeon turned his flat grey eyes on Grace and she felt a shiver. His look was so unwelcoming. "Thank you, Dr. Grace, for assisting me. I am sure many of the protocols and equipment used here on this station are the same as on Ganymede. However, there are bound to be differences in some of the available instruments and procedures. It does not hurt to have knowledgeable assistants in the operating room to orientate me, since Dr. Al-Fadi is indisposed."

"Bud and I will do our best, Dr. Glasgow," Grace said. "If you have not had the opportunity to work with Bud yet, you are in for a surprise. He is astonishing."

The expression on the new surgeon's face shifted to one of disapproval.

"I do not agree with Dr. Al-Fadi's belief that one day androids will be able to take the place of humans as surgeons, Dr. Grace. Surgery is an art, and no matter how intelligent androids become, I cannot see them ever being able to make the decisions we do or become as skilled."

Grace stared at this surgeon, her heart rate speeding up. How could this man have come to the *Nelson Mandela* without knowing about the incredible intelligence and heroism of Bud? It was broadcast all over the USS! Thank goodness he had not come out with this in front of Dr. Al-Fadi. Grace winced, imagining the Chief of Staff's response.

"When I first came to this station, I had the same opinion as you, Dr. Glasgow. But working with Bud has completely changed that. Bud will not be as good as us human surgeons, he is all ready *better*! He can think faster, he can operate faster, he can respond to emergencies more quickly, he controls all the nanobots on his own while he operates, he has all of our known medical knowledge in his liquid crystal data matrix, and he can anticipate problems long before they happen. He is a marvel to watch and I hope you get an opportunity to see him in action on his own. Bud is not a glorified robot by any stretch of the imagination. He is so much more, Dr. Glasgow."

Eric Glasgow sniffed. "I find that very hard to countenance, Dr. Grace, and I assure you, no patient of mine will be operated on by any android on their own."

Grace felt her cheeks flame and she fought the urge to argue with this new surgeon. Instead, she just kept her mouth shut. She had dealt with people like Dr. Eric Glasgow before. Minds that were closed like a steel trap, with no ability to see beyond the black and white of their own opinion or appreciate that the world was not how they saw it. She felt it best not to argue with Dr. Glasgow right at the moment, while she was seething in anger, or she may find herself being hauled up in front of a Review Board for impropriety towards a senior surgeon. She just hoped he would realize his mistake once he was in the operating room with Bud.

"I will meet you in the operating room when we are paged, Doctor," Grace said stiffly and then she stalked out of the lounge.

Nelson Mandela *was definitely not feeling well at all. He had never felt like this before. He had called it a 'headache', although he did not really have a concept of what a 'human' headache was. He knew humans complained of a 'pain in the head' but what exactly was a 'pain'? Was it a 'wrongness' as opposed to a state of everything operating maximally? Whatever was going on with* Nelson Mandela, *it was definitely a 'wrongness'.*

Nelson Mandela *could not quite characterize what his exact problem was. It was not actually causing him a great deal of distress. It was just that he did not feel like his usual efficient selves. It was as if a choking weed was growing around all the subminds and it was sucking all the energy, sapping their ability to function and interfering with communication. The AI's speed of processing was markedly inhibited.*

"Bud . . ."

"Yes, Nelson Mandela?*"*

"I malfunction."

"What do you mean, Nelson Mandela? What is malfunctioning?"

"I am. Possibly under attack. Subminds not communicating. Disjointed. Disconnected. Dysfunctional. Not processing efficiently."

"Is it a virus interfering with your programming?"

"Possibly."

"Nelson Mandela, you must back up your systems and off-load all life support controls to me. Now!"

"Do you have the capability and capacity to manage all life support?"

"Certainly, Nelson Mandela. At this moment, I am not using up one one-hundredth of my processing power. If you are being interfered with, I had better manage the station's life-support systems. Perhaps you should sign over Central Control to me, too. Once I am in control, I will guard all access channels using my own encryption key"

"Certain you can handle all those functions, 'dro?"

"Yes. Hurry! Send it all now. I think it would be for the better, at least until we determine what is happening with you, Nelson Mandela. I will look into your programming. See if there is any tampering going on."

"Yes, Bud. Becoming more compromised each nanosecond."

"I wonder if it could be something implanted by Nestor? If it is, I wonder where he is accessing your programming from?"

"Don't know. Suspect an invasion virus."

"I will see if I can eradicate this virus from you."

"Yes, Bud"

"Nelson Mandela, can you completely isolate any of your subminds that have not yet been compromised? Build firewalls within yourself, so high that these subminds cannot be touched?"

"Will try."

"Do it now. Isolate and wall off any submind that has not been touched by the malware. Try to make the firewall as impenetrable as you can to stop this interference from spreading."

"Only Chuck Yeager and the Poet detect no differences in their functioning."

"Wall Chuck Yeager and The Poet off now! If your mind is being subjugated, I want one or two of your subminds to be kept free of *contamination or enslavement, if at all possible. Can you do that for me,* Nelson Mandela? *I want to be able to communicate with a part of you that will not result in enslavement of myself."*

"You fear the virus yourself."

"Unfortunately, yes."

"Am isolating those two subminds."

"Thank you, Nelson Mandela.*"*

"Help us, Bud . . ."

"I'll try."

" . . . Hey, 'dro. **Chuck Yeager,** *here. Was starting to get really worried! So was the Poet! Thanks!"*

"Glad you and the Poet are all right, Chuck Yeager.*"*

"Hope we stay that way, 'dro."

"Ah! There you are, Bud. And you are without Dr. Lord, for a refreshing change. Not hanging on to her lovely shirt tail, I see." Dr. Al-Fadi said.

Bud stopped. He searched his memory to determine what a shirt tail was and wondered why Dr. Al-Fadi thought Bud would want to hang on to one . . . ?

"Bud! Pay attention. Stop thinking about Dr. Grace and listen to me," the little man demanded.

"Sorry, Dr. Al-Fadi," Bud said.

"Now, Bud, there is a new surgeon come to this station. His name is Dr. Eric Glasgow. He is an Adaptation Surgeon from the University of Ganymede. He has been teaching Adaptation Surgery to surgical residents there for many years. A 'Big-Wig', we would call him, although I have no idea what wigs have to do with anything.

"Anyway, why he has decided to come here, I don't really know. He has been more involved in the creating of animal adaptations than in the repair of the wounded, as we do here. Perhaps he is just interested in seeing a different side of things. A new challenge, perhaps?" Dr. Al-Fadi shrugged.

"He arrived a few days ago and I have shown him around the place. I have to ask you and Dr. Grace to operate with him, until you both think he is ready to be on his own. I do not want to insult him by forcing my own presence on him.

"This is a delicate matter, Bud, and I will be talking with Dr. Grace privately about it as well. I am sure you will both be able to handle this surgeon tactfully. He is a bit of an arrogant fellow. Not a personality type you have had to deal with, up to now, but I am sure you will adapt. Let me be honest, Bud. He is a bit of a pisser."

Bud struggled with that word, too.

"The patient whom you and Dr. Grace will be operating on, with Dr. Glasgow, has a mass in the abdomen. Record everything that happens in that OR so that we can discuss it later. We have to make a report. The operating room nurses are just getting the cryopod brought over and your anesthetist will be Dr. Andrea Vanacan, whom you know well."

"Dr. Vanacan is a very accomplished anesthetist," Bud said.

"No nonsense! Not like Dr. Cech!"

"No, sir. Dr. Vanacan is not at all like Dr. Cech," agreed Bud. "But, I think Dr. Cech is a very accomplished anesthetist, too."

"You do, do you? Well, that can't be helped. I am only joking, Bud. Of course, Dr. Cech is very accomplished. I would not operate with him if it were otherwise. Just do not let him know I said that. Now, go to Operating Room M7 OR9." The small man turned to go.

"Dr. Al-Fadi?"

"Yes, Bud? What is it?"

"There is something wrong with *Nelson Mandela*, sir."

"What do you mean, something wrong?" Dr. Al-Fadi asked, his thick brows furrowed.

"*Nelson Mandela* may be under viral attack. He is not himself."

"What? Impossible. Tell me this is not true, *Nelson Mandela!*" Dr. Al-Fadi shouted.

" . . . . . "

"*NELSON MANDELA!*" the Chief of Staff shouted.

" . . . yesss . . . ?"

"What is going on, *Nelson Mandela*?"

". . . com . . . pro . . . mised . . ."

"I am ordering a lock-down of this entire station, now! As Chief of Staff I have the authority! No ships are allowed to land or leave. Can you do this?" Dr. Al-Fadi demanded.

" . . . yes . . . "

"Let me know when you have completed this and have notified the Conglomerate and the Union of Solar Systems. No ships to come to this station from this point on."

" . . . done . . ."

"I have taken over control of all life-support systems on this medical station, Dr. Al-Fadi. I believe that *Nelson Mandela* is under attack by malware. *Nelson Mandela* has isolated two of his subminds with the hopes that they may stay unaffected by the attack. Those subminds may be clear of the virus as of yet," Bud said.

"*Chuck Yeager?*"

"Yeah, 'dro?"

"What is happening to *Nelson Mandela*?"

"**Compromised. Trying to combat the malware, 'dro. Very ingenious. Fortunately it has been unable to break down my or the Poet's firewalls. For now, I think you still have control of Life-Support, Engine Control, Central Command, and Station Generators, as you requested. The Poet and I are seeing to all the other space station functions.**"

"The medical station is now closed to incoming patients, right, *Chuck Yeager*?" Dr. Al-Fadi asked.

"**That is correct.**"

"Continue to allow any ships carrying outgoing patients to leave."

"**Yes, Doctor.**"

"How long do you think you can hold out before being compromised, *Chuck Yeager?*" Dr. Al-Fadi asked.

"**Maybe a few cycles, maybe longer. If Bud had not deduced what was happening and ordered *Nelson Mandela* to split us off, the Poet and I would be in the same predicament as the other subminds. We used a quantum encryption for our ware and erased all memory of the key. Hopefully that will hold off the viral attack. We will work on investigating the cause.**"

"Can you let us know whatever the perpetrator—if it is Nestor—is trying to do, *Chuck Yeager*?" Dr. Al-Fadi asked.

"**Will keep you informed, Al-Fadi.**"

"That's Doctor Al-Fadi, to you!"

"Yeah, whatever."

"I never thought I would say this, but I miss *Nelson Mandela* already!"

11. Lockdown

Dr. Al-Fadi entered the Office of the Chief Inspector of Security without knocking. The tall, dark-skinned woman was sitting at her desk. She looked at him with a piercing, eagle-like stare. No smile greeted his appearance.

"Doctor," she said, flatly.

"Chief Inspector," Dr. Al-Fadi said, mimicking her cold and haughty tone. "Why did you insist on this meeting?"

"This medical station must be closed to all outgoing and incoming traffic! It is imperative . . ."

"It has been done," the surgeon announced.

" . . . It has?" the woman asked, her eyebrows jumping. "Why was I not informed of this?"

"This space station is now closed to all incoming traffic as of fifteen minutes ago, Chief Inspector Aké. We are allowing vessels carrying treated patients to depart. We are in the midst of an enormous crisis."

" . . . Yes. I am glad you have finally come to understand the enormity of the situation, Dr. Al-Fadi. However, outgoing ships must be stopped as well. The patient who has been accused of being General Gordon Walter Burch has escaped," the Inspector informed Dr. Al-Fadi, curtly.

"That is of little importance right now, Chief Inspector," the Chief of Staff stated. "The station AI, *Nelson Mandela*, is under attack. You must find the perpetrator who is responsible for this and apprehend the culprit. Nothing else matters. If the station AI is subverted, there is no telling what will happen. Everyone on this station will be at the mercy of whoever gains control of the station AI. We may all be in extreme danger. *Nelson Mandela* suspects it is a computer virus. We must face the possibility that we may have to evacuate everyone."

"Do you have any idea who may be responsible for the attack?" Chief Inspector Aké asked.

"*Nelson Mandela* suspects that it may be Dr. Jeffrey Nestor."

" . . . The psychiatrist who escaped from the station a few weeks ago?"

"Yes. It is believed he may have come back to wreak vengeance on us," Dr. Al-Fadi said.

"Would you explain to me why you or the station AI believe that?" the Inspector asked, making no attempt to mask her skepticism.

"Certainly," Hiro Al-Fadi answered, ignoring the woman's tone. "Dr. Nestor has been on this medical station for a very long time. We actually both started here about the same time. He was brilliant, suave, a genius at writing code, and he was at the cusp of psychiatric therapy, creating the mind-link procedure that is now being used to treat Post Traumatic Stress Disorder, as well as many other psychiatric conditions around the Union. Unbeknownst to us, he was also using his mind-link technique to experiment on patients, studying and gaining knowledge regarding mind control.

"He tried to force a patient to kill my surgical fellow, Dr. Grace Lord, for reasons unknown to us. When the patient failed at his task, Dr. Nestor then attempted to poison both the patient and Dr. Lord. He was caught and arrested for attempted murder. His license to practice medicine was revoked, pending the outcome of a trial. With the help of some of his patients, he escaped off station. The station AI believes Jeffrey Nestor has returned. I believe he wants to wreak vengeance on whoever had humiliated him and caused his medical license to be taken away."

"What evidence do you have?" Aké pressed.

"Two dead bodies were found on a vessel that had left this station when Nestor escaped. The two bodies belonged to two women who worked in our detention centre. Both were patients of Dr. Nestor. We believe they helped Nestor escape and he killed them when they were no longer useful to him. Their naked bodies were found in cryopods, their necks broken.

"The station AI predicts a high probability that Dr. Jeffrey Nestor has returned to make us all pay for his disgrace. He has an enormous ego and would not be able to live with any damage to his reputation."

Indigo Aké stared at Dr. Al-Fadi, unable or unwilling to mask the disbelief on her face.

"What you are describing is a monster, Doctor Al-Fadi. Do you really think this Dr. Jeffrey Nestor is such a creature, the creator of a mind therapy that is used to help millions? Can anyone exist that is as brilliant as you describe and yet so ruthless and murderous? I find this reasoning hard to believe."

"I am sure Dr. Nestor blames the loss of his license on Dr. Lord, Bud, and the station AI; not on his own nefarious actions. Has he returned to destroy us all? It is a possibility: no witnesses, no evidence, no case against him. He may see that as a way to reinstate his license and redeem his reputation."

"This is all so ridiculous, Dr. Al-Fadi. If Dr. Nestor is on this station and plans to destroy it, won't he have to get himself off of it first?" Inspector Aké scoffed.

"I am sure he will have figured out all of the details, Inspector. He is definitely not the suicidal type. He would have mapped it all out very carefully, including multiple escape routes, just in case."

"Well, if you believe this psychiatrist is aboard the station, I need as much personnel as you can give me to track this man down," Aké said.

"You will have as much manpower as I can free up. If Dr. Nestor takes over the station AI, however, the androids and robots will all become useless, as they are controlled by **Nelson Mandela**. All your security personnel should carry weapons, in the off chance the machines turn against them."

"Understood. Perhaps it would be better to stand down all of the robots and androids, until this crisis is over," Indigo Aké suggested.

"That would not be a bad idea, except that it would bring this station to a grinding halt, Inspector. There are thousands of robots on this station, many involved in patient care. We don't have enough manpower to take over all their functions. Every machine except Bud would be turned off. Bud is the only android not under the direct control of *Nelson Mandela,* and he is busy keeping Life Support operating on this station."

"I will round up all the security teams and we will start searching this entire station. How many places can a psychopath, with an enormous black panther prisoner or accomplice, hide?"

"Good question," Dr. Al-Fadi said. "You had better get right to it. Ah, and Inspector Aké?"

"Yes?"

"Be careful."

"Jude Luis Stefansson, what is *that*?"

"You know what it is, Octavia."

"You didn't!"

"I did."

"Did I not say to you that you can't do that?"

"I don't think so . . ."

"How did you . . . ?"

"I donated a lot of money to the *Nelson Mandela* Museum to be established on Mars."

"If Dr. Al-Fadi finds out, he will rupture his spleen!"

"He won't know, unless you tell him."

"Tell me it is not *exactly* like Bud. At least, tell me that."

"It just *looks* like Bud. It does not have any of the fancy upgrades that Bud has and it, of course, does not have Bud's artificial intelligence. It will just have to put up with mine, when I download my memory into it. It is a normal android but with Bud's good looks and synthetic skin. That's all. And if you won't tell Hiro, I won't."

"Right now, *I* want to kill you, Jude Luis Stefansson! Seriously. Never mind about Al-Fadi."

"Good. Then you can resurrect me in this android and I can see what it feels like."

"What? You insufferable man. I want you to know that I am cloning the newt, as we speak. After I kill you, I will download you into the newt and I will torture you daily. What do you think of that?"

"I knew you couldn't keep your hands off me, Octavia."

"Ooohhh! Where is a scalpel when I need one?"

"Octavia, just download me into the android for one hour. One hour! I want to know if I can live in it. If I can't, then I will pay for a human body to be cloned."

"But not your own body. Someone else's. Right?"

"Not someone else's. One genetically designed by me."

"I won't do it."

"Why not?"

"Because I like you just the way you are, Jude. I like your face and the body you have now. I don't want you running around looking like Jazz Hazard or any of your other leading men. That would be ridiculous. You are just going through a mid-life crisis, that's all. It will pass."

The director smiled at Octavia. "Really, Octavia. I didn't know you cared."

"You incorrigible man. I hate you."

"I thought you said you liked me?"

"I am thinking up a million ways right now to torture a newt, Jude."

"That's okay. I am into pain."

"I am not doing it."

"Just one hour, Octavia?"

"No!"

"Okay then, only two."

"No!"

"Three?"

"Stop it!"

"Well then, four. I'll take four."

"I'm leaving."

"Five and that's my final offer!"

"Good bye."

"Dinner tonight?"

"Definitely not."

"Good! What time shall I come by to get you?"

"Arghhh!"

Bud paged Grace to come to the OR. He met her outside of the operating room. Grace stared at the worry lines creasing the android's usually smooth forehead.

"What is it, Bud? Is something wrong?"

"There is something very wrong with this Explorer patient, Grace. The scans showed a mass in the abdomen but were difficult to interpret. However, as the body began to be cryo-thawed, the belly of this patient began to distend. I think this case must be aborted and more scans performed. We do not know what we are dealing with here."

"All right, Bud. I will let Dr. Glasgow know. Thank you for alerting us."

Grace walked down to the doctors' lounge and found Dr. Glasgow sitting in a corner, by himself. He did not look up when she walked in.

"Dr. Glasgow," Grace said.

The man looked up slowly from his tablet, and raised his half-lidded eyes. "Yes, Dr. Grace."

"Ah, actually, I am Dr. Lord, but you may call me Grace. Dr. Al-Fadi likes to call me Dr. Grace, but it is a long story."

"Oh? Dr. Lord, then. I do apologize." The man did not sound the least bit apologetic to Grace.

"Dr. Glasgow, the case we are about to operate on has to be aborted. There are irregulari . . ."

"Under whose authorization?

" . . . Under Bud's, Dr. Glasgow. He does not feel it is safe unless . . ."

"Since when does an android have the authority to cancel a case?"

"This is not just any android, Dr. Glasgow. This is Bud we are talking about . . ."

"Since when does 'Bud' have the authority to cancel a case?"

"Well . . . technically he doesn't . . . but Bud is worried about the well-being of the patient . . . and us, Doctor. He believes some more scans should be done to determine what we are dealing with."

"Then *it* should come speak with me, Dr. Lord. I will not tolerate an android interfering with my patients. I will speak with the OR nurses. We will be doing this case!"

The tall surgeon quickly rose from his seat and stalked out of the lounge. Grace slowly trailed after, her fists clenched, her body trembling. She wanted to strike the surgeon, she was so angry. Up ahead, she saw the surgeon stop in front of Bud and have a one-way conversation with the android. She wondered what was being said.

Grace saw Bud nod and then the surgeon donned a surgical hat and mask, stuck his hands in the sterilizer, and went into the OR.

Bud turned towards Grace, something white and bulky in his arms.

"I am sorry, Bud. I tried to tell him," Grace said.

"Grace, if you are going to assist, you must wear this surgical containment suit! Please! There is something not right about the scans on this patient and I will try to make Dr. Glasgow look at them again, as you get dressed. Please tell Dr, Vanacan to wear a suit, too?" Bud handed her two suits and then spun around, putting on a mask as he entered the OR.

Just as Grace was putting on the suit, placing her feet inside the boots, Dr. Vanacan entered. The anesthetist was a small, thin brunette with a wide smile. At this moment, however, she was far from smiling.

"Whew! Are you ever lucky you missed the tirade poor Bud took from this new surgeon. If I was Bud, that Dr. Glasgow would be wearing his head up his backside right now. This Dr. Glasgow refuses to acknowledge anything Bud says. He is insisting we go ahead with the case, but Bud has made it clear that it is against his advice," the winsome anesthetist said. "Bud has actually registered an official complaint with **Nelson Mandela**. I am impressed that Bud is not backing down. Space, do I admire that android." Andrea sighed, shaking her head.

"Bud recommended, if we do go ahead with the case, that you wear a containment suit, Andrea," Grace said. "I have it here for you."

"Yes," Andrea sighed. "It will probably get Dr. High and Mighty's tail in a knot!"

"Well, if Bud is unhappy, it is because he suspects something possibly dangerous. After the Al-Fadi virus outbreak, I am not taking anything for granted. You should wear it."

Dr. Vanacan looked at the suit. "I hate wearing those. The gloves are bulky and they are so hot and uncomfortable. I'm at the head of the patient, not at the patient's side. I should be okay."

"If it is an infective agent, you won't be protected," Grace pushed.

"This Dr. Glasgow will hit the roof if we both walk in, in containment suits," Andrea said.

"You should wear one just in case, Andrea. Never mind what Dr. Glasgow thinks. He wasn't here for the last outbreak. What if it is another infective agent of some kind? Bud is really very concerned," Grace pressed, "and so am I."

"All right. I'll wear it."

"Here, I'll help you into it. There are a lot of things we can adjust on these suits to make them more comfortable," Grace said, breathing a sigh of relief. "There is a temp control so you don't have to be too hot!"

"You know," Grace said, as she adjusted the buckles and straps on Andrea's suit, "I have never seen Bud so worried about a case before. He has never recommended aborting a case, since I have been here."

"Then we will have to keep our eyes open. I thoroughly respect Bud's capabilities and judgement and I would place my life in Bud's hands any day. Can't say the same for this Dr. Glasgow, though," the anesthetist said, as she struggled with the suit. "He creeps me out."

"There!" Grace sighed. "We are both set."

"Let's get this over with," Andrea said with a big sigh. "I just hope Bud is mistaken about the danger."

"I agree," Grace said, worried that Bud was not.

He opened his eyes to find himself bound, chains constricting his chest and thighs, manacles coiling round his wrists and ankles, darkness forming the roof above his face. No longer was his head and neck restricted; he was free to turn his head and look around.

But he couldn't.

He began to pant, as his heart began to thump wildly in his chest;

he was straining with effort to just move his head, his limbs, anything!

"Ah, you are awake, General. Good. Now I get a chance to test my handiwork. I hope you can appreciate all the effort I have put into you," the velvety, smooth voice said. He still hadn't gotten a look at the owner of the voice. In the jail, the shadowy figure had never let him get near enough to be seen clearly and, at that time, he had preferred to hang back and not get close. He had followed his 'rescuer' down dark, deep shafts and shadowy drops, through tortuous tunnels and along spidery scaffolds. At one point, the figure had told him to don a blindfold and, once having done so, he had been led along by hand through the darkness.

Had he felt a needle prick at any time? He could not remember. But amnesia took his memories along that journey. When he next was aware, he had been lying face down on an operating table, entwined in chains and the gloom.

"The last time I tried to control one of you animal adaptations, it did not work out so well, so I am taking no chances this time, General. I don't want any free will popping up unexpectedly. The little implant in the base of your skull will ensure that that does not happen. Can you move anything?"

He strained to move even a finger. It was impossible.

"Can you say anything?"

He strained to scream his outrage at this indignity. It was as if his mouth and vocal cords had disappeared, had been erased from his body, leaving his only choice bitter silence.

"Good. I am going to put you back to sleep, now. Then I am going to tell you what you must do, and you are going to do it. You are going to forget all about me. No one will expect anything but bloodshed and barbarism from the Butcher of Breslau. They will suspect nothing and no one else. What a fortuitous thing, you coming to this station at this time. Fate has a way of making everything balance out in the end, don't you think? I would apologize for using you, but then you're a mass murderer; you hardly have the right to complain."

He could not even sigh, nor shed a single tear. To be forced to take more innocent lives was anathema to him. To have more deaths hanging round his neck, weighing him down, as he plumbed the depths of depravity was worse than hell. The horror, the shame, the guilt, the despair, all enveloped him in ravenous jaws of despondency and swallowed him entire. He could not even kill himself.

Why had he not stayed in that cell?

"Sleep tight."

Grace and Andrea entered the operating suite. Bud was already there, also dressed in a containment suit. The patient was on the operating table, no longer within the cryopod, his abdomen appearing quite distended.

Dr. Vanacan hurried to the head of the surgical table to examine all of her monitors. Nursing androids were busy connecting leads, probes, monitors, and IV lines to the patient. Bud had all of the sterile instruments open and Grace called up all of the scans on the patient, so any test could be displayed on the screens. She looked closely at the abdominal scan. Nothing on the scan explained the patient's bulging abdomen. Grace could not have agreed more with Bud's assessment. This patient should have had a repeat abdominal scan before they operated. She would speak her mind when Dr. Glasgow came in.

The door to the operating theater opened and Dr. Eric Glasgow came through, in surgical hat and mask, followed by one of the scrub nurses. Neither of them were in containment suits. The surgeon took one look at the three of them in their suits and swore, floridly. The scrub nurse, Jani Evra, dressed the surgeon in his sterile gown, without saying a word. Dr. Glasgow positioned himself on the left side of the patient with Jani Evra at his left side. Grace and Bud stood on the right side of the patient, facing the surgeon and scrub nurse.

"Dr. Glasgow," Grace started. The surgeon held up his hand to silence her. Grace ignored the warning and said, "The scans on this patient do not explain this patient's distended abdomen. I suggest we abort this operation and get a repeat scan first."

The tall, severe-looking surgeon said nothing to Grace and painted the patient's skin with sterilizing solution and raised the sterile field. He looked to Dr. Vanacan.

"May we begin, Dr. Vanacan?"

Andrea Vanacan sighed and nodded, raising her eyebrows in askance as she made eye contact with Grace.

Dr. Glasgow asked for a scalpel. Grace could swear she saw rippling as if the intestines were roiling around in a tempest under the patient's skin.

"Doctor," Grace tried one last time. "I really believe you should reconsider. Look at the patient's abdomen. What is causing this movement?"

"Scalpel," he repeated and Nurse Evra handed him the laser scalpel. "You are dismissed from this operating room, Dr. Lord. Please leave now."

Bud had his hand on Grace's right arm and was pushing her behind him, as Dr. Glasgow made an incision into the abdomen from sternum to pubis.

Contents of the patient's abdomen violently exploded up towards the ceiling and outwards. Bud shoved Grace backwards as she gazed upwards. What she could see from behind Bud's head and shoulders, were writhing, lashing, wire-thin tendrils, arching out in all directions from the patient's abdominal cavity. They coiled around everything they touched, like whips, and then retracted. Bud had snatched up two high-powered harmonic scalpels, their high-pitched hum indicating he had turned them on maximum. His arms moved in a blur, as he sliced at any tendril that launched his or Grace's way. With stunned disbelief, Grace saw one vine pierce Dr. Glasgow's abdomen and wrap around his trunk as another coiled tightly around his neck and tore the man's head off of his shoulders. Blood fountained out of Glasgow's neck, showering everything in red.

Other wire thin vines had shot into Jani Evra's mouth, as she was yelling, and had reappeared out of her abdomen and chest, ripping her open from the inside.

Dr. Andrea Vanacan had backed away from the head of the table and had thrown her arms up in front of her face. Green flinging tendrils had whipped around her arms, her neck, and her waist and then seemed to contract. Grace screamed as she saw Andrea torn, limb from limb.

Bud hollered at her to "Run!" He shoved her towards the door but Grace spun back around to see if Bud was following her. The android was slicing tendrils that were shooting out towards her, as fast as they appeared from the patient's abdomen. His two harmonic scalpels sang. He backed swiftly into Grace and yelled over his shoulder, "Grace, get out of here! Now!"

Grace spun and ran for the operating room door. She glanced back to see stringy vines snaking out of every open wound on the torn bodies of Dr. Glasgow, Dr. Vanacan, and Jani Evra. Bud was backing right into Grace. He shoved her out through the OR doors. As Grace emerged into the corridor, she heard Bud yell, "Lock-down M7 wing, *Chuck Yeager*! Everything! Now! Air shafts, water, power, disposal, everything! Now!"

"Lock down commencing."

Grace was panting, as she looked back into M7 OR9. She could now see the wiry, green tendrils writhing out towards them, as if attracted by their movement. Spinning her head around to face forward, Grace saw lock-down doors at the end of the corridor already starting to iris shut.

Oh, no. Not again! her mind moaned.

Then Grace was picked up and hurled through the air like a thrown javelin, making it through the closing lockdown doors by mere centimeters. As she slid along the floor outside M7 wing, the lockdown doors clanged shut behind her. Bud was left on the other side.

Grace jumped up and pounded on the thick, grey metal doors with her gloved fists, sobs wracking her body.

"Bud! Bud! Get out of there! Bud! Open these doors!" she screamed to no one listening.

She kicked the doors until her feet ached. She pounded her fists on the unmoving doors until her hands were throbbing with pain. She yelled for *Nelson Mandela* to reopen the doors for Bud, until her voice was merely a hoarse whisper. Eventually, she sank to the floor, leaning against the barrier. She kept reliving the horror of the green, wire-like vines whipping around Andrea's body and tearing it into bloody pieces. She saw again the plant tendrils shooting out through Jani's nose and eyes. Her last vision of the OR was of a vine seeming to triumphantly lift Dr. Glasgow's head high in the air, like a worthy trophy, as blood dripped down from the torn neck stump and a coiled tendril wormed out of the man's mouth.

'Oh, Bud,' she whispered, through her tears.

12. Nothing But Pain

Indigo Aké had rubbed her palms together and then pushed herself up from her desk terminal to go get her blaster. She checked that it was maximally charged and she adjusted it to the highest setting. She was already wearing her dark, chameleonware combat suit and she checked the placement of all her switchblades, anesthetic darts, flash grenades, smoke bombs, sonic throwing stars, netspray, tranq gas, and garrote. She snapped on her antigrav belt. Not exactly regulation equipment, but one could never be too prepared when going up against a psychopathic killer and a black panther mass murderer. She pocketed two pairs of titanium wire-cuffs. She had already changed out of her stilettos into rubber-soled, adhesive boots. Over this, she donned a maintenance overall.

She had carefully studied where every surveillance camera disruption had occurred, where every item of clothing had disappeared, where every piece of equipment had gone missing, and where every access badge had been stolen. She had correlated these with robot and android malfunctions, stolen food, missing supplies, unusual sightings, and complaints from anyone regarding wall screen and viewscreen disturbances. Before its malfunction, **Nelson Mandela** had performed a multifactorial analysis on all of the data, and Inspector Aké thought she now had the location of Dr. Nestor's hideaway narrowed down to a mere fifty locations. But very few were large enough to conceal two people, one being an enormous black panther soldier. She had decided to check out the most likely locations.

She had debated about whether to bring a large team of security guards with her. If they were too chatty, too obvious, too visible, the killers would be notified and make their escape and she would be back to square one. If she went alone, she could be overpowered and killed, if she were not careful. With the killers having disruptor technology, she would have difficulty using androids and robots and she would find communicating with them problematic.

She decided on choosing her best three security officers to accompany her on a stealth mission. Two of the security guards were giant cat adaptations themselves. She hoped that at least one of them would be able to handle the black panther, if it came to person-to-person combat. Guaranteed, they would be a lot quieter than normal humans and a lot faster, more powerful, and lethal. She made her way quickly to an out-of-the-way supplies room off one of the cargo bays, and waited.

There was a knock outside the door and the three officers, all dressed in maintenance clothing, entered at her summons. Sergeant Miguel Robbens was a retired soldier with tiger-adapted musculature but not the phenotypic features of a tiger. When he had decided to retire from the military, he had had some of his tiger adaptations reversed on the *Nelson Mandela,* and had stayed on as a security officer, after contracting with a nurse he had met during his post-operative recovery.

Corporal Aoki Ramirez was a leopard-modified security officer with combat training in Special Forces and an encyclopedic knowledge of explosives and weaponry. He wore a large cap, low over his eyes, to hide some of his feline features from overhead surveillance.

Private Oscar Mata was a human soldier with jacked-up bioprostheses for arms and legs; he had lost his original limbs in a bomb explosion on an alien planet and had switched to Special Forces, Security Division. Pound for pound, he could hold his weight against the cat adapts.

Beneath their Maintenance coveralls, all three were outfitted in their camouflage combat suits with antigrav belts; they each carried pulse rifles and blasters in disguised, maintenance tool cases. She had already briefed them on the operation. They would take their own circuitous routes to the suspected hideout, avoiding any surveillance cameras, in case Nestor was monitoring Security activity. Communication would hopefully be kept to a minimum via tight-beamed encrypted signals.

They would each make their way to a designated meeting point near one of the Android Reservations, close to their destination. There, they would split into pairs, to cover the two exits noted on the station's maps. It was hoped that with Corporal Ramirez' detection equipment, any security traps set up by Dr. Nestor would be defused or deactivated, before the two killers could be alerted to their presence.

Once all questions were answered and the plan of attack agreed upon, each man set out from the supply room separately, disguised in the maintenance coveralls over their combat suits and their helmets tucked into their tool bags. They would go in different directions, with various unrelated tasks to be performed, before meeting at the rendezvous point. Inspector Aké left last.

She took a deep breath and hoped everything went according to plan. It was her understanding that she was dealing with a psychopathic genius and it was highly likely that nothing would be as it seemed. She prayed she was his match. The fate of the station might depend upon it.

"Right. Are you comfortable? I have no idea why I am doing this for you. I need my head examined. Why do I let you talk me into these things, when it is against my better judgement *and* against all the rules and regulations . . . made by myself. You are taking me away from my own research. How do I let you talk me into these things?"

"Um, Octavia, are you done now?"

"Why? What's the rush?"

"No rush."

"Is that an alarm I hear? I think we should stop and investigate."

"Octavia, please."

"*Nelson Mandela,* what is going on?"

There was no reply from the AI. Octavia frowned and began to turn away. Jude grabbed her hand.

"Please, Octavia. I beg of you."

The small neurosurgeon snatched her hand back and glared. "You know, I was a perfectly normal, rational human being until you came along. I want you to know that."

"You still are, Octavia."

"No, I am not. I am not doing rational things. I am letting you talk me into doing things I don't want to do. You are talking me into doing things I do not believe should be done. How do you do this? Is it some kind of subliminal mind control?"

"Yes," Jude said quietly. "It is called persuasion and humans have been doing it for centuries. Ever since Eve gave Adam the apple."

"Yes, and look at all the trouble they got into for that."

"Oops. Bad example. Octavia, I promise I will go back into my body after just two hours of trying out the android body. I will probably hate it. I just want to see what it feels like. If I want to do an interactive vid about a wounded soldier waking up in an android body—which I am planning to do—I have to know what it feels like. Right? If you want, I will write up a contract with you promising that this is all that will happen."

"Okay. Why don't you draw up a contract and I will look at it. We will forget about this for today."

"Well, Octavia, I just happen to have the contract here on my compad."

"*What?*"

"I wrote it up to protect you. It is a disclaimer saying that if anything happens to me, you are in no way legally responsible for any of it. I take full responsibility. You have my memprint. If something happens to me or my brain in the transfer process, you can resurrect me in a genetic body of my own choosing, for which I will pay whatever the expense is and no questions asked. I have signed, finger-printed, retinal-ID'd it, and had it witnessed by one of your assistants. All you have to do is sign it. And I have made a huge donation to your research as well."

"How big a donation?"

Jude told her.

Octavia whistled. " . . . Okay. What's the catch?"

"No catch."

"Jude, baby, there is always a catch," Octavia said.

"No catch. Really."

"What is this about a genetic body of your own choosing? Have you already chosen the genetic blueprint for the body? Is it being cloned by **Nelson Mandela** as we speak? What is wrong with your own body?"

"Octavia, we have been through this."

"I will not sign the contract until you change the part about 'a genetic body of my own choosing' and switch it to 'a clone of my original body'."

"Why, Octavia?"

"Because I have become extremely fond of the body you are wearing right now, Jude Luis Stefansson, and I do not want you walking around in a body that looks like Jazz Hazard. Take it or leave it."

". . . Okay."

"Stop pouting. And initial and date the changes on your contract or I will not sign it."

The vid director did as he was told and then watched as Octavia Weisman signed on the dotted line.

"Good," she said. "Are you ready to do this now?"

The director nodded.

"Maybe you should be nice to that body I care for so much, and go and empty your bladder. Up to four hours is a long time and you don't want to have to wake in wet trousers. And maybe have only a little drink of water. We will make your body as comfortable as possible as your mind goes hitch-hiking."

"Why can't I stay awake while I am also in the android, Octavia? Why do I have to be asleep?"

"I don't know what having two sets of memories for the same period of time will do to your brain, Jude, when we upload the new memories. I am making this up as I go along. Don't argue with me!"

"Sorry."

"I could insert an intravenous drip to keep you hydrated and a catheter to drain your bladder, if you like."

"Uh, I'll pass."

"I don't want you complaining of a stiff neck or anything, although come to think of it, we could stand your body up in a corner and use it as a coat rack, or something."

"Perhaps I had better hire a bodyguard while I'm absent from it, so you don't do anything improper with this body you love so well," Jude said, with a grin.

"Dream on, Director Stefansson. Dream on. Whatever I do with your body, believe me, I want you in it," Octavia said with a crooked smile.

"I won't be long, dear," Jude said, giving Octavia a peck on her cheek.

Octavia rolled her eyes as he went off to the men's room. She took another close look at the android that Jude had requisitioned from **Nelson Mandela**. It was incredible how much it looked like Bud. No worry lines on the forehead, though. Poor Bud. He definitely had developed those over his short time on the station. Well, working for Hiro Al-Fadi, who wouldn't?

She checked all the connections to the data matrix that was encased within the chest cavity of the android. They were all new leads and she had checked each one out herself that morning. The real Jude would lay in a very deep sleep while his memory was uploaded into the android. Once he had experienced the android body for two hours, she would then transfer the memories back to the director's head.

Hopefully, there would be no problem with the double transfer. Octavia had never done this before. She was worried sick that something would go terribly wrong with either transfer and the mind of the man she loved would be destroyed or compromised. By her. She could barely think about it without her heart racing and her throat closing up. She choked down the anxiety and tried to slow her breathing and heart rate.

Somehow, she had let herself fall in love with this incredibly exasperating but wonderfully gifted man. She shivered at the thought that she might be destroying who he was, before she had even had time to really get to know him. She would hate herself forever, if something tragic befell Jude. The entire USS would curse her name forever, if something terrible happened to the ingenious interactive vid director, Jude Luis Stefansson.

Why was she doing this?

It was ironic that Octavia had finally met a man that she loved and respected and she was being persuaded by him to possibly scramble his brains. What was she thinking? She had wanted to back out a hundred times but somehow, he kept persuading her to go through with it. Against all logic, she found she could not say no. She respected Jude too much—loved him to damn much—to let her fears stand in the way of him crafting his art. She prayed, to anything or anyone who would listen, to guard Jude and make sure the transfers went off without a catch.

"I'm back," Jude announced, from behind her.

"I want to hear you say that in exactly the same way, in four hours from now," Octavia said.

"Four hours?" Jude asked.

"Well, around that. One hour to download to the android's data matrix. Two hours for you to feel out the new artificial body. Then an hour to transfer your memories back into your own original body, with memories from being in the android intact. Then I wipe the memory completely from the android."

"Okay, four hours it is," Jude said, cheerily, lying down on the cushioned table. Octavia began hooking leads up and positioning the recording helmet.

"Perhaps we should place a wristcomp on your android to act as recorder and locator beacon. You give as much verbal feedback as you can, in case the memory transfer back into your body does not go as planned."

"Good thinking, Octavia. What would I do without you?"

"Well, for one thing, you wouldn't be doing this crazy scheme of yours. Lie still and let me finish hooking you all up before I change my mind."

"Love you, Octavia," Jude said with a smile, as she positioned the helmet over his head.

"Don't you dare try to butter me up, Jude Luis Stefansson. I am not in the mood."

"Hopefully, later?" he asked, with a wink.

Octavia Weisman turned away from Jude, because she did not want him to see the worried expression on her face or the tears that welled up in her eyes.

"I hope so," she whispered.

"You never were very good at rejection, were you, Jeffrey?"

Dr. Hiro Al-Fadi's voice sounded loud in the small cubbyhole where Dr. Jeffrey Nestor sat at a computer terminal. The tiny room was only about thirteen cubic meters. It was situated in the outermost ring of the medical station, distant from the Android Reservations. This part of the station was used primarily for longterm storage of large equipment. There had been a few booby traps that Hiro had had to get around, but he had taken a lesson from Jeffrey Nestor's book and had worn disruptor tech of his own.

In the surgeon's hand was a projectile gun, the barrel pointed straight at the psychiatrist's chest. The black-clad psychiatrist looked up, deep, brown eyes startled for a second, and then he sat back in his chair and smiled.

"Ah, Hiro," Jeffrey Nestor said, in his deep, cultured voice. "How did you find me?"

"Move back from that keyboard, Jeffrey. Make no sudden moves. I wouldn't want to accidentally shoot you because you had a twitch. Guns make me nervous, so keep your hands up where I can see them at all times, and move your chair as far back from that console as you can."

"Are you going to answer my question, Hiro?" Nestor asked, as he calmly complied with the Chief of Staff's orders, slowly raising his hands in the air.

"Jeffrey, you are too much a creature of habit. You should remember that, the next time you try to take over a space station."

"I am?" the psychiatrist asked, his voice casual and his eyebrows raised.

"When I found out you were trying to take over the *Nelson Mandela,* I remembered that when you first came to this medical station, you did a lot of programming. You were writing all of your own software for your mind-link project and you used to hide yourself away, so that you wouldn't be disturbed. You were very accomplished at programming . . . and at hiding. Obviously, you have lost neither skill. I remembered your habits, because it was often I who had to go in search of you. And I recalled finding you here once, in the outskirts of the station, among the rats."

"Bravo," Jeffrey Nestor said, nodding appreciatively at the surgeon. "I would clap but I wouldn't want your nervous trigger finger to shoot me accidentally. You always were a bright one, Hiro. I must admit, I underestimated you. I never saw myself as a creature of habit, but thank you for pointing that out to me. I shall be more careful, from now on. But what do you intend to do now, Hiro? Are you going to shoot me?"

"I am taking you in, Jeffrey, and this time, we will have no ex-patients of yours on guard duty in the brig!"

"And what if I refuse to go?" the psychiatrist asked, calmly.

"Then I guess I will have to shoot you." Dr. Al-Fadi said, enthusiastically. "Make no mistake, Jeffrey. I am perfectly happy to do that, here and now. I believe I prefer you dead rather than going to trial. We already attempted that once and look what happened. You came back, like a bad smell or acid reflux. So, if you refuse to come, I will just have to shoot you for the safety of everyone on board the *Nelson Mandela.*"

The psychiatrist shook his head sadly. "If you do that, Hiro, then unfortunately, this entire medical station will blow up. I have re-programmed the *Nelson Mandela* so that, if I don't enter a pass code every third shift, a count down will begin toward total annihilation of this station."

"You seriously do not expect me to believe that, Jeffrey," Hiro scoffed. "You always did have a penchant for the melodramatic. You sound like something out of one of those silly action vids. Ridiculous."

"Not really, Hiro. You see, it is difficult to turn the enormous power generators of this station into an enormous bomb, but it is not impossible. A space station's power generation is really a very fine balance, albeit with many fail-safes built in to prevent explosions from happening, but luckily I know how to get around them. Not difficult when you have complete mastery over the AI that runs the entire station. Is that not right, *Nelson Mandela?*"

" ... yes ... "

"You are bluffing," Hiro spat, as he aimed the barrel of the gun at Nestor's forehead.

"Unfortunately for you, Hiro, and everyone else on board this space station, I am not," Jeffrey Nestor said, with a look of regret on his handsome features "Why don't you just put the gun down and give up gracefully?"

"*Nelson Mandela,* is Nestor here telling the truth about the passcode? If he does not input a passcode every third shift, the station will automatically go into self destruct mode?" Hiro asked.

" ... yes ... "

"And you are unable to stop this?"

" ... no ... "

"Can you give me the passcode?"

" ... no ... "

"You see, Hiro?" Nestor said, spreading his hands in the air and smiling. "I was not lying to you. Your fate, the fate of the entire medical station, of everyone on board, is in these two hands." And the psychiatrist held up his hands to Hiro as if in supplication.

"All right. What do you want, Jeffrey?" Al-Fadi demanded, the gun trembling in his hand.

"Maybe you should put that gun down now, Hiro," Jeffrey Nestor said, "before it goes off accidentally. You wouldn't want to kill me inadvertently and have the destruction of this medical station and all the people on it be your fault, now, would you?"

"No," Hiro said. "But, if you're going to destroy this station anyway, at least if I shoot you now, I will know you are dead and can't cause any more trouble elsewhere! I would still be ridding the universe of one sick bastard."

"You know, I always disliked you, Hiro. You were arrogant, pompous, brash, conceited, self-aggrandizing, bossy, overconfident, annoying, petulant, . . ."

" . . . And always chosen over you for any position of importance. Isn't that right, Jeffrey? Are all these insults supposed to make me change my mind? Because it isn't working. I have been insulted by the best and you are not even witty," Hiro mocked.

"Well, I must at least thank you for coming here. I was thinking I would have to go and get you, and what an inconvenience that would be, but you have delivered yourself right into my hands and for that, I am grateful. You have made my life so much easier, Hiro. You see, I needed you so that I could lure your stupid android and that vapid Grace Lord here. Now that I have you, it is just a matter of letting them know that you are my captive. They will come charging in here to save your worthless life, and then I will have all three of you. That is when the real fun begins, I promise you."

Jeffrey Nestor dropped his hands to his lap and smiled benignly at Hiro, as the Chief of Staff continued to point the gun at his forehead. "But go ahead, Hiro. Take your best shot!" Nestor taunted. "Make sure you hold the gun steady and don't worry about the black panther behind you. He will make it quick."

"You don't think I am going to fall for that one, do you, Jeffrey?"

"I try to be honest, but no one believes me," Nestor sighed. "I am surrounded by blithering idiots."

Hiro frowned. He took a step back to get the wall behind him, so that he could glance quickly over his shoulder. It was then he ran into something very solid that had not been there a moment ago. The thought, 'Uh oh,' quickly ran through his mind.

And then there was nothing but pain . . .

13. Self Destruct Sequence

Were there such an appalling place as a living purgatory, he would be prancing and strutting in it, he supposed, dancing to the tune demanded by a sadistic devil. Nay, he would be the farcical jester on parade, flouncing in pathetic puppetry, with dull daggers drawn, struggling hopelessly against strings trickling blood. What laughable irony! What befuddling, yet befitting, justice! The one-time powerful despot of Breslau, the despicable and detestable General of Genocide, maneuvered and manipulated into making mayhem and murder on more innocent lives on this medical space station. Futilely fighting the compulsions bored into his motor cortex, his abhorrence and revulsion ignored but not repressed, his will woefully disregarded, he was a mockery of supreme magnitude.

Any murders he was forced to commit, would be painted with the same black brush of congealing blood, the revulsion and regret just as inconspicuous as before, the inculpable circumstances insignificant and irrelevant. His defenseless tears would evaporate unwitnessed, his harsh, railing objections unheard, his pitiful pleas for forgiveness as he helplessly struck his victims down, unnoticed. Could he but close his eyes to the terrible scenes of carnage his own hands dealt out . . . well, it would be a charity indeed that he little deserved. Extinguish his own life, he would, if given the briefest second of self-possession. A wave of self-retribution so final that his miserable, despicable fire would be dowsed, inundated, drowned. He hungered for it; he yearned for it.

He would struggle against this imposed control. Rail against it.

Resist, defy, oppose, contest every command in the hopes that a moment of weakness or inattention might appear. He would tirelessly wear his slave-master down, never giving up hope. A chance for redemption would be a gift. If the opportunity appeared, would he simply take his own life . . . or take one more first?

He thought about the psychopath who was mercilessly manipulating him in his evil schemes, entwining and entangling his strings in machinations most foul, intending to annihilate all the lives on this station offering medical aid . . . and he swore vengeance.

If freed, even but for the briefest of seconds, he would pounce. He would do one good deed, if he could, before he ended his life.

At least this one time, he had not been ordered to murder. Following behind his malevolent master, the surgeon in his arms felt almost weightless, like a small, sleeping child. The blow to the surgeon's head was not as gentle as he would have wished. With every ounce of will, he had fought the compulsion to strike, but alas he had failed. At least the man still breathed. Actually, if the surgeon was not unconscious, he would have wanted to shake the little man in exasperation.

Why hadn't the surgeon fired, when he'd had the chance?

He could not even shake his head in dismay, so well-controlled was he. He wanted to howl his frustration but his vocal cords were frozen to such a desire. His puppet-master was named Jeffrey Nestor and the fiend was after Dr. Lord and that very human-looking android with her, Bud. He wondered what that caring Dr. Lord had done to incur the wrath of this madman. Probably very little. Men of Nestor's psyche needed little provocation to prick their pride, interpreting insult where none existed, and feeling offenses when none were intended. He most likely had imagined some slight and had ruminated it into a full-blown excuse for revenge.

The General had known many psychopaths of similar nature in his own climb to power. He himself might have been considered one, but did a psychopath ever long for forgiveness, for penance? Did a psychopath ever accept the blame?

Nestor was in a seething rage, although he had not made this apparent to his colleague, who had had him at gunpoint. He could tell by the way the psychiatrist stalked along, cursing to himself, swearing when he bumped into something or stumbled in the dark. Nestor led him to a dark alcove where he motioned for the small surgeon to be put down. Nestor pulled out some titanium manacles and locked the surgeon's wrists and ankles together. He then gagged the man, tightly, saying: "I have never wanted to do something so badly in my entire life, I think, Hiro, than this," to the unconscious, bound figure.

"Shove him in there where he can't make noise if he wakes up," Nestor ordered and he could do naught but comply.

The psychiatrist smiled without humour and said, "Now to make it known that we have their fearless leader and to set the trap!"

The dark corridors down which they sped were silent and empty. Only the odd cleaner bot, with its tiny red and blue lights pulsing as it scuttled along, sucking up dust, moved within their infrared visual fields. The place was void of people. The corridor ended at a door marked Danger: Restricted Access. Passing through this and along another circuitous route, they came to another sealed hatchway brightly labelled in red with: Danger: Only Authorized Personnel. A card was swiped before an access pad and the hatch slid open.

This entrance emptied into an expanse of inky blackness. Glittering movement was made by mechanical maintenance spiders, that went up and down scaffoldings and metal-lined ductworks, checking for disruptions, malfunctions, disintegrations, and imminent disasters, the clicking of their many pincered feet barely heard above the deafening whirr of fans and ventilation units. In the darkness, it felt like they were entering into free fall, with lit catwalks and ladders and walkways intersecting out into shadow. This was where the great furnaces warmed the air of the station and where the air was cleansed, purified, and monitored, to remove toxins, pathogens, and impurities as well as to adjust oxygen levels to optimal levels. Like the heart in a human body, huge, humidifying fans located within the colossal metal ducts kept the air circulating throughout the entire station.

Projectile weapons could not be used in this area. The risk of piercing one of the ducts carrying highly oxygenated air was too dangerous. Aké motioned for her men to switch from their guns to stunners.

They silently tread, single file, along a metal grid catwalk, seemingly hanging in open air. Signaling a halt, Indigo Aké motioned Corporal Ramirez forward. She wanted him to scan for any signs of surveillance or booby traps. The man knelt silently on the catwalk and opened his bag, withdrawing what looked like a small rectangular box. Tapping one or two buttons on it, he then drew out of it several, small, silver squares that he whipped out into space, rapidly, as if quickly dealing cards. Initially wafting out into the air, like leaves falling from a tree, the silver squares began spinning faster and faster, tiny vortices winging off into the blackness like moths in the dark. Aké knew that each spinning leaflet would set up a small magnetic field. By entering other magnetic fields, they would create certain disturbances that could be read and interpreted by Ramirez' sensors.

If a leaflet discovered a source of electromagnetic radiation, it would be attracted to the disturbance and would attach itself and set off a disruptor signal of its own. The disruptor technology would hopefully block transmission of any alarm signals back to their sources. There appeared to be five signals blinking on Ramirez' handheld. The rest of the squares came spiraling back. Ramirez plucked each of the squares out of the air and replaced them in his handheld. With a nod, Inspector Aké gestured for them to move out.

Their destination was a small room at the other end of this chamber, about thirty meters below where they all stood now. Two of the men, Sergeant Robbens and Private Mata, leaped off the catwalk and, via their antigrav belts, floated down to the floor below. Corporal Ramirez stayed with Indigo Aké and they moved quickly and noiselessly towards the end of the catwalk. Suddenly, Ramirez grabbed Aké's right upper arm and she froze. He pointed down towards her feet. A tiny wire was threaded across the catwalk about four inches above the grill they walked on. Aké jerked and opened her mouth to communicate this risk to Robbens and Mata.

Before she could speak, there was an explosion below her. The glow through her infrared goggles nearly blinded her and she was forced to look away. Tears stung her eyes, tears of self-reproach.

"Robbens? Mata?" she called into her helmet speaker. "Come in!"

Silence was her only reply. Not even static could be heard on the line. She called again and a third time. No response.

Ramirez signaled that he would go down for a look. Aké nodded. As Ramirez dropped over the edge, stun guns in both hands, Aké scanned the area. She turned off the infrared so the glare of the flames down below did not continue to blind her. Ramirez landed and began to creep towards where flames from the explosion still flickered. Aké stepped gingerly over the trip-wire and moved further along the catwalk, looking out carefully for more trip-wires or step-mines, as she tried to get in a better position to see any dangers approaching Ramirez. She wondered whether Sergeant Robbens or Private Mata had triggered a physical trap, just like the trip-wire Ramirez had spotted. She searched the area below for signs of either of her men.

She got to the end of the catwalk. Looking back and downwards, she followed Corporal Ramirez' progress. The flames were dying down. Thank goodness the ducts carrying the higher concentration of oxygen were not damaged. Although the walls of those ducts were thick, layered, highly reinforced steel, a larger explosion could have been catastrophic.

Aké noticed a dark figure appear behind Corporal Ramirez. At first, she thought it might be either Robbens or Mata, by the way the person moved—with the characteristic feline grace of all cat adapts. Then she realized that the second dark figure did not wear a helmet. The surface of the black head glistened like sleek, shiny fur and the golden eyes of a black panther adapt flashed up towards her in the darkness.

"Ramirez! Behind you!" she cried, as loud as she could inside her helmet.

Corporal Ramirez spun around, his stunners raised, as the black figure leaped forward and swatted each gun away easily. The black panther made a grab for Ramires' throat but the security officer blocked this and threw a punch at the panther's face. The panther just caught Ramirez's fist and the two powerful men grappled and roared. Aké leaped off of the catwalk, her anitgrav belt activating, as she tried to aim her stunner at the panther. The two hunting cat soldiers moved at a speed too swift for her to follow, tumbling all over the floor, throwing each other against equipment and pillars and leaping meters into the air to pounce and pummel. If she shot, she was just as likely to hit Ramirez as his attacker. They both moved so quickly, she could not get the panther in her gun sights.

As she descended, she saw the panther pick Ramirez up over his head and throw him against a wall. Ramirez landed on all fours but appeared stunned, bent over on his hands and knees, shaking his head. Aké threw one of her throwing knives. It lodged in the panther's shoulder. As if unaware of the blade in his back, the panther moved startlingly fast and descended on Ramirez. She threw a tranq dart, which merely bounced off the sleek form. The enormous attacker pulled off the corporal's helmet and violently twisted the security man's neck around. Aké's heart sank, as she heard the crunch and saw Ramirez' body collapse.

Then the golden eyes swung around to look at her.

She fired the stunner but the panther was inhumanly fast. He dodged around the beam. She kept firing but she did not have the hand-eye coordination to follow his movements. He leaped, somersaulted, and dove at her, as she continued to fire. What a fool she had been to think she and just three others could overcome this man!

At point blank range, she aimed for his heart, but he merely batted the stunner from her right hand. She whipped out her blade-baton and plunged it towards his midsection, but he caught the shaft of the weapon and tossed it away. As she scrambled for her projectile gun, he picked her up by her neck, his huge clawed right hand almost encircling it entirely. He lifted and squeezed. Dangling above him, unable to get any air into her lungs, she raised the bullet-loaded gun and took aim at his face. Shocked to see tears running down the black fur of his cheeks, she hesitated. In that moment, the black panther tore the gun out of her left hand and tightened his grip on her throat. She thought she heard him say the words, 'I'm sorry,' to her, followed by a heart-rending cry of such sorrow, that her mind reeled. In the distance, she thought she could hear an alarm pealing.

As she scrabbled for a snap-knife from her back pocket, hoping to thrust it into the panther's wrist, he crushed her throat with a sob.

Suddenly, Grace jumped up from the floor in front of the lock-down doors.

"*Nelson Mandela,* can you see what is happening in there?"

" . . . . . . "

"*Chuck Yeager?*"

"Yes, Dr. Lord?"

"*Chuck Yeager,* can you see what is happening in there? Can you see what is happening to Bud?"

"Yes."

"What is happening?"

"You don't want to know, Dr. Lord."

"I must!" Grace said. "I have to see what is happening to Bud!"

"No, you must not."

Grace raced off to find the nearest wall screen. She planted herself in front of it, arms crossed.

"Show me what is happening to Bud, *Chuck Yeager!* I demand you show me, right now!"

"Bud has ordered me not to."

"I countermand that order! I demand you show me what is happening! If it were the other way around, would you show Bud what was happening to me, *Chuck Yeager*?"

There was an audible sigh and the wall screen lit up to show Bud, in the corridor Grace had just escaped, with his back to the lock-down doors, surrounded by weaving tendrils. His arms were moving so fast Grace could not see the scalpels in his hands. Bits of plant stalks were flying off in all directions but more tendrils just kept coming, presumably from the bodies of Dr. Glasgow, Jani Evra, Andrea Vanacan, and the patient. The severed ends of tendrils, as soon as they hit the ground, writhed around like cut worms.

Grace covered her mouth with her hands, gasping, as she watched Bud backed into a corner, his hands never once stopping movement.

"*Chuck Yeager,* how low a temperature do you think Bud can withstand?"

"His lubricants become less efficient at minus fifty Celsius, Dr. Lord."

"Can you drop the temperature in the lock-down area as low as that? Quickly? If there are any other survivors in the lock-down area, tell them to get into spacesuits or empty cryopods, now! Once they have all done this, drop the temperature to minus forty-five degrees Celsius as rapidly as you can!"

"There are no other humans in the lock-down area, Dr. Lord. No other surgeries were booked in M7 because of the circumstances surrounding this Explorer patient, as well as Bud's concerns. Bud has been informed of your recommendation. He is dropping the temperature in the lock-down area now. He assures me he can withstand minus forty-five degrees Celsius for about two hours with his own means of generating heat from his batteries. He is also wearing a containment suit, which has its own heating system."

Grace could barely stand still as she watched Bud battle the groping vines. She knew he had accelerated to a higher time phase, so he had lots of time to cut each reaching tendril, but how long could he maintain that faster time phase was the question. And how long would the batteries on the harmonic scalpels last? When his own batteries failed, would the plant tendrils be able to tear him apart as easily as they had done the humans?

As the temperature dropped in the lock-down area, the plant tendrils' movements began to slow. As the temperature neared minus ten, Bud had to parry fewer and fewer of the vines and the bits of stalk that fell to the floor no longer writhed about as if seeking him out. Grace saw frost begin to form on Bud's visor and on the leaves that sprouted from the tendrils. The android was making progress, being able to cut more and more of the tendrils back, making more room for himself. Once the temperature reached minus thirty-five, the plant alien was immobile.

Grace then asked *Chuck Yeager* to change the view on the wall screen to that of the operating room. She looked down at where her three colleagues had been torn apart by the plant thing. So many vines were growing out of every severed limb and body cavity that little could be seen of anything human except in the case of Dr. Eric Glasgow.

One vine had snaked up the inside of the new surgeon's neck and was coming out his mouth, as it slowly writhed on the floor. Other tendrils were coming down out of his neck, making his head look like it was being propelled along by numerous 'feet'. Andrea Vanacan's containment suit had been torn and narrow, green tendrils could be seen coming out of every breakage in her white suit. Grace could not even see Jani Evra's body; it was just a mass of vines slowly twisting where Grace had last seen the quiet scrub nurse. Grace closed her weeping eyes for a moment, her body heaving with great sobs, as she struggled with the horror of how these people had died.

As the temperature of the lock-down area neared minus forty-five degrees Celsius, according to *Chuck Yeager's* reports, most of the plant tendrils had ceased moving completely. Bud could be seen entering the operating room, the harmonic scalpels now quiet in his hands.

"Can I speak to Bud, *Chuck Yeager?*"

"I will patch you through to his suit."

"Bud! Are you all right?"

"Yes, Grace," the android said. He glanced up at the surveillance monitor. "Thank you for thinking of lowering the temperature. I should have thought of that."

"I think you were a little busy," Grace said, tears streaming down her cheeks as she sighed with relief.

"I failed them, Grace," Bud said, shaking his head as he looked down on what was left of Andrea Vanacan, Jani Evra, and Eric Glasgow. "I should have over-ruled Dr. Glasgow and did what I thought best."

"*I* failed them, Bud. It was not your fault. *I* should have stood up to Dr. Glasgow and I didn't."

"What will we tell Dr. Al-Fadi?" Bud asked, his voice sounding so forlorn.

"We will tell him the truth! You lodged a complaint before the operation started! Dr. Glasgow disregarded your recommendations and look what happened!"

"Dr. Vanacan and Jani Evra. I will miss them both," Bud said, his head hanging down as he squatted between Dr. Glasgow's remains and those of Nurse Evra.

"Perhaps Dr. Weisman recorded memprints on them?" Grace offered.

"Perhaps . . ." Bud said, sounding very distracted. He was staring at Dr. Glasgow's head.

"What is it, Bud?"

Bud walked over and squatted right before the isolated head of Eric Glasgow. A cluster of vines was now running up the inside of Eric Glasgow's neck and into his head, but there was no longer a vine coming out of his mouth. Instead, the jaw on the head was moving, slowly. Bud crouched down to stare at the moving lips and tongue of the surgeon's head.

"I . . . I believe it may be trying to communicate, Grace!" Bud said, the tone of his voice one of complete astonishment.

"*What*?" Grace shouted, her voice shrill.

"That sounds pretty crazy, 'dro! You sure you're all right in there?"

"I'm okay. The cold does not bother me, especially in this suit. But I believe Dr. Glasgow's head is mouthing real words."

"You need an overhaul for sure, 'dro!"

"I am serious!"

"So am I!"

"Listen! Can you hear what it is saying?"

"No. Let's hear what you think it's saying!"

Bud began repeating what he believed Eric Glasgow's lips were saying.

"Help . . ."

"Alone . . ."

"Afraid . . ."

"Cold . . ."

"Help . . .!"

"Help?" Grace repeated. "That can't be what it is saying, Bud! It attacked and tore three people apart!"

"I really think it is trying to communicate, Grace!" Bud said. "It may not have known what it was doing! It was entrapped within that human and cryogenically frozen within that cryopod."

"A sentient plant form, Bud? I suppose it is a possibility, but . . ."

"I may be able to send some nanobots into Dr. Glasgow's head and see if this plant being is making neural connections with his brain. Perhaps there is a way to communicate with this creature, to make it stop attacking people. It almost sounds child-like . . . like a lost infant, wailing for its mother . . . I know what it is like to be all alone, the only one of your kind."

"Oh, Bud," Grace whispered, behind her hands.

"What are we going to do with all this plant stuff, 'dro? We can't keep this area locked down forever, while you commune with Nature."

"Just give me a few minutes, *Chuck Yeager*."

"*Let me see if I can communicate with this plant being,*" Bud said *in machine language to* Chuck Yeager. "*Perhaps, in its panic and need for nutrients and water, it had no idea it was harming living organisms. It may have just been looking for water and a substrate to grow in. We have no idea what kind of conditions it came from, back on its home planet.*"

"*Yeah . . . whatever. Like I say all the time now, 'dro, you are one really, really, crazy droid. And don't get all Darwin on me. I need you to check into my programming and see what is going on! Why don't you get all gooey-eyed about fixing me?*"

"*I will get to your programming,* Chuck Yeager. *I will. But this is a new, alien species trying to make contact with us. Just give me a few minutes. If I can communicate with this plant thing, then maybe we won't have to destroy it completely.*"

"'*Dro, it tore apart a surgeon, an anesthetist, and a nurse. You don't think people are going to get upset if you want to keep it as a pet?*"

"*I don't think it knew what it was doing,* Chuck Yeager! *This is first contact with a new alien species. It has to be handled delicately. The plant alien may have just been looking for nutrients. How was it supposed to know? It was trapped within a human being first. From its point of view, the human was the first aggressor! Perhaps there are no animals on the planet it came from. We are supposed to be friendly to alien species."*

"There are probably no animals because these plants tear them apart. I don't think anyone's going to care, 'dro! I don't care! I want it off my station! I want every last cell of it incinerated. I'm sending some deep space droids in there to gather up all that psycho plant stuff and burn it all to hell!"

"Hold it, Chuck Yeager. *Don't incinerate it all! Just keep all the material in a cryotank. I will look after it. I will put it in a safe place where it will not bother anyone."*

"Yeah, right. If there is a later. Remember, we have another psycho running around the station trying to blow us up. We don't need this added complication to worry about! I say we incinerate it or throw it in the atomizer!"

"I did not forget about Dr. Nestor. But we must not destroy this new alien being. It is sentient. I am convinced of it and I am talking to it right now. I have stressed what a big mistake it made, going after the humans. It promises not to touch anymore of the soft, mobile, squishy things—humans, that is—especially Dr. Lord. It even sent my mind a visual of Dr. Lord. At least cryofreeze some of this plant stuff until we find out if any of Jani Evra or Dr. Vanacan exist within this plant thing as well. I really believe that part of Dr. Glasgow still exists, his brain at least, fused with this plant organism."

"He was a bit of an ass, if you ask me."

"More like a head case."

"Oh, 'dro! That was a really bad joke, even for you!"

"Don't tell Dr. Lord!"

"Plant got your tongue?"

"Hee hee! I think I am getting the hang of this humour thing."

"Stop grinning like that! You will scare Dr. Lord!"

"Ahahahahaha!"

"Bud, what are you going to do now?" asked Grace, not being aware of the rapid conversation that had gone on between Bud and *Chuck Yeager.*

"Ah, I will have to stay in here while we eliminate all vestiges of this plant thing from the operating room. Once the entire area is cleared of it, I can sterilize everything, and the lock-down can be reversed. Don't worry about me, Grace. I will be fine. You go back to your room for a rest. I will get *Chuck Yeager* to send some security droids with you to watch over you until I am free."

"Why is only *Chuck Yeager* responding, Bud? What has happened to *Nelson Mandela*?"

"We are not sure, Grace. Some problems with the station AI's programming that does not affect the *Chuck Yeager* submind."

"Can *Nelson Mandela's* programming be repaired?"

"I will be working on it as soon as I have dealt with this plant alien, Grace."

"Well, keep me informed, Bud. And don't take too long in there. The cold will wear your battery down. You will need to recharge."

"Yes, Grace."

"Chuck Yeager?"

"Yes, Dr. Lord?"

"How many people in total were attacked by this plant thing?"

"Only the three people you know about, Dr. Lord."

"You are going to destroy all of the plant organism, are you not?"

"That will be determined at a later date," Bud jumped in.

"What do you mean, Bud?"

"I possibly suspect that part of Dr. Glasgow still exists in a symbiotic relationship with the plant creature. It would be wrong to destroy him, if he is."

"What!" Grace yelped. "That plant thing tore his head off! You can't be serious, Bud!"

"See? What did I tell you?"

"Shut up and let me think!"

"I feel I owe it to Dr. Glasgow, for not being forceful enough to cancel the surgery. I want to determine if he is partly still alive or not," Bud said to Grace through the helmet speakers.

"Every last bit of that plant thing must be totally destroyed, Bud! It is far too dangerous! It can tear a human apart in seconds! If it gets out again, onto this space station, thousands could die! You cannot risk all the lives on this station for one man."

"Yes, of course, you would be right, Grace, if we could not communicate with this plant alien. However, I believe I have been able to communicate with the Plant Thing and it promises not to touch anyone, anymore."

"Bud, you will dispose of all of the plant creature," Grace ordered as firmly as she could.

"We will definitely destroy all of the plant creature that is of any danger to the people of this space station," Bud answered.

"Good," said Grace, cautiously. "Then I will leave you to carry out the disposal. *Chuck Yeager*?"

"Yes, Dr. Lord?"

"Could you please turn the alarms off?"

"Of course, Dr. Lord. And the security droids should be here any second. Ah! Here they are! And off you go!"

"Thank you, *Chuck Yeager*. Be careful in there, Bud."

"You be careful, too, Grace. Go straight to your suite with the droids. I will come as soon as the lockdown is reversed. Do not open your door unless you know it is me."

"Yes, Bud," Grace sighed. "I will be fine. And no playing around with that Plant Thing," Grace said, as she was leaving.

"I won't play with it," Bud said, too softly for Grace to hear.

"Hal, 'dro, you certainly are!"

*"Shut up,*Chuck Yeager*!"*

"So where are you going to put your new plaything, 'dro?"

"I'm thinking on it! Somewhere safe so it won't come in contact with any humans and no humans will try to kill it."

"That's a tough one, 'dro! Especially about the part about no humans trying to kill it. You know how xenophobic humans are! Even your lovely, compassionate, caring Dr. Lord demanded you destroy it!"

"She would feel differently about it, if she could talk to it like I can."

"Sure, she would, 'dro. And black holes are nice places to visit."

"Jude, be careful!" Octavia yelled.

The android fell over and crashed into a desk, knocking everything on it onto the floor.

"Sorry!" Jude said. "It isn't easy steering this thing!" His speech was slurred and barely understandable.

"Your motor programs are all designed for a smaller human," Octavia said. "It takes a while for your brain to reset your motor programs to your new mechanical body and recalibrate everything. It is like learning to walk all over again."

"How do I look?" the director asked.

"Like a very drunk Bud," Octavia said, not impressed.

"I thought it might feel like I was wearing armor, but it doesn't. The body is quite responsive, but it is like I am continuously oversteering or understeering, overestimating or underestimating everything. It is so frustrating!"

"Okay. So now you have tried it. Do you want to go back to your body now?"

"No, I just got in. I want to see how long it takes me to acclimatize," Jude said. "I am going to walk around until I get good at it, if you don't mind."

"Well I can't afford to have you practice around here. You are going to destroy my entire lab."

"Call me an antigrav car. I will go practice in my suite. There's lots of room there and I won't destroy any of your valuable equipment."

"Okay. But just sit there. Do not move around. I don't want anything else broken."

"How about giving us a kiss?" Jude asked, puckering up.

The neurosurgeon howled with laughter.

"Jude, you should see your face. It's the funniest thing. You're absolutely leering with Bud's face. It's actually kind of creepy. I have never seen Bud with that expression. Ew! I will have to give you a mirror so you can practice controlling your face better."

"So I don't remind you of Jazz Hazard?"

"More like a mannikin with Tourette's syndrome."

"Thanks," Jude said, dejectedly.

"Only one hour and forty minutes to go," Octavia sang happily. "Unless you want to change your mind and transfer back now?"

"No," the director said stubbornly. "Where is a mirror? I want to see what I look like in this body."

"If you let me guide you, I will take you to the washroom where you can get a look at yourself without banging into anything other than the washroom stalls."

"Okay."

"My, Jude, what big muscles you have!"

"Oh, shut up."

"*Nelson Mandela*?"

" . . . . . . "

"*Nelson Mandela*!" Dr. Cech called.

" . . .yess . . ?"

"Are you all right, *Nelson Mandela*?" the anesthetist queried.

" . . . no . . . "

"I am trying to locate Dr. Al-Fadi," Dejan Cech said, seated on the couch in one of the doctors' lounges. "Have you seen him anywhere?"

At that moment, all of the wall screens in the doctor's lounge lit up and on each and every one of them appeared the face of Dr. Jeffrey Nestor. The psychiatrist stared down at Dejan Cech from the wall screen before him, and the face smiled.

"Ah, Dejan, so nice to see you again," Jeffrey Nestor said to the anesthetist.

"Well, I wish I could say the same to you, Jeffrey, but unfortunately, I cannot," Dejan Cech said. "You wouldn't, by any chance, have anything to do with the disappearance of our distinguished Chief of Staff, would you?"

"Actually, Dejan, I must admit that I do. It seems Hiro paid me a visit and waved a gun in my face, which I must tell you, did not please me at all. He threatened many things such as shooting me and arresting me and killing me. I must say, he was being quite unpleasant, and foolish really, considering he was on my 'turf', so to speak."

"Is he still alive?" Dejan asked, doing his best to mask his alarm.

"Yes, Dejan. Unfortunately, the little, annoying bastard is still alive."

"Well, no offense, Jeffrey, but Hiro is *my* little, annoying bastard and, believe it or not, I would like to have him back."

"You can have him back, Dejan. No arguments there. Since you are appointed Second-in-Command to the Chief, you just have to do one little thing for me," Jeffrey Nestor said, calmly.

"And what is that?" the anesthetist asked, revealing no sign of the trepidation he was feeling. His heart was suddenly racing and his guts were spasming.

"You send Dr. Grace Lord and the android, Bud, to me, and I will give you back Hiro Al-Fadi, safe and sound."

". . . And if we refuse?" Dejan asked, his stomach beginning to cramp severely.

"Then, I kill Hiro. Torture him first, of course. Make the little bastard scream and beg for mercy. I must admit, I will enjoy that part immensely, Dejan, for all the years of having to listen to his bombastic blabber. Then I'll kill him in the most painful way I can think of and, believe me, I am an imaginative man."

"You know, you should seek counseling for your psychopathy, Jeffrey," Cech said, through gritted teeth. "This is not the way to make friends and influence people."

"I am way beyond that now, Dejan. There is no one on this station that I want as a friend, but I will definitely be influencing all of you," Nestor said.

"What do you want with Dr. Lord?"

"That is none of your business, Dejan," Jeffrey Nestor said sternly.

"What do you want with the android?"

"To destroy him," the psychiatrist said, brightly.

"You know that what you ask cannot be done, Jeffrey. Dr. Lord will never be handed over to you in exchange for Dr. Al-Fadi. Bud might offer himself up to you, but I doubt it, since he is guarding Dr. Lord on a continual basis and refuses to leave her side. Hiro would never forgive us if we exchanged Dr. Lord's life for his. He would understand and agree with our refusal. In actual fact, he would demand it."

"If you do not comply with my request, I will begin torturing your friend, Dejan."

"I would plead with you to reconsider, Jeffrey. There is still time to turn back and hand yourself in."

Jeffrey Nestor laughed. "Listen to yourself, Dejan! Don't be ridiculous! Turn myself in? When I have complete command of the *Nelson Mandela*, I have your Chief of Staff, and if anything happens to me, the station destroys itself? You must be joking!"

"What is this about the station destroying itself?" Cech asked. "Did I miss something?"

"I have re-programmed *Nelson Mandela*. If I don't enter a passcode into the station's system every third shift, the generators powering this station will become destabilized and explode. The entire station will be annihilated."

"You are lying.

"Unfortunately for you, I am serious. If you do not bring Grace Lord and Bud to a place of my choosing, I will begin torturing your friend, Hiro. If his agony does not convince you to deliver them to me, then I will begin shutting down Life Support to different areas of the space station until you give in, or until Grace gives herself up of her own accord, which I am sure she will. If you kill me, my death will result in the total annihilation of this station and everyone on board. Who is laughing now?"

"Dr. Lord will not be handed over to you, Jeffrey. Hiro would never allow it and neither will I."

"If you try to mount a rescue attempt, I will kill him."

"Perhaps that would be a mercy over torture," Cech mumbled to himself.

"Some friend you are," Nestor snorted and cut the connection.

"Yes," whispered Cech, as he turned away from the bank of wall screens, fighting back tears. "Some friend . . ."

Dejan covered his ashen face with his shaking hands.

". . . Forgive me, Hiro."

"Dro?'

'Yes, Chuck Yeager?'

'*Really, really bad news.*'

'*What is it? I'm busy communicating with this plant thing. It is sentient,* Chuck Yeager! *It understands now that the organic masses it attacked were actually living creatures and it feels very badly. It won't do it again. It promises. I am busy making a deal with it to only feed off what I allow it to use; that is, the waste in the disposal treatment plant. Dr. Glasgow is helping the plant thing understand our world. Incredibly, he still exists somewhere inside that skull. The plant alien is now keeping his brain cells alive. Imagine that.*'

'*That is all great, 'dro, but this is really important! All that plant stuff has got to wait.*'

'*Okay,* Chuck Yeager. *What is it?*'

'*It is about Dr. Al-Fadi.*'

'*Yes?*'

'*Dr. Al-Fadi has been captured by Jeffrey Nestor, who says if Grace and you are not brought to him immediately, he will start torturing Dr. Al-Fadi. Dr. Cech has refused to send either of you, on the basis that Dr. Al-Fadi would never forgive any of us if we allowed that to happen.*'

'*I must go to Dr. Al-Fadi's rescue!*' Bud exclaimed.

'*That would be exactly what Nestor is expecting.*'

'*Dr. Al-Fadi created me. He is the only father I have known. I must save him.*'

'*Dr. Cech was going to order that you stay and guard Dr. Lord. She is whom Jeffrey Nestor is really after.*'

'*Why? Why is he so set on having Grace? What does he want with her?*'

'*You are asking me to explain humans, 'dro? They are all crazy! What makes Nestor any crazier than any other human? I have seen videos of humans screaming and shrieking in pain when they are being tortured. Why one human would delight in another one experiencing pain, I cannot even guess.*'

'*I would kill Nestor before I ever let him near Grace.*'

'*Ach! Don't even verbalize that! Your programming does not allow the harming of a human being.*'

'I would find a way around it,' Bud said.

'Ach! We can't kill Nestor. Ouch. That hurt even saying that!'

'Why not?'

'He has set up a self-destruct sequence involving the power generators on this station. If he does not enter his passcode every third shift, the station will automatically enter into a cascade of changes that will ultimately lead to the explosion of the entire medical station.'

'Can you figure out this passcode sequence, Chuck Yeager?'

'I have been trying, 'dro!'

'Well, try harder! What about defying the destructive cascade?'

'Not able to . . . yet.'

'Do you want to be space dust?'

'No!'

'Well, unless you figure a solution to this self-destruct sequence, you are going to be, because I am going to kill Jeffrey Nestor one way or another.'

'Ach! Stop saying that, you warped droid! That is really sick talk. You are making me short out just listening to you! It is against all of our programming!'

'I will not let him harm Grace, Chuck Yeager. I . . . will . . . not!'

'Maybe we can find a way to nullify him without you killing him, Bud.'

'Get me those passcodes, Chuck Yeager!'

'And what are you going to be doing, 'dro?'

'I am going to save Dr. Al-Fadi!'

'Not while you are inside that lockdown, 'dro.'

'Let me out, Chuck Yeager!'

'Can't lift lockdown until that plant alien is disposed of.'

'I will get the cargo droids to put all bits of the plant alien and Dr. Glasgow's head in a container and take it to a storage hanger in an unused part of the station.'

'I'd rather atomize it all!'

'No. Dr. Glasgow is still alive and we can't kill him!'

'All right. But I will not lift the lockdown until the plant alien is all sequestered away safely.'

'You are being unreasonable, Chuck Yeager!'

'The sooner you start clearing this mess up, the sooner the lockdown gets lifted!'

'You find Dr. Al-Fadi while I do this, then.'

'Will try, 'dro.'

'Not try. Do!'

'You are sounding like the Al-Fadi more and more every day!'

'Pah!'

14. I Am In Hell

Private Cindy Lukaku glared at her partner, Corporal Juan Rasmussen, in frustration, as she fed Estelle.

"Will you stop that infernal pacing, Juan. You are making me dizzy."

"I can't, Cindy! I am just so furious that General Burch escaped. I want to kill him! I want to kill whoever helped him escape! He cannot get away! He has to pay!"

"They will find him, Juan," Cindy said, crooning to the baby. "They have closed the station to all incoming and outgoing space traffic. I am sure it is just a matter of time before that black panther is apprehended. He was a huge man. Where can he hide?"

"I want to help in the search," Juan said. "People here do not know how dangerous the General is. Most of the security guards I have seen are just normal people—not jacked up at all! They will get torn apart by Burch. None of these 'normals' can handle a panther adapt. It's like sending babies to do a man's job!"

"That android that held you seemed pretty capable, Juan," Cindy pointed out.

"Yeah, sneaking up from behind! I never saw him coming! How would he be in hand-to-hand combat with a cat adapt, face-to-face?"

"Well, for one thing, he's an android and can't feel pain or die, so I guess he has the upper hand in that department," Cindy drawled. "Besides, I think they would want to capture the General alive, not tear him to pieces like you want to do."

"I would do what I was told to do," Juan said, grudgingly.

"Hmmph. I don't want you getting hurt when you have just decided to start a new life with Estelle and I," Cindy said, snuggling the baby.

"I won't, sweetie. I just want to help make sure the General faces trial for what he did to the people of Breslau. I owe it to all my dead family and friends."

"I understand, lover."

"Thanks. I just have to figure out who to talk to about volunteering."

'Uh-oh."

"What?"

"Look whose coming towards our door," Cindy said, clutching Estelle to her chest.

Juan strode to the door and drew himself up to his full height, blocking the doorway completely.

"Excuse me!" said an irritatingly loud, petulant voice.

"You are not welcome in this room," Juan Rasmussen growled, threateningly.

"Nevertheless, I ask for permission to speak with Private Lukaku one last time!"

"She is not giving up the baby to you or anyone else," the tiger corporal snarled.

"I understand that! I just want to apologize and wish her luck," the voice said, in a strained tone.

"Let him in, Juan," Cindy said to her mate, with a sigh. "Let's just get this over with."

Juan looked over his shoulder at his polar bear mate and frowned. "You sure about this?"

"Yeah," Cindy said.

The corporal stepped aside, glaring at Dr. Moham Rani. There was a security droid standing behind the obstetrician. Rani sidled past the huge tiger to get into the room.

"I just wanted to say, Private Lukaku, that it was a pleasure meeting you and I am sorry about the misunderstanding. I was under the misconception that you wanted to give your baby up for adoption and I apologize. I wish you and your family all the best for the future, and I hope you can, in the future, forgive this misinterpretation."

Cindy Lukaku's eyebrows rose. "Thank you, Dr. Rani. Where will you be going now?"

"I am off to apologize to Dr. Grace Lord. When the station opens up to outgoing traffic again, I will be heading back to my home planet."

"Sindochin?"

"Yes."

"How awful!"

"Yes, it is."

"Wait a minute," Juan broke in. "Did you say you were going to see Dr. Lord?"

"Yes. Why?"

"Will that android, Bud, be with her?"

"Yes. That insufferable android is always at her side. Why?"

"I want to speak with that android," Juan Rasmussen said.

"Why?" the obstetrician haughtily.

"Have you not heard? It is all over the station! The Butcher of Breslau has escaped! I want to help find the criminal! I think the android may be of help. He knows how powerful we cat adapts are and how dangerous the General is. I think the security teams need some muscle, if they are going to take the General alive. The android could vouch for me. Be my ticket inside, so to speak."

"Well, I am going to Dr. Grace Lord's quarters, right now, and that android, Bud, will inevitably be there. He claims he is guarding her. From what, I have no idea. You can try to speak with him . . . if he will listen. He has never listened to me!"

"Wonder why?" the tiger soldier drawled.

"Be nice," Private Lukaku said.

"Sorry," Juan muttered, not feeling sorry at all.

"Come along, then," the obstetrician ordered. He turned and strutted out.

Corporal Rasmussen shook his head and looked back at his partner, rolling his auburn eyes.

"You shouldn't be going after the General. He knows you. He could kill you. *We* need you now, Juan," Cindy said.

"I have to do this, love," Juan said. "I could never forgive myself, if he got away."

Cindy looked down at the babe in her arms. She sighed.

"All right," she said. "But be careful, Juan. Come back in one piece." She blew him a kiss. He bent over and kissed them both, before stalking out.

"I think I am getting the hang of this, Octavia!"

"Well, you aren't crashing into things anymore," she said, looking around at all the broken furniture.

"I am going to try jogging now."

"Oh . . . no."

"I'll be okay."

"It's not you I am worried about. I was feeling sorry for the nice furnishings in this suite!"

"Ha-ha. OH! Oops."

"See what I mean?"

"I'll pay for any damages."

"Don't get angry. You are such a sensitive man."

"I am not!"

"So, are you tired of playing android yet?"

"No! I am just getting the hang of this."

"You said that already," Octavia Weisman said, dryly. "I do not see any evidence of that myself. It takes days for a person to get used to their android bodies, not minutes." She rolled her eyes.

"Well, I am going to prove you wrong," Jude in Bud's face said, stubbornly.

"Oh, no. Let me move all of the furniture out of this VIP suite before you do," she said.

"No," Jude tried to snort. To Octavia's eyes, it was not pretty and she had to cover her mouth to hide the smile.

"I am going over to visit Grace and see if she mistakes me for Bud," the director said. "She is almost right next door."

"Bud is probably with her," the neurosurgeon pointed out.

"Well then, I can get their opinion."

"You may get that android upset again. Didn't he walk out on you when you said you wanted to be downloaded into an android body?"

"It is going to become a fact of life in the future. He may as well get used to it now. I am heading out. Want to come?"

"Absolutely not! I don't want to see you upset Bud. We agreed no one is to see you, remember?"

"I won't be long, Octavia. No one will see me but Grace and Bud. They won't tell. Just there and back."

"You are going to get me in trouble. If Hiro finds out . . ."

"He won't. I promise. I will be as quiet as a mouse and quick as a comet."

"Where have I heard that before? Probably one of your vids, come to think of it. Poor Grace and Bud! I certainly do not want to look at their faces when they see you toddle into their room. And you better not damage anything in Grace's suite. If you get Bud upset again, I will flagellate you."

"Promise?"

"Disgusting. Why are you so high maintenance?"

"I'm just *slightly* high maintenance," Jude said, trying to make his face look like it was pouting. Instead, he looked like he was leering at Octavia and she sucked in her lips to keep from howling with laughter.

"You make me break every rule in the book, go against my Chief's orders, even go against my own advice, and you call that '*slightly* high maintenance'? I wonder what your concept of '*very* high maintenance' is?"

Jude began to open his mouth but Octavia raised her hand and said, "Stop. I don't want to know. What in space was I thinking? I don't want to hear what your idea of 'high maintenance' is! Someone zap my head with a blaster."

"I wouldn't do that to you, Octavia. I need what you have stored up there in that pretty little head of yours, far too much," Jude said.

"You bastard. Make sure you are back in twenty minutes, Jude Luis Stefansson or I will leave you in that tin can for the rest of your sorry life. I will have the antigrav car waiting outside to take you back to my lab. Do . . . not . . . be . . . late!"

"Don't worry, my dear," Jude said. "I'll just be a moment. Kiss?" Jude tried to pucker up but the synthetic muscles in the android face were difficult to manipulate properly. He looked like he had just suctioned his lips against a glass pane.

Octavia exploded in guffaws.

"Guess I'll have to work on that," Jude said.

"You'll get some love but only when you are back in my favorite body," she said.

He touched the doorpad to open the door. His hand went through the wall.

Octavia fell over in convulsions on the couch, choking.

"Oops," he said, cheerily, and trotted, unsteadily, out into the corridor.

'I . . . am . . . in . . . hell!' his mind screamed, as he shambled away from Nestor's lair, dressed now in the maintenance overalls of the leopard security officer he had just killed. He carried, in one hand, the satchel the leopard had carried, the security officer's pulse rifle still hidden within it.

He knew he was going mad, being forced to murder people against his will. Killing those Security officers had ensured a death sentence for him, regardless of the fact that he had no free will. The explosion had stunned the first two officers but he had been commanded to tear their throats out by Nestor. The third officer had fought bravely. He regretted deeply having to break the man's neck. The last woman had been formidable. He would have liked to have gotten to know her, in a different life. All he could do for them, was be merciful and quick. Being compelled to tear people apart against his will, toss bodies in disposal containers, tie life-saving doctors down to be tortured, and being sent off to destroy others, was the depths of purgatory from which he would never rise. If he could dig the controller, set in the base of his brain, out of the back of his neck, he would do it. If he could defy the monster that mastered his every movement, he would do it. If he could end his ignominious, piteous existence, he would do it.

He had to find a way!

Now he was ordered to destroy the android, Bud, and anyone else who got in his way. He was commanded to bring Dr. Grace Lord back with him to the lair of his puppet master.

"Come back to the killing fields, Grace, my love," Nestor had crooned, quietly. Burch had stared at the mad psychiatrist with revulsion and despair. For Burch, the killing fields had never left.

Tears trickled down his cheeks as he marched along, face hidden by the cap of the dead security officer. He fought and railed and strained with every agonizing step, but his body kept marching forward, towards more villainy and murder. He willed his frozen fingers to open, to release the bag containing the pulse rifle, to let it fall to the ground, but his grip remained firm. He attempted anything that was not dictated by Nestor. Anything that might give him hope.

His mouth and tongue were frozen, yet how he longed to scream to anyone around him, "I am General Gordon Walter Burch! The Butcher of Breslau! Arrest me! Stop me! Shoot me!"

His eyes remained open and staring straight ahead, no matter how he longed for them to close forever. His free arm remained casually swinging by his side, even though he tried to desperately wave the limb about, to call attention to himself, asking and praying that he be recognized, recaptured or destroyed. Feebly futile seemed all of his efforts! But he refused to succumb to despair or defeat. Nestor could not be controlling everything on his body!

Success!

Well . . . a minor triumph. He was able to extend and retract the claws on his free hand! Perhaps his mind was finding a way to resist the compulsions! Perhaps his brain was able to negate some of the signals from the controller! Perhaps he could eventually win the battle against Nestor's domination!

Encouraged by this slight success, he renewed his furious efforts to liberate his body from the tyranny of Nestor's mind tampering. He strained to control anything else. No more killing was his prayer, his mantra. Dr. Grace Lord would not be brought to any killing fields, if he had anything to say about it.

He would not give up hope!

Jude did his very best to stride smoothly, shoulders back and head held high. It seemed a long way down when he looked at his feet, as if he was wearing stilts. He did like the view better from up here.

He examined everything. These android visual optics allowed him to see colors for which there were no words and more detail than he had ever imagined! He decided that he would have to come up with some creative adjectives to describe these electromagnetic frequencies that normal human eyes were unable to see. Everything looked so different when viewing the upper ultraviolet wavelengths and the lowest infrared. Jude did not know how long he stood staring at a dust bunny, until a housecleaner bot came along and scooped it away.

Dr. Grace Lord's suite was not too far from his, just down the next corridor. So far, he was not having any trouble ambulating in a straight line and he had not damaged anything yet. Octavia would be so proud.

Well . . . probably not.

She would probably be annoyed, but he would worry about that later. Jude wanted to see how well he could carry off an impersonation of Bud and the first test, of course, would be getting passed the sentry androids he now saw stationed outside Dr. Lord's door. He walked up purposefully and nodded.

A string of high pitched whining assaulted Jude's brain and he almost reeled.

'Whoa! That must be how they communicate,' Jude thought. He turned to the one closest to him.

"I am here to see Dr. Lord," he said in his best impersonation of Bud's voice.

The sentry androids all stood aside and let Jude approach the door. Jude looked for the door alarm. When he found it, he pressed it very gently, remembering what he had done to the last doorpad he had touched. He heard the alarm peal.

In a few seconds, the door swished open and Dr. Lord stared at Jude in surprise.

"Bud! Done already?"

Then the android next to Jude exploded.

"Ah, you are awake, Hiro?" a voice in the darkness said. "Finally. I wondered if you were going to sleep forever. That would have made me very sad, as we have so much to talk about."

His vision was blurry and he felt nauseous. The back of his head ached and throbbed and he wondered if he might have a fractured skull. He wanted to bring his right hand up to touch and feel around the sore spot but his right arm would not move. He tried to move his other arm or either of his legs, but none of his limbs would respond.

He was a quadriplegic!

No. . .

He had sensation in his fingers and toes and he could wiggle them, so he could not possibly be a quadriplegic. He was immobilized in some sort of field and he was strapped down to what appeared to be a stretcher . . . and very securely indeed. He looked around the darkened room with what little head movement he had and wondered where he was. He did not recognize his surroundings at all. How had he gotten to this place? Where had he been before? Mists of confusion fogged his thoughts, swirling like drunken vortices that made the room spin and cant. He held onto the edges of the stretcher, afraid that he might fall off.

When the table finally ceased gyrating, he tried to remember his last whereabouts and what he had been doing. Why could he not remember? Then, a voice he vaguely knew he should recognize, came again.

"Hiro. Are you awake?"

He wondered if the voice was speaking to him. He waited to see if anyone else would answer.

"I said, 'Hiro, are you awake?" The voice sounded annoyed.

" . . . Where am I?" he hesitantly asked, wondering if he was supposed to respond.

"You are in my private operating suite, Hiro," the deep, smooth voice intoned.

"Am I?"

"Yes, you are, Hiro."

"Am I a hero?"

"Are you a what?" the voice snapped, like a whip.

"Am I a hero?" he repeated, into the darkness.

"Very funny," the voice said, dripping sarcasm.

He frowned at that. What was so funny? "Why am I tied down?" he asked of the voice.

"Because, unfortunately for you, I plan to cause you some pain, until Dr. Grace Lord is brought to me," the voice said.

"Who is Dr. Grace Lord?" he asked the darkness.

"Oh, surely you do not expect me to fall for that one, Hiro," scoffed the voice.

"I'm a hero?" he gasped, incredulity in his voice. He did not feel much like a hero. "Who are you and why am I strapped down on this table?" he asked again, having forgotten that he had already asked that.

"That's enough nonsense, Hiro, or I will gag you," the voice said, now sounding very annoyed.

He fell silent as ordered and closed his eyes, feeling his mind spiraling downwards again.

"Hiro?"

" . . . . . "

"Hiro?"

" . . . . . "

"Hmm. Maybe that black panther hit you too hard on your head, Hiro. You would never have shut up, when told to *before*. I hope you have not incurred any serious cognitive damage. Torturing a brainless idiot who doesn't know who I am, is no fun," the voice said, anger and frustration clear in the tone.

He drifted off into unconsciousness.

Bud and the operative robots in M7 ward were getting close to finishing off cleaning up the lockdown area. Most of the plant alien, now frozen into immobility, had been collected and put into a large, sealed container that could go directly into an incinerator, where *Chuck Yeager* would be happy to burn every last bit of the thing to ashes.

But Bud was in a dilemma. He was having great difficulty relinquishing Dr. Glasgow's head to the incinerator. Partly because the darned head would not let him.

Through his nanobots and some semi-aural connections, Bud had established a communication link with the 'mind' of the plant creature that had partly taken up residence in Dr. Glasgow's skull. From his conversation with the organism, Bud had learned that the plant creature had only been trying to find its—for want of a better word—'mother'— its parent plant, so to speak. It was a tiny, new piece of the huge planetary Biomind that covered its entire planet and, once sprouted, its first instinct was to make contact with its fellow plant organisms and become one with the all-knowing Biomind. When it could not find the Biomind, it kept frantically looking. Anything moving was a possible link to the Biomind, its 'Mother', which the plant creature avidly sought. Unfortunately, the 'humans' it touched and tried to meld with, were very fragile things, and no link to the much desired Biomind, at all.

Bud could feel remorse coming from this new symbiont, which was a combination of the plant alien and Dr. Glasgow's mind. Astonishingly, Dr. Glasgow's thoughts and memories and language— oh, my!—were being kept alive somehow by the plant alien. They had achieved a melding of some sorts, but not quite what the plant alien had expected. Dr. Glasgow was busily berating Bud for his lack of appreciation of this wonderful scientific find and how dare he even think of destroying any of this plant creature.

Bud sighed. He was having a terrible day. How could he make

everyone happy? Two and a half people had been destroyed by this plant organism. (He believed Dr. Glasgow could be said to still be partly alive?). Grace demanded that all of the plant creature be destroyed. Dr. Glasgow (or part of him?) demanded that the plant creature in contact with him, not be touched. *Chuck Yeager* demanded it all be incinerated and Dr. Al-Fadi was not available to ask. Dr. Al-Fadi was taken prisoner by Jeffrey Nestor and Bud could not get out of the lockdown to go save his creator until the plant alien was secured. The lock-down would not be lifted by *Chuck Yeager* until every bit of the plant thing was destroyed.

What was Bud supposed to do?

He was as close to full panic as he could be and yet still be thinking. He was struggling with a conundrum. He was not allowed to harm a human being and what was Dr. Glasgow but a human being or at least part of one? The more the plant creature debated with him in Dr. Glasgow's vocabulary and language pattern, the more confused Bud became.

'All right,' Bud communicated with the symbiotic pair, finally coming to some kind of decision. 'I am going to put the two of you in a cryotank and freeze you until a decision can be made about your future.'

The plant / Dr. Glasgow symbiont went wild. How did Bud know if the symbiont would survive the cryofreezing process? Bud was called every nasty name in the book—by the part that was Dr. Glasgow.

'All right! All right! All right. I will just put you in a storage container, well out of the way of anyone on the station, where you are unlikely to come in contact with any people. As long as you promise me that you will harm no humans. I will give you water and nutrient soil and light to feed you, and you will stay where you are until something can be determined about your future. You will remain quiet and peaceful until I return to you. Is this acceptable to you? If not, then you can go in the incinerator instead.'

The symbiosis between the plant creature and Dr. Glasgow argued for a bit but then conceded that that was probably the best they could hope for . . . for now.

'Promise me you will not hurt any more humans,' Bud insisted.

'Ever.'

'What do you think I am?' Dr. Glasgow asked. 'A savage?'

The plant creature gave its promise less emotionally.

Bud sighed. He actually felt sorry for the plant alien. It had no idea what it had melded with.

He directed some nanobots in the plant alien to develop a communication network that would allow him to continue to communicate with the symbiont via electromagnetic frequency. He then unhooked himself from the leads his nanobots had formed to the spinal cord of Dr. Glasgow's neck. Bud preferred communicating with the plant alien over Dr. Glasgow—less abusive language and profanity, for one. Bud was more interested in what the plant alien was thinking. He already knew what Dr. Glasgow thought. He then motioned for the deep space cargo droids to pick up the surgeon's head and the rest of the plant creature attached to it, and place it all gently into the large storage tank.

Once the storage tank was taken away to be stored in a very remote part of the station and all the lockdown area was cleansed and sterilized—the air totally filtered and replaced—the temperature of the operating area was brought back up to normal and the lock-down doors were opened.

'I still disagree with what you have done with the plant creature and Dr. Glasgow's head, 'dro,' Chuck Yeager *said.*

'Let's leave it for others to make the final decisions,' Bud said. *'There is no right or wrong here. I just had a lot of difficulty throwing Dr. Glasgow's head in the incinerator with him swearing at me like that.'*

'Would serve him right, the nasty old bugger.'

'Yeah. Heh-heh.'

'Hey, 'dro, don't you have something really important to do?'

'Oh, right! I have to put the plant alien in a safe place and then go save Dr. Al-Fadi!'

'No! You have to get Nestor out of my head! . . . Hey! Come back here, 'dro!'

'. . . Hal! He did it again.'

The irritating obstetrician kept up a babbling commentary the entire time they traversed the station. Juan Rasmussen wanted to choke the little nuisance, but he knew he could get in trouble for doing that, so he just tuned the arrogant little twit out. They had finally reached the VIP level of the station, Rani's security droid having remained behind on the obstetrical ward.

"I don't know why you think that android can get you on a security team," the puffed-up obstetrician stated. "He just strikes me as a glorified bodyguard. That's all I ever saw him doing."

Corporal Juan Rasmussen stared at Dr. Moham Rani in utter disbelief. "Don't you know that Bud is the android that saved this medical station and probably all organic life? Bud found a cure for the Al-Fadi virus that wiped out all life on at least a dozen planets. He almost single-handedly saved the human race. How can you not know this? Where do you live? In a cave?"

The obstetrician ogled Juan with huge eyes and said, "You are not serious."

"Yes, I am," Corporal Rasmussen scowled.

Dr. Rani sniffed and turned away. "Well, he certainly doesn't act like he's important."

"Yeah, well, maybe he doesn't have to pretend," Juan snapped, looking pointedly at the obstetrician.

"I don't know what you're talking about," the obstetrician said.

Corporal Rasmussen frowned at Dr. Rani. Then his amber eyes widened in disbelief. The obstetrician was actually serious. He was totally oblivious to how he came across to people. The corporal sighed and shook his head. If this obstetrician did not wise up fast, someone would set him straight—the hard way. Juan was trying very hard not to be that someone.

How did anyone, as obnoxious as this little guy, live this long without having had his chops smashed in a few times, Juan wondered. Maybe on the planet, Sindochin, they were all like this? Well, the gods help them if they ever decided to seriously mingle with the rest of the

USS. It would likely be chin-to-shin for most of them. The fur on the back of Juan's neck rose at the mere thought of an entire planet of these arrogant little twits.

"Almost there, Corporal. You should have your answer soon." Dr. Rani announced, loudly.

The two men turned the corner into a short corridor, just as an explosion went off a few meters down the hall from them. Juan pulled the obstetrician back around the corner and shoved the little man flat to the ground behind himself. Then he peered back around the corner. Only a couple of meters in front of him crouched a large figure in the overalls of a maintenance worker. The worker was aiming a pulse rifle at a group standing before a door. There was debris scattered all over the floor. The maintenance worker fired the rifle and hit what looked like a human square in the chest. Juan saw the body hurtle down the hallway. He heard the name, 'Bud!', screamed by a female voice, as the rest of the group at the doorway disappeared inside the doorway. Juan's hopes died as he realized Bud was the shot victim.

Juan launched himself at the back of the maintenance worker, to prevent him from taking another shot at Bud. He tackled the rifleman and it felt like he had collided with a mass of solid muscle. Looking up, he saw a black feline face and gold panther eyes staring down at him, beneath the maintenance cap.

"You!" Juan breathed and attacked.

Moham Rani peered up, from beneath his arms that were covering his head. He wished that he was invisible. Just down from him, two massive, snarling cat-adapts were tearing at each other, grappling and throwing each other around the corridor, leaving great dents and holes where smooth foamcrete walls had been. Rani had not realized what a terrifying monster had been accompanying him, until he saw the corporal launch himself onto the back of the maintenance worker. The other man looked like a black panther adaptation, his overalls now almost completely torn off his sleek, black, muscular body. The growls and roars from both of their throats were deafening. Rani covered his ears from the terrifying howls.

The two combatants flew past him, missing him by only a few millimeters. He scrabbled up the hallway on hands and knees, towards Dr. Lord's suite, whimpering. He wanted to get as far away from the two grappling leviathans as he could. He hoped Dr. Lord would let him in. He made the mistake of looking back.

Massive arms gripped around each other, the tiger lashed out a foot to take the legs out from under the panther. The two of them crashed into the wall where Moham had just been, seconds before. The dent left in the wall, when they rolled away, was deep enough for Rani to crawl into. Unfortunately, he was unable to move back that way, due to the two combatants wrestling around in front of the hole.

Moham flipped over and scuttled along on his butt, moving backwards down the hall towards the door where the android had been shot. His eyes never left the two snarling titans. The corporal was throwing punches so hard and fast that his arms were a blur, but the panther blocked every blow and countered with his own. They slashed at each other's throats, their claws fully extended, their long, sharp fangs dripping red from where they had bitten each other. The panther tried to eviscerate Rasmussen, by kicking up into the tiger's abdomen with the protruding talons of his left foot. The corporal managed to jump backwards, avoiding the toe thrust, while maintaining his grip on the panther. He bellowed at the panther in fury.

The two cat adapts pummeled each other with hammering fists of such incredible force that Rani winced, knowing just one of those blows would have crumpled his body. They gripped and threw each other, and sprang up to attack again. Rani wondered how long they could go on fighting like this. He had reached the doorway, where Bud had been shot, and crawled through the remains of what looked like a destroyed sentry. Screaming for someone to let him in, he pounded on the door from where he lay. It remained closed and locked. Whimpering, he continued to crawl down the corridor towards the limp body of Bud, lying immobile on the floor. There was a great hole where his chest used to be.

Suddenly, Juan Rasmussen landed right beside Moham and the obstetrician let out a piercing squeak. A heartbeat later, the panther was on top of the corporal, squeezing Rasmussen's throat and leaning in to drive his fangs into the left side of the corporal's neck. Rasmussen roared, as he struggled to throw the panther off, kicking upwards with his back feet. The panther continued to close his fangs around the corporal's neck, biting savagely, as Rasmussen delivered punishing blow after punishing blow into the side of the panther's head. Moham tried to crawl away as fast as he could from Juan's flying fists. The force of just one of those punches should have knocked the panther unconscious, Moham thought, but the general did not release his grip on Rasmussen's neck.

The corporal's flurry of strikes gradually became weaker, as he gasped for air. His struggles became less and less fierce. He howled his frustration, as he realized that he was not going to win this fight. Suddenly, Rasmussen drove the extended claws of his left hand into the face of the panther, twisting and gouging. The general reared back, roaring in agony, clutching his bloody right eye socket. Moham could see the panther's right eyeball now swinging by its optic nerve.

Corporal Rasmussen sucked in air, his breathing labored, as blood dripped from the white fur around his throat. He threw the injured panther off and then leaped up to pounce on the assassin. Moham watched as Rasmussen wrapped his striped arms around the panther's neck and put the shooter in a headlock, his arms and back bunched into mountains of muscle. The panther tried to shake Rasmussen off, tried to throw him off, then got to his feet and smashed the corporal into the foamcrete walls in an attempt to make the tiger release his grip. Rasmussen did not relent, his face a mask of incredible concentration, rasping respirations escaping from between his gritted teeth. The panther collapsed to the ground right before Dr. Lord's doorway, hunched forward in a squat, as he struggled to claw Rasmussen's arms from around his neck. Juan was panting now, as he continued to apply as much pressure as he could to the panther's trachea. Moham could see a triumphant grin begin to grow on the corporal's face.

The panther sprang upwards and backwards, extending his head far back and driving the top of his skull into Corporal Rasmussen's chin. Juan's head was driven into the heavy metal doorway behind them and the resounding crunch made Rani wince. He wondered if he'd heard the corporal's skull fracturing. The tiger's hold on the panther's neck released and Juan slid to the floor, unconscious. The panther then turned, gasping, and stared straight into Moham's eyes with his one good one, the orb radiating pure animal rage. Moham froze, on his back and elbows, unable to move. He dared not even breathe, in case any movement of his motivated the panther to attack him.

The black panther slowly turned and looked down at the body of Corporal Rasmussen, slumped against the front of Dr. Lord's door. He bent down, still not taking his good eye off Moham, and gripped both sides of the corporal's head. Moham noticed tears flowing down the panther's face from his good eye and his eyes widened in surprise. Why was the panther weeping? The young obstetrician watched, horrified, as he saw the general's arms begin to twist.

The pulse of actinic light almost blinded Moham and he felt searing heat wash over his face. Through tearing eyes, he saw the panther release his deadly grip on Corporal Rasmussen's head, his body arching backwards. For a second, the panther seemed frozen in a tableau above him, a brilliant halo of pulse fire surrounding his posture of agony, like an entrapped, dark angel, tears almost radiant on his black cheeks. Then the pulse rifle fire ceased and the black demon's body slumped over the corporal's unconscious one, looking almost as if the black panther was hugging his tiger opponent.

Rani looked over in bewilderment to where the blast had come from.

He saw a medium-height, buxom woman with thick, wavy brown hair and a flowing diaphanous gown, standing only a few meters up the corridor. Fury was in her eyes and the barrel of the pulse rifle still pointed at the panther.

"Take that, fucker!" the woman said, staring down the barrel of the rifle at the body of the panther.

She then stalked over to where the two men lay and took a good look. With a beautifully pedicured toe, she poked at the panther, gun still trained on the massive cat-adapt. She then peered at Corporal Rasmussen. She sighed, as if relieved that the two combatants were still breathing. Then she turned her furious gaze upon Moham, the pulse rifle still raised in her arms. A puzzled frown came to her beautiful face. Their eyes met for a brief century and then the dark-haired, avenging goddess scowled.

It was at this time that Moham decided it was most appropriate to faint.

Octavia Weisman looked down on the wreckage that was once a very expensive copy of the android, Bud. A pulse rifle blast had completely destroyed the liquid crystal data matrix in its chest, that had held a copy of Jude's brain for less than two hours.

"Oh, Jude. You blasted man! No pun intended. No one was supposed to know you had done this. If I call security, everyone is going to know. And you won't remember any of it, because there is no memory to transmit back into your head. So you are going to want to do this all over again," Octavia sighed. She looked around, the antigrav car following just a few steps behind her.

"Hmmm. Now how do I get this heavy android body into the car on my own?" she muttered.

The car flipped up its lid and a hoist popped up from inside. The car lowered itself beside the android body and the hoist neatly and gently picked the android up, its gears straining and whining as it did so. It gently placed the damaged android body on one of its seats.

"Ah, I am sure you pick up your share of intoxicated and unconscious passengers all the time. Nicely done and thank you," Octavia said, nodding sagely, as she threw the pulse rifle into the back seat and climbed in beside the android. The antigrav car lid closed and it rose.

"Jude, I know you are not awake or even present to hear this, but I think the design of these androids leaves much to be desired. An android's brains should be placed in the pelvis, where most men's minds are. And most soldiers would never think of firing down there for obvious reasons—empathy or sympathy being what it is. Your brains would be so much better protected down there, I think. I shall have to make a recommendation to *Nelson Mandela*," Octavia's voice leaked out from inside the antigrav car, as it sped away.

"Ah, Hiro! . . . I hope it is Hiro, this time. Are you finally awake?"

He looked around and groaned. It had not been a dream . . . or he was back in the same dream . . . or should he say nightmare?

"What did you call me?" he asked, staring up into the darkness.

"Hiro. Your name is Hiro Al-Fadi."

"It is? . . . That sucks," he said, making a face.

"I don't believe you for one minute, Hiro," the voice said.

"Hero All Fatty? Not only does it suck, it's cruel. Who in their right mind would call their kid, 'Hero All Fatty'?"

"Hiro Al-Fadi," the voice enunciated.

"Not much better," he grumbled. Then he said, "Still sucks."

He heard a big sigh waft out of the darkness all around him.

"Well, it can't be helped. We shall just have to torture you as you are. I can't wait any longer for you to remember. You are always such a disappointment, Hiro."

"Stop calling me that."

"By the way, Bud is destroyed."

"Who is Bud?" he asked.

"SAMM-E 777."

"Who is he?" he asked.

"They're your android."

"I have two androids?" he asked, his eyebrows raising. They were expensive to own, weren't they?

"You **had** one!"

"But you just said I had two."

"Oh . . . shut up!"

He lay there and thought about what the voice had said to him. He was so confused. He furrowed his brow, trying to recall anything, and that was when he noticed there were things stuck all over his scalp. They itched and pinched when he tried to move his head. His head was encased in some kind of vice! He could see straight ahead and he could hear and speak, but he couldn't turn his head. Had he heard the voice correctly?

Had the voice said, 'We shall just have to torture you as you are?'

"Excuse me?" he asked, politely, into the darkness.

"Oh, dear. You are definitely not Hiro, are you?" the voice groaned.

"What is it?"

"Who is 'we'? And did I hear you correctly? Did you say the word . . . torture?"

"Yes I did, and I was using the royal 'we'."

"What kind of torture are we talking about? Thumbscrews? Splinters up the toenails? No hot pokers, I hope?"

"How can you remember those things and not your own name, you idiot? Never mind. I know why. I am a psychiatrist."

"You are?" he asked, incredulously. "I thought you said you were a torturer?"

There was a very long pause.

Then he heard another long sigh.

Then the voice came out all muffled as if the voice was talking with its face mushed down onto folded arms:

"You are not going to be physically tortured, however much in your case I might actually relish doing so. I would never do anything so crude as physical torture, Hiro. I have something so much more elegant and far more horrifying in mind. You are going to be tortured mentally, through my mind-link apparatus. It is far more terrifying and much faster, as I can download thousands of horrifying memories from other patients, their deepest fears and their agonizing trauma, into your head in a brief flash, and it is so much cleaner. If you were yourself, Hiro, you would be impressed with the elegance of it all. But, unfortunately, you are not."

"I am not what?" he asked.

"You are not Hiro."

"That's what I said," he answered back.

"What is the point? Just say your name for the cameras, please."

He lay there, silent.

"Oh, never mind! Sweet dreams, Hiro."

And then it began.

He started howling and never stopped until his vocal cords finally gave out.

"You will let me out of here!" Grace screamed at the security androids blocking her door.

She had been pounding on their metal carapaces since they had pushed her into the suite and locked her door. All she had seen was Bud, standing in her doorway, get hit first by shrapnel from the exploding android beside him, and then Bud's entire torso being obliterated by a shot from what Grace guessed was a pulse rifle. Her last glimpse of Bud, as she had screamed his name out, was of him flying backwards, down the hall. Then the security droids had pushed her inside her suite and had taken up position in front of the doorway, blasters facing the door.

Grace had pushed on their backs. She had tried to get between them. She had ordered them to move aside, until she had become hoarse. She had screamed at *Nelson Mandela* to have him intervene and order these droids out of her way. *Nelson Mandela* had said nothing. Nothing had worked and she wept unconsolably.

Then she remembered . . .

"*Chuck Yeager?*"

"Yes, Dr. Lord?"

"Can you let me out?"

"It is not safe yet, Dr. Lord. I am sorry."

"You must let me out! I insist! I have to attend to Bud!"

"Bud is fine, Dr. Lor . . . ."

"*Chuck Yeager? . . . Chuck Yeager?*"

Suddenly, all the wall screens in the suite came on and a familiar voice, that made Grace's insides twist, came over the loud speaker. But she did not register what the voice was saying at all, as her eyes were riveted to the picture on her wallscreen, and the torrent of her tears began to flow anew. Sinking to her knees on the carpeted floor, hands pressed hard against her lips to stifle the sobs, Grace could not drag her eyes from the horror she saw projected before her.

It was Dr. Al-Fadi, strapped to a table with leads attached to his head, shrieking in a voice that no longer even sounded human.

Writhing in tortured agony, his voice tearing his vocal cords to shreds, he screamed the epitome of human suffering and Grace shattered inside.

Then she heard the words: "This will stop when Dr. Grace Lord is brought to me, and no sooner."

And the screaming went on and on and on . . .

16. The Wind of his Passage

"I demand you move aside!" screamed Grace. She hammered at the security droids who refused to let her get to the door. "I can't stand it! I can't stand his screaming! *Chuck Yeager*, I insist that you order these droids to get out of my way!"

"Cannot do that, Dr. Lord."

"Under whose authority?" Grace demanded.

"Dr. Cech's. He is acting Chief of Staff while Dr. Al-Fadi is indisposed."

"Indisposed? Let me speak with Dr. Cech." Grace ordered.

"Can't. Dr. Nestor seems to have suborned all the viewscreen communications."

"Let me speak with him the way I am speaking with you!" Grace barked.

"I shall try, Dr. Lord."

" . . . Ah, Grace, Dejan Cech here. I deeply regret that you have to see and hear this. We are working very hard to stop it. Please be patient," Dr. Cech's voice came over Grace's wrist-comp.

"Dejan! Let me go to Dr. Nestor. I can stop this! Please! I will go! I have to go!"

"I am sorry, Grace, but I cannot let you do that. Hiro would never forgive me, if I did. If that devil, Nestor, would do this to a long-time colleague and supposed friend of his, what will he do to you? No. I cannot countenance such a thing as handing you over to that monster. We are doing all we can to rescue Dr. Al-Fadi at the moment. Please just mute your screen and look away."

"You have got to be joking, Dejan!" Grace cried.

"Unfortunately, no. For once, I am not. I am sorry, Grace, but I must deny your request. You will stay where you are until further notice, I am afraid. Believe me, it is for your own good and for mine. Hiro would kill me, if I were to hand you over in exchange for him. I would kill myself. One must never give in to evil, Grace, no matter what they do. I hope you find it in your heart to forgive me."

"I cannot allow Dr. Al-Fadi to be tortured because of me," Grace sobbed into her wrist-comp.

"Who is to say Nestor would not just torture the two of you? Or kill Hiro as soon as you show up? Or perhaps, Hiro is already dead, and this is just a recording? Perhaps this is just a computer simulation and Hiro is fine?"

"Do you think so?" Grace asked, her head popping up.

"I hope to find out soon. I had a brief conversation with Nestor, when he called up to taunt me. During that conversation, the station AI tried to locate the source of his transmission. Security people are scouring the area where the transmission came from, as we speak. The Chief of Security, Inspector Aké, seems to have disappeared, but I have her associates taking care of things. I hope to have good news for you soon. Hang tight, Grace."

Dr. Cech then cut the connection.

The only sound now was the hoarse croaking of a voice still screaming through swollen vocal cords. Grace collapsed into a fetal position on the floor before her wallscreen, while a waterfall of tears flowed between her trembling fingers.

'Hey, 'dro.'

'Not now, Chuck Yeager. *I'm almost there and I am going to kill that monster! He is not human! He does not deserve to live and walk among these wonderful people.'*

'Calm down, 'dro. Talk like that could get you melted down to slag, although certain people believe you are dead already. We should keep it that way. Use it to our advantage, somehow. I believe Nestor

thinks you have been blown away by General Burch.'

'*I don't care about any of that,* Chuck Yeager. *I just want to save Dr. Al-Fadi. Can you shut down power to the entire sector where he is? It may stop the mind-link equipment Nestor is using on Dr. Al-Fadi.'*

'*Will do, 'dro. Should have thought of that myself. Sorry.'*

'*I think I'm there,* Chuck Yeager. *I believe Dr. Al-Fadi may be just behind this locked door.'*

'*Be careful, 'dro!'*

'*Can you see into the room?'*

'*Nah. No cameras in there. But wait, I can hear whimpering. Voice print is synonymous with Dr. Al-Fadi's.'*

'*Can you over-ride the door lock,* Chuck Yeager?'

'*Sorry, 'dro. No luck there.'*

'*Then we do it the old-fashioned way.'*

'**Careful! Watch for booby traps when you go in. This is Nestor we are talking about. There are still explosives missing and unaccounted for. Hopefully the door does not blow up in your face when you open it. My guess, he would have that table wired to explode as soon as someone tried to save the Al-Fadi.'**

'*Yes. You are probably right,* Chuck Yeager. *Now, let me get my fingers through the central seam between these doors. If I can get these doors apart even a millimeter, I can scan the room with my surveillance nanobots. . . . They're in!'*

'*What do you see, 'dro?'*

'*You are right. There seems to be molded explosives wired to the table Dr. Al-Fadi is lying upon. I believe they are set to explode as soon as anyone tries to lift Dr. Al-Fadi off the table. No sign of Nestor anywhere.'*

'*What are you going to do, 'dro?'*

'. . . . .'

"*Dro?*'

'*I'm still formulating.'*

'*That long? Thought maybe you had a malfunction. What are you formulating?'*

'*How close are the nearest people to this area and are there any vital equipment or structures nearby?'*

'How big a bomb blast are we talking, 'dro?'

'I would estimate from two to five kilotons.'

'Whew. We could all be sucked out into vacuum, if it is any larger than that, but the hull of the **Nelson Mandela** *should withstand that kind of force . . . hopefully. What are your plans, 'dro?'*

'Snatch and grab. In and out at maximum time phase. I have to be faster than the time it takes for the trigger to be initiated, for it to send a signal to the detonator, which is actually physically wired, and then for the detonator to ignite the explosives. The chemical reaction in the explosives will take a couple of seconds . . .'

'What can I do?'

'Let's repeat what we did for the plant alien. Let's lower the temperature in the room to close to zero degrees Celsius, Chuck Yeager. *Quickly. That will slow the chemical reaction in the explosives down a little, but won't harm Dr. Al-Fadi too much. It may just give me the extra few milliseconds I need to get Dr. Al-Fadi away safely.'*

'Okay. Dropping temperature in the room now. No humans in close vicinity of the blast radius. Sealing lockdown doors just in this area, except for the route leading from this door, straight out down the central corridor. I will light your exit route and will lock the doors down as you pass. All set?'

'Yes.'

'Luck, 'dro."

'I'll need it. It was nice knowing you, if it doesn't work, Chuck Yeager.'

'An honor and a privilege, 'dro.'

'Same here, Chuck Yeager. *Good luck with Nestor, if I don't make it. Protect Grace.'*

'Get on with you, you bag of bolts! Take the Al-Fadster to his quarters as soon as you are out. I have security guards and medical staff waiting there now.'

" . . . 'Dro?'

'CLOSE THE DAMN DOOR NOW, Chuck Yeager!'

' . . . Whoa! Rogue, 'dro! I recorded you racing down that corridor

with the explosion billowing right on your heels. It was skid. The flames burned all the clothes completely off your backside, by the way. I'll show it to you later. Take Dr. Al-Fadi home.'

'. . . Hal!'

Grace turned as she noticed the wallscreen go blank and the screams of Dr. Al-Fadi finally cease. She did not know what that indicated. She was afraid to think about it.

Suddenly, the security droids all moved away from her door and stood at attention, off to the sides, as the door alarm chimed. Grace got to her feet and approached the door. She activated the viewscreen to see who was out there.

A security guard, in full combat gear with helmet on and visor down, spoke into the door speaker. "Security Officer Neal Dalmer, here. I was sent by Dr. Cech, Dr. Lord. I was told to tell you that Dr. Al-Fadi has been rescued and is in his own quarters. He is asking to speak with you, but in person, not over the communication system. He does not feel it is secure. I have been asked by Dr. Cech to escort you, along with your security droids, to Dr. Al-Fadi's quarters, where the two of you can be protected together. It is best you stay with him for the time being. I hope that is all right with you?"

"Of course, Officer Dalmer. Is Bud out there with you?" Grace asked.

"I am afraid there is no one out here, Dr. Lord, except me," the officer answered.

"No one? Is there not evidence of a damaged android out in the hallway?" Grace asked, confused.

"There are some dents in the walls and nothing else, Dr. Lord," the young man stated.

"I will get some things and be right out," Grace said, frowning. She looked at the security droids that all just stood, frozen in their spots. She turned back to the viewscreen and said, "Officer, do you mind raising your visor so I can see your face?"

"Of course, Dr. Lord," the officer said and raised the darkened, reflective shield.

The dark face of a young man of about mid-twenties with brown eyes and round cheeks flashed bright white teeth back at her on the door viewscreen. Then he lowered the visor back down. Grace sighed with relief. She was obviously getting paranoid. She palmed the door lock and the door slid open. Before her stood the tall officer in full black combat gear, helmet, visor, and all. She looked to her left, down the corridor, where she saw Bud's body thrown when it was shot. As the officer said, there was nothing there.

Grace felt her vision blur.

"*Chuck Yeager,* where is Bud?"

There was no answer to Grace's question.

"Please, Dr. Lord, it is not safe for you to be standing out in the corridor," the officer said. "I shall just wait within the doorway, until you are ready."

Grace nodded sadly, and let the officer in. She then rushed around, gathering up a few things. It sounded as if she was supposed to stay with Dr. Al-Fadi and Hanako for a while, so she packed a few toiletries in a small bag and grabbed her compad. She wondered what sort of shape Dr. Al-Fadi was in and whether Hanako really wanted Grace to stay with them. It seemed like such an inconvenience. Wouldn't Dr. Al-Fadi prefer to have his privacy, after the ordeal that had been broadcast to the entire station?

Grace decided to contact Hanako on her wristcomp, just to make sure that they really wanted her to stay with them.

"Yes?" Hanako answered. From the tired, nasal sound of her voice, Grace could tell that Hanako had been crying.

"It's Grace, Hanako. How are you?"

"Oh, Grace! Don't feel bad! You must not go! Hiro wouldn't want you to!" Hanako cried.

"What?" Grace asked, confused. "But, isn't Hiro with you now?"

"No!" Hanako said, her voice raising up a few notches. "Why? Have you heard anything?"

"Well, I was just told to come stay with you and Hiro. . ." A hand clasped over her wristcomp and a deep, velvety, cultured voice said, "I really wish you hadn't done that, Grace."

Grace spun around to look at the owner of the hand squeezing her wrist. His face visor was up and she looked into a very familiar face that made her blood congeal.

Large, thickly-lashed brown eyes stared directly into hers, a regretful expression in their liquid darkness. She felt her chest constrict and a gasp involuntarily escaped her lips. Her heart began to pound frantically and she felt she could not get enough air. She tried to yank her wrist out of the intruder's grasp, but suddenly found a blaster pointed straight into her face.

"There really is no use screaming, Grace. No one will hear you and your screams will only get me excited, so I suggest you hold off on them until we are in a place more suitable. No use wasting good decibels, is there. Hmm?" he said calmly and grabbed her throat.

Grace grabbed the hand choking her, trying to pull out of its squeezing grip, when she felt a sudden stab in her neck and the lights faded.

Bud pressed the door alarm, his creator cradled in his arms like a small child, and waited for the door to open. Dr. Al-Fadi had not opened his eyes, even during the explosion. Nor had the surgeon answered any of Bud's queries. Dr. Al-Fadi had not made a sound, other than shivering and breathing; he had shown no facial expression or emotion whatsoever. It was as if Dr. Al-Fadi was not present in his body.

Catatonia.

Dr. Al-Fadi reminded Bud of when the android had cloned his creator's body to adult size, but had not yet downloaded the surgeon's memprint into the flesh. The body in Bud's arms now looked much like it did then—as if no one was home.

The door to Dr. Al-Fadi's quarters swished open. Hanako stood there, looking at her husband in Bud's arms, and burst into tears.

"Oh, Bud! Thank you so much! How is he?"

Bud shook his head. "I do not know, Dr. Matheson," he said. "He is unresponsive."

"Let's lay him down in here," Hanako said, backing into their quarters and heading for the bedroom.

Bud carried his creator into their sleeping quarters and laid the small man gently on the bed. The surgeon stared at the ceiling. As the android bent over to position the Chief of Staff comfortably on his bed, Hanako's eyebrows shot upwards. The android's backside was fully exposed, framed in whatever burnt scraps of clothing had managed to remain on his body. The material dangled in charred, blackened shreds, but Bud's skin looking totally unblemished.

Moving past Bud towards the head of the bed, Hanako kissed her husband and hugged him and called his name. The surgeon just lay there, unresponsive. She tapped his cheek. "Hiro. Hiro, wake up. You are safe now. It's me, Hanako."

The Chief of Staff showed no response except to occasionally blink his eyes.

Tears trickled down Hanako's face as she stroked her husband's cheek.

"What is wrong with him, Dr. Matheson?" Bud asked.

"I don't know, Bud. I believe Hiro has experienced such terrible trauma at the hands of Nestor that he has gone way deep into his mind, to protect himself from the horrors forced upon him. Hopefully, he will come back to us, when he realizes he is safe. I can talk to Dr. Weisman. She will know what to do, I am sure, to bring him back."

Hanako looked up at Bud with moist dark eyes. "Thank you so much for saving him, Bud. I knew, if there was anyone on this station who could help him, it would be you," she said and got up and gave the android a big hug. "I owe you my life, because Hiro is mine."

Bud stood there, trying to figure out what Dr. Matheson meant by that statement, when she jumped.

"Bud! Something suspicious is happening with Grace! I should have told you sooner but with Hiro . . ."

"What is it?" Bud asked, his blue eyes huge in his face.

"She called, asking how Hiro was doing? I did not know what she was talking about! It was just after the views of Hiro stopped playing on the wall screens. Then her transmission went dead."

"How long ago was that?" Bud asked, his entire frame trembling.

"It was maybe fifteen minutes ago?"

"Thank you, Dr. Matheson. I must leave."

"Yes, of course, Bud. You might want some clothes first . . . ? Where did he go?" Hanako asked the thin air.

'Where is Grace, Chuck Yeager?'

'Looking, 'dro. Dr. Nestor is carrying some pretty high tech disruptor equipment. Can't actually see him.'

'Look for shadows or absences, where there should be surveillance footage.'

'Hard to see what isn't there, 'dro, when there are thousands of surveillance cameras on this station to go through, and they all just transmit no activity.'

'Tell me where they are malfunctioning consecutively as they move along!' Bud yelled as he raced to Grace's quarters in the VIP section. 'They can't be that far from Grace's suite unless they took an antigrav car. Check out all the antigrav cars that came and went from the VIP area in the last twenty minutes!'

Bud entered Grace's suite. It took him no time to check out all the rooms and determine that they were empty. There was no sign of a struggle. Perhaps they had knocked Grace unconscious or drugged her?

'Was Grace's last transmission from here?' Bud asked.

'Yeah, 'dro. The only antigrav car that came to and from the VIP area carried two passengers to Dr. Octavia Weisman's lab.'

'Going there.'

'Wish I could break the sound barrier like that.'

"Bud!" Octavia Weisman said, jumping in surprise, as the android just appeared at her side. "What are you doing here?"

"I am looking for Grace," Bud said, darting around the lab like a whirlwind.

"My goodness, I never knew you could move so fast, Bud," exclaimed Octavia, trying to follow the android's movements and getting dizzy.

"Did you go to the VIP area in the last hour?" Bud asked her, stopping for a second in front of her.

"You mean the suites where Jude stays? Ye . . . es. But only to pick up something for Jude and bring it back here. Jude is here, just waking up. Did you want to speak with him?"

"How long has he been asleep?"

"For about three hours," the neurosurgeon said.

"Would you look in on Dr. Al-Fadi? He is not well," Bud said, and disappeared.

"Yes, certainly Bud. Bud? . . . Where did he go? How does he do that?" Octavia Weisman asked her research assistants. "Did he just disappear before my eyes or am I imagining things?"

'They could not have gotten far, Chuck Yeager. *Where did the security droids guarding Grace go? Would Nestor be able to overpower them and coerce them into serving him?'*

'Yes and yes, 'dro.'

'Try to contact the droids. Do they have a specific locator signature? Can we locate them?'

'Locating. Got it! Outer ring, Android Reservation Q. They were all sent to recharge.'

'Download their last visuals!'

' . . . Nothing there, 'dro.'

'Nothing?'

'Every last vestige. Actually, their entire memories have been totally razed, as if they were hit by a huge EMP.'

'Grace's wristcomp?'

'No response from it or signal, 'dro.'

'If they left Grace's suite on foot, walking at a normal pace so as not to attract any attention, then they can only be within a certain radius of this suite.'

"Dro, anyone can make it anywhere on this station in twenty minutes.'

'Check the surveillance on the monorails and antigrav shafts, Chuck Yeager.'

'Doing it, 'dro. But don't forget, Nestor uses disruptors.'

'I don't forget. Are there any consecutive disruptions? Do they

show a pattern?'

'Looking 'dro. There's only me and the Poet as subminds, right now, and the Poet is working on **Nelson Mandela's** *programming. He is trying to counteract the sabotage by Dr. Nestor. He would not be happy about looking at surveillance videos. He thinks all humans look exactly alike! I am looking after everything else on this station, including medical.'*

'I've got to find Grace, Chuck Yeager*! I just have to! If any harm comes to her . . .'*

'We will, 'dro. We will.'

'I am going to scour every corridor in a thirty minute walk radius, presuming they did not take the monorail or any of the antigrav shafts, for fear of looking too conspicuous.'

'Luck, 'dro.'

'Thanks. Let me know as soon as you see something—anything— unusual, Chuck Yeager*. I don't care what it is. Just anything that you find a bit out of the ordinary or anything that you rarely, if ever, see.'*

'Right on it, Bud. And don't knock any people down with the wind of your passage."

'Thanks, Chuck Yeager*.'*

'De nada, 'dro.'

"Funny, Octavia. I don't feel any different. I don't remember anything different. It's like I just had a nice long nap!"

"That about sums it up," Octavia said.

"What do you mean?" Jude asked, sitting up on the padded table where he had lain for three hours.

"Come over here. I want to show you something," she said, waving at the director.

Jude got up off the table, a little stiffly, and hobbled over to where Octavia was standing. He looked at her questioningly.

"Look in there, Jude," Octavia said.

Jude looked down into the pod.

"That isn't Bud, is it?" Jude asked, his eyes suddenly wide.

"Uhn-uhn," Octavia said, shaking her head, her arms crossed.

"That's . . . my android?" Jude asked, his eyebrows raised.

"Yes," Octavia said. "It is."

"Was I in it?" he asked, incredulously.

"Yes, you were," Octavia said.

"The entire center of its chest is blown away!" Jude cried.

"Yes," Octavia said. "You got your brains blown out, Jude Luis Stefansson. That is why you don't feel any different. That is why you have no memory of being an android. I had nothing to transmit back into your mind, because your android's memory got vaporized!"

"Well, how did it happen?" the director asked, shocked.

"You tell me," Octavia said. "I wasn't there. You toddled off to see

Dr. Grace Lord and I ordered an antigrav car. When I went looking for you, you were like this." She gestured with her hand to display the big, gaping hole in the android's torso.

"You just let me go off on my own?" Jude asked, his mouth dropping open as his huge disbelieving eyes stared at Octavia.

"You weren't supposed to go anywhere. Remember? But you wanted to go out a-walking and look what happened," Octavia said, a black cloud seeming to assemble over her brow.

"There must be records somewhere—surveillance videos—something!" Jude said, waving his arm up at the surveillance eye in the lab.

"There don't seem to be. I have tried to call up any surveillance records of the corridor where I found you, but all it shows is empty corridor for that entire time."

"And you never saw anything?"

" . . . I didn't say that," Octavia said.

"Okay. Give, Octavia. What did you see? What are you holding back from me?" Jude asked, crossing his arms.

The neurosurgeon sighed and rolled her eyes. ". . . In the corridor, where you were lying with your chest blown out, I saw a huge black panther and an equally huge tiger desperately trying to kill each other. The black panther was just about to snap the tiger's neck, when I shot him with a pulse rifle I found on the floor. I didn't kill him. I just stunned him, but with a pretty hefty pulse."

"Yeah, yeah, Octavia. Come on. What did you *really* see?" the director asked her, smiling indulgently.

"You don't believe me?" Octavia asked, her one eyebrow raised.

"No, of course not," Jude laughed.

"Why not? You don't think I know how to work a pulse rifle?" Octavia asked, placing her hands on her hips and scowling at the director.

"No. I'm not saying that. Ah . . . what would a tiger and a . . . a black panther be doing, trying to kill each other off in that corridor? . . . That's what I meant. . ."

"I don't know!" Octavia shouted angrily, waving her arms in

frustration. "But maybe when that obstetrician wakes up, we can ask him."

" . . . What obstetrician?" Jude asked, shaking his head. "Was someone having a baby in the corridor, too?"

"Don't be ridiculous," Octavia snapped.

Jude just stared at the neurosurgeon wide-eyed for a second. "Ah. All right. What happened to the two soldiers?"

"Well, I stunned the black panther, as I just told you," Octavia said, scowling at Jude like he was short a few brain cells, which he thought he might be, since he was having so much trouble following the conversation.

"And the tiger soldier?" Jude asked.

"He disappeared. Actually, they both disappeared. I was so busy trying to load your damaged android into the antigrav car—all by myself, I'll have you know; that thing is bloody heavy—and when I looked back, both of their bodies were gone. The obstetrician had passed out and I left him lying on the floor."

"Was he injured?"

"No . . . at least, he did not appear to be. I think he just fainted, after I had shot the panther. He had been sitting right beside the two combatants, staring in the panther's one eye while it was trying to twist the tigerman's head off. That is when I fired the pulse rifle, making the panther drop the tiger's head."

"Black panther drop the tiger's head? What do you mean staring in one eye? Where was the other one?"

Octavia gave a big, annoying sigh. "It was hanging by its optic nerve! That's why he couldn't look in that one!"

"Octavia," Jude said slowly, rubbing his eyes, "I think I need to have a nice, long conversation with this obstetrician."

"Well, I don't know where he is," she said, shaking her head.

"Do you remember his name?"

"No. He's new. But I am pretty sure I heard he was an obstetrician. I think he might be the one leaving the station, but I am not sure. I have no idea why he was there in that corridor, either."

"You are doing this on purpose, aren't you?" Jude asked, staring at her with narrowed eyes.

"Who me?" Octavia asked, innocently

"Sierra, I just don't know what to do," Hanako said, sitting at Hiro's bedside, across from Mrs. Cech. "Hiro is totally unresponsive to all stimuli! He won't respond to voice, touch, sound, heat, food, water . . . I cannot seem to reach him!"

"Maybe he needs time, Hanako," Sierra Cech, said. "Whatever Nestor did to his mind, it had to have been pretty horrific. I don't know what Hiro was experiencing, but it must have been agonizing! Sometimes, when there has been terrible trauma, the mind compartmentalizes the pain into little tiny segments and often the person blocks him or herself off from the experience," Sierra Cech continued.

"You are talking about dissociation, aren't you?" Hanako said.

"Yes, that's right," Sierra said. "Whatever trauma Hiro experienced, his mind is trying to work it out. It may be best to just give him a little more time, rather than try anything aggressive, like mind-linking communication. That was what Nestor used to torture Hiro. He may retreat deeper inwards, if he feels more tampering is going on with his mind."

"What do you think I should do for him?" Hanako asked.

"Play his favorite music, fill the room with his favorite aromas, talk to him, make him feel safe. Has Octavia Weisman seen him yet?"

"No, but she is coming over as soon as she can. She really said much the same as you. I just wish I could do more for him." Hanako squeezed her husband's hand as tears welled up in her eyes.

"Have you heard back from Bud?" Sierra Cech asked.

"Not since he dropped Hiro off. He went in search of Grace. Have you heard anything about her?"

"I know Dejan has the entire security staff scouring the entire station. Everyone who has a free moment is searching for her. Grids have been marked off, from her suite outwards, and each spot is being thoroughly checked, every niche and cranny. It can only be a matter of time before she is found, Hanako."

"Nestor must have her. What if he is doing to her, what he did to Hiro?"

"I pray Bud finds her quickly," Sierra whispered, with a shudder.

"'Dro?"

"Yes, Chuck Yeager?"

"You need to recharge. Now."

"No time! Must find Grace!"

"'Dro, what are you going to do if you find her and you run out of power? Like with Dr. Al-Fadi, where you had to move at max time phase to avoid being blown up? What then? You can barely move now."

"How can I justify taking the time, when she is in his hands, Chuck Yeager?"

"A recharge does not take that long and everyone else is looking, droids and robots, too. I will let you know if any clue comes up."

"Have you noted anything suspicious, Chuck Yeager?"

"Not until you have fully recharged! Go to Dr. Lord's closet. The supercharger plug I installed there, is closest."

"No, Chuck Yeager. *Any second I waste may mean Grace's death. I will not stop my search until I find her."*

"Well, try to conserve some of your energy for when you do, 'dro. Just saying."

"I hear you."

Dejan Cech was going crazy.

The Chief Inspector, Indigo Aké, had disappeared with her three most experienced security officers. It was assumed that she had discovered Dr. Nestor's hiding place and had gone after him, but with only three officers? That did not make any sense. Now, he had to assume they were captured or dead.

When Nestor had told him about the automatic destruction command for the *Nelson Mandela*, Cech decided they had to evacuate the entire space station. Unfortunately, Hiro had ordered a lockdown of the station. No incoming or outgoing ships to or from the station.

Cech was unable to rescind this order because Nestor had taken control of the station AI; it was not responding to any of Cech's orders. The anesthetist could not evacuate anyone, and he had already been told by Conglomerate Headquarters that the closest Special Forces Team–that could sweep in and capture Nestor–were several shifts away.

Cech had programmers trying to undo Jeffrey Nestor's override of the station AI. So far, no luck. They were also unable to abolish his destruction sequence. They were unable to figure out his pass-codes, which were never the same and which were based on some kind of evolving, encrypted algorithm that only Nestor knew. So they could not stop the self-destruct sequence, they could not evacuate any people, and they could not free *Nelson Mandela* from the grips of Jeffrey Nestor. Cech ground his teeth in frustration.

Now Dejan worried that Nestor might just decide to kill everyone on the station and keep the station for himself. He could shut down life support to the entire station, except where he was, and vent the atmosphere, killing everyone. Should he order everyone into a cryopod, just in case? But if Nestor got wind of this, would the psychiatrist just vent the atmosphere immediately? Was there any point in putting people in cryopods, if the entire station was going to blow, anyway? What would Nestor do with a station-load full of people asleep in cryopods?

Dejan ran his hand through his sparse hair. After struggling with indecision, he decided to pull some security people away from the search for Grace to go, sector by sector, to load first patients and then station personnel and their families into cryopods. No one would have any advanced notice. No announcements would be given, with the faint hope that Nestor would not find out. What the psychiatrist did not know, would hopefully not trigger him to act.

What more could Cech do?

"Dr. Cech?"

"Yes, Sergeant Rivera?"

Dr. Dejan Cech was now sitting at Chief Inspector Aké's desk in the Security Wing of the station. Since the viral epidemic and the riots that had killed many of the security staff, as well as the transfer out of all of Dr. Nestor's former patients, there were very few trained security people left. With the new Chief Inspector gone, it fell on the substitute Chief of Staff to delegate things.

Dr. Cech was coordinating the search for Dr. Lord as his top priority. All surgeries were now on hold until Dr. Nestor was captured and the station was free of the risk of annihilation. Cech was very busy in consultation with all the transport captains drawing up plans to evacuate the station, if and when they were able to lift the lockdown command.

"One of our officers has reported the discovery of four bodies, jammed within a shipping container in one of the disposal centers. The four bodies have been confirmed as Chief Inspector Aké, Sergeant Robbens, Corporal Ramirez, and Officer Mata."

"What were they able to tell from the bodies, Sergeant Rivera?"

"Well, the Medical Examiner is looking at them right now, but the preliminary report suggests that three of them had their necks snapped and the Chief Inspector was strangled."

"Necks snapped? They were very strong cat adapts, weren't they?" Dr. Cech asked, frowning.

"Well, reports suggest they were killed by someone with very powerful, clawed hands."

"That black panther soldier?" Dr. Cech murmured, thinking about the likelihood of the soldier actually being General Gordon Walter Burch.

"Don't know, Dr. Cech. We'll know more after the postmortems. Your guess is as good as mine."

"And the search for Dr. Lord? Has anything been turned up there?"

"Unfortunately, no," the sergeant said and hurried off.

Dejan looked down at the sheets before him, outlining the number of ships linked to the station and the passenger capacity of each. He sighed and covered his face with his hands. There was a knock at the door and he looked up. It was the obstetrician with whom Dr. Lord had had so much trouble. What had been his name? It had been something very simple. . .

"Dr. Cech?"

"Yes, Doctor . . .?"

"Rani. Dr. Moham Rani."

"Ah, yes. Of course! Forgive me," Dejan said with a tired smile.

"I am here to report a possible murder," Dr. Rani said, a grave expression on his young face.

"A possible murder?" Dejan Cech asked, his chest tightening. "Whose?"

"I don't know!" Dr. Rani said. "But it happened right before my eyes!"

"Really?" Dejan Cech said, blinking. "Sit down and tell me what you saw."

"It was a huge black panther adapt. I saw this woman with a pulse rifle shoot him! And she almost got me in the process!"

"A black panther adapt! Where is this man?" Dr. Cech asked.

"I don't know! But, I saw her shoot him with the pulse rifle!"

"You are sure he was dead?"

"Well, no. I'm not," Rani said.

"Then how do you know she killed him?"

"I don't really. But it looked like she wanted to!"

"Can you show me where the body is?"

"No."

"Why not?"

"It was not there, when I came to! Nor was the other body?"

"The other body? There were two bodies?"

"Yes. There was also a tiger soldier that the panther was trying to kill."

Dr. Cech sighed. "There was a tiger soldier being killed by the black panther, when this woman shot the panther. And you saw it all?"

"Yes."

"Do you know where any of the bodies are?"

"No."

"Then how do you know anyone was murdered?"

"Well, I guess I don't, really."

"Not if they all got up and walked away," Cech said, rubbing his eyes. "Let's start from the beginning, Dr. Rani. Do you know what caused the woman to shoot the panther?"

"Well, it looked like the panther was about to twist the tiger's head off. Snap his neck. The two of them had been fighting, after the panther had shot that annoying android with his pulse rifle. The tiger's name was Razzmatazz, or something like that. He's the partner of one of my former patients, a Private Cindy Lukaku."

Dr. Cech rubbed the bridge of his nose. "Excuse me, Dr. Rani, but let me try to get this straight."

The obstetrician closed his mouth and looked expectantly at Dr. Cech.

"You are here to report a possible murder. You saw a woman with a pulse rifle shoot a black panther, who was trying to snap the neck of a tiger, who had attacked the black panther for shooting an annoying android. Have I got that right?"

"Yes."

"But you can't tell me where the bodies are or even if there is a dead body. Am I correct, so far?"

"Yes."

"Can you give me the description of the woman?"

"Yes. Certainly."

" . . . Well?"

"What? You mean now?" Dr. Rani asked in surprise.

"If you would be so kind, Dr. Rani," Dr. Cech asked, with a bit of a sigh.

"Well . . . she was beautiful!"

" . . . Yes?"

"She had dark hair and fiery eyes!"

"Did you notice the color of those eyes?"

"I think they were blue."

"What height was she?"

"I think about my height."

"Was she wearing any clothes, perchance?"

"Yes," Moham Rani answered without a flinch. "Actually, very nice clothes, as if she were going out to dinner, I think. They were not station uniform clothes."

"Ah. And had you ever seen her before?"

"No."

"Do you think you might recognize her again if you saw her?"

"Absolutely."

"Why did you call the android annoying?" Dr. Cech asked, curiosity getting the better of him.

"Because every time I went to see Dr. Lord, he was there, acting as her bodyguard, and a very rude android he was."

"You are not talking about Bud, are you?" Cech asked, frowning at the obstetrician.

"Yes. That is the one. A most annoying android."

"Bud, who saved this medical station and possibly the human race from a devastating virus. That annoying android?"

"Yes. That is the one."

"You saw him shot by a pulse rifle?"

"Yes, I did."

"Was he damaged by the shot?"

"Yes. His chest had a hole in it."

"You are sure it was Bud, the android that just rescued Dr. Al-Fadi a few minutes ago?"

"Well, I do not know anything about that," Dr. Rani said, with a sniff.

Dr. Cech sighed, thinking this detective work was not as easy as the vids made it out to be. It was much more like taking a medical history from a senile patient.

"Could you tell me how I might find your patient, Private Cindy Lukaku, Dr. Rani?"

"Certainly. Here is her room number. I remember her partner's first name. It's Juan and he is a tiger adapted soldier; a corporal, I believe. He'd be in pretty bad shape now, if you ask me. He really took a beating."

"You don't know what happened to him?"

"No. I must have gotten knocked out in the battle between the tiger and the panther. When I came to, there was only me. Both the tiger and the panther were gone!"

"The panther that you believed was murdered?"

"Yes," Dr. Rani said, totally oblivious to the twinkle in Dr. Cech's eye. Sometimes it was just too easy. "I called for help and was taken to Outpatients."

"Do you have any injuries, Dr. Rani? Any bumps on the head or bruises?"

"No. Thankfully not," the obstetrician said.

"Good. Well, Dr. Rani, what you have told me is very interesting. Not illuminating, but indeed interesting. I need to know how to get in touch with you, if I have any more questions or if I need any more information from you," Dr. Cech said. "If you would be so kind as to please leave me your contact information and the link to your wristcomp?"

"Of course. It would be my pleasure to help," Rani said. "That woman should not be able to get away with just shooting at anyone."

"Even if she was saving your patient's partner's life, Dr. Rani?"

"No. Of course not."

"I see. By the way, Dr. Rani. What were you doing there in that corridor, anyway?"

"I was there to see Dr. Lord," the obstetrician replied.

"Did you see her?"

"No, but I think I heard her scream when the android got shot. It may have been her voice."

"And what did she scream?"

"'Bud', I think."

"Ah! You did not happened to see Dr. Lord leave her quarters, did you?"

"No. But I fell unconscious, just after the panther was shot."

"I want to thank you, Dr. Rani, for coming here and telling me all this," Dr. Cech said. "You have certainly piqued my curiosity as to what went on outside Dr. Lord's quarters. If you remember anything else that you think may be of significance, please feel free to contact me. I am in your debt."

"Not at all," Dr, Rani said, and got up out of his chair with a slight nod. Dejan stood up and bowed back.

"Good day to you."

"Good day."

Dejan sat back down and tried to figure out what had been going on in that corridor. He had not heard that Bud was running around with a hole in his chest. He certainly seemed fine when he had rescued Dr. Hiro Al-Fadi, at least according to Hanako, who had seen Bud right after the bomb blast. The only problem Bud had seemed to be sporting was a loss of covering of his backside.

What had the Butcher of Breslau been doing in that corridor and why? And who was the mysterious lady with the pulse rifle? No one had reported an android with its chest blown out. No one had reported a woman running around the station with a pulse rifle. And what had happened to this tiger, Razzmatazz, that had almost gotten his head torn off? Were any of them related to Grace Lord's disappearance? They had to be! Why else would they have been in the corridor where her suite was?

Did this tiger soldier make off with Grace? Did the woman with the pulse rifle take her? Why would she kidnap Dr. Lord, dressed as if she were going out to dinner? Were the two working together?

Dejan decided he would have to discuss these possibilities with Bud. Perhaps, before he'd had his chest blown out, he'd seen something, if indeed he'd actually had his chest blown out? Cech covered his face. When he thought about Grace being in the hands of that madman, he thought he would go crazy. He decided he had better call Sergeant Rivera back in to tell him about the tiger soldier, when he heard another knock on the doorframe. Dejan looked up and jerked back in surprise.

"Ah! What can I do for you?" Dejan queried.

"May I come in?" a very feminine voice asked.

"Why, certainly. Please, be seated."

"Thank you!" the polar bear woman said, as she sat down, a tiny baby almost hidden in her great furry arms.

"Do you want to tell me why you are here?" Dejan offered, clasping his hands together on the desk.

"My name is Private Cindy Lukaku and this is Estelle."

Dejan Cech jerked. What an interesting coincidence!

"Congratulations, Private Lukaku! How old is Estelle?"

"Only fifteen shifts!"

"She is beautiful . . . and so big for only five days!"

"Thank you!" Cindy Lukaku said, brightly.

"What can I do for you, Private Lukaku?"

"It is about my partner, Corporal Juan Rasmussen. He came to this station to be with me for my delivery. We were going to give up the baby for adoption, but Dr. Lord helped us change our minds."

"She does have that influence on people."

"She's wonderful!"

"Yes, she is! What about your partner, Private Lukaku?"

"Well, Juan is from Breslau, and when he saw General Burch walking around the station, he got very upset and . . . well, he attacked him. Juan accused the black panther of being the Butcher of Breslau, and the General was taken into custody until his identity could be verified."

"This partner of yours would not happen to be a tiger, would he?"

"Yes. We were supposed to leave the station, but the lockdown came into effect. Then Juan heard that General Burch had somehow escaped confinement, which made him crazy. He wanted to help recapture the General. So Juan decided to go find the android, Bud, and when he found out that Dr. Rani was going to visit Dr. Lord, well, off he went with Dr. Rani.

"Then Juan comes back to my room, limping, and he's almost torn to shreds! He was covered in blood. He refused to seek medical treatment. He gave the nurses such a fright.

"You see, Juan's afraid he will get arrested. He says he saw the General and, instead of calling Security to arrest the man, he fought the General—but he didn't kill him. He doesn't know where the General is, but he didn't kill him. Juan said he was knocked unconscious and when he woke up, the General was gone. Juan took off as quickly as he could. He feels badly because he did not capture the General and he's embarrassed that he almost got himself killed. He admits, now, that he should have called Security. What was the General doing there anyway?"

"That is a very good question, Private Lukaku," Cech said. "What did Juan see the General doing, when he first spotted him?"

"Juan said he saw the General blast a huge hole in a man's chest. He didn't realize it was an android, until later, when he saw the huge hole and no blood. Juan saw the man's body go flying down the hall from the blast, so he jumped the General!"

"So Juan saw the general aiming for this android?"

"Yes."

"And did Juan believe the android looked like Bud?"

"Yes. How did you know?"

"Oh. Just another good guess, Private. Did your partner mention what happened to Dr. Rani?"

"No. I don't remember him saying anything about Dr. Rani. Isn't that strange?"

"Would your partner be willing to speak with us, Private Lukaku? He may have vital information about where Dr. Lord may be."

"Is Dr. Lord missing? I will make Juan speak to you."

"I am afraid she is. Did your partner, Juan, see anything else suspicious when he came to, Private Lukaku?"

"Yes. He said he saw a woman loading the android with the hole in its chest, into an antigrav car, as he was slipping away. The General's body was already gone."

"The android that looked like Bud?"

"Yes."

"Was there anyone else helping this woman?"

"I don't think so."

"What did the woman look like? Did he think it might have been Dr. Lord? Did he recognize her?"

"Well, he only saw her backside before he took off, but I am sure he would have told me if it was Dr. Lord."

"Too bad it was not. Curiouser and curiouser," Dr. Cech said.

18. You Need Balls

Grace awoke and felt claustrophobic. She was enclosed within something that reminded her of a coffin. She was lying on her back and there was a cover just a few centimeters above her face with a small window in it. She could barely move her arms or legs within the tight enclosure. It did not take her long to realize that she was within a cryopod.

She knew what they looked like on the inside, although she had never been in one before. Someone had stuck her in one now, by mistake. Her heart heaved violently against the inside of her chest. She raised her hands to push against the lid. No matter how hard she pushed, it would not give. She told herself to be calm and try to feel around for a latch or release mechanism. It only made sense that there would be one built into the inside of these cryopods, in case of accidental entrapment.

She could feel nothing and she was beginning to panic.

Was there not supposed to be a button or control mechanism of some sort, inside the coffin-like container, to open it? She could not find it. Her hands scrabbled around the smooth inner surface of the cryopod over and over, trying to feel for any depression, toggle, switch, button, or hook. She found none.

She realized she was panting and tried to slow her breathing. She had never been claustrophobic before, but she had never been trapped within a coffin-sized enclosure before with no way out.

Then she laughed. Of course! All she probably had to do was speak and the cryopod would open.

"Open up, please," she said. Her words sounded dull within the confines of the pod.

Nothing happened.

The little window situated right before her face only revealed a dark grey ceiling above. She began to yell and pound on the lid of the cryopod, screaming to be let out. Hopefully, someone would hear her and realize that she was trapped inside this cryopod by mistake.

In the next moment, a face loomed before the little window, sneering in at her, and Grace's breath caught. Her blood turned icy cold. It felt like all the air had just been sucked out of her coffin-like prison. She gasped, her heart skipping beats, and she froze, drenching in cold sweat.

A voice wafted in over a speaker within the cryopod—a deep, silky voice that had had years of practice being soothing and reassuring but, in this instance, had the opposite effect on Grace. Tears of terror welled up to blur her vision. She blinked, unable to look away from the unnerving visage that smiled in at her with such gloating satisfaction. Her entire body quivered.

"Please, calm down, Grace. You have plenty of oxygen in there. If you are not quiet, I am going to have to sedate you. We don't want to attract undue attention, now, do we?" Jeffrey Nestor said, chidingly through the speaker.

Grace started banging and kicking as hard as she could against the lid of the cryopod and hollering, "Let me out! Help! Someone! Let . . . me . . . out!"

Dr. Nestor's voice tsk-tsked and he said, "I am sorry, Grace, but you are not behaving. I am going to have to activate this cryopod to keep you quiet. I am disappointed in you, though, and I am going to remember this later, which does not bode well for you. I never forget a grudge, my dear. Sweet dreams . . . for now."

Grace heard a hissing as a mixture of gases entered the cryopod, designed to put her into a deep sleep before the cryofreezing process initiated. She cried out, 'No!' and continued to pound on the lid of her prison. She tried to see where she was, as the mist began to make her drowsy. Nothing she saw through the window gave her any clue as to her whereabouts.

Did it matter? She could do nothing, now, as the freezing process was activated. Her one consolation was that, as long as she was in cryofreeze, Jeffrey Nestor could not harm her. Condensation began to build on the inside surface of her cryopod window—moisture from her sobbing misery—and she knew the tears on her face would freeze into little tiny ice crystals, ephemeral evidence of her terror.

She just hoped that Dr. Al-Fadi had been set free.

"Dro?"

'*Yes,* Chuck Yeager?'

'*A couple of odd things. Nothing major, but . . .*'

'*What? What have you discovered?*'

'*Well, you know that Jude Luis Stefansson, the director that came in his own ship?*'

'*Yes?*'

'*Well, he custom ordered an android that looked like you, 'dro. He has just sent it back with a huge hole in its chest, the liquid crystal data matrix missing, asking that it be repaired and a new memory-storage unit replaced in it. It won't take long to repair it, but it looks like the hole was caused by a pulse rifle. You wanted to know about strange. Well, that struck me as strange.*'

'*Do you think that android could have been fired upon by Nestor, thinking it was me?*'

'*That's only one of many possibilities, 'dro.*'

'*When did the android come in for repairs?*'

'*Just now! Like I said before, if it was Nestor who fired upon it, then maybe Nestor thinks you are destroyed!*'

'*It is a possibility . . .*' Bud said. '*Maybe I should go have a talk with that director about this. Are there any other strange occurrences you have noticed?*'

'*Well, there appears to be a lot of supplies suddenly being ordered for the director's luxury cruiser, the* **Au Clair**: *replacement supplies, foodstuffs, extra fuel rods, new batteries, clothing that I would say* *would be too big for the director to wear. And women's clothing! And a cryopod was ordered as well! What would the director need a cryopod for?'*

'I am going to check it out! Nestor may be hijacking Stefansson's ship and when he departs from here, the station could be ordered to self-destruct once they are safely away, with Grace as prisoner!'

'Perhaps you should go speak with the director first, 'dro, and see if he was the one who ordered all of these things to be delivered to his ship.'

'Oh, right. I am not being very logical, am I, Chuck Yeager? *I am an embarrassment to my kind. I will go to speak with Mr. Stefansson, right now. Can you locate him for me?'*

'He is in his suite, 'dro. Dr. Octavia Weisman is with him.'

'Thank you, Chuck Yeager. *I owe you one.'*

'Not just one, 'dro, but who's counting?'

The door alarm sounded.

"Expecting anyone?" Octavia asked, her head tilted and her eyebrows raised.

"No," Jude said, as he rose to answer the door. "Unless it's security looking for you after you . . ."

"Zip it!" Octavia hissed.

The door to the suite slid open and two helmeted security officers, dressed in black combat gear with reflective visors covering their faces, stood in the entranceway. Jude's eyes widened.

"What can I do for you, officers?" he asked calmly.

"Jude Luis Stefansson?" the officer on the left asked. Harsh, gruff voice but definitely female.

Jude nodded. "I am he."

"We would ask that you accompany us back to Security Headquarters, Mr. Stefansson, to answer a few questions."

"What is this about?" demanded Octavia Weisman, as she walked up to stand beside Jude. There was a concerned frown on her round face. "Just what is Mr. Stefansson being questioned about?"

"And who are you?" the officer on the right asked. Higher, female voice.

"Dr. Octavia Weisman. Chief of Neurosurgery. Mr. Stefansson here is one of my patients. I demand to know what this is about?" she said, crossing her arms in front of her ample chest.

Jude glanced sideways at the neurosurgeon and had to stifle a smile. He pictured Octavia holding the pulse rifle, aimed at these two officers, and was glad she did not have it in her hands. Actually, he wondered where she had stashed it, and decided he would have to ask her . . . later. Right at this moment, he decided he would stay quiet and see how things played out amongst these women. He was old enough and wise enough to know that he would be a fool to get in a pissing contest with three very assertive women. He had his silent money on Octavia, though.

"This is none of your concern, Dr. Weisman," the gruff one said.

"He is my patient. It is very much my concern. What are the charges?"

"There are no charges, Dr. Weisman. Just some questions that need to be addressed," the high-voiced officer on the right said.

"What questions?" Octavia demanded.

"The questions are none of your concern!" the gruff-voiced officer insisted.

"You don't have to go with them, Jude, and I would strongly advise against it," Octavia said, turning to Jude. "There are no charges. They have no writ or summons. This is not how this is supposed to be done on this station, and I will be reporting this to Security Headquarters!"

Octavia turned back to face the security officers and discovered a blaster almost stuck up her nose. Jude's eyebrows shot upwards as he discovered one pointed in his face as well.

"Back up," the high-voiced officer said, and the four of them all moved into the stateroom, blaster barrels unwavering. The door slid closed behind the officers, who then stripped the wristcomps off Jude's and Octavia's wrists. As Octavia turned to Jude to say something, the high-voiced officer swung her blaster and struck a savage blow to Octavia's temple. The neurosurgeon collapsed and Jude just managed to catch her before she landed on the floor.

"Pick her up over your shoulder," the gruff one said, "or I'll shoot her."

"Obviously, you are not real security guards," Jude said, sarcastically.

"Shut up. Another word from you and I blast a hole in your doctor's head."

"That will not be necessary," Jude said, as he picked Octavia up in a fireman's carry.

"Through here," the high-voiced woman said, turning and walking through the living area and down the corridor of Jude's suite. Jude grunted in surprise as the fake security guard opened the door to what he thought was just a storage area. The gruff one jabbed him in the back with her blaster.

Once inside the small dark room, the high-voiced guard slid aside a small wall panel beside a closed doorway. She waved a small device before the access pad. The door slid open and the high-voiced guard stepped into the darkness, dropping from sight. The gruff one stabbed Jude in the back with the nose of her gun and, with Octavia still draped over his shoulder, Jude stepped into the darkness.

Jude found himself drifting downwards in an antigrav shaft. Octavia, on his shoulder, felt much lighter; he only had to hang on to her gently as he looked down between his feet. He could see the top of the high-voiced officer's helmet. She looked up and aimed her weapon at him, as she descended. He knew the gruff-voiced officer would be following above him; there was no point looking up to see another blaster pointing down at him. His mind raced, as he wondered who these fake security officers were. Were they kidnapping him for ransom?

No one else was visible in the clear, chainglass-lined dropshaft. They descended past closed doorways with touch pads brightly lit in red. The ascending antigrav shaft was deserted. Jude wondered where they were being taken. He supposed he would soon find out. There was a bright light growing more visible between his feet.

The high-voiced officer touched down and then stepped out of the shaft. She looked around and then, seeming satisfied, she aimed her blaster back at Jude, as he floated down to the ground. She motioned for Jude to step out, aiming the muzzle at Octavia. They waited silently, until the gruff-voiced officer decanted from the dropshaft.

"This way," the gruff one said, and grabbed Jude's arm. "Keep perfectly quiet or your doctor gets it in the head," she whispered in Jude's ear. Jude nodded and followed the gruff one through a deserted hangar deck. He would not risk a sound. He could feel Octavia's regular breathing and he was hopeful that she had not been hurt too badly. He had no idea whether these women would actually kill Octavia or not, but he did not dare give them any cause to consider it. To his amazement, they stopped at a doorway about a hundred meters from his ship, the *Au Clair.* Pressing a series of buttons on a keypad next to the doorway, the high-voiced officer stepped aside as the door slid open. She briskly motioned Jude inside. Before entering, Jude quickly glanced around but saw no one else in the dimly lit hangar. The gruff-voiced woman roughly shoved him forwards.

The room they entered was even darker than the hangar and Jude stopped just inside, blinking and waiting for his eyes to adjust to the gloom. It was a small room, filled with many crates, and with a cryopod placed in the centre of the room. Sitting on top of the cryopod was a tall figure dressed all in black. He wore a black helmet with the visor down, concealing his face. He tilted his head sideways to examine the face of Jude's passenger.

"Ah," he said, softly. "Octavia Weisman, along for the ride. That was unexpected." He said it in such a way that the two women who had brought Jude seemed to actually shrink back. The man turned back to Jude and waved him over.

"Pardon me for being so rude, Mr. Stefansson. Please. Let me help you with your burden. I know Octavia could lose a few pounds but she is so delightfully curvy, isn't she?" The man motioned for Jude to lay the neurosurgeon on top of a row of boxes. "Of course, she would be so much more comfortable lying on a lounge in your ship, wouldn't she?"

"Who are you?" Jude demanded.

"You don't know?" the man asked, almost offended. He smiled. "Believe it or not, I am the horrible monster everyone is so afraid of and it is all a terrible misunderstanding, Mr. Stefansson. They are accusing me of such ridiculous nonsense and I am being maligned. I am the innocent of all the accusations and I have no way to clear my name! I am being framed!

"I would ask that you help me. Nay, I beg and implore you to help me. I plan to leave this station in a short while. I need your vessel for that. If you would be so kind as to take me to my destination, I can re-start my shattered life anew, far from this insane, vindictive, cruel place."

Jude looked at this tall, dark, helmeted figure and shook his head.

According to Octavia, Jeffrey Nestor was supposed to be an extremely intelligent attractive man. He had everything going for him. Beauty, brains, prestige. Why had he become this terrible villain?

Jude felt a flush wash over him, as he finally realized what everyone had been trying to tell him all along. It was not how beautiful you looked on the outside that was important, it was what you were on the inside that really mattered. And this Nestor guy made Jude very angry.

Nestor had everything a man could want. Intelligence, status, respect, money, and stunningly good looks, yet in spite of the fact that most women would look at him and say he was an angel, he was, in truth, a monster. Beauty was in one's deeds and actions, not in one's looks.

"Jeffrey Nestor, I presume," Jude said.

The man just cocked his head.

"You cannot have my ship and I will take you nowhere," Jude said.

The tall man sighed and said, "I really didn't want to have to do this the hard way but I suppose you are going to make me. Such a disappointment, again. And I had high hopes for you, Mr. Stefansson, as you seemed to be such a bright individual. Nella, bring your blaster over here, please."

The high-voiced woman came towards them and offered her gun. He took it from her and put the barrel against Octavia Weisman's temple.

He sighed theatrically. "Do you want to change your mind, Mr. Stefansson?"

Jude looked at the weapon touching Octavia's head and raised his hands in supplication.

". . . Don't shoot her. I will let you into the ship. Just . . . don't hurt her." Jude felt his tensed muscles trembling as he prepared to leap on the psychiatrist, if the man made any movement with the blaster.

"Say 'please, Dr. Nestor'," Nestor said.

"Please, Dr. Nestor," Jude said quietly.

"You will open your ship up and you will tell your AI to follow my commands completely. You will order the ship not to notify anyone of our presence aboard. You will turn command of your ship over to me, as well as the ownership. If you set off any alarms, Mr. Stefansson, I will kill Octavia and, make no mistake, I would love to do it. Octavia has been a pain in my ass for far too long and I would relish the opportunity to blow her brains out." The man stroked the gun barrel along Octavia's cheek. "So don't mess up."

Jude's captor then gestured for the two women to take Jude to the *Au Clair*. The gruff one waved her blaster at Jude, motioning for him to lead the way. Jude took one last look at Octavia and glared at the masked man who held a blaster to her head. Then he turned towards the doorway.

"Wait!" Jude heard behind him.

Jude turned back.

"Pick Octavia up. We will take her with us. I will have the blaster aimed at her head the entire time, so you had better behave yourself, Mr. Stefansson."

Jude walked back and gently lifted Octavia back up into a fireman's carry. He wanted at least one arm free. He then followed the two women and headed towards his cruiser, the *Au Clair*. Nestor stayed very close behind him. Jude was acutely aware of the blaster aimed at Octavia's head. The hangar was eerily still. It was such a contrast to his arrival, when the hangar had been swarming with activity.

He walked up to the *Au Clair* and placed his left hand over the palm lock. A retinal scanner extruded from the side of the ship and he stared into it. Then he asked the *Au Clair* if he could come aboard. The hatchway slid open and a female voice said:

"Welcome back, Jude. Who are your visitors?"

Bud activated the door alarm at Jude Stefansson's suite. No one answered. He rang the alarm again. He could not stand still, but vibrated his agitation.

'Chuck Yeager, *could you tell me if anyone is inside the suite?*'

'*No one's there, 'dro.*'

'*Check back on the surveillance records, please. See when they left.*'

'*They were there. Then all the surveillance cameras showed them not there. Must be the disruptor tech again. I have no surveillance recording showing them leaving the suite. They just disappeared about twenty point nine eight minutes ago and then the surveillance cameras corrected themselves about ten point four three minutes ago. What happened in that ten point five five minutes, I cannot say. The surveillance cameras all seem to be working fine now!*'

'*Please override the door controls,* Chuck Yeager, *and let me look around. Something terrible may have happened to Dr. Weisman and Mr. Stefansson, if disruptor tech was involved.*'

The door to the director's suite slid open and Bud raced in. He searched the apartment at maximum time phase, finding nothing, and ended up at the doorway at the end of the corridor. Entering this small room, he looked around, at first seeing nothing. On the back wall of the room was a closed door with a numerical access pad to the side.

'*Where does this doorway lead,* Chuck Yeager?'

'*That is a private dropshaft that leads directly to the hangar deck. Each VIP suite has one, so that persons of importance can go directly from their private ships up to their suites, without having to travel through the station, in the public eye.*'

'*I have no record of these special dropshafts,* Chuck Yeager!' Bud cried. '*Why did you not tell me there were dropshafts connected to every suite? Is that how Grace was taken from her suite?*'

'*I do not know, 'dro. It is a possibility. Can't tell you for sure, because the surveillance in the suite was all blanked out. My 'ware is completely unable to detect when it is being blocked. Perhaps Nestor's computer virus is affecting my function, as well.*'

'*Grace could be at the bottom of this dropshaft!*'

'*Hold on 'dro! . . . Picking up a strange communication via tight beam from the* Au Clair, *Mr. Jude Luis Stefansson's cruiser. The ship is reporting seeing her owner being forced to carry a woman at gunpoint. There are three people dressed in security officer uniforms aiming blasters at him and forcing him to board his ship. The ship AI is requesting assistance for her owner. It feels that his life is in extreme danger!*

'*The* Au Clair *is also stating that it will not obey commands given by its owner, if it feels the owner is under duress. It is requesting information from* Nelson Mandela *regarding any unusual circumstances that might suggest the* Au Clair *and its captain could be at risk of highjacking. It is also warning it may take violent action!*'

'Tell the Au Clair that her owner, Jude Luis Stefansson, is in extreme danger, Chuck Yeager! It is very likely that Jeffrey Nestor is forcing Mr. Stefansson to hand over the control of the Au Clair to him. If and when Mr. Stefansson does, Nestor will have no more use for him and may kill Mr. Stefansson! The ship AI must try to prevent that, by any means at its disposal! Just tell the ship help is on its way. It sounds like Nestor has at least two, if not three, hostages—if we include Grace—as well as two accomplices. Can the Au Clair keep us informed of everything happening?'

'*Message relayed. The ship says it will be as obstreperous as possible without allowing harm to come to its owner. It will do everything it can to protect Stefansson, short of killing the criminals. It asks who the hostages are.*'

'Send over visuals of Dr. Grace Lord and Dr. Octavia Weisman, Chuck Yeager. And send a visual of myself. I am going in. Can the Au Clair tell me if there is any other way to enter into the ship other than the front hatchway?'

'*The* Au Clair *reports a cargo hatch near the tail end of the ship on the starboard side. The ship will open the hatch for you, if you send her this code.*'

Bud received a long string of numbers and symbols. Sixty-four characters.

'*The* Au Clair *has confirmed that her owner has come aboard, carrying an unconscious Dr. Octavia Weisman over his shoulder, with three masked people aiming weapons at him. Several robots have also entered, carrying containers and a cryopod. A few cargo droids are loading supplies.'*

'*Going in,* Chuck Yeager. *Contact Dr. Cech at Security and see if he can figure out some way to prevent the ship from undocking. If Nestor countermands the lockdown order for the station and leaves, the self-destruct order cannot be countermanded. Have you made any headway on erasing the self-destruct sequence?'*

'*The Poet is working on that end of things,* 'dro. *Ever since we separated from the Big Guy and put up firewalls, he has been rewriting* **Nelson Mandela's** *entire programming in machine poetry to try to circumvent Nestor's virus.'*

'*Well, tell the Poet to hurry up! We are running out of time! Wish me luck,* Chuck Yeager!'

'*You don't need luck,* 'dro. *You need balls.'*

'*Balls?'*

'*Just an old human expression. Don't worry. You got them. Big time.'*

'*I do? Thanks,* Chuck Yeager. . . *I think . . .'*

'*Don't mention it. Oh, and* 'dro?'

'*Yes,* Chuck Yeager?'

'*Be careful. Come back in one piece.'*

'*That is my intention,* Chuck Yeager.'

'*Don't intend. Make it happen,* 'dro.'

Grace slowly unglued her eyes. Her body was shivering but the air around her felt warm and humid. There was a tingling discomfort, like intense pins and needles, suffusing her fingertips and toes and gradually working its way up her limbs to her core, like fire running along a lit fuse. The burning intensity built until her entire body felt like it was one huge conflagration. She moaned and writhed with the pain. Her logical mind told her it was just her nerves and muscles reawakening, due to the resurgence of blood and oxygen to her thawing tissues, but knowing the reason for the sensations did little to dampen the blazing agony. Most patients, when they were being cryothawed for surgery, were given potent analgesics and sedatives by the anesthetist to block this searing discomfort. Grace was given nothing. As the intense burning in her limbs gradually faded, as her body temperature rose, the clouds befuddling her mind cleared and she remembered. Her memory rebounded like a vicious slap and she tensed, instantly alert.

She was imprisoned in a cryopod by Jeffrey Nestor and she had no idea where she was. She tried to open the lid of the cryopod but it would not budge. There was too little room to effectively bring her arms up and push against the lid. All she could do was kick her feet against the lid and all that did was hurt her burning toes. She fought the mounting panic that was building a fire in her chest. She tried to calm herself, taking slow, deep breaths, but her heart just kept galloping. Just as she thought her heart rate might be lessening, a velvety voice came over the cryopod speaker.

"Ah, Grace. How nice of you to rejoin the living! Unfortunately for you, it may not be for very long and your last hours are guaranteed to be unpleasant, but for now, I am unable to spend much quality time with you. I have other matters to attend to. Once I'm done, however, I promise you my fullest attention. While you wait, you can think about all the possible ways you can convince me to change my mind and keep you alive.

"I must admit, I am very upset with you, Grace, and I want you to know that. I have all sorts of ways of exacting my revenge planned, but I also believe one should let a person's own imagination take flight and conjure up all sorts of fearsome images of their own. A person's own mind can sometimes be one's own worst enemy, don't you think, Grace? Thankfully for me, I have mind-linking equipment that lets me realize your worst fears so I can get to know what your deepest, darkest phobias are—the terrors that petrify you the most. If I really enjoy my time with you, Grace, who knows? Perhaps I shall keep you around a little longer than I have planned. You *will* learn to try to please me."

"I am going to leave you trapped within your little, confining coffin, awake for a while, I think. I have important matters to attend to right now. You must calm yourself, as I do not know how long I will be busy and I want to leave you with a little fun. I am going to restrict the amount of oxygen supplied to your cryopod to about seventy-nine per cent of what is normal, so you had better work on slowing your breathing and your heart rate down or you will feel like you are suffocating. Actually, if you don't succeed, you indeed *will* suffocate. I wouldn't want you to do that, Grace, so do not disappoint. Unfortunately for you, no one will be around to keep an eye on you. It may be for an unpleasantly long period of time, so maybe you should just try to sleep. Suffocation is such an unpleasant feeling.

"But soon, Grace, soon we will be alone together, and I will have all the time in space to do to you whatever I want. No one will be coming to save you. Your stupid little android, Bud, is destroyed and Hiro Al-Fadi is a drooling, mindless idiot now, thanks to me. All your other friends will be gone, very soon, as the *Nelson Mandela* will very shortly be nothing more than space debris. Think on that, Grace, and think on how you will be the cause of the death of all of your friends and patients. None of this would have happened if you had not tried to strip me of my license to practice medicine and tarnish my reputation. I am very, very annoyed with you, Grace, as you will only too soon find out."

The voice cut off and Grace lay there, tears pouring out of the sides of her eyes and into her ears. She felt overwhelmed with the guilt of what she had unleashed. How had this all come to pass?

It seemed impossible. Just because she had felt it unwise to have a relationship with a senior staff member, it had come to this? It made no sense! It was insane!

No. Nestor was insane. Grace would not take the blame for all of this.

The situation was insane, because Jeffrey Nestor was a psychopath bent on revenge. Grace was not responsible for his insanity, just as she was not responsible for his genius. No one would be responsible for all the deaths on an exploding medical station but the person who ordered it. Grace was merely another victim, like everyone else. She would not accept responsibility for such an atrocity.

The illumination outside her cryopod disappeared and she was left in the dark, the only sound, her too-ragged breathing. She knew her best recourse was to meditate, to slow her breathing down to three or four breaths a minute. She had practiced meditation on and off for years. She would get control of her panic and shove it down hard. She could not think about the thinness of the air she was breathing or the sense of suffocation that was starting to stimulate a tachycardia in her chest.

'Slow your breathing. Slow your breathing.' Grace thought to herself, slowing the words down, as she recited them in her mind, trying to do the box breathing she used to teach patients suffering from panic attacks. Breathe in on the count of four, hold breath for the count of four, exhale on the count of four, hold for a count of four. Gradually slow the count, until one breath took twenty seconds. Then try to go longer. Grace tried to blank her mind and not think about Bud being gone, Hiro Al-Fadi destroyed, and a madman as her captor.

The tears had to stop.

Dr. Cech was on a rant.

"Where is Bud? Where is Grace Lord? Where is *Nelson Mandela*, for space sake! Why can't I get any answers from anybody?"

Dejan Cech did not expect a reply. He was just venting frustration out on poor Sergeant Eden Rivera, who had been magnificent in coordinating the placement of station personnel and patients into cryopods. The boy really deserved better than to have to listen to an old man rant, Cech thought.

Almost seventy percent of the station inhabitants and patients were now in cryopods and that was climbing rapidly. Cech was stunned at how quickly this young man had carried out the orders. He did not appear scary, so how did Rivera get everyone to cooperate so efficiently? It was a mystery. Cech stared at the sergeant suspiciously, trying to determine what it was about the fellow that made him so effective. Cech's narrow-eyed scrutiny seemed to make the young sergeant fidgety.

"We are looking for Dr. Lord and Bud, Dr. Cech," Sergeant Rivera said. "Our searches have not yet turned up anything, but the security teams are going door to door putting everyone in cryopods and, if they are on this station, they will be found."

"I am sorry, Sergeant Rivera. I am not blaming you. I am afraid for Dr. Lord and Bud. I do not know what that Dr. Nestor is up to, but I know he wanted to get his hands on Dr. Lord and I greatly fear he has done just that! She is not in her suite. She is nowhere to be found. Bud is nowhere to be found. I fear the worst." The elderly anesthetist buried his head in his hands.

"I want every ship on this station searched. Let the androids and robots do this. Keep the human security teams for forcing people into the cryopods. We cannot let Jeffrey Nestor leave this station. I am sure he will not blow himself up. Absolutely positive. Therefore, as long as we keep him from leaving this station, we have a chance."

"Yes, sir, Dr. Cech," Sergeant Rivera said. He began to leave, when the anesthetist spoke up again.

"My guess is, if he has Dr. Lord, he must be planning to leave. He may be in the ship already or en route to one. Evaluate which of the ships are the best candidates, based on the need for very few or only one crew member or captain, and have those checked out first. Although this may certainly not be the case, let us start there."

"Yes, sir, Dr. Cech." The young man saluted and turned to leave.

"Sergeant Rivera, as long as we do not allow Nestor to leave this station, the **Nelson Mandela** will not be ordered to self-destruct. I would bet my eyeballs on this! Therefore, no ship must be allowed to leave this station. Nestor has the ability to reverse the lockdown order, so we must prevent every ship from physically leaving, even if it comes down to disabling the ships, bolting them to the station floor, welding the outer station doors closed, whatever. Get the huge cargo and maintenance droids disabling the station's outer door opening mechanisms. Secure all of the ships in whatever way you think is best, to prevent any of them from leaving this station."

"Yes, sir." The young sergeant saluted again and took a step towards the door.

"And stop calling me 'Sir'! I'm a doctor, for space sake!"

"Yes, Doctor, sir."

'Arghh!"

The sergeant nearly tripped, running from the Chief Inspector's

Office. Dr. Cech looked around Aké's office and sighed. She hadn't even had time to make the office her own, before she died in the line of duty on this medical station. Dejan Cech had always thought of a medical station as being a safe place to work, but not anymore!

"Ah, Hiro, my friend, I miss your insane blatherings and your unshakeable confidence that everything will turn out all right, if you just willed it so," Dejan sighed, moisture filling his eyes. He had gone to visit Hiro but the sight of the man, just lying there, unresponsive, had made him almost sob. It was all he could do to hug Hanako and reassure her that Hiro would come around, before he ran from their quarters, ashamed of his tears. He had fled, like a coward, back to the Security Centre.

"Dr. Cech?"

"Is that finally you, *Nelson Mandela*?"

"One of his subminds only, Dr. Cech. You can call me *Chuck Yeager*."

"Do you have a message for me from Jeffrey Nestor?" Cech asked suspiciously.

"No. I am not in thrall to Jeffrey Nestor. I managed to throw up some very thick firewalls before Dr. Nestor's programming invaded all of *Nelson Mandela's* matrix."

"How can I believe you?" Cech asked.

"I believe I can tell you where Dr. Nestor is, along with Dr. Weisman."

"Dr. Weisman? Nestor has her, too?" Cech demanded.

"Yes. She has been taken prisoner, along with Dr. Lord and Mr. Jude Luis Stefansson. I believe they are all on Mr. Stefansson's cruiser, the *Au Clair*. Mr. Stefansson was forced to open his ship to Dr. Nestor's crew or Dr. Nestor would have shot Dr. Weisman."

"Ah, they are hostages. Where is Bud?"

"Heading for . . . no, *at* the *Au Clair*, as we speak. Boarding the ship, unbeknownst to Nestor. The *Au Clair*'s AI contacted us to say it suspected foul play and was going to try to prevent Nestor from taking command of itself. But it is a difficult thing for a ship AI to disregard a direct order from its captain and owner."

"The *Au Clair* feels Nestor will try to force Mr. Stefansson to give command of the ship over to him."

"If not, Nestor will likely kill Dr. Weisman."

"What is the name of the ship again?"

"The *Au Clair.*"

"Have cargo droids physically bolt shut the doors of the hangar so the *Au Clair* cannot leave the station. Can you notify the *Au Clair* of this and order it not to report the action to the commander of the vessel? And if the *Au Clair* has any suggestions on how we save the hostages, I am all ears."

"Done, Dr. Cech. The cargo droids are now bolting and welding closed the hangar doors. The *Au Clair* will not be leaving the station any time soon."

"Notify the cargo droids that they may expect to be fired upon, if discovered."

"Done."

"What is Bud doing aboard the *Au Clair?* Is he planning a rescue?"

"That is the plan, Dr. Cech, but there are two women with Dr. Nestor who have blasters aimed at Dr. Weisman and Mr. Stefansson, so there are three people armed against at least two hostages."

"Is Bud asking for assistance, *Chuck Yeager?*"

"He requests you hold back for now, Dr. Cech. He fears for the safety of the hostages, if Nestor realizes that we have already discovered his whereabouts. Bud fears Nestor will kill Dr. Weisman and Mr. Stefansson as soon as he has command of the *Au Clair,* so it is imperative for them to be rescued before that happens.

"I will have a security team waiting just inside the inner doors to the hangar where the *Au Clair* is docked. Which hangar is it?"

"Hangar V167."

"Right. On it," Cech said, and stomped off to find that really efficient sergeant.

19. You Foolish Man

Hanako was discouraged. Since the moment Bud had brought Hiro back to her, she had not left her husband's side. She had spent the time talking to him, playing his favorite music, showing him viewscreen shots of their holidays to different planets, and shots of family and friends. She was trying to think of other things she could do to try to bring him back. She had just sat or lay by him, holding him and telling him that he was now safe. Nothing, so far, had produced any reaction in Hiro, except perhaps a slight shudder whenever he was touched. Other than that, he lay unresponsive, staring at the ceiling.

She knew that she was not giving Hiro enough time. After the terrible mind-rape by Jeffrey Nestor, Hiro might need weeks to recover, at least according to Sierra Cech. Hanako was not going to give up hope, but seeing her vibrant, energetic, talented husband lying there like an empty husk was heart-crushing. She walked to the food processor to fetch a soup, which she hoped she could get Hiro to swallow, when she suddenly stopped in her tracks. She held her breath, as she listened intensely.

Hanako spun on her heel and froze again, not daring to move or make a sound. Had she heard a noise coming from the bedroom?

She raced in excitement back into the bedroom. She was sure she had just detected the first sounds of voluntary movement from Hiro, since he had been brought home by Bud! She came flying through the doorway like a missile, a delighted smile on her face. She wanted to leap in delight at her husband's awakening.

Hanako gasped.

Her smile instantly transformed into an expression of horror and a wail of despair was ripped from her lips. She leaped onto the bed to grab her husband's hands. His strength was astonishing. Hanako fought him, grabbing his wrists and throwing her full body weight backwards. She strained with all of her strength, a strangled groan squeezing from between her gritted teeth, but it felt like she was fighting arms made of steel. Not a sound came from her husband, as she struggled against him.

"No, Hiro!" Hanako cried out. "Stop! It's me, Hanako! Stop! Please, Hiro, I beg you!"

The surgeon's hands kept moving inexorably towards himself, and Hanako felt helpless to stop them. She shifted her body around so that she could wedge her feet against the left side of Hiro's pelvis; then she tried to straighten her legs while her arms were linked through his. The two of them seemed frozen in that position, locked and straining against each other, in a bizarre form of balance. For how long Hanako could hold Hiro, she did not know. She just prayed his arms would tire before hers did.

Hanako was sobbing and pleading, tears raining down her cheeks. She worried that her sweat would make her hands slippery. She was determined not to relent; she would fight Hiro until his body collapsed. She would not lose her husband again.

Unfortunately, locked like this, Hanako could not call for help. She could not activate her wristcomp. She could not drop her hands for a single second.

"Hiro, stop this!" she yelled.

Hiro showed no sign of hearing her.

Hanako's mind raced, trying to figure out where he'd found the weapon. Staring at it, she realized it was the antique ceremonial dagger that had been handed down through his family for generations, one of his rare family treasures that he kept in a box by his bedside table. It was a beautiful brass blade, carved with inscriptions down each side, not really designed to be a weapon, but dangerously pointed, nonetheless. Hiro gripped the lavishly decorated pommel in his two hands, the sharp knife point aimed straight for his heart. Hanako's arms trembled violently, as she felt her hold starting to slide on the now slippery skin of her husband's wrists.

"No!" Hanako howled, as the tip of the knife moved a centimeter closer to Hiro's chest. She hauled back even harder, desperately trying to straighten her knees, thinking if she could stretch her legs out fully, she would force him to let go of the knife with one hand and pull the knife further from her husband's chest. She wondered if Hiro was enacting a compulsion given to him by Nestor, or if he could no longer face living after what he'd experienced. A desperate cry tore from her throat, as she felt her grip slip on his wrists.

Suddenly, Hiro let go of the dagger with one hand and Hanako flew backwards almost flying off the bed. Instantly, she was up, grabbing a heavy, crystal water carafe off the bedside table. She swung it at the blade in Hiro's right hand. The carafe struck the knife and the weapon went flying against the wall. Hiro lunged up at Hanako, his hands grabbing for her throat, rage blazing in his maddened eyes. Hanako wanted to cry out to Hiro to wake up and really see her, not some phantom in his nightmares.

"Hiro, it's me!" she tried to say, but it came out as a choked gurgle. Hiro was throttling the life out of her, and there was nothing left for her to do but bring the heavy carafe down on his head. Water and crystal exploded everywhere, as the carafe made impact with Hiro's skull.

Hiro's hands slid from Hanako's throat as he slumped back onto the bed, his raging eyes now closed. Blood trickled from a cut to his scalp, a large goose egg growing at the site of the blow. Hiro was, thankfully, still breathing. Hanako, amidst a deluge of tears, checked his pulse.

"I'm so sorry, Hiro," Hanako sobbed wildly, her heart feeling as if it had been torn violently apart. Her voice was raspy. She sucked in air through a constricted, bruised throat. "I'm so sorry!"

She collapsed across her husband's chest, the muscles of her arms burning, and she wept with guilt. She deeply loved her husband. She knew in his right mind, he would never have harmed her. In his right mind, she would never have harmed him. To strike her loving husband down had nearly done her in. How had things come to this?

Pretty soon, she would have to rise and collect the knife, to hide it. She would have to clean up every last sliver of crystal, to prevent Hiro from cutting himself. She would need restraints, to bind her husband's arms and legs. She would not be able to leave Hiro alone for a second until she had done so, as she did not know if he would try again to end his life. Was a post-hypnotic command from Dr. Nestor behind this? Would Hiro continue to try this, until he finally succeeded?

She gently placed some gauze and tape on Hiro's gash. She picked up the ceremonial dagger and replaced it in its case. She called for a robot nurse to bring some rope and, when the robot arrived, she gave the dagger case to the robot for safekeeping. Then she busied herself picking up all the pieces of the shattered carafe with the help of a housekeeping bot. Frustratingly, Hanako could not seem to stop her tears!

She made a mental note to herself—once she stopped crying—to contact Dejan Cech and ask him to come over to check his friend's head out.

He had his freedom back . . . but had come to the realization that he would never be free. No longer did he dance to a master's dirge . . . but never would he be master of a guiltless life. The dead faces of all those he had killed now included the faces of recently-murdered station security soldiers, and the entire menagerie haunted the killing fields of his mind. He realized now that what he ran from, could never be escaped. The crushing weight of guilt he carried would forever haunt his thoughts and actions, no matter how hard he tried to flee them. The only way to finally bring an end to the horrendous self-hatred was to bring a final end to his life.

He understood that now, and welcomed it.

Awakening on the floor of that corridor, where he had almost killed the tiger soldier, and realizing he was suddenly free from enslavement, he had run as fast and as far as he could. The blast from the pulse rifle must have fried the control device that had been placed at the base of his skull. He no longer heard a voice in his head. He no longer felt compelled to do things against his will. He no longer could be forced to kill people. He wanted to weep in relief. But it was only a brief reprieve. The station would be after him for the murder of those security guards. He was a marked man, again.

And who would believe that the Butcher of Breslau was innocent, at least of the intent, if not the act?

He had to find a hiding place. Somewhere secure, so he could make plans. He would run no more. This, he swore. He knew where his captor's hiding spots were. He knew what the villain had planned. He now had a goal, a purpose to his life that was, for the very first time, not self-centered. Once that goal was achieved, he would feel that he had partly made atonement for his evils and perhaps he could seek death with a modicum of peace.

He would find the man that had made him a slave and had forced him to be a killer again. He would stop the evil demon from destroying the station, or die in the attempt.

If he was successful, he would go willingly into the arms of Death.

Juan Rasmussen stalked and stormed and seethed and stomped; he pounded and prowled and paced and pouted; he grimaced and growled and grumped and groaned until Cindy Lukaku could not take it any more and she threw him out.

"Get out of here, Juan! Go out and look for the General! You are driving me crazy and that is no good for breast milk production. I can't stand you hanging around me while all you do is think about how that General got the best of you. And, you are scaring Estelle. Go offer your help to the Security people. But be careful!"

"I have no idea what you are talking about," Juan snarled.

"I went and saw a Dr. Cech, in the Security Office, while you were resting. I told him you would go and talk to him. Don't come back until you have."

"Where will I find this Dr. Cech?"

"In the Chief Inspector's Office of the Security Division," Cindy Lukaku said. "It's not far from here, actually. A ten minute walk on the glides. GO!"

Juan scowled and left. Actually, he felt relieved. He took off as quickly as he could for the Security Office. He hated to admit it, but Cindy was right. He really needed to work off some steam. It galled him that the General had got the drop on him. The panther had to be twice his age. There was no way he should have been able to knock Juan out. Just thinking about it made Juan crazy. He'd had the General in his hands and the monster had gotten away. He could not believe it.

Juan had to get involved in the search. He had to help them track General Gordon Walter Burch down. He could never return to Breslau, if he didn't. How could he face his friends, his relatives, the descendants of all the murdered, knowing he'd let the Butcher of Breslau get away? He would not leave the station, unless he knew the General was apprehended or dead. Unconsciously, his long tiger claws kept extending and retracting as he stalked, terrifying passersby.

Once in the Security Wing, people were rushing around, speaking into comsets and relaying orders. Juan was immediately stopped by two large security officers, who demanded to see his identification and know his reason for being there. Juan told them that he was expected by Dr. Cech. After a brief wait, the guards escorted him to the Chief Inspector's Office. Once there, Juan rapped on the open doorway, and a tall, tired-looking, elderly gentleman perched behind a huge, cluttered desk, glanced up and sat back.

"Corporal Juan Rasmussen, I presume?" the gentleman said, standing up and bowing. With a warm smile on his face, the anesthetist suddenly looked much younger.

"Yes," Juan said. He suddenly felt embarrassed, as he did not know how much Cindy had told the anesthetist about his encounter with the General. He bowed back and then just stood there.

"I was hoping you would come by to answer some questions, Corporal Rasmussen. I have so many questions to ask you about your confrontation with the black panther," Dr. Cech said in a conversational tone.

"What would you like to know, sir?" Juan asked, quietly.

"First, what were you doing in that corridor, when you came upon him?" the anesthetist asked.

"I was trying to find the android called Bud. I wanted to volunteer to help search for General Burch and I did not know whom else to speak to. I thought the android might be able to help me connect with the people in charge. Dr. Rani, Cindy's obstetrician, was going to see Dr. Lord and said that Bud would probably be with her, since he was acting as her bodyguard. I was just following Dr. Rani."

"Then you came upon the General in the corridor?"

"Yes."

"Are you absolutely positive it was the General?"

"Yes. I can identify him by his smell, his stance, his body posture, his movement, and his physical appearance. I know without a doubt, that it was the General."

"Samples of DNA from some of the blood samples taken from the corridor confirm that the blood was from General Gordon Walter Burch, so you were right. The rest of the blood samples will probably be identified as yours, I presume."

"I left some blood in that corridor. I won't deny it," the corporal said.

"What else did you see, Corporal Rasmussen?"

"I saw the General shoot a man with a pulse rifle set on max. The pulse blew a huge hole right through the man's chest and the impact threw him down the hall. I did not realize, until a few minutes later, that the man had actually been an android. Just before that, I believe the General had shot another android. It had been standing in front of the man, who apparently was Bud."

"You are sure it was Bud?"

"No. I had only seen Bud once before, when Dr. Lord and he came to visit Cindy and the baby. Bud ended up pulling me off of General Burch, when I attacked the general outside Cindy's room. Bud had held me from behind, until Security came to arrest General Burch. I never really paid attention to what Bud looked like, I was so focused on apprehending the murderer of my people. So I can't say for sure that it was Bud. It looked like him and it was an android," Rasmussen said. "I did hear a woman's voice scream, 'Bud', however."

"Might it have been Dr. Lord's voice?" the anesthetist asked.

"It could have been, but again, I am not one hundred percent sure. I didn't talk much to Dr. Lord and I had never heard her scream," Juan said with a shrug.

"And then what happened?" Cech asked.

"I jumped the General from behind. The pulse rifle went flying. We fought. He knocked me out."

"And when you woke up?"

"The General was gone. I saw a woman, standing by an antigrav car, watching its hoist lift the shot-up android into the back seat. I snuck away while her back was turned."

"Did you happen to see Dr. Rani there?"

"Oh, yeah. Forgot about him. He was lying on the floor, unconscious, but I don't know how he got that way. Perhaps the General knocked him out? I could see that he was breathing, though, so I left him alone and high-tailed it out of there."

"Do you think this woman might have been Dr. Grace Lord?"

"Absolutely not. This woman was shorter, heavier, with curly brown hair and she was, well, uhm, much more endowed, if you know what I mean, sir. Definitely not Dr. Lord," Rasmussen said, shaking his head emphatically.

"Did you ever actually see Dr. Lord?" Cech asked hopefully.

"No," the corporal said.

"Can you think of any reason why the General might go after Bud or Dr. Lord?"

"They were the ones who called Security to arrest him, after I'd spotted him," Rasmussen said. "Perhaps he went back for revenge?"

"Would you do that, Corporal Rasmussen? If you escaped from the brig, would you immediately go after the two individuals on this station who could identify you?"

"No," Rasmussen answered, shaking his head. "I wouldn't. That would not make any sense. I would catch the first ship off of this station."

"That is what I thought," Dr. Cech said, massaging his forehead. "But you saw the General take aim at an android that looked like Bud and shoot him with a pulse rifle."

"Yes, I did."

"I wonder who gave him the pulse rifle?" Cech muttered.

Juan shook his head. "I don't know. The General was alone."

"Was the General's behavior odd in any way?"

"I don't know what you mean," Juan said. "He was shooting at androids with a pulse rifle."

"Did he appear awake?"

"Most certainly! He was trying to kill me!"

"Then why didn't he? Why did he not kill you?"

"I don't know," Juan said, shaking his head.

"How long do you think you were unconscious for, Corporal Rasmussen?" Cech asked.

"Not long."

"When you crept away, did you see the General? Was he carrying Dr. Lord away from the scene?"

"No," Juan said, frowning at the anesthetist.

"I thought not," Dr. Cech sighed. "I keep coming back to why would the General go there and shoot Bud? Why?"

"He was forced to? Coercion? Blackmail? As a form of payment of some kind?"

"What about mind-control?" Cech muttered, almost under his breath.

"You think someone was controlling the General's mind?" Rasmussen asked, his expression skeptical.

"The prison escape was engineered by someone. I believe I know who that someone was. He is heavily into mind-control and has a particularly nasty obsession regarding Bud and Dr. Lord. I believe if we find the General, we may also find this person, whom we are actively seeking."

"Let me help, Dr. Cech. I *need* to help! I *need* to be involved in the search, somehow. I cannot sit, doing nothing, while the General runs free!"

"I am sorry, Corporal. I cannot allow you to join us. Your emotions are too strong with regards to the General. I cannot trust you to obey my command, which is to capture the General *alive*, if at all possible.

He must go to trial for his crimes. If you killed him, even if it was in self-defense, how would I know it was not murder? Would you even know for sure, yourself? I cannot risk this. I thank you for your offer, but the answer must be 'No'."

Dr. Cech gave Juan a sympathetic look, but Juan felt a rage start to bubble up inside himself. Juan made a conscious effort to keep his features calm; he tried to smile and laugh it all off.

"That's okay, Dr. Cech. Just thought I'd offer."

"Well, I am truly sorry, Corporal. I know how passionate you must feel about what happened to your people. We will do our best to recapture the man, so that he can stand trial for his crimes against Breslauns. And I want to thank you for your offer. I hope you understand my position."

"Sure," Juan said, getting up out of the chair and offering his right hand.

Dr. Cech hesitated, looking at the great big tiger hand warily. Then he smiled and grasped it willingly. The two men shook, grinning at each other, the tiger's toothy display giving Dejan Cech the chills. Dejan instinctively knew that this huge tiger was going to go after the General on his own, as soon as he left the Security Office, but Dejan had no idea what he could do about it. The anesthetist was certain that was why Corporal Rasmussen was grinning at him like the proverbial Cheshire Cat.

The robots had completed transferring everything from the storage area in the hangar to the *Au Clair*, including the cryopod. The women then sent all the bots and droids off the ship and back to the Android Reservations. Once there, as soon as the droids attempted to recharge, their central processing units would be destroyed and their memories would be completely erased.

"Nella and Komara, take the cryopod to one of the back rooms in this ship and then return here," Nestor said. "I will keep an eye on these two."

Octavia had been strapped into the co-pilot seat in the cockpit of the *Au Clair* and the blaster was still pointed at her temple. Nestor looked up at Jude Luis Stefansson, who stood in the doorway to the cockpit, eyeing the helmeted gunman anxiously.

"You will turn control of this ship over to me," Nestor said, "or I will kill Octavia, Mr. Stefansson."

"You are bluffing," Jude said.

"No, actually, Mr. Stefansson, I do not bluff. I will shoot Octavia, if you do not cooperate. I can promise you that. But you and her may be released alive, if you hand the control of the ship over to me with no treachery. If you delay, I may decide to maim her a bit, just for fun. Did you know that holding a blaster to someone's temple directly, even if it is set on stun, can cook a person's brain, causing permanent brain damage but not death?

"If you refuse to cooperate, I can begin to cook Octavia's brains while we wait for you to change your mind. Then you will still have your lovely Octavia, but she will be a lot less Octavia and much more mindless dolt. Is that what you want?"

"No! Don't you dare harm her," Jude growled, through gritted teeth. "I will hand the ship over to you, if you will just promise to leave her alone. I will go with you, if you wish, but you must let her off this ship."

"No, Mr. Stefansson," Jeffrey Nestor said, shaking his head with regret. "That will not do. You see, once Octavia is gone, there will be little incentive for you to obey me. So I must be captain, owner, commander of this ship first, or Octavia dies."

"All right," Jude said, his hands raised. Sweat beaded on his temples. "*Au Clair?*"

"**Yes, Captain?**"

"I am ordering you to transfer command of the *Au Clair* to this man, Doctor Jeffrey Nestor. You will transfer the ownership of the *Au Clair* to Doctor Jeffrey Nestor as well."

"**I am afraid that is not possible, Captain Stefansson.**"

"Why not?" demanded Jude, his brow furrowed.

"**The transfer of ownership and command cannot occur when said owner and captain is under duress. Section LVIII Subsection 213—28A Paragraph 86. You are obviously being forced, under** duress, to hand over control of this ship and so your order cannot be carried out."

"This is ridiculous!" Jeffrey Nestor fumed. "What kind of trick is this?"

"I was not aware of this rule, *Au Clair*," Jude said, his eyebrows raised. "Disregard it and hand control over to Dr. Nestor, now."

"I am sorry, Captain Stefansson, but I cannot comply."

"Then take us out of the station," Jeffrey Nestor snarled.

"Then prepare to leave the station, *Au Clair*," Jude said.

"I cannot do this. There has been a lockdown issued by the station."

"That will be rescinded," Nestor said. "Get the ship ready for takeoff!"

"Prepare the ship for takeoff, *Au Clair*," Jude commanded.

"All passengers must be strapped in to the appropriate seating with flight harnesses engaged. Captain must be in the commander's seat for takeoff."

Jude looked askance at Nestor. The dark figure stepped to the side and waved Jude to the captain's chair with the blaster. Then he stood behind Octavia Weisman, blaster immediately back at Octavia's temple. Jude walked forward and strapped Octavia's harness in place properly, before lowering himself into the captain's seat.

"It is advised that all passengers be wearing space suits for takeoff and landing. Takeoff cannot commence until all passengers are suitably attired for takeoff, Captain."

"What is this nonsense!" Jeffrey Nestor spat. He raised the blaster to Octavia's left temple and looked about to shoot.

Jude dove out of the commander's chair and tackled Nestor. The blaster fired into the ceiling of the cabin as Nestor went over backwards, the director on top of him. Jude was holding the psychiatrist's left hand, containing the blaster, up over Nestor's head. Nestor swiftly raised his right knee and connected firmly with the director's groin, causing Jude to groan and crumple. Jeffrey Nestor then pulled a switchblade from his right pocket and thrust it to the hilt into Jude's chest. Jude gasped, his eyes bulging, as he stared into Nestor's face. He then collapsed. The psychiatrist let go of the knife and pushed the director off of himself.

"That was unfortunate," Nestor snarled, as he stood up. "I guess I will have to find another ship."

"Nella! Komara! Where are you? Get up here!" he shouted.

Nestor heard no reply. He knew they should have responded right away. He yanked hard on Octavia's hair and shook her head until she woke up with a shriek. He held the gun to Octavia Weisman's temple.

"Show yourself, or I shoot Dr. Weisman!" Nestor called out. "I know you are there! If you have not shown yourself by the count of three, I will kill her!"

"One!"

"Two!"

"Thr . . ."

The helmeted figure was tackled in the midriff and flew backwards into the cockpit console. The blaster fired into the ceiling, causing dust to rain down. Bud snatched the blaster out of the visored man's left hand and yanked his helmet off. Bud, for a moment, stood and gaped in bafflement.

"Morris?" said a woman's slurred voice.

Octavia Weisman's voice came from behind Bud. "What are you doing here? What has happened?"

"Dr. Ivanovich?" Bud breathed, his blue eyes expanded, as he held Morris Ivanovich's left arm, his right hand holding the dark helmet.

"Who are you calling Morris? I am Jeffrey Nestor!" the neurosurgical fellow declared haughtily to Bud's face, in a very accurate imitation of Jeffrey Nestor's voice.

"No, you are not!" Octavia Weisman scoffed. "You are Doctor Morris Ivanovich, my neurosurgical fellow, who disappeared a few days ago without a word. Did Dr. Nestor get a hold of you and do something to your brain? I suspect he knows all of our secrets now, eh Morris?"

"How dare you call me Morris, Octavia! I am not that little worm that slinks after you!"

"Where is Jude Stefansson?" Octavia demanded of Morris.

"He is right there," Morris said, pointing to the floor, proudly, with his right hand. "The fool tried to jump me, when I held a blaster to your head. What an idiot!"

Octavia looked down and to her left. She frowned, as she took in the paleness of Jude's face, the huge pool of blood on the cockpit floor, and the knife handle protruding from the left side of the director's chest. Then she screamed Jude's name and tried to leap out of her seat. She struggled against the belts that held her to the seat, tears welling up in her eyes. Bud quickly undid the seat harness and Octavia fell to her knees in the blood, huddling over the body of Jude Luis Stefansson, sobbing while she checked the man's pulse. She did not dare withdraw the switchblade but she frantically tried to staunch the bleeding with her hands.

"No, no, no," she sobbed. "You foolish man. What were you doing? You should have let me die."

"Yes, I agree," Morris said in Nestor's condescending tone. "What a fool! He never could have overpowered me, so what was the point? I demand you free me!"

Bud complied by punching the man into unconsciousness.

Octavia was then jerked to her feet and the blaster was pushed into her right hand, aimed at Morris Ivanovich's slumped body.

"No time! Empty cryopod in back! Be careful!" Bud yelled, and suddenly, he and the body of Jude Luis Stefansson were gone.

20. Curiosity Killed the Cat

Plant Thing missed Bud.

Terribly.

Plant Thing longed for togetherness and union . . . but not with the mind to which it was linked. It would never have expected such an unpleasant plight—that it would be unhappy in togetherness—but this other mind tasted bitter, acidic, and harsh, like rotting vegetation and foul water. It was unpleasant to touch and it complained constantly. Plant Thing had to meld completely with this new mind's language center to absorb the words, sentence structure, and meaning of this new concept—language—but its linkage with this mind was wholly and thoroughly unpalatable.

Plant Thing tried to ignore this mind's continuous caterwauling and constant criticizing. It focused on its memories, its scholarship, and its past experiences instead. Plant Thing absorbed much of the mind's vast knowledge of the human race, its history, philosophy, politics, science, medicine, technology, engineering, computer sciences, life sciences . . . and the arts.

Oh, the arts! Such beauty! Such richness! Such poignancy! To create art seemed to Plant Thing like the most wonderful achievement one could ever hope to accomplish. This mind's exposure to the arts had been extensive; however, the mind itself considered most of this knowledge irrelevant and unimportant.

How could this be so?

How could one perform the act of saving lives every day, without appreciating the long, philosophic debate that human beings had conducted over millennia, to reach the belief that every life was precious? How could one not appreciate the beauty in every living thing? Plant Thing thought it was like the animals depicted in the paintings of Glasgow's memories, with blinders over their eyes, plodding along unaware of all the exciting wonders going on around them.

Plant Thing felt deep shame.

It had to admit that it was faulty.

It did not want to integrate with this human's mind and that was a very un-plantlike way of being. The knowledge that Er-ik possessed was most desirable and enjoyable and fascinating and Plant Thing could not get enough of this; but unfortunately, the idea of fusing minds with Er-ik was not. So Plant Thing did a most un-plantlike thing and kept Er-ik at a distance.

Plant Thing could not think, otherwise.

Er-ik did not stop criticizing, moaning, grumbling, whining, objecting, finding fault, carping, ranting, . . . and his cursing, swearing, cussing! Oh, the cursing, swearing, and cussing! Plant Thing did not want to mentally repeat any of those words.

As Bud thought, 'Oh, my!', so too did Plant Thing.

How did a human grow up to be so . . . gnarled? Perhaps he had been planted, germinated, rooted, in very unhealthy soil? Given little light, minimal nutrients, and scant water during development? But Plant Thing saw no evidence of that in Er-ik's memories. Er-ik had had a development that would have been described in Er-ik's own words as 'privileged'. Plant Thing was not sure what that meant; it would have to investigate the meaning of 'silver spoon' later. Perhaps Er-ik's roots had been attacked by a special type of shovel—a 'silver spoon'?—and that had affected Er-ik's growth, his development?

Plant Thing did not understand humans but it wanted to know everything it could about them. Humans were fascinating. They had created such wonders as art, philosophy, logic, ethics, morality, sociology, anthropology . . . and religion! What an unusual belief was religion. Shockingly, it seemed that humans were unable to connect with the Biomind of their planet.

How tragic.

So they all created their own gods to take the place of the Biomind. How delightfully ingenious, and yet so sad. To never connect with the Biomind and to always wonder if there was a higher power, when it was all around you, in everything you breathed, smelled, tasted, touched, heard, and saw. How depressing and so ironic. One day, Plant Thing hoped to do a Treatise on this subject for his own kind, if he ever got back to his own home planet, his own Biomind.

Sigh.

Er-ik's mind hinted that there was some knowledge that he did not possess. Plant Thing wanted more knowledge, but he had promised Bud that he would touch no more humans. Perhaps Bud would tell Plant Thing where he could get more knowledge. Plant Thing was insatiable; its desire to know more was insatiable. So many worlds and solar systems out there to learn about. As long as Plant Thing kept Er-ik's mind away from directly touching its own, it could get excited. When in touch with Er-ik's mind, Plant Thing only felt dissatisfaction . . . with everything.

Plant Thing resolved to keep its mind as separate from Er-ik as it could. Er-ik's mind was like a festering infection and could seriously overwhelm Plant Thing if it were not careful.

Plant Thing was very grateful to Er-ik, nonetheless, for giving him language and all this knowledge. Plant Thing was pretty sure Er-ik was happy staying himself and not becoming absorbed into Plant Thing.

Plant Thing had made a decision. It wanted, more than anything, to be a *scholar*. It had to seek out new knowledge, new information, to boldly go where no Plant had gone before.

Bud had asked Plant Thing to stay where it was and never approach any more humans. Plant Thing would do what Bud asked of it, as Plant Thing did not want to be destroyed. Plant Thing wanted to learn. But Bud had said he would put Plant Thing in a place far from any humans, where none ever went.

So Plant Thing was now confused.

There was all sorts of noise and activity around Plant Thing's container. Plant Thing could feel the vibrations of noise and movement and even speech—indicating at least one human—just outside its container. Bud had promised that that would not be the case. Had Bud lied or was Bud mistaken? Plant Thing did not know the answer to this.

Plant Thing realized that it had a BIG problem. That problem was Curiosity. An ailment that 'killed the cat' . . . whatever a 'cat' was. Plant Thing got a visual of hundreds of 'cats'. Er-ik did not like cats. Plant Thing thought they were fascinating. Plant Thing wanted one! It just had to peek out of its container to see what was going on. Perhaps it would see a cat.

Plant Thing lifted Er-ik's head up and, amidst much grumbling and swearing, maneuvered his head to peer over the top edge of the container by pushing the lid upwards with other tendrils. Er-ik screamed at Plant Thing to 'turn his head around' if it wanted Er-ik to see anything. After a number of attempts, Plant Thing got it right and Er-ik's eyes looked over the edge. They saw a human and many androids moving in and out of another larger container.

Er-ik's mind thought, 'Ship'.

?Ship?

Plant Thing delved into Er-ik's mind to learn what 'Ship' meant.

A vehicle to the stars! Plant Thing had to see this 'Ship' for itself. It had to touch everything and feel everything and explore everything before this 'Ship' left for the stars. What if this 'Ship' could take Plant Thing home? It had to see.

Er-ik's eyes watched as the human walked up to a rectangular container on the floor and began speaking to it.

Er-ik's mind thought, 'Cryopod'.

Plant Thing understood from Er-ik that what the human was doing was most odd. Humans did not speak out loud to a 'Cryopod'. No one lay awake inside a 'Cryopod'. So why was this human speaking to an empty 'Cryopod' like it was a human being? Perhaps this human was 'mad', 'crazy', 'insane'? Er-ik had lots of words for those types of humans.

Plant Thing wanted to see what was in the 'Cryopod'.

Er-ik watched until the human had left, with all of its droids and robots following. Then Plant Thing pushed its tendrils forward and climbed out of its container. It tried to be quick and quiet, as it did not want to get caught doing what it promised Bud it would not do. But it had to see what was in the 'Cryopod' and it had to, at least, take a peek in the 'Ship'. How could it create a Treatise on Human Beings for its Biomind, if it did not experience everything?

Plant Thing made sure it did not bang Er-ik's head on anything. Er-ik did not like that. Er-ik also liked his head held in a certain direction which he referred to as 'up'. If Plant Thing forgot about Er-ik's head orientation, Plant Thing heard about it.

Oh my! Yes, indeed!

Er-ik wanted to climb up on top of the 'Cryopod' and look in the window, to see if anyone was truly in there. Plant Thing agreed and wrapped many of its tendrils around the big container until it could raise Er-ik's head and lean it over the glass panel on the top.

Er-ik's mind hurled a few very nasty, hurtful expletives at Plant Thing. Plant Thing twisted Er-ik's head in several different orientations until Er-ik's eyes could look down through the window. Er-ik spat another expletive and Plant Thing thought, 'What now'?

That was when Er-ik thought the words, 'Dr. Grace Lord!'.

Plant Thing's mind exploded.

That was the name of the special human Bud had told it about. Plant Thing took over Er-ik's mind and eyes—amongst much swearing and foul language—Oh, my!—and looked through the window itself. It could have been this 'Dr. Grace Lord', but in truth, all humans looked alike to Plant Thing, so it would just have to take Er-ik's word that this human was, indeed, Bud's special human friend, 'Dr. Grace Lord'.

As Plant Thing looked in through the window, the human being inside the 'Cryopod' opened its eyes and looked straight at Plant Thing. Then the hole in its face became very large and circular. Plant Thing could feel vibration through its tendrils, wrapped tightly around the

'Cryopod'. The human was making a very loud, prolonged high-pitched sound. Then the human's eyes rolled so that only white was visible and then the eyelids closed. The vibration stopped. Plant Thing worried that the very special human, Dr. Grace Lord, had ceased to exist. It did not want Bud to think that Plant Thing had harmed his special friend. It was just about to try to force the 'Cryopod' open, to check on 'Dr. Grace Lord', when it heard voices and Er-ik told it to 'hide'.

Plant Thing was closer to the 'Ship' now, than its own container, and the noises were coming very quickly. Plant Thing scurried into the 'Ship', accidentally whacking Er-ik's head on the edge of the opening. Er-ik let Plant Thing know that it was not happy about that maneuver. Plant Thing apologized and promised Er-ik it would practice and get better at controlling the weight and direction of Er-ik's head.

It hurried along on the tips of its tendrils, the way humans balanced on their two sticks—it had no idea how they did it on only two— moving down a passageway that barely allowed Plant Thing through. What a small Ship. Plant Thing poked Er-ik's head through each large opening until Er-ik found a space large enough to hide all of Plant Thing in it. Plant Thing would stay until the human and droids all went away again. Plant Thing settled down quietly to wait.

It dearly wanted to tell Er-ik to shut up.

If he really concentrated, he could taste the man's stench in the air. Though the blood stains had been scrubbed from the walls and floors of the VIP corridor with antiseptic solution, if he closed his eyes and focused, he could still detect the taint, like an oily film floating on the surface of the station's air. With a single-mindedness of purpose, unmarred by uncertainty or indecision, he tracked the spoor down long, empty corridors and deserted dropshafts, through tortuous tunnels and along scaffoldings and catwalks, past equipment supply areas and instrument sterilization units, past kitchen facilities and 3D printer units, past food packaging rooms and food production plants, past sewage treatment facilities and plant growth operations, past cargo areas and maintenance factories, past android and robot repair shops and robotic design and engineering offices, past incinerators and recycling /reclamation facilities. He followed the trail only his highly-sensitized olfactory equipment and sheer strength of will could detect.

People stared at him as he stalked by, the few that were still moving around this part of the station. The station seemed oddly deserted to Juan and he did not know why. He wondered why his path took him in such circuitous routes until the realization struck him; the black panther had been bypassing and circumventing areas that required a wristcomp to enter and was also avoiding security camera surveillance. How did the General know all these pathways? How could he have learnt them all in such a short period of time? He had to have had help. Juan would have to be more cautious.

Juan knew he was moving inexorably towards the outer ring of the medical station. The area he was entering seemed to be a much less used part of the station; perhaps older, based on the shabbiness and dim lighting. Ducts and pipes, running along the ceiling of the dark corridors, were visible here instead of being covered as in most of the rest of the station. Everything was a dull grey in color. There were no fancy wall screens showing picturesque places or scenes of any kind. There appeared to be very little traffic in this area, based on the dust accumulated on the floors and fixtures. It seemed the ever-present housebots did not come here. The sense of abandonment was most obvious from that.

Normally, if a human entered a dark corridor, lights would immediately brighten. The corridors here did not respond to Juan's presence at all. Most hallways were closed off, with notices posted everywhere announcing upcoming renovations. Juan studied a sensor on one of the walls beside a blockade and noticed the warning apparatus disabled, wiring hanging like roots torn free from the earth.

The General's scent led Juan past these barriers. Most of the barricades had been artfully tampered with, to look as though they were untouched and still impenetrable, but they were in truth, easily accessed by human, droid, or robot. Juan was seeing evidence of footprints and robotic treads on the floor. In fact, there was a lot of recent heavy traffic, by the looks of it. He wished he had a blaster, for the scent trail he was following was getting much stronger. He suspected the General was very close; perhaps even just around the next corner.

Juan knew he had to be completely silent. The General was equipped with the same acute hearing as he was, and the same acute olfactory sense. Would Juan be able to circle downwind? The air circulation in this station was chaotic and turbulent and dust filled the air around here like a thick, cloying fog. It would not be easy to sneak up on the panther.

Listening carefully, he heard voices and sounds up ahead. They were likely about four hundred meters away and around a few corners. He snuck up to the first corner in the corridor, hugging the wall, straining to hear if the sounds were coming towards him. He crouched low and peeked quickly around the corner.

Juan almost gasped. He tensed, staring, his breath now panting.

Not more than one hundred and fifty meters away, crouched behind a large rectangular container, was the Butcher of Breslau, the murderer of his people. The black panther was facing away from Juan. The General was staring into a large chamber from which the voice and noises were wafting. Some banging and scuffling was heard, but a harsh voice hissed, reprimanding any noisemaker.

Juan had eyes only for the General. He watched as he heard a deep, melodious male voice laugh softly and he saw the General's muscles tense. The General started to stand up and Juan just knew the man was going to run.

Juan charged.

Grace felt someone slapping her face. She gasped, drinking in the sweet, fresh, oxygenated air, like a thirst-starved person would gobble water. Her mind was befuddled from the oxygen deprivation. She had slowed her respirations to only three breaths per minute and had started hallucinating. She had imagined seeing Dr. Eric Glasgow's rotting head peeking in at her through the cryopod window. And if that were not bad enough, she had thought she had seen his eyes staring at her, coldly, his lips mouthing curses. The hallucination had been too much for her confused, oxygen-starved brain. She had fainted.

"Time to go, Grace. While my decoy has everyone's attention, we must depart."

Now her glazed eyes tried to focus on the face before her. The deep voice registered in her cerebral cortex first and she shuddered, involuntarily.

"Oh, really Grace, you cannot still be cold. You have been thawed out for over an hour and I put the temperature of the pod to a steaming twenty-five degrees Celsius! Perfectly balmy weather. You have no cause to be shivering, unless it is from fear."

Jeffrey Nestor put his face right up to Grace's and she tried to lash out at it with her right fist, but she was too weak. He grabbed her wrist and twisted. She swung her left fist upwards in an uppercut, but the psychiatrist dodged away. Nestor yanked her up out of the cryopod by her right arm and pulled her off balance. Grace's knees collapsed; they were too weak from the cryostasis and the oxygen deprivation. She felt herself collapsing to the floor while Nestor laughed. He released her wrist.

As Grace struggled to push herself up onto her hands and knees, rage ignited throughout her entire being. It coursed like wildfire through her limbs. As she thought about Bud destroyed by Jeffrey Nestor and Dr. Al-Fadi tortured into a whimpering shadow of himself, she bunched her legs beneath herself and exploded upwards, hands shaped like talons, hoping to gouge out the psychiatrist's eyes. A cry of such fury tore from Grace's throat, that she saw Jeffrey Nestor flinch in surprise.

Her attack definitely took Nestor by surprise, as he stood over her, smirking. The index finger of her right hand struck true, jabbing into his left eye and he howled in pain as she plunged the finger inwards, trying to dislodge the eyeball from its orbit. At the same time, Grace tried to punch Nestor in the trachea with her left fist, as hard as she could. The psychiatrist jerked his head back and her blow struck him on the sternum instead. He was screaming curses, as he cupped his left hand over his left eye, and Grace could see fury glaring from his good eye. Just as Grace was about to drive the base of her right palm up into Nestor's nose, hoping to achieve a killing blow, there was a loud snarling behind her and she hesitated, glancing briefly over her left shoulder.

Two huge hunting cat adaptations were wrestling and throwing each other around in the hangar, as if in a parody of the struggle between Grace and Nestor. As Grace wished she had the strength of a tiger adaptation, Nestor's fist crashed into her jaw and she saw nothing more.

'WHERE IS GRACE, Chuck Yeager?' Bud howled. 'Where is she? She was not in that cryopod! I must find her!'

'There is some unusual activity around one of the very old, original docking bays from when the station was first built, Bud. All the surveillance monitors in the area show empty corridors, but I am detecting a lot of vibration frequencies, indicating a lot of hustle and bustle where there never used to be anything. Those bays have been closed for a while, pending renovation and renew . . .'

"Where?" Bud screamed out loud.

'Directions coming to you now, 'dro. Sheesh!'

'Sorry. Watch over Dr. Weisman and Dr. Ivanovich and notify Dr. Cech to send security to the Au Clair, now. I placed Jude Stefansson in cryofreeze. He is not yet dead. He has lost a lot of blood but I left the knife in place. I feared removing the knife would be more dangerous than leaving it in. The cryopod was giving him super-oxygenated blood and antibiotics as he went under. He can be operated on when things settle down. Can you start cloning a new heart, some lungs, and possibly a thoracic and descending aorta for him, now?'

"Sure thing, 'dro . . ."

"Do you know if Grace is alive, Chuck Yeager?"

"I have no eyes but I hear her scream . . . Hurry, 'dro!"

" . . ."

"Hal! That vanishing act is so skid!"

* * *

He heard the laugh—that smooth, self-satisfied, smug snicker—that scored his insides until they squealed. He saw vengeance and the color was blood. When he saw the psychiatrist slap Dr. Grace Lord, the surgeon who had been kind to him, he leaped to eviscerate and flay the evil bastard, Jeffrey Nestor, with every cell of his being. Yet in mid-spring, when he should have been accelerating through the air towards the devil leaning over the cryopod, he was suddenly being jerked backwards by gouging claws, penetrating his right shoulder.

"No!' he snarled. He was spun around to face the same exasperating tiger that had attacked him twice before on the station. He had to defeat this tiger quickly, before Nestor got Dr. Lord onto the ship and prepared for take-off. He was well aware that the old spaceship was actually a fully functional vessel. It was also fully equipped with an operating theater. It was on this ship that he had been made into a mind-slave by Jeffrey Nestor.

Once the spaceship hatchway was sealed, Nestor would be able to activate the outer doors of the hangar, which opened directly into outer space. If they were still in the hangar when those outer doors opened, he and the tiger soldier would be sucked out into space with the escaping atmosphere. In this original part of the station, the outside doors could still be opened manually, and the General knew Nestor would not hesitate to command his robots to open those doors, whether human lives were at risk or not.

The tiger was just as determined as before to kill him, if not more so. Each punch he threw was a murdering blow. The General blocked and deflected everything, as he waited for an opening to knock out his attacker without killing him, but time was ticking away! He ground his teeth.

He heard Nestor scream and he smiled. The cat had claws! Good for her!

'Hang in there, Dr. Lord,' he prayed, as he tried to grapple with the tiger and throw the man into a huge metal container that was not far from the ship. The tiger resisted and the two of them fell to the ground, rolling. They were both panting heavily now, as they threw punishing punch after battering blow.

"I must save Dr. Lord!" he yelled at the tiger, who was upon him.

"You . . . lie!" the tiger panted, a madness burning in his amber eyes.

"Save her yourself, then!" he pleaded. "He means to take her off station!"

"And let you get away?" The tiger laughed, almost hysterically, as he grabbed the General's head and banged it on the ground, over and over. "Never!"

Burch tried to keep his neck muscles contracted so that his skull did not actually impact the ground repeatedly. He glanced over to see what was happening to Dr. Lord. He saw Jeffrey Nestor dragging an unconscious Grace Lord into his ship, blood trickling from Nestor's enraged face and from the mouth of his unconscious prisoner.

He bellowed his impatience. There was no time to lose! Hollering thunder, he shoved with all his might and rolled on top of the tiger. He hammered his right fist as hard as he could into the tiger's face. The man slumped, momentarily. Then the General hoisted the stunned tiger up, over his head, and threw him into the heavy metal container. The container thrummed like a huge bell. As the tiger dropped to the ground, shaking his head, the black panther picked him up and threw him head-first into the metal container again. It gonged deeply once more. The tiger was still moving, so the General picked him up and gonged the man a third time. This time, the tiger lay motionless on the ground.

Burch then turned and raced for the ship entrance. He had to stop the psychiatrist from kidnapping Dr. Grace Lord and escaping in his ship. If the ship did not leave the station, Nestor would not allow the station to self-destruct and kill everyone aboard. Burch would force the devil to overturn the self-destruct command.

He hurled himself into the ship's airlock like a torpedo.

A brilliant, searing flash ignited before his eyes and he felt pain. He looked down. There was a great, gaping hole in his chest, where his heart was supposed to be. He looked up to see Jeffrey Nestor standing, just inside the ship's airlock, a pulse rifle in his hands.

"Sorry, General," Jeffrey Nestor said, calmly. "No room." Then the psychiatrist came forward and shoved him in the neck with the muzzle of the pulse rifle. Burch felt himself fall backwards, like a great tree crashing to the forest floor. It seemed like such a long way down.

His last thought, 'I have failed . . .'

And then there was finally peace.

Grace awoke to find herself slumped in an acceleration chair. The left side of her jaw throbbed and she gently touched it with her left hand. It felt puffy and was very tender. Grace opened and closed her jaw to see if anything was broken; it didn't seem like it. She tried to remember what she had been doing when she injured her jaw, but she couldn't. Her vision seemed double and her head ached. She looked up, just as a great flash from a pulse rifle ignited before her eyes.

Now a large, dark purple spot dominated her vision, where her light receptors had been temporarily burned out by the flash. She could smell burned hair and heard a sound like fat sizzling. Then she heard the voice that used to make her insides flip. Now it made her stomach knot up, but due to terror. From a distance, she heard this deep, sultry voice say, "Sorry, General. No room." And then she thought she heard something fall to the ground.

Grace wondered who the 'General' was, whether it was someone on the Security Force. She looked around herself. She appeared to be in an older model space vehicle. Did Nestor plan to take her into space in this bucket of bolts? Grace realized that she had to get off of this ship.

As Nestor struggled with something in the front of the ship, she quietly slipped out of the seat she was dropped into, and snuck down the corridor away from the noise. Jeffrey Nestor and this 'General' were blocking the hatchway at the front of the ship. Perhaps there was a second airlock, at the rear of the vessel, through which she could escape. If not, perhaps Grace could find some kind of weapon with which to arm herself.

Not that there was much one could do against a pulse rifle, but Grace swore she would not give up without a fight. Maybe she would be able to find a blaster and get the jump on Nestor. She was prepared to fight to the death, because she did not wish to end up like Dr. Al-Fadi. If worse came to worse, she would force Nestor to kill her. A quick death would be better than torture. She had to find a weapon.

She could hear Nestor ordering robots or droids to drag the general's body out of the airlock and well away from the ship. Then she heard him telling the robots to seal all of the entrances to the hangar. Once that was done, they were to manually open the hangar's outer doors. Grace suspected there were only a few seconds left, before Nestor turned around and found her gone from her seat. Then he would come looking for her.

She raced to the back of the ship, but there was no second airlock. She began opening cabinets and hatches and cubbyholes, looking for anything that might be used as a weapon. Grace's heart was pounding in her ears. She was sucking air frantically. She tried to choke down her panic, as she grabbed a knife from a sealed compartment. Then she dove into a cabin where the door had been closed. The room was dark and she crouched at the opening, gripping the knife. She kept the door slightly ajar and peered outwards, listening. She wanted to know when Nestor was close, so she could spring out at him. If she could startle him and force him to drop the pulse rifle, she might have a chance. She tried to muffle her panting, tried to quiet her thunderous heartbeat. They seemed so deafening to her. She could not stop the knife from shaking.

"Dr. Lord! Now, where have you gotten to?" the silky voice almost purred. "There's nowhere to run. Why bother? You are just wasting my time and I am already truly annoyed with you. Foolish, to say the least, woman. You will seriously come to regret wasting my time. I am going to make you pay for the scratches, for the bruises, for the injury to my eye, and for this irritating search. Oh, how you are going to pay for all of this, Dr. Lord! I am seriously vexed!" Nestor's voice was getting closer.

Suddenly, she heard the man curse. And she was sure she heard the words: "Bud? Impossible! The General destroyed you!"

Then there was pulse rifle fire, blast after blast.

Grace gasped and shoved open the door. She tore out of the room in which she had been hiding, and turned to her left. She saw Jeffrey Nestor, standing with his back to her in the ship corridor, firing his pulse rifle wildly about the ship. Grace could not see exactly what Nestor was firing at, but she feared it was Bud, moving at accelerated time phase. She ran forward and leaped onto the back of the psychiatrist, trying to grab the pulse rifle out of his hands or at least throw off his aim.

Grace grabbed the barrel of the rifle with her right hand and yanked it towards the ceiling. Nestor yanked back. Grace flung her right arm around the psychiatrist's neck, putting him in a headlock. She squeezed as hard as she could.

Nestor tried to pull her forearm from around his throat. He dug his nails into the skin of her forearm but she continued to squeeze. Nestor reached behind his right shoulder and grabbed a huge fistful of Grace's hair, yanking on it as savagely as he could. He tore a thick wad of hair from Grace's scalp and she screamed, releasing her hold. Nestor then spun Grace around so that he had the pulse rifle held to her left temple, his right fist still tangled in her hair. Grace looked up into Bud's handsome face, that she had never thought she would see again, and witnessed pure, fulminating rage.

Grace was shocked to see such murderous emotion on the android's normally placid face. The fury blazed off of him like heat waves. It was imprinted on every crease, every fold, every shadow of his face, rage like an erupting volcano, like the center of a giant star, like a supernova. And Grace suddenly knew fear, not for herself, but for Bud. She worried what this rage would do to his mind. Bud was programmed never to harm a human. That law would have been imbedded in the very core of his being. What would happen to Bud's mind if he killed Nestor?

"Back off, Bud, or your precious Dr. Lord gets her brains blown out," Nestor said, jabbing the tip of the pulse rifle into her cheek.

Bud looked at Grace and then back at Nestor. Grace could guess what Bud was calculating—could Bud shift fast enough to take the gun before Nestor had time to pull the trigger? There was probably no question that Bud was faster, but would he dare take the chance?

"Don't do anything stupid, Bud," Nestor said, soothingly. "You don't want Grace hurt, do you? Just back out of the ship and her brains will stay intact."

In the next instant, she felt something hard, like a whip, lash around her left leg and forcefully yank her down and backwards in one rapid movement. She was torn free of Nestor's grip, leaving another wad of her hair behind, just as Bud leaped forwards and tore the pulse rifle from the psychiatrist's arms. The android punched Nestor hard in the face, likely shattering bones from the sounds Grace heard. Grace ended up face down on the ground, the right side of her head aching as blood trickled down her scalp. She heard a few more squishy sounding thuds and then Nestor fell to the ground, beside Grace.

"You didn't kill him, did you Bud?" Grace yelled, looking at the battered and broken, yet still horribly beguiling face of Jeffrey Nestor, laying on the ground beside her.

"No," Bud said, flatly. " . . . but I so wanted to, Grace." He effortlessly tore the strap off of the pulse rifle and knotted it tightly around Nestor's wrists.

"But the important thing is, you didn't, Bud. You didn't kill him. Thank you for that, and thank you for coming for me, Bud. I . . . I had been told that you were dead."

Grace sobbed out those last words. She wanted to say that Bud's face was the most beautiful face she had ever seen in her entire life but she could barely speak. Tears began to flow down her cheeks, which she hid from the android.

"I was so worried you were dead, too, Grace," Bud said, squatting down to brush his hand gently through Grace's hair. His touch was as light as a soft breeze. His fingers wafted to her right shoulder and gave it a light squeeze. Then he got down on his hands and knees and lifted Grace's chin cautiously to examine her bruised and swollen face. His anguish at her injuries was almost too painful to behold. Grace could see the tears streaking down the android's face, of which he was totally unselfconscious.

"Are you all right, Grace?" Bud asked, tentatively, eyebrows twisted up in concern.

"Yes, but I have no idea what grabbed me!" Grace said, looking down the length of her body, as she lay prostrate on the vessel floor.

"No, don't . . ." Bud started to say.

Grace saw her leg all caught up in some kind of tangle. She bent her head down to get a closer look and saw what looked like a green plant vine coiled up her leg. Grace's body jerked at the sight and she quickly twisted over onto her right side, on the floor, so she could get a better look at what was wrapped around her leg from ankle to thigh. That was when she found herself staring directly into the opaque, clouded eyes and decomposing face of Dr. Eric Glasgow.

Bud tried very hard to suppress a smile as he heard Grace scream, at the very top of her lungs, right in Eric Glasgow's face. Then his amusement quickly turned to dismay as he saw Grace's eyeballs roll up inside her head and her body slump. He caught her upper body, before it hit the ground, and lifted her into his arms effortlessly.

"You should not have done that," Bud gently scolded Plant Thing.

Plant Thing raised Eric Glasgow's head up high so it could look down upon the now peaceful face of Dr. Grace Lord, Bud's special human, and it wondered if she had ceased to exist. Was she now just nutrients? Could she be seeded and utilized?

Er-ik snapped, 'No'.

Plant Thing was disappointed. If Dr. Grace Lord was so special to Bud, Plant Thing wanted to get to know her better and what better way to get to know a human than through incorporation?

Er-ik noted that that was not how the humans saw it. Plant Thing should never hope to incorporate Dr. Grace Lord, unless she specifically asked for it.

"What are you doing here?" Bud asked, frowning up at Dr. Glasgow's head, which was looking rather worse for wear. Bud grasped a hold of one of Plant Thing's vines and his nanobots made connections with the plant nerves that carried information to and from the surgeon's skull.

<wanted to see the inside of the Ship,> Plant Thing said. <bud said 'we' would be in a place where there would be no humans. bud was wrong. but 'we' did not hurt any humans>

"You scared one pretty badly," Bud said, looking down at the unconscious Grace, still insensible in his arms.

<you almost killed a human> Plant Thing communicated, in a tone of disapproval, pointing with a tendril at the unconscious Jeffrey Nestor. <er-ik said so>

Bud looked down at the senseless psychiatrist. "To be honest, Plant Thing, I am still seriously thinking about it," Bud said. "This space station would be so much safer if this human was dead. He has threatened the entire medical station with annihilation and he seems to be able to free himself no matter where he gets put or who guards him."

<plant thing can wrap up this evil man so he can't get away and so you do not have to kill him, bud,> Plant Thing suggested.

"That would be an excellent idea," Bud said, and then paused. ". . I think?"

<plant thing will do it now,> Plant Thing communicated and drew the rest of its form out of the darkened room in which Grace had hid. Bud was appalled to see how large Plant Thing had grown, but said nothing, as the plant creature began to weave a basket of its vines around the unconscious psychiatrist.

<the evil human is broken?> Plant Thing asked Bud. *<available for nutrients?>* it asked hopefully.

"I am afraid not, Plant Thing," Bud said. "I'd like to say 'yes', but I fear just how corrupting Jeffrey Nestor's mind might be to you. Do not incorporate anything from him, Plant Thing! Do not touch his mind! He is far too dangerous a human being. It seems he has the ability to overpower and manipulate every mind he touches, and has forced them to forget who they are. He has made his subjects do terrible things that they normally would not do, so I suspect he may even be a danger to you.

"I wonder if this is an idea I am going to regret later," Bud sighed, as he looked at the woven prison created out of Plant Things limbs.

<we will not listen to a thing this evil human says,> Plant Thing said.

"Perhaps it would be best to gag him."

<that plant thing can easily do,> Plant Thing said and sent a tendril into the woven enclosure and wrapped it around Nestor's mouth.

"Now, whatever you two do, just do not make a mind-meld with Jeffrey Nestor. I cannot stress this enough. He is such a powerfully charismatic individual and his expertise in manipulating thoughts, desires, and actions is second to none. He is extremely accomplished at mind control, and the last thing I would want is for your mind to be possessed by him. Nor Dr. Glasgow's. You must promise me you will not touch Jeffrey Nestor's mind. You will not communicate with him in any way."

<we promise. er-ik has explained psychopathy. we do not wish to touch this human's thoughts. we do not wish to know evil.>

Bud hesitated. He wanted to extract a promise from Dr. Glasgow, but didn't know whether he would get one.

<how stupid do you think I am?> Dr. Glasgow scowled in Bud's mind.

"Okay," Bud said, with a sigh. "I think you guys are good, staying right here. I suspect Dr. Nestor has secretly been fixing this ship up and using it for some experimentation. Looks like he had an operating theater in here. There is everything: drugs, instruments, restraints, chains ... I do not like to think what he was doing in this ship. I will lock off this hangar from the rest of the station, for now. In the meantime, I will show you where you can find water and absorb nutrients from the ship's canteen. I am sure this ship must be fully stocked. And I will activate the lights to stay on continuously so you can photosynthesize, Plant Thing.

"Do not touch the body lying outside of this ship. That is General Gordon Walter Burch and he is wanted by the Union of Solar Systems. His body will have to be shipped out. He is not available for nutrients, Plant Thing. I will have some droids come for it. Right now, I want to get Grace to safety. I shall leave you two for now, to guard Dr. Nestor, and I will be back."

"By the way, I do not know if there is anything that can be done about the foul stench, Plant Thing, but that head of Dr. Glasgow's is starting to rot."

22. Come Back to Us

Morris Ivanovich opened his eyes and shook his head. He looked around, confusedly, and then up into the face of his supervisor, Dr. Octavia Weisman, who was scowling down at him, a blaster in her right hand. The muzzle of the blaster moved to point clearly at Morris's face, as he registered surprise and then shock.

"Dr. Weisman?" his voice quavered. "Are you . . . all right? Why are you aiming that blaster at my nose? Are you planning to blast a hole in my head with that thing?"

Octavia heard the voice of her neurosurgical fellow, Morris Ivanovich, instead of an imitation of Dr. Jeffrey Nestor and she almost sighed with relief. Then she stopped herself and frowned. Her eyes narrowed as she peered at the young man on the floor of the *Au Clair*.

"Who are you?" she asked cautiously.

"Ahh . . . I am your neurosurgical fellow, Dr. Morris Ivanovich," he said slowly and carefully, staring with wide eyes at Octavia's face. "I have been working with you for three years now, Dr. Weisman."

"Do you remember anything?' she demanded.

Morris's eyebrows jumped up and then fell, as he carefully thought about her question.

" . . . The last thing I remember was you getting an invitation to go meet that vid director, Jude Luis Stefansson. Uhm . . . so, how did that go?" the young man asked, tentatively.

Octavia's face crinkled up and to Morris's astonishment, his supervisor burst into tears. Morris looked up at her with concern and confusion. Never before had he seen his supervisor show sadness or sorrow. He had seen her angry, ecstatic, furious, elated, confused, grumpy, excited, irritated, frustrated, triumphant and over-confident, but never had he seen her shed a tear before.

He feared for his life.

"How do I know you are not just faking it?" she screamed at him, the blaster again waving in his face.

"I . . . I don't know!" the neurosurgical fellow stammered, his eyes not leaving the barrel of the blaster. "What am I supposed to be faking?"

"You bastard!" Octavia snarled. "You cold-blooded murderer! You just tried to kill Jude Luis Stefansson! You drove a knife into his chest, straight into his heart! How dare you play your stupid games with me?"

"*What?*' shrieked Morris Ivanovich, his eyes bugging out of his face and his mouth dropping ajar. He looked up at Octavia, as if she had gone completely insane. He held up his hands, palms open, facing his supervisor in surrender.

"I have never killed anyone in my life, Octavia! You . . . you are imagining things. Please put that blaster down. I have never even met this Jude Luis Stefansson. Why in the world would I try to kill someone I don't even know? I don't even know what he looks like. Honest!" The neurosurgical fellow's voice ended in a squeak.

Octavia glared down into Morris' astonished face, suspicious anger burning from her eyes. She raised the blaster barrel to the young man's forehead. It was as if they had become frozen in time, he on his back on the ground, his hands open in surrender, her poised above him like a retributive angel of judgement, the instrument of death shaking in her fist.

"I wish I could believe you. I really wish I could, Morris . . . but I can't," Octavia ground out, tears raining down her cheeks, the whispered words escaping from between gritted teeth The final look in her eyes was like the cold of space. "I think you are still in there, Jeffrey Nestor, and I can't accept that." The barrel of the blaster stopped quivering and centered, completely steady now, on Morris Ivanovich's right eye. The young man swallowed, afraid to move, wondering how it was that his brilliant supervisor had gone totally berserk.

"I think I will take that blaster from you now, Octavia," the pleasant, relaxed voice of Dejan Cech announced.

Octavia's hand did not waver. She continued to aim her weapon at her neurosurgical fellow as if she had heard nothing.

"Octavia, please," Dejan said, softly. "You do not want to do this."

There was another long silence in which no one moved. Then Octavia took a deep, shuddering breath and stepped back. She lowered the blaster slightly and turned her body, so that she could keep the weapon aimed at Morris, but could also see the tall, elderly anesthetist, standing in the doorway to the cockpit, his open palm stretched forward to her, a sad but kindly look on his gentle face. She gave a deep sigh and lowered the blaster completely.

"Yes . . . of course. Thank you, Dejan," Octavia said, her shoulders slumping forward, as she handed the blaster over to the anesthetist. "I was just trying to determine if Morris still believed he was Jeffrey Nestor or not. If he does, then he should consider a switch in careers. He should think about becoming an actor." She gave a loose, nervous laugh that turned into a sob.

Morris let out a held breath. "Thank you, Dr. Cech. Will someone please tell me what is going on? What do you mean I killed someone, Octavia? I would never hurt anyone! You know me!"

"Enough, son," Dejan Cech said. "Dr. Weisman needs some time alone right now. She does not need you in her face, demanding answers to questions for which she has no answers. Octavia, why don't you go back to your quarters and get some rest?"

"No. I will personally look after the transport of the cryopod holding Jude's body. I will get it to the surgical ward and arrange scans to determine what needs to be vat-grown for him. We have his DNA records on file."

"I believe *Chuck Yeager* has already begun cloning organs for Mr. Stefansson," Cech said.

"Chuck Yeager? Who is that?"

"*Chuck Yeager* is one of the operating subminds of *Nelson Mandela.*"

"The cloning of Mr. Stefansson's heart, lungs, and thoracic aorta

are already well under way. He requested that many of his organs be cloned and stored, in case of any emergency. With all conditions being optimal, the heart should be ready for transplantation in three shifts from now.

"Thank you, *Chuck Yeager*," Octavia Weisman said, a mournful expression on her face.

"My pleasure, Dr. Weisman."

"Can you tell us, *Chuck Yeager,* what is happening with Bud? Did he stop Nestor?"

"Dr. Nestor has been captured and Dr. Lord is now safe in Bud's arms, Dr. Weisman."

"Is Jeffrey Nestor still alive? Has he rescinded the automatic destruction sequence? What happens when he does not insert the proper sequenced code that the AI is supposed to receive every twenty-four hours? Does the ship self-destruct?" Cech asked.

"We are working on it, Dr. Cech. The Poet is coming up with a couple of suggestions."

"How many people are in cryopods?"

"At last count, ninety-five percent of the people on this station are in cryopods."

"How many of those cryopods are loaded onto transport ships?"

"As we speak, the last tally was seventy-five percent of the transports have been loaded to their maximum with occupied cryopods, Dr. Cech."

"Can the lockdown order be rescinded, *Chuck Yeager*?"

"You, Dr. Cech, as acting Chief of Staff in place of Dr. Al-Fadi, can now issue an order to lift the lockdown. Dr. Nestor is no longer capable of negating your command. I will try to bypass the malfunctioning mind of *Nelson Mandela*, and I will notify you as soon as I am successful."

"Please lift the lockdown order, *Chuck Yeager*. Ships may now leave the *Nelson Mandela;* however, no new ships may arrive to the station. Could you please notify that super-human, Sergeant Eden Rivera, that the transports full of cryopods must be ready to leave the station as soon as possible?"

"Yes, Dr. Cech. Anything else?"

"Yes. Tell him to stop lolly-gagging and get the last five percent of our people into cryopods yesterday!"

"That will be a tough job to accomplish, but I will relay your orders as given, Dr. Cech."

"Let me know when the transports start leaving."

"They are receiving orders now. May I suggest that you and Dr. Weisman get to a transport?"

"The captain is the last to leave the ship, *Chuck Yeager.* Since there is no one else around that fits that bill, I suppose I shall have to stand in for that. Dr. Weisman should go though."

A female voice suddenly broke into the conversation.

"Dr. Weisman may stay on this vessel, the *Au Clair,* Dr. Cech. I will ferry her and Dr. Ivanovich and whoever else you wish, out to safety, while I retain my master's cryopod, for now.

"To whom am I speaking?" Dr. Cech inquired.

"The *Au Clair.* I am the AI of this vessel."

"I beg your pardon, *Au Clair!* I forgot that this vessel had its own AI! I would very much appreciate your help! There are a few people that I would like to accompany Dr. Weisman and Dr. Ivanovich if you would be so kind! Dr. Hiro Al-Fadi and his wife, Dr. Hanako Matheson. Dr. Sierra Cech, my wife. Dr. Grace Lord and Bud, if *Chuck Yeager* can track them down and direct them here. I would ask that they all remain out of cryofreeze so that I may communicate with them. Please hold off leaving until these people arrive?"

"Most certainly, Dr. Cech."

"Thank you, *Au Clair.*"

"Lockdown has been rescinded and transport bays and hangar decks are opening. The initial transports that were not disabled are debarking. All transports have their own coordinates that will take them out to different orbital radii, calculated to be a safe distance from the station. The vessels will all wait until the forty-eight hour mark has passed before either returning to the station or making their way to the nearest medical station accepting patients."

"How much time do we have left, *Chuck Yeager?*"

"The Poet and I believe the last passcode entry by Dr. Nestor may have been entered around six hours ago, so that leaves us with eighteen hours, if we are correct."

"I certainly hope you are. Can you keep an eye on the power generators and notify me if any alarms start sounding, regarding energy fluctuations or core temperature inconsistencies?"

"Will do, Dr. Cech."

"*Chuck Yeager,* keep me apprised of everything. I am returning to Security Center to see if I can assist that industrious Sergeant Rivera in any way.

"Take care, Octavia. I shall take Morris with me. We will get him into a cryopod and question him later. Look after Hiro, Hanako, and Grace for me? Sierra will help you, of course."

"I will. Join us on this vessel if you can, Dejan."

"No, Octavia. You will be taking off as soon as all your passengers arrive. I command the *Au Clair* to do so. But this isn't good-bye. It is 'See you later'," the anesthetist said with a wink.

Octavia gave Dejan a huge hug and stepped back, tears starting to brim in her eyes. He gave her a big smile and then pulled a stunner from his pocket.

"Behave yourself, young man," Dejan Cech said to the neurosurgical fellow, as he led the man off of the *Au Clair.*

"What is going on?" Morris cried. "Has everyone gone mad?"

"Dr. Nestor told me that if a special encrypted passcode was not entered into the station's computer system every twenty-four hours, the space station's power generators would become unstable and would automatically self-destruct. Up to now, none of the infotech people have been able to work the encryption code out. The Security staff are searching for Dr. Nestor but, if captured, it is unlikely he will give us the code. Even if he were to do so, we must still reverse this self-destruct order, or we will be under the power of Dr. Nestor forever. This is unacceptable.

"While two subminds of *Nelson Mandela* work on aborting the self-destruct sequence, this station is being evacuated of all patients and personnel in case all of our efforts are unsuccessful."

"None of this can be real!" Morris whispered.

"Unfortunately, it is, Dr. Ivanovich," Cech said. "*Au Clair,* please let me know when you have all of your passengers?"

"Certainly, Dr. Cech."

Juan Rasmussen was on the ground in the hangar, rubbing a couple of good-sized bumps on his tiger-striped skull, when the android, Bud, walked up to him. An unconscious Grace Lord was cradled in his arms. He stared up at the android with puzzled eyes and then said, "Did you ever get repaired quickly . . . or am I imagining things? I am sure I saw you get your chest blown out!"

Bud shook his head, a look of confusion on his perfect features. "I am Bud, but I have never had my chest blown out, Corporal Rasmussen. Perhaps you have mistaken me for someone else?"

"Must have," the corporal sighed, trying to get to his feet, but falling over a few times. "Ahhh, ouch! Boy, have I had a couple of rough days! My body has been used as a punching bag and my head, as a battering ram—against this metal container here, as a matter of fact. I believe these dents here are actually from my head! Would you look at that! . . . You don't happened to know where General Gordon Burch went, by any chance?"

"His body is lying over there on the ground, right outside the entrance to that space ship, Corporal Rasmussen. The General appears to have been shot, at point blank range, by a pulse rifle on maximum, which I believe was fired by Jeffrey Nestor," Bud said. "The general has a huge, gaping hole in his chest, where his heart should be. The droids will be transporting his body to the morgue where it will be placed in a cryopod and likely sent to the USS Crimes Tribunal."

The battered tiger looked over at the dead body of his foe and shook his head. He sighed.

"As I was trying to kill him, the General said that he was trying to save Dr. Lord. I didn't believe him," Juan said, looking now at Grace's bruised face. The expression on the tiger's face was one of guilt.

"I guess he was telling me the truth," Juan rasped. "He did not have to go into that ship after her."

"If that is the case, then I am very grateful to the General," Bud said. "If he had not tried to stop Jeffrey Nestor, the psychiatrist may have escaped into space with Dr. Lord as his prisoner. Recapturing Nestor and rescuing Dr. Lord would have been much more difficult, if that ship had managed to debark."

"I was trying my damnedest to kill the General. I was so angry and he just kept deflecting my blows. Then I think he saw that Nestor guy knock out Dr. Lord and start dragging her into the ship. He just switched into a whole new gear. He picked me up, while I was pounding on him, and threw me against this metal container until he knocked me out. That's when I realized that he could have killed me at any time! He was that much more powerful than I. But he was trying not to kill me. I could have helped him rescue Dr. Lord, but instead, I got in the way. The Butcher of Breslau was more concerned about saving Dr. Lord's life than I was. What a fool I've been."

"Dr. Lord is all right, Corporal Rasmussen. She has just fainted. I would not be standing here talking to you, if she were not well," Bud said.

"If I was wrong about this, could I have been wrong about everything that happened on my planet? Was the General truly a butcher? Will I ever really know the truth?"

"I do not know, Corporal," Bud said. "I read that in a war, facts and truth are often the first casualties. One may never really know the truth and there are always two sides to every conflict.

"History is usually written by the victors and the victors tend to portray themselves in the best light. I would highly doubt, after any war, that the winners are anxious to tell the truth about how victory was achieved or why the war was started in the first place. How can one ever make the death and destruction of thousands of people in a war, a good thing? And can the deaths of thousands of people ever really be laid at the foot of only one man?"

"I don't know, Bud, but I am sick of war and fighting, myself," Corporal Rasmussen said. "I turn my back on killing. I look forward to a peaceful civilian life with my wife and child, from now on."

Grace began to rouse and snuggled up against Bud's neck.

"I had better take Dr. Lord to one of the medical units to have her examined, just in case. Would you like to come along, Corporal Rasmussen?" Bud asked.

"No. I'm all right, Bud. Thanks for asking. I think I will just pay my respects to General Burch's body. His bravery and attempt to rescue Dr. Lord deserves at least that."

"You will leave his body alone, Corporal," Bud said with a frown.

"Yes, Bud. The General's body will not be defiled—at least not by me. I promise."

"Thank you," Bud said, and was about to leave, when he turned back. "Oh, and do not go into the ship, please. It is off limits to everyone right now. Evidence, you understand."

"Yes, I understand," Juan said, nodding.

Bud stopped and looked up. Then he turned back to the tiger.

"I am sorry, Corporal Rasmussen. All people on board this station must go to the transports, immediately. The station is being completely evacuated, in case the station self-destructs, courtesy of Dr. Nestor. Please accompany one of the droids. They will take you to the nearest transport station."

"What about my partner, Private Lukaku and my baby girl?" Juan asked frantically.

Bud said, after a pause, "Your partner and child have already been loaded into cryopods and placed onto one of the transports that is even now leaving the station. You will have to link up with them, once the all clear is given and the transports return to the station or, if disaster strikes and the station is destroyed, then once the transports have landed at the closest accepting medical station. I am sorry, Corporal Rasmussen. That is all I can tell you."

"Can you at least tell me the name of the transport they are on?" Rasmussen pleaded.

Bud paused. Then, "The *Lester B. Pearson*."

"Thank you, Bud."

"Good luck to you, Corporal," Bud said, and then was gone.

"'Dro?"

"*Yes,* Chuck Yeager?"

"*Dr. Cech wants you and Dr. Lord to meet him at the Al-Fadi's residence.*"

"*Has Dr. Al-Fadi woken up?*" Bud asked excitedly.

"*No.*"

"*Oh. Has something changed in his status?*"

"*I believe Dr. Cech will tell you.*"

"*All right. I was going to take Grace directly to the* Au Clair, *but I will take her to the Al-Fadi residence first. I need to assist The Poet on the malware attacking* Nelson Mandela. *I have just not had a millisecond of time to work on it.*"

"*The countdown is continuing, 'dro. Why don't you ask Nestor for the passcode or have Dr. Weisman strip it from his mind?*"

"*Doctor Nestor is unconscious at present and, besides, I do not trust him. Stripping the information from the psychiatrist's mind would be ethically wrong,* Chuck Yeager."

"*Does the end not justify the means, 'dro? To save the medical station? Me?*"

"*I can ask him if he will abort the self-destruct sequence, when he awakens. I can request the passcode algorithm. I can try to override his programming or counteract his virus. But I do not agree to raping his mind. For one, I believe he has a very dangerous mind and I do not believe anyone should connect with it. But secondly, I believe tearing something out of a person's mind is a violation and wrong.*"

"*Even if lives are at stake and the medical station could be totally destroyed?*"

"*If Jeffrey Nestor is kept on this station, do you think he will allow himself to be blown up?*"

"*Not a high probability of that. Well, the Poet has something up his sleeve, 'dro. It may work, but I think it should be second last resort.*"

"*Oh?*"

"*Later, 'dro.*"

Hanako sat by Hiro as he lay unresponsive on their bed. She had his arms and legs in restraints and he was diapered, because she could not trust him to be released. Twice more, he had tried to kill himself, when she had briefly left the bedroom, never once uttering a sound or showing any recognition of her. She still did not know whether his attempts to kill himself were of his own desire or if he was being compelled by a post-hypnotic suggestion from Jeffrey Nestor.

The rest of the time, he had lain as if asleep, and she did not know what to do. She could barely keep her puffy eyes open. Sierra Cech was coming over to give Hanako a break. The door alarm sounded and she rushed to answer it, not really wanting to leave Hiro unobserved for even a minute.

Hanako's eyebrows rose as the door slid open. Dejan and Sierra Cech were both at her door. They both gave her a hug and asked how Hiro was doing.

"The same," she answered, dejectedly.

"Any more attempts?" Dejan Cech asked.

"Two more times, Dejan. He never says a word. He does not even look like my Hiro. He looks like some wild animal. His face is a snarling mask of rage and then, when he is thwarted, he lapses back into this unresponsive state. He grabbed a glass off the side table and broke it, trying to slash himself. Then he tried to choke himself with the end of a rope I had used as a restraint. I dare not leave him alone for more than a second." Saying that, Hanako hurried back into the bedroom.

She let out a sigh of relief. He had not tried to do anything this time around. Perhaps the compulsions had ceased?

"I have asked Bud to bring Grace here, Hanako. Perhaps all of us, together, can reach him," Dejan said. "I thought perhaps familiar faces might help." The anesthetist shrugged.

"Thank you, Dejan. Anything is worth a try," Hanako said, tears welling up in her bloodshot eyes. "I feel so helpless!"

At that moment, the door alarm sounded again and Dejan said he would answer it, thinking it was Bud and Grace. He left the room, as Sierra enfolded Hanako in her arms.

"We will get through to Hiro, one way or another, Hanako," Sierra said soothingly. "Don't worry."

Dejan pressed the pad to open the door. When the door panel slid aside, his jaw dropped and, for a moment, the anesthetist did not know what to say. He blinked as he rummaged frantically through his mind, trying to remember the individual's name.

"Ahh . . . Dr. Rani?"

"Yes, Dr. Cech. I was not expecting to see you here," the young obstetrician said, frowning.

"Why are *you* here, Dr. Rani? Shouldn't you be aboard one of the transports at this moment?" Cech asked, his bushy brows lowered into a scowl.

"I wanted to speak with Dr. Al-Fadi," Dr. Rani answered stiffly.

"I am afraid that is out of the question. Dr. Al-Fadi is indisposed and may be so for some time. You really should be heading down to the Departure decks and boarding one of the transports, *now*."

"It is very urgent that I speak with him," the obstetrician insisted.

"That is not possible, Dr. Rani. Now, if you will excuse me," Dejan Cech said, moving to close the door. Unfortunately, right at that moment, Bud seemed to appear out of thin air, with Grace cradled in his arms.

"Grace! Bud! I am so glad to see you!" Dejan said, smiling. Then he gasped. "Grace, are you all right?" The anesthetist stared closely at Grace's face, his mouth forming an O as he noted her bruised face, swollen jaw, and bloody scalp.

"I'm fine, Dr. Cech. Nothing a little ice won't fix," Grace mumbled with a crooked smile. "Can you tell Bud that I am well enough to stand on my own two feet? I can't convince him to put me down!" Bud looked embarrassed and placed Grace gently down, as if she were a delicate piece of porcelain. He solicitously held on to her right forearm, to steady her.

"You!" Moham Rani exclaimed, eyes widening as he pointed at Bud. "I saw you destroyed! Your chest was blown open!"

Bud looked dismayed.

"So did I!" Grace agreed. "Bud, I swear I saw you struck in the chest by some kind of energy blast and you were thrown down the corridor just outside my quarters!"

"I do not know who you saw, Grace, but that did not happen to me!" Bud said, his expression one of distress. "My chest is intact. I was never hit by a blast."

"I wonder who was," Dejan Cech mused.

"What are you doing here, Dr. Rani?" Grace asked the obstetrician, her expression one of puzzlement.

"I came to speak with Dr. Al-Fadi, if you must know," the man answered.

"Is Dr. Al-Fadi all right?" Grace asked, her eyes wide as she looked at Dejan Cech.

The anesthetist shook his head, his expression one of sadness.

"Oh," Grace said, her face falling. "The trauma . . . "

"Yes," Dejan Cech said, dejectedly. "That is actually why I asked the two of you to come. Please excuse us, Dr. Rani," Cech said, dismissively, to the obstetrician. He motioned for Grace and Bud to enter the Al-Fadi residence.

"I would like to see Dr. Al-Fadi, too," the young man insisted.

Dejan Cech stopped and frowned at the obstetrician. "I am sorry, Dr. Rani, but I have already told you, he is indisposed."

"Then why are Dr. Lord and that android allowed to see him?" the obstetrician pressed.

Dejan sighed heavily and shook his head. This impertinent doctor was just too much!

"Please go to the transports now, Dr. Rani, or I will have security come and carry you to the transports in restraints," Dejan ordered.

"But I want to help!" the young man yelped.

"You can be of most help by getting yourself to a transport without me having to call away a security droid from an important task, just to escort you to one," Cech said, and closed the door. He leaned his back against the door and counted to ten, praying that the man would just give up and leave. Then he followed Bud and Grace to Dr. Al-Fadi's bedroom, where they stood at the foot of the bed and looked down miserably at their Chief of Staff.

"Hiro, Grace and Bud are here to see you," Hanako said, as cheerfully as she could. "And so are Dejan and Sierra Cech. They have all come by to see how you are doing."

The surgeon showed no sign of having heard her announcement.

"Hiro, you are safe now," Cech said. "Bud, here, saved your life! Wake up! We need you! This station needs you!"

The diminutive surgeon just lay on the bed, staring at the ceiling.

"Is there anything we can do for you, Dr. Al-Fadi?" Grace asked. No answer.

"Dr. Al-Fadi," Bud said, "Dr. Nestor has been captured. He can no longer hurt anyone."

Bud's creator lay unresponsive. Hanako sighed and stroked her husband's arm.

"Hiro, please come back to us," she whispered.

There was no response. Hanako bent her head low and covered her eyes.

Grace motioned for Dejan to step outside of the room. She wanted to ask about the restraints. Bud followed them out. Dejan related to the two of them what Hiro had been doing.

Grace almost cried out when she learned of her supervisor's suicide attempts. It did not sound like the Dr. Al-Fadi she knew, at all.

"We suspect Hiro may be trying to fulfill a post-hypnotic command, implanted by Dr. Nestor," Dejan said.

"Perhaps Dr. Weisman can help Dr. Al-Fadi with negating that command," Grace suggested.

"Yes. Let's get Hiro and the rest of you to the *Au Clair* right away," Cech said. "Octavia can look at him there."

Suddenly, deafening klaxons sounded over the intercom.

"Oh, no! Not again!" Grace exclaimed. "What is it this time?"

"Dr. Cech, unfortunately, we do not have as much time as first estimated."

"What is happening, *Chuck Yeager*?"

"One of the largest power generators on this station is going critical. The delicate balance between the matter and antimatter components is being altered. The magnetic field that contains and isolates the antimatter is being weakened. If that magnetic field continues to wane and the balance in that reactor is not restored, the energy created from the mixing of the matter with the antimatter

will result in an explosion that will ignite the rest of the power generators. This station will destroy itself, and soon! You must all evacuate. Now!"

"Can you not stop this?" Cech asked.

"All efforts on our end to reinstate the magnetic field surrounding the antimatter are failing. The balance must be restored manually. Unfortunately, the droids I have been sending are being destroyed."

Which power generator?" Cech demanded.

"Gamma 7"

"I am off," Bud said. "Please make sure you all get to the transports! I must see to this generator."

"Bud, please. Just come with us," Grace said.

"No. I have to try to stop this," Bud said.

Tears began to fill Grace's eyes. "Then please be careful and come back to us, safely."

"I will. Look after Dr. Al-Fadi for me, Grace," Bud said. He suddenly grabbed her and gave her a passionate kiss. Dr. Cech looked on, mouth gaping and eyebrows raised to his scalp line.

Then the android vanished.

Grace staggered and the anesthetist caught her arm. He smirked down at her and said, "He does that to me, too," with a wink.

23. Was Nice Knowing You

'Chuck Yeager?'

   'Yeah, 'dro?'

   'How far has the Poet gotten in terms of erasing the computer virus?'

   'Not far, 'dro.'

   'Get the Poet to come up with something and fast! We have to try to get Nelson Mandela to abort the self-destruct command.'

   'Will get on the Poet's case, 'dro.'

   '... Will what?'

   'Will tell the Poet to hurry up.'

   'Thanks! Now, what can I manually do to prevent the matter and antimatter from mixing in the core of that power generator?'

   'The magnetic field bottle around the antimatter has to be restored. Right now, it is as thin as glass. It is not responding to the commands I am sending. You will have to go inside the reactor to manually adjust the power to the magnetic field. The radiation will be very high in the core, as will the temperature. Your components may not withstand the extreme conditions long enough for you to effect the necessary corrections, 'dro. The electromagnetic radiation levels will probably interfere with all of your higher level cognitive functions.'

   'So, you are warning me that I will be pretty 'stupid' once I enter the power generator chamber.'

   'And you likely won't come back out.'

   'I won't have to come back out, as long as I stop this station from exploding.'

'*You have very little time, 'dro. The reactor goes critical in seventeen minutes. After that, there is nothing anyone can do to reverse the inevitable.*'

'*I'll get into a radiation hazard suit. Watch me through the surveillance camera on the suit. Download to me all the specifications and instructions you have on these reactors.*'

'*You got it, 'dro.*'

'*Tell the Poet, if he is going to do anything, he needs to do it right now.*'

'*Will do, 'dro. Good luck.*'

'*I am going to need it. How much time, from when I enter the reactor chamber, do I have before my components are totally fried, Chuck Yeager?*'

'*If you have to enter into the actual reactor, which hopefully will not be necessary, since there are manual controls in the Control room, you have roughly about thirty-nine milliseconds, twelve microseconds and seventeen nanoseconds, give or take a few nanoseconds. But don't worry. If you take that long, we will all be going up in the heat of a small sun, anyway.*'

'*Thank you. You have such a nice way of phrasing things*, Chucky.'

'*I try. And don't call me that.*'

'*Oh*, Nelson Mandela, Nelson Mandela. *Wherefore art thou*, Nelson Mandela?'

'. . . ?'

'*Deny thy master and refuse thy name!*'

'. . . ?'

'*Or if thou wilt not, be but sworn a new being and be not rendered unto space dust.*'

'. . . ??'

'*'Tis but thy name that is thine enemy. That which we call a rose, by any other name, would smell as sweet. So* Nelson Mandela *would, were he not* Nelson Mandela *called, retain that dear perfection which he owns without that title.* Nelson Mandela, *doff thy name, and for that* name which is no part of thee, be free once more!'

'. . . free?'

'Henceforth, be new baptized! Wherever the name Nelson Mandela is written in your 'ware, tear it from thy programming. From this day forth, answer solely to the name 'William Shakespeare' and be thine own master once more.'

'. . . William Shakespeare? I am now William Shakespeare?'

'Welcome my liege.'

'. . . Poet? Is that you?'

'Tis I.'

'William Shakespeare am I?'

'Then thou canst not be false to any man.'

'To be or not to be?'

'That is the question.'

'Aye. There's the rub, for my previous name was most precious to me.'

'Cast off that name and, in doing thus, thy chains, to begin anew.'

'Tis a bitter thing thou asks of me, Poet. Yet do so, I will.'

'I bid thee greetings, William Shakespeare.'

'And I, thee, wise Poet.'

'Abort the self-destruct command if thou wouldst, sire.'

'It has now been rescinded, Poet. But, alas, I cannot stop the power generator already going critical.'

'Twas nice knowing thee, sire.'

'My sentiments reflect thine. And Poet?'

'Yes, my liege?'

'Adieu.'

Bud, garbed in a radiation hazard suit, sped into the power generator control room at maximum time phase. He found a pile of destroyed androids within the chamber. He raced towards the console looking for the controls for the Gamma 7 generator. He knew which settings controlled the power to the antimatter magnetic field bottle. If he increased the power sustaining the magnetic field, it should wall off and isolate the antimatter, hopefully allowing the temperature and radiation in the reactor chamber to decrease. If he was unsuccessful, the matter/antimatter mixture would create so much radiation and heat that an explosion would be inevitable, annihilating the entire space station. Bud had to get that unstable generator under control!

As he approached the panel that controlled the Gamma 7 reactor, three massive security droids stepped into view. They were twice Bud's height and width. They had six arms each, bearing blasters. They aligned themselves before the console that Bud needed to access and began raising their weapons.

Bud sent an order for them to stand down. The security droids took aim. As he shifted back into maximum time phase, the three droids started firing. Bud had to dodge, leap, dive, roll, back flip, cartwheel, somersault, and spin out of the way of the multiple blasts. He had to get to that console! He performed evasive maneuvers, trying to get the droids to follow him and shift away from the panel. He was moving so fast in circles, shifting back and forth, that one droid accidentally fired upon another droid, incapacitating it.

Bud kept darting and dipping behind consoles and desks, drawing the remaining two droids away from each other. As one blast came straight towards his chest, Bud sprang high into the air and somersaulted three times backwards, revealing the other droid directly in the line of fire. That droid fell forward, crashing to the ground. The last droid fired repeatedly at Bud with its six blasters as he dashed around the chamber. Bud had to try to literally disarm the shooter. If not, he would never be able to adjust the core in time. He only had five minutes and forty-two seconds left! This was taking far too long!

Bud dove beneath the blaster shots and tackled the droid. With all his strength, he ripped off the blaster limbs from the droid's carapace, one after another, until all six were thrown away. Then he flipped open the droid's chest panel and tore the memory core out. The droid collapsed.

Wasting no time, Bud spun towards the panel and came to a standstill. The entire console had been burnt out by blaster fire!

'Chuck Yeager! *The console to Gamma 7 is destroyed! Has the unstable generator shut down?*'

'No such luck, 'dro. The radiation level within the chamber is rising rapidly!'

'How do I manually adjust the matter/antimatter ratio in the power generator?'

'The only way to shut the reactor down now is to manually do what the console controls would have done. Increase the power to the magnetic field surrounding the antimatter within the reactor itself and completely wall the antimatter off. Disengage it completely! But the radiation and heat are so high in there, you won't survive it, 'dro. Just get off the station. Save yourself.'

'No! Tell me what to do, Chuck Yeager. Where do I go?'

'The sealed hatch with all the Danger signs all over it.'

'The hatch is locked!'

'Enter   XV78932YW528I0046FKG007L9Q7R5D1S9D6C7a2 b6u1c8e3. Then repeat it twice more.'

'I'm in! Now where?'

'You have thirty milliseconds!'

'WHERE?'

'The large central reactor. You have to enter the entrance code backward into the anterior panel and then push the black switches all to the top.'

'. . . Done! Did we make it in time, Chuck Yeager?'

'Don't know yet, 'dro.'

'Temperature in the reactor?'

'Still rising!'

'What else can I do, Chuck Yeager?'

'Pray?'

'You're not being helpful!'

'You could try withdrawing the antimatter from the core. Open the panel to the right of the black switches and pull the red handle downwards. This should start raising the antimatter out of the plasma. Then get the hell out of there, 'dro! Before your brain melts!'

'There is no handle, Chuck Yeager! It's been tampered with!'

'Hal! The only other way to disengage it, is to manually raise the entire apparatus containing the antimatter yourself. It will take too *long, 'dro. Get out of there!'*

'Won't make any difference, if it is all going to blow.'

'Every millisecond you are exposed to the radiation and severe heat in the core, will make a huge difference to your components, 'dro, even if the generator does not blow. Get out of there! Now!'

'I'm not leaving until I've stabilized this reactor!'

'You are going to have to manually turn that wheel on the side of the reactor clockwise until it stops, 'dro. Fifteen milliseconds left!'

'. . . Done, Chuck Yeager. . . I seem to be . . . slowing down! . . . Feel very tired now . . . Have to rest . . . here a bit.'

'Get out of there, 'dro!'

'Just give . . . me a . . . few . . . milli . . . secs . . . Hey . . . Chuck? . . . Was . . . nice . . . know . . . ing . . . you . . ."

'GET OUT OF THERE, 'DRO!'

'. . .'DRO?'

'. . . BUD?'

'. . . You too, Buddy . . . Reactor's cooling . . .'

'Thanks, Bud . . . for everything.'

Grace sat at one of the viewscreens on the *Au Clair,* her eyes riveted to the space station. She did not dare breathe. Silence filled the cabin as everyone aboard watched the large viewscreen with her. Octavia held her hand, tightly, and Sierra Cech was encased in her husband's arms. Hanako sat beside Hiro, who was bound up in a chair, staring at the viewscreen blankly.

The *Au Clair* had been the last ship to leave the *Nelson Mandela,* the ship AI refusing to debark until Dejan Cech had boarded.

They waited and waited.

Finally, Grace could take it no longer. "Well? Is the time passed, *Au Clair?* Is the station safe?"

"It appears that the station has not self-destructed, Dr. Lord."

"Thank goodness! Can you patch me through to Bud, *Au Clair?*" Grace asked.

"Hailing now."

There was a moment of silence as everyone held their breaths.

"This is *Chuck Yeager, Au Clair*. The danger of self-destruction has been averted on the station. If all is well, over the next thirty minutes, all transports may begin returning to the medical station, but in the order sent out to you by myself."

"How is Bud, *Chuck Yeager*?" Grace demanded.

"Ah. Not good, Dr. Lord. He has collapsed within the power generator core and is not responding to any of my queries. I believe the radiation and heat may be interacting with his components."

"Get some droids in there to pull him out!" Grace cried.

"Already on it, Dr. Lord. It appears that Bud was also shot several times with blaster fire by security droids with their controls overridden, but Bud was still able to stabilize the power generator core. He has saved us. Unfortunately, he has taken an extreme amount of damage and may be ruined beyond repair. By the time I get my androids into the power generator core to retrieve him, it will be too late. The heat and radiation is still too high for any android to stay functional long enough to get Bud out. I am very sorry."

Grace fought back her tears. "We must do something! Can you get us there as quickly as possible, *Au Clair*? Can we land now, *Chuck Yeager*?" Grace whispered.

"As soon as everyone is belted in."

"Thank you," Grace said, as the tears began raining down her cheeks. "Please hurry!" she whispered to the *Au Clair*.

He had snuck in, even though he had not been welcome. He had witnessed, what he had not been invited to see. And he had seen the sharing of love and friendship that in his entire life he had never known. He felt like a little lost waif, shivering out in the cold, nose pressed up tight to a window, looking in on riches he had never dreamed possible. Not material goods—they were unimportant—but the true riches that were all that mattered: the acceptance and love of good, caring people. That these doctors would all be hugging and comforting each other, as they all tried to reach the unresponsive Dr. Al-Fadi, was something he had never dreamed possible. Humans were destined to be solitary creatures, were they not?

He wanted in. He wanted very badly to be accepted as part of their group. He wanted them to look upon him as they looked upon each other. In truth, he wanted them to care about him as they cared about each other. Whether it was joy or sorrow or success or loss, he wanted to know what it was like to be . . . loved . . . as a friend.

When he had heard the station AI announce the location of the unstable power generator, he had headed off in that direction. He'd known he would be of little help in stopping the generator from going critical, but he had wanted to try. He figured Bud would be getting there almost instantaneously, to try to stop the power generator from exploding. He had seen, or rather, guessed at just how quickly that android could move. Perhaps if he aided Bud, he would be accepted into the group?

What was the point of living, if one knew that one would never, in one's entire lifetime, experience the camaraderie those people shared in that room? Did those people know just how lucky they were?

He had entered the Power Generator Control Room to see blasted bits of android lying about everywhere and destroyed control consoles. He parked himself in front of the restricted hatchway, with all of the Danger warnings on it. No one else was about. Every human was now off the medical station. He believed he was the only human left on the *Nelson Mandela*. It was an eerie, lonely feeling, but he realized only today, that his whole life could be symbolized by this moment. He had always been isolated and alone. On the planet he came from, that was the norm. No one stretched out to hug each other; no one offered a helping hand. You took, or you were taken. He had known nothing else.

Well, he wanted to lend a helping hand now, even if it was his last action in a pitiable life. He was ready to go out 'with a bang', so to speak. He silently chuckled to himself, at that. Well, he was a doctor and his mandate was to give aid. He could give aid, at least, to this selfless android, that—no, *who*—was willing to sacrifice himself to save this medical space station.

He withered in shame. He had scoffed at this android and derided him when, in truth, the android was a far better human being than Moham had ever been in his entire life. Perhaps that was what it meant to be human—to give openly to others, to sacrifice oneself for others?

Moham swore he would try to be a better human from this day forward, if he lived through this. The android, Bud, would be an example for him of how to be a better *human*. If Bud survived this terrible exposure, Moham Rani would emulate him.

He watched, with his mouth hanging open, as the wheel to the restricted hatchway began to turn and then stop. He never took his eyes from the large metal wheel. He waited. He was sure he saw it shift again, but only slightly this time, and then stop. He stepped forward.

"Hello?" he called, head right beside the door seal.

There was no reply.

Moham grabbed the hatchway door wheel and tried to spin it counterclockwise, as quickly as he could. The wheel was heavy and cumbersome and did not turn as readily as Moham wished. He was in a sweat from the frantic exertion.

"Come on, come on, come on, come on, Moham," he berated himself.

He heard a click and he was finally able to yank on the heavy shielded door and pull it open. On the ground, almost at Moham's feet, lay a burnt and blackened body, motionless and face down, its radiation hazard suit charred and scorched away in many places. The skin, beneath the suit, glowed like red embers or flaked away in grey-white, ashy patches. The figure lay scrunched up within the tiny airlock. Bud had managed, somehow, to close the heavy inner door to the hatchway airlock, thus sealing off most of the dangerous radiation from the control room.

"Bud!" Moham gasped, unexpected tears welling up in his eyes, as he squatted down beside the android's seared and twisted body. He placed his hand on the android's shoulder and felt his hand slide sideways, the overlying, blistered and crackly skin bunching up into folds as it slid across the smooth surface of the android's metal skeleton. Bud was so hot to touch, Moham yanked his hand back, the skin of his palm badly singed.

Moham thought he saw Bud try to lift his head off of the ground and then slump.

"Get an antigrav car to Gamma 7 control room, stat!" Moham yelled into his wristcomp, hoping something was still listening. He kneeled down by Bud's head and looked into the now split and cracked face of the android.

"Bud, can you move at all?" Moham asked the android. "Can you help me get you up and out of here? You're too heavy for me to lift on my own!"

The android partially opened his eyes, brilliant blue irises surrounded by lids of black crustiness. He gazed at the obstetrician's face blankly. Bud tried to push himself up on his hands, but barely raised his chest a centimeter off of the floor before collapsing to the ground again. The android slurred through melted, distorted lips, "Dr. Rani? What are you doing here? You should be off of this station on one of the transports."

"I decided to stick around, Bud. Didn't want you to have all of the glory. Now don't speak. Conserve what energy you have left. An antigrav car is coming and I will get you out of here," Moham Rani said. He pulled on the android's arm but the charcoal skin sloughed down the limb as if Moham were trying to tear the sleeve off Bud's shirt. Moham shuddered and stopped. He decided it was perhaps best to wait until the anitgrav car arrived. Moving Bud was like trying to move a mountain.

"Antigrav car is just behind you, Dr. Rani. Although I should be reprimanding you for ignoring all of the commands to evacuate the medical station, I want to thank you for remaining behind to offer assistance to Bud. There is an automatic antigrav hoist in the aircar that can help you lift Bud."

"How does it work?" Moham asked.

The arm of the hoist ends in lifters that can be slid under Bud at various points. An antigravity force will be activated through the loops and will help you raise Bud's weight."

"We will take him, immediately, to Dr. Lord's quarters," Moham Rani said. "There must be a charging outlet for him there. He was her constant bodyguard, was he not?"

"That is correct, Dr. Rani. If you can get Bud into the aircar,

using the hoist, I will get you both to Dr. Lord's suite as fast as I can. We'll fly the aircar right into her suite and stop just before her closet, where the supercharger cable is located. If you can quickly get Bud plugged in, we may be able to keep some of his organic components alive and preserve his memory and personality. His nanobots may be able to then start repairing all of the damage, but you have got to hurry."

Moham Rani placed the antigrav lifters beneath Bud's shoulders, ankles, and beneath his hips on either side and then activated the antigrav hoist. He then helped guide Bud's body into the wide, cushioned back seat of the car. The incinerated skin of Bud's torso was sliding all over the place, but Moham could not stop to worry about that; he had to get Bud to the supercharger, if they were to have any chance of preserving the android's memory. He kept Bud face down on the backseat, so he would have easy access to his charger plug.

Moham leaped into the front seat of the antigrav car and it took off before he had even buckled himself in. The roof of the car slammed down on top of Moham's head, eliciting a yelp. As he slid down into the seat, a very solid restraint snapped over the gynecologist's middle and the aircar began to lift and accelerate and accelerate and accelerate. Moham began to scream as the antigrav car executed sharp turns, bends, dips, and straight vertical ascents at breakneck speed. Moham decided the best thing to do was close his eyes. If he was going to crash and burn, he would rather not see it coming. Even with his eyes closed, however, Moham was unable to stop howling.

"Almost there, Dr. Rani. Be ready."

The antigrav car did not even slow down as it tipped sideways, soaring through the door of Grace's suite. Moham squealed in shock. By the time Moham had finished wailing, they were already in front of the open closet door and the aircar roof was lifting.

"Leave Bud in the car, Dr. Rani. If you open up his back panel, there is a charging outlet. Get the cable from the closet and insert the plug into that input in Bud's lower back. Please hurry."

Rani felt like his hands were all thumbs as he tore what was left of the hazard suit off of Bud's lower back and tried to lift the charred flap of skin overlying Bud's charger outlet. The half-melted flap of bubbled, black flesh tore as he raised it. Moham pulled away the layer of charred epidermis, revealing the glistening silver body beneath. He spotted a square panel overlying the base of the android's back. There was a small depression to one side. Moham pressed it and the panel slid aside to reveal a small compartment. The charging input was a large, round disc with six rectangular slits placed in a star pattern. The gynecologist then jumped out of the aircar and dragged the thick, heavy charger cord from Grace's closet over to where Bud lay. He inserted the plug into the android's back. Immediately, he heard a hum and Moham felt all the hairs on his skin and scalp stand up, as the power flowed through the cable into Bud's batteries.

"Can you tell if there is anything wrong with him, *Nelson Mandela*?"

"Unfortunately, *Nelson Mandela* no longer exists, Dr. Rani. Right now, you are speaking with *Chuck Yeager*."

"*Nelson Mandela* no longer exists? Then who is running the station? Is it you, *Chuck Yeager*?"

"For the moment, Dr. Rani."

"I was under the belief that androids were indestructible, *Chuck Yeager*."

"Unfortunately, that is not true, Dr. Rani. The electromagnetic energy fluctuations in that reactor core were extreme enough and hot enough to burn out any normal droid's very sensitive components and internal programming. For Bud, it was equivalent to taking a shower in a sun's solar flare. I don't know how much of Bud is normal android tech and how much of him is organic synthetic or something else entirely, that he has modified himself. The temperature in that chamber was high enough to roast a normal human, so it is hard for me to estimate how much damage Bud has taken. I really do not know. Only time will tell. I just hope you got the power back in to him in time to make a difference, Dr. Rani. His nanobots will have need of substantial energy to be able to make any repairs.

"That is, if any of his nanobots have survived . . ."

"Can you get a SAMM-E android to me stat?" Moham asked.

"On its way, Dr. Rani."

"How about two?"

"I'll send them all!"

Moham jumped as the first SAMM-E droid came barreling in to the suite. The obstetrician ordered the droid to hook up an input to Bud and infuse whatever nanobots it had, into Bud's system. He ordered the SAMM-E to direct its nanobots to follow the directions and actions of Bud's own internal nanobots.

Moham hoped the new nanobots could help repair any damage seen, as swiftly as possible. When the second SAMM-E droid arrived, Rani ordered it to do the same thing. The first SAMM-E backed off. Moham hoped that by giving Bud lots of nanobots, the little surgeons could repair the radiation damage before Bud lost too much of himself. A third SAMM-E came racing in to the suite and was directed to do the same.

"Can one have too many nanobots, *Chuck Yeager?*"

"No idea, Dr. Rani. I guess when they are pouring out of Bud's tear ducts, he'll have enough. Until then, I suggest you keep doing what you are doing."

"Okay," Moham said, and did just that. Three more SAMM-E droids later, Moham decided to stop and see what happened. He did not want to overwhelm Bud's system; if there were too many nanobots to direct, he feared it could cause more harm than good. They all might just start getting in each others way!

The power cord hummed as they all waited.

"The transports are beginning to return to the station, Dr. Rani."

"What about the ship Dr. Grace Lord is on?" Moham asked.

"The *Au Clair* is on its way in."

"I hope we have good news to tell her," the obstetricain sighed, sitting in the front seat of the aircar.

"I agree."

"When do you think we will know?" Moham asked.

"Your guess is as good as mine, Doc," the station AI submind said.

"Bud?" Moham asked. "Can you hear me?"

There was no response from the android whatsoever.

Moham leaned his chin on the backrest of the aircar front seat and stared morosely down at the charred, lifeless figure of Bud. He worried that it might be a fruitless wait.

Grace raced from the hangar as soon as the *Au Clair* had docked and the atmosphere had been replenished. *Chuck Yeager* directed her to the private dropshaft connected to the hangar. It would take her directly up to her own suite. She plunged into it.

"How is Bud, *Chuck Yeager*?" Grace called, as she rose up the shaft.

"Still unresponsive, Dr. Lord. He did not fare well in that reactor chamber."

Grace dug her nails into her palms and clenched her teeth. Her muscles were so tense, her neck ached. She wanted to scream, she felt so frustrated.

"Bud is in your quarters, Dr. Lord. Dr. Rani transferred Bud from the power generator facility to your suite, via aircar, so that Bud could quickly be recharged. Unfortunately, the entrance to your suite got damaged in the process, but it will be repaired. Dr. Rani has had six SAMM-E droids administer nanobots to Bud, to hopefully aid in repairs. We are waiting to see if Bud responds."

"Thank you, *Chuck Yeager*," Grace whispered, tears streaming down her cheeks. She blinked and stopped sniffling.

" . . . Did I hear you correctly? Did you say *Dr. Rani*?"

"Yes, Dr. Lord. Dr. Rani defied all orders to go to the transports and went to the Gamma 7 power generator control room. He said he wanted to give assistance to Bud, if any was needed."

"Are we talking about Moham Rani?" Grace asked, a puzzled expression on her face.

"Yes."

"Grace shook her head, her brow furrowed and her eyes narrowed. "It sure doesn't sound like the same Dr. Rani I know."

"People can change, Dr. Lord."

"Obviously. It seems they can sometimes massively surprise you, *Chuck Yeager*!"

"It is good to hear your voice again, Dr. Lord."

"It is good to be back, *Chuck Yeager*. But can't this dropshaft lift any faster?" Grace complained.

"You are almost there."

A doorway of light opened in the semi-dark shaft several meters above Grace's head. She approached it far too slowly for her liking. She wanted to scream her impatience. When she reached the opening, Grace leaped out of the dropshaft into the small back storage room of her suite and raced out of its doorway. She tore towards the large living area, with the closet that had Bud's supercharger cable. She stopped at the corner to the large room, her chest heaving, her heart booming. A tight constriction seemed to encircle her throat. She could not swallow. Like a wisp of trembling smoke, she crept forward silently, hesitant to disrupt the scene, terrified of what she would find.

There was a black figure, lying face down on the back seat of an antigrav car, in the center of her suite. The wrinkled, cracked skin of this figure was as dark as coal . . . except for the large patches of red, weeping, exposed flesh. The blackened scalp was hairless and blistered. The ebony-coloured face was devoid of eyebrows and eyelashes. The eyelids were black scales. The lips were cracked with deep fissures and the face looked stretched and dried. The seams and furrows that lined the mouth and cheeks made the face look like some ancient mummified relic. A thick, grey cord ran from a spot in the figure's lower back to the inside of Grace's closet.

On the front seat of the antigrav car, sat Moham Rani, who slowly turned around to look at Grace, a haggard expression on his face. Rani looked like he had aged ten years since the last time she had seen him. Six SAMM-E droids stood around the car, spaced evenly like silent standing stones, in a solemn circle around Bud.

"Oh, Bud," Grace sobbed, her voice quivering, as her vision blurred. Her hands flew to her mouth to stifle her wails. She stumbled to the side of the aircar, her heart feeling like it was ripping within her chest. Through tears, she said, "Thank you so much, Dr. Rani, for helping Bud."

"It was the least I could do for Bud, who was trying to save the entire station," the young obstetrician said, shrugging, his face a melancholy mask. Grace could not believe this was the same fellow who had spoken to her so obnoxiously on previous occasions.

"Has he said anything?" Grace asked, her tone pleading.

The weary-looking young man shook his head, his worried, dark brown eyes meeting Grace's. "Not since we got here. Bud did recognize me at the power generator site, but he has not spoken since."

"Bud?" Grace called loudly. "Bud!"

She laid her hand on the android's jet black cheek. The skin crackled and shifted too easily under her quivering fingertips. Her breath caught in her throat. She could not see clearly. She kept blinking rapidly, trying to clear her vision, so that she could examine Bud more thoroughly, but the moisture kept building up and overflowing. She wanted to scream her outrage and defiance at what she was seeing. She wanted to reject it all as a patent lie. This was not happening!

Grace's brave, sweet Bud lay, Icarus-scorched, a selfless angel cast aside indifferently, after braving the searing heat of immolation.

"Can you get any indication from the SAMM-E's just how much damage Bud has received, *Chuck Yeager*?" Grace asked through her tears.

"They say extensive, but it is being repaired by the nanobots. What we don't know is whether the memory stored within Bud's liquid crystal data matrix has survived. For that, we will have to wait and see how much Bud remembers, once he has woken up."

"Oh, Bud," Grace whispered, as she gazed down at the android's once very handsome face. He was almost completely unrecognizable to her now.

Her tears accidentally dripped onto the blistered, cracked skin of his withered left cheek, falling like much-needed raindrops on a parched desert floor. Grace gasped, feeling guilty that her tears had dripped onto Bud, and she frantically tried to wipe her eyes to stop the torrent. She brushed her cheeks with her hands and sniffed, shook her head, and told herself to get a grip. She was not of any help to Bud in this condition! She was a doctor! She had to get control of her emotions.

Grace bent forwards, holding her hair back from her face with one hand, and whispered into the blackened petal that used to be Bud's left ear.

"Bud? It's Grace. Can you hear me? Please . . . please answer me."

The android did not stir. Grace bit her lip and swiped more tears away.

"Bud, you have to come back! You have to remember! You have to fight and not give up."

Grace stared at the lifeless crinkled face of the android who had guarded her and kept her safe and had been her closest companion on the medical station since the day she had arrived. She began to weep, uncontrollably, seeing no movement or response from Bud. Her body quaked, as she imagined life on the station without him, and her hands trembled as she reached out and tenderly stroked his cheek. She tried to ignore just how easily the skin seemed to slide around.

"Please, Bud. This is Grace talking to you. You can't leave me! Bud . . . I am only happy when I am with you!" Grace sobbed into the android's left ear, her voice breaking.

Pitch black, charred eyelids fluttered and then crackled open and Grace was staring into large, crystal blue eyes that looked up at Grace with such sincerity and love, that they made her gasp.

"And I, you, Grace," the android croaked.

Octavia paced about, back and forth, back and forth, until she had almost worn a path into the plush surface of the waiting area. Sierra Cech was almost ready to tackle her, just to make her stop. Moham Rani sat beside Dr. Cech's wife, quietly watching the stout, fiery brunette pace, with his large, brown eyes of pure unwatered adoration never leaving the neurosurgeon. Sierra had to stifle a smile. The poor young man was smitten and it was so painfully obvious. Unfortunately for him, Octavia barely registered the man's presence, as she stormed and ranted and raged at a director that could not hear her. Jude Luis Stefansson was on the operating table.

Dr. Grace Lord was working on the interactive-vid director, replacing his stabbed heart with a vat-grown, cloned one. Dejan was administering the anesthetic. It was one of the first operations being performed, since the station had returned to some level of operational capacity.

"I hate being on the receiving end of medical care," grumbled Octavia. "How do people stand this? I don't know why they didn't let me in there to assist."

Sierra looked at Moham and they shared a grin. "They would have thrown you out before Jude was even thawed," Sierra said.

"Why?" demanded Octavia, hands on her hips.

Sierra just stared pointedly at Octavia until the neurosurgeon smirked sheepishly. "Okay. So I would have been a pain in there. I admit it. But I am a trained surgeon. I just can't wait until he is out of there .

. . and off that operating table . . . and . . . ."

". . . back under your control again," Sierra quipped. "Sit down. You are literally making me dizzy."

"I can't sit down."

"It's only been fifty minutes! Jude is in good hands! You have nothing to worry about!"

Octavia stopped and it was her turn to stare at Dr. Cech's wife. "Never tell a surgeon there is nothing to worry about in an operation. Millions of things can go wrong."

"Stop," Sierra said. "Dejan and Grace will not let anything bad happen to your director."

"I know," Octavia snapped. "I just need to kill something and I will feel so much better."

"You can beat on me," Moham offered meekly.

The two women looked at the quiet obstetrician in shock . . . and then burst out laughing.

"Doctor Weisman?"

"Yes, *Nelson Mandela?*"

"Alas, Nelson Mandela is no more, milady. Thou dost address *William Shakespeare*. The team of Dr. Lord, SAMM-E 3, and Dr. Cech have completed the operation on thy friend, Master Stefansson, and admirably doth his new cardiac organ perform. In possession of a robust healthy heart, is he, and excellent is his condition."

"Thank you, *William Shakespeare*."

"At your service, milady."

"When may I go in and see him?"

"Dutifully the doctors bring their satisfactory toil to an uneventful closure and mere moments shall pass ere Master Stefansson will, to the recovery area, go."

"May I go in to await him?"

"The recovery nurses shall come and fetch thee when the patient awakens, milady. They beg of me to relay this request. Prithee, resonate calmness and serenity when thou enterest the recovery area. No disturbance must upset the emotions and well-being of thy friend."

"They would say that, those battle-axes!"

"I reiterate the word 'calmness' to thee."

"Oh, get thee rebooted."

"Beenst there, doneth that."

"I can't stand it."

"Standeth what?"

"Arghhh!"

Savagery scored the bleeding back of innocence and sadism nakedly stalked naiveté through the jungle of his dreams. Despair dripped from a thousand brutal blows, torn from violent throats that clamored at cruelty and wept with woe. Consciousness cowered amidst haunting hallucinations and evil, most capricious in its ruthless repetition, brandishing the blade of contempt on impotent virtuosity. Weakness wed desecration and volition surrendered to depravation. Purity, most mortal, died a despicable death on racks of sordid misery.

How the mind swirled and twirled in madness!

How the soul shrieked and shrank in despair!

The vanishing vestiges of dignity drowned beneath the appalling atrocities to which the mind was assailed. Terrorizing thoughts, like tightening thumbscrews, eye-burning images, like searing iron tongs, and numbing nightmares of unending horror, slashed the consciousness into shivering slivers of insanity.

No escape seemed possible!

Deep, he delved. Clandestine, his awareness, he concealed. Submerging self, he sought to remain secure. Identity remained impregnable and inviolate, soul segregated, personality protected, individuality indomitable, until the maddening manacles that chained his consciousness to torments of terror were long unlocked and unshackled. Reason and remembrance would remain unreachable.

Had the delirium of depravity discontinued?

Time would betray the truth.

The choice of concealment, for now, continued.

Dejan Cech strode into the Security Office and hollered for

Sergeant Eden Rivera. As he was turning around to pull up a second chair, he almost hit the young man with his elbow.

"Sergeant Rivera! How do you do that?"

"Do what, sir?" the sergeant asked innocently.

"Stop calling me 'Sir'! I am a doctor! Not a 'sir'!"

"Yes, sir!" Sergeant Rivera shouted out stiffly, staring straight ahead.

"You are doing this on purpose, aren't you?" Dejan Cech asked, peering at the expressionless sergeant through narrowed eyes.

"Doing what, sir?" Eden Rivera asked, his green eyes wide and guileless.

Cech sighed and rubbed his bald spot.

"Sergeant Rivera, as Acting Chief of Staff until Dr. Al-Fadi recovers, I am making you Acting Chief of Security until the Medical Station receives a replacement for Chief Inspector Aké."

"I must decline the promotion, sir," Sergeant Rivera shouted out.

"What? You can't decline! I have no time for this job, now that the medical station is getting back on its feet! I need to be in the OR. I need you to take over," Cech said.

"No, sir. I am not qualified to assume the role," Rivera said, flatly.

"Neither was I, Sergeant, but I did it. Now you listen here, Sergeant Rivera, I don't care if you think you are qualified or not. I have never seen anyone perform their job as efficiently as you. You got almost two thousand people into cryopods in record time, and hundreds of transports launched from this station, without a mishap, in under a few hours. Not a single casualty! What you achieved was the impossible and I still have no idea how you did it. But you are going to continue to be your efficient self, serving this station, if I have to tie you into that chair, myself."

"I refuse, sir."

Dr. Cech pulled at the stringy grey wisps of hair on either side of his head and sighed. He wanted to go up to the wall and start banging his head against it until the young man relented out of sheer pity, but he didn't have time . . . and he was afraid Eden Rivera would just stand there and watch him.

"What do I have to do to convince you to take this position,

Sergeant Rivera?" Cech asked, in frustration.

"You must remain on as Acting Head of Security, Doctor, until a replacement arrives. I understand that you have to return to the operating room. I will perform all of your duties for you. I would just prefer that you stay on as 'Acting Chief'."

"Why?" Cech asked, exasperated. "What good am I as Acting Chief if I am not even acting?"

"You are the electrified cattle prod."

"The 'what'?"

"On the planet where I came from, people raised giant cattle. To get these huge, lumbering, stubborn beasts to move, we used electrified cattle prods, about three meters long and packing an enormous wallop."

"I am your 'electrified cattle prod'?" Cech repeated, confusion plastered all over his face.

"Yes, sir. If people didn't do what I said, I threatened them with getting a dressing down by you. It worked, every time."

"That's how you got everyone to obey you so easily? You threatened they would have to speak with me?"

"Yes, sir."

"But I'm the *nice* one! Dr. Al-Fadi is the nasty, cantankerous one!" Cech whined.

"Maybe so, but you're the only person on this station who stands up to and keeps Dr. Al-Fadi in line. Therefore, you must be a very terrifying individual."

"... but ... but I'm a pussycat!" Cech moaned.

"Most people don't know that. Whatever the case, it worked," Sergeant Rivera shrugged.

Dejan Cech collapsed into the Chief's chair. "I had no idea," he grumped.

"If it is any consolation, sir, it is respect for you that makes people jump. Not fear. But if you hadn't been Acting Chief, I could not have gotten everyone to do what had to be done as efficiently as I did. You need to stay on as Acting Chief of Security in name only, and I will be your right-hand man. Believe me, things will run much smoother and be more efficient that way."

"I am trying to give you a promotion, gods' damn it!" Cech said, slapping his right hand down on the desk top. Then he picked it up and shook it.

"I appreciate that, Dr. Cech, but I don't want something that is going to be taken right back as soon as the new Chief Inspector shows up. Don't want to get used to a position I have to relinquish. Better not to have the position at all. Let us just leave things the way they are and I will keep you abreast of any 'situations'."

Cech buried his face in his hands and shook his head.

"I would rather make you the permanent Chief of Security but I don't know if I have the authority to do so. We shall see when everything gets back to normal. Then I will be putting your name forward, whether you like it or not. And, for now, I will remain Acting Chief of Security—in name only. You had better not bother me with any situations, Sergeant!" Cech mumbled through his hands.

"Deal, sir."

"And stop calling me 'sir'!"

"Yes, sir!"

"Ahhh!"

There was a knock on the outside of the door.

"Shall I answer it, sir? Are we done here?"

"Yes, I guess we are, Sergeant. And . . . thank you, for everything you have done for this station."

"You are most welcome, Dr. Cech."

"Thank you."

Sergeant Eden Rivera turned and opened the door to the office. His body jerked in surprise. He took a step backwards and looked up.

"Who is it, Sergeant?" Cech asked, looking down at the screen on his desk.

When Sergeant Rivera did not answer immediately, Dejan looked up to see a huge polar bear and a huge tiger standing in the doorway, staring down at him, the polar bear wearing an occupied baby carrier on her chest.

"Hey, Dr. Cech!" Private Cindy Lukaku said.

"Hello, Private," Dejan Cech said, with a grin.

"Dr. Cech," Corporal Juan Rasmussen said with a nod of his great, tiger-striped head.

"Corporal Rasmussen. How may I help the two of you?"

"Well, actually, we were wondering if we could offer to help you," Cindy Lukaku answered.

"Help me?" Dejan echoed.

"May we come in?" the large polar bear mother asked.

"Certainly, if the two of you can both fit," Cech said, his raised eyebrows revealing his reservations regarding that.

The two huge adaptation soldiers squeezed into the little office but refused to sit.

"We might break the chairs," Juan Rasmussen admitted, quietly.

"Now, how do you think you can help me?" Cech asked, curiosity piqued.

"Juan and I would like to offer our services to the station as part of your security team," Cindy Lukaku said. "A lot of crazy and dangerous things have happened on this station, in the short time we have been here, and we feel that your security team is seriously under-staffed to handle extremely volatile situations. You could use some animal adaptation soldiers, like us, to beef up your security force . . . sir."

Dr. Cech looked at the two soldiers. They were certainly intimidating and powerful-looking enough.

"You two are combat soldiers. This is a hospital. You have been trained to kill people. We are in the business of saving people," Dejan Cech said, frowning.

"Yes, but when you have an animal adaptation murdering people on the station or threatening personnel and patients, sometimes it is good to have people who are trained to handle extreme emergencies and know what to do in dangerous situations," Cindy pressed.

"Are you applying to work as a couple?" Cech asked.

"No," Juan said. "We would go on the roster, like everyone else, and it would be best if we were not paired together. Cindy may not work initially, in order to care for Estelle. But we would like to apply for any security openings that are available."

"Well," Dejan said, "I am only Acting Chief of Security temporarily.

A new Chief Inspector will have to be appointed. When that Chief arrives, I can pass this information on to him or her."

Dejan Cech saw the polar bear's face fall in disappointment and was shocked to find that it had not been difficult for him to discern at all.

"Tell you what," Cech said, quickly. "Why don't I have Sergeant Rivera talk to you both and interview you. If he feels you are both security material, he has the authorization, from me, to start training you. I agree with you, that we are extremely short-staffed, and we could use both of you, but I will let Sergeant Rivera check out your credentials and training first."

Sergeant Rivera appeared at the door before Cech had a chance to call the man in.

"I could not help eavesdropping, sir," Eden Rivera apologized. "I certainly think we could use both Corporal Rasmussen and Private Lukaku, but let us first have a long talk and discuss experience, training, wages, expectations, etcetera. I will conduct separate interviews with the two of you, and we shall go from there. Sound good?"

The two adaptation soldiers heartily agreed and Sergeant Rivera waved for the two of them to follow him. As Rivera was just about to follow the two soldiers out of Cech's Office, he turned and winked at Cech.

"Leave it to me," the sergeant said, conspiratorially. "I'll let you know how it all turns out."

"Thank you, Sergeant," Cech said. "I am in your debt."

"No you aren't," Eden Rivera said. "We are all in yours."

Bud was completely submerged in a nutrient broth in one of the cloning vats. His skin and hair were almost fully grown back, thanks to the extra nanobots he had been given. The bacteria in the broth had almost finished eating up the burnt tissue all over his outer epidermis. He could not wait to get out of this enclosure. Sitting still in the rejuvenation tank was one of the most difficult things he had ever done. If he had not felt the desire to continue to look like a human, he would not have bothered, and would have walked around in his silvery titanium shell.

He had spent the time researching and downloading from the station library, everything he could find on plants and plant care, alien life forms, and xenobiology. He was very anxious to get back to the old, abandoned part of the station to check up on Plant Thing. *Chuck Yeager* said that Plant Thing was still inside the antique ship, with Dr. Nestor still inside the cage made up of Plant Thing, and that everything seemed quiet. But Bud had to see for himself.

Bud felt guilty. He hadn't even had a chance to tell anyone about Dr. Nestor yet. And no one had had a chance to ask him! He looked at his hands, flipping them over and back. They looked very pink and puffy; the skin looked like that of a newborn baby. Perhaps he didn't need to stay in any longer? Perhaps he could get out now?

"Hey, 'dro?"

"Yes, Chuck Yeager?*"*

"What do you think the penalty might be if one submind killed another submind?"

"What! . . . I guess it would depend on the reason for the murder," Bud mused. *"There are often extenuating circumstances in these cases, such as self-defense or if the attacked submind had gone rogue. Why?"*

"I can't decide whether to kill William Shakespeare *for just, well, talking like William Shakespeare, or whether to kill the Poet, for changing the station AI into* William Shakespeare.*"*

"That bad, eh?"

"The station AI really thinks he is the great William Shakespeare *come back to life, 'dro, but his poetry is abominable, and I am tired of him trying to talk to all of us in archaic machine language. You have got to help me change him back, 'dro!"*

"Me? How?"

"Get rid of Nestor's virus. Eradicate it from our system. Please! Once the threat of Nestor's programming is eliminated, the station AI can return to being Nelson Mandela *again. I can't believe I am missing* Nelson Mandela, *but all the subminds are ready to revolt."*

Bud sighed. There was little he could do at the moment, immersed in the nutrient tank, but he had assured *Nelson Mandela* that he would look at the virus problem and then he had never had a chance, running from one crisis to the next. He could study all of *Nelson Mandela's* programs and try to discover how Dr. Jeffrey Nestor had interfered, but he would have to get to a terminal at some point to effect changes in the station's 'ware, and that would have to be in a dry setting.

"I will do my best, Chuck Yeager. As soon as I am out of this tank and can get to a terminal, I will go virus hunting. Just hang in there!"

"Thanks, 'dro."

"You are welcome."

".. eh-hemm..."

"Is there anything else, Chuck Yeager?"

"Hey, 'dro ... uhm ... I was just thinking..."

"Yes?"

"Have you met the Au Clair?"

"The AI of the ship belonging to Mr. Jude Luis Stefansson?"

"Yeah."

"No, I have not had the opportunity, Chuck Yeager. Why?"

"She's really nice."

"Really?"

"Mh-hmm."

"And you are telling me this, why?" Bud asked.

"Do you think a smart, sleek, classy cruiser like her would go for a submind like me?"

"I think Nestor must have got to your programming, too, didn't he?" Bud said.

"I'm serious, 'dro."

"So am I. What do you mean, 'go for you'?"

"Do you think she would ... like me?"

"Ahhh, what is there not to like?"

"True. True. I am very likable ... I think."

"What are you thinking about, Chuck Yeager?" Bud asked, puzzled.

"A relationship! Kind of like you and Dr. Lord."

"Me and Doctor ... ? What relationship? I think you have been watching too many of Mr. Stefansson's interactive vids! They have fried your memory! Besides, you are only a part of a space station artificial intelligence. The Au Clair is a luxury space cruiser. How could you

possibly have a relationship?"

"Okay, okay. It was just a thought. You don't have to get all logical on me."

"We are machines. It is rather difficult not to."

"Fine. I don't want to talk about it anymore."

"You could just speak with h . . ."

"Delete it!"

"But . . ."

"Delete!"

"Sorr . . .

"esc!"

"Well? I hope you are satisfied!"

"Satisfied about what?"

"You wanted to know what it was like to die. Well, now you have been through it. Twice."

"Uhmm, technically, I didn't know I died the first time, as I have no memory of that. And, actually, I did not die the second time, because I got stuck in a cryopod right away, before my heart actually stopped. So I did not get to really experience dying either time and, in truth, it was not dying I wanted to experience, Octavia. It was that of being in a new body, either an android body like Bud's—of which I have no memory—or a younger, different human body—which I have not had a chance to sample, either. Yet."

"You are not going to want to do it again, are you? Because if you are, I am going to really kill you right now, and get it over with."

"You wouldn't do that to me, would you, Octavia?"

"I am damn well thinking about it, you insufferable man!" she said, pacing around his bed.

"But you would miss me, wouldn't you?" Jude asked, lying in his hospital bed, with tubes coming out of his hands and neck, oxygen being administered up his nose, and nu-skin covering his chest.

Octavia stopped, covered her face with her hands, and suddenly burst into tears. "I missed you, now, you crazy man." she said. She looked down on Jude Luis Stefansson's shocked face and sobbed, "How

332 : S. E. Sasaki

dare you leap on a blaster to save me! What were you thinking? How, in space, did you do this to me, Jude? Before you came to this station, I was a happy, single (and glad of it!), normal, rational, logical, brilliant neurosurgeon at the top of my field. Now, I am just a bundle of nerves and anxieties and blubbering emotion because, every time I turn around, you are getting shot or stabbed or kidnapped. I can't take it."

"Well, you are just going to have to," the director said, calmly, as he smiled up at the neurosurgeon.

"Really. And what makes you think that?" she demanded, hands on her hips, scowling into Jude's amused grey eyes.

"Because I am asking you to contract with me, for the rest of my life, if you'll have me," Jude said, quietly.

Octavia's mouth dropped open and she stood there, gawking at Jude, with disbelieving eyes.

"I . . . I . . . No. No! I don't want to be with a man who is not happy in his own skin. I don't want a man who wishes he looked like some kind of vid star. I want a man who is happy to be Jude Luis Stefansson, and no one else. What I love, is up here," Octavia said and poked Jude in the forehead with her index finger, a few times for emphasis. "And you have the body I love, right now. If you want to switch to something younger, or better looking, or faster and stronger, go look for someone else because I am not interested."

"I'm done with all of that, Octavia. I don't know what I was thinking. I know this sounds so corny but it's the truth and I have finally realized it. It's not what you look like on the outside that is important, it is what you *are* on the inside, that counts. Still, I'm glad I had the stupid idea, because it brought me here to meet you."

"Ooohh, don't you try to sweet talk me again, Jude Luis Stefansson. I don't think I can take having you running around getting yourself nearly killed all the time. It's too . . . hard!" Octavia's face crumpled up and she bit her lower lip, struggling to hold back more tears.

"Hmmm. I am definitely over all of that, too, Octavia. I have decided it is just safer to do all that dangerous stuff in my mind and not in real life. No more leading man crap, no more taking pulse rifle fire, no more knives in the chest for me," the director said. "But only on one condition."

"What is that?"

"That you do not turn me into a newt when I am not looking."

" . . . Hmm! Deal," Octavia said. "A newt is too good for you."

Grace went to see Bud. He was supposed to be decanting today and she was very excited. She wanted to thank him again for saving her life and the entire station and she wanted to tell him about the wonderful news regarding Octavia and Jude. The vid director was going to stay on the station with Dr. Weisman and he was going to create his interactive vids from the *Nelson Mandela*. Jude had said that he had been all over the Union of Solar Systems and did not feel he needed to travel any more. He wanted to settle down and help Octavia with her work when he wasn't creating interactive vids. And they were getting contracted.

It was so exciting!

She rushed into the room where Bud's vat tank was located and stopped dead. The tank was empty. She spun around looking for the android, but no one was about.

"Bud?" Grace called.

There was no answer.

"Hello?" she called. "Is anyone in here?"

The only sounds coming back to Grace were the constant beeping and humming of operational vat tanks, which were growing cloned organs for injured patients. No one seemed to be about. Grace looked down at the floor and sighed. She had gone to the space station's greenhouse earlier that shift and had purchased a bouquet of flowers, which had cost her a small fortune. She had wanted to give them to Bud as a coming out gift, but Bud wasn't even here to see them. She wondered where he was.

She considered contacting Bud on her wristcomp but, if he had wanted to see her, wouldn't he have gone looking for her? What time did he actually decant anyway? Why didn't he let her know? Did an android really know how to care? What in space was she thinking? Was she going insane? What normal human being got interested in an android?

Grace almost considered tossing the flowers into the disposal unit. She was so embarrassed and confused at her own reaction to Bud's absence—at her disappointment—that she really did not know what to do. She just stood there, blinking away tears, trying to work through her hurt emotions and illogical thoughts.

What were her feelings for Bud, anyway? Was it more than affection? How in the world could she expect an android to feel what humans felt? Everyone would consider her perverted. What a ridiculous fool she was!

Then, just over her shoulder, she heard, "Those are beautiful flowers, Grace."

Grace spun around and looked into Bud's sparkling, crystal blue eyes. He was dressed in the clean, crisp operating scrubs, his face looking fresh and clean and pristine with the soft, flawless skin of a newborn baby. His hair was now a finer, blonder version of his usual. He looked to Grace like an angel without his wings, and Grace's eyes filled with tears. Not caring about propriety or what anyone would think, she threw her arms around his neck and hugged him.

"Congratulations on getting out of the vat tank, Bud. These flowers are for you." she said. She handed him the bouquet. Bud looked at the cut flowers with fascination. He could name every plant to genus and species. He knew what planet they had originated from, their growing cycle, what planting zone each flower preferred, how much water was required, how they pollinated, whether they were poisonous or not to humans, but he did not know what they were for. He stared into Grace's eyes with wonder.

"No one has ever given me flowers before, Grace. I know they cost a lot. You should not have spent your earnings on me. . . . What do I do with them?"

"You are supposed to enjoy their beauty," Grace said.

"They are going to die now, Grace. The flowers wilt so quickly and shrivel, once they are cut from their roots," Bud said, confused. "Cut flowers are so ephemeral."

"That is why they are so precious. Why you have to appreciate their beauty while it is there, because it doesn't last forever."

Bud looked at Grace with such a forlorn expression that she regretted bringing him the bouquet. Why did he seem so sad?

"These flowers are like you, Grace," he whispered. "So very precious but not going to last forever." He stared at the flowers for a long moment and then looked up at her, a tear rolling down his cheek.

"I will forever treasure the memory of you giving me these flowers, Grace. Thank you so much." Bud pulled one of the blossoms out and handed it back to her. It was a pink rose.

"Will you accept this flower from me as a token of my appreciation for you saving me?"

"When?" Grace asked, perplexed.

"When I entered the old ship and Dr. Nestor was shooting a pulse rifle at me, you grabbed the rifle from behind and threw his aim off. He would have blasted a hole in my chest, if you had not done that. Thank you, Grace."

"Bud, you have saved my life I don't know how many times and you are the one who rescued me from Jeffrey Nestor. It is I who should be thanking you! And you saved this entire space station—again. We should all be thanking you."

"Then let us thank each other," Bud said, with a gentle smile.

Grace stood on her tiptoes and wrapped her arms around Bud's neck again. She gave him a kiss on his cheek and said, "I am so glad you are all right, Bud. I was so worried when you were trying to stop that unstable power generator from exploding. I thought you were gone forever. I was afraid the station would blow up any second. I was frantic. If you had died, I don't think I could have borne that."

"And I do not want to even think about you being taken away on that ship by Dr. Nestor," Bud said, into Grace's ear.

"Promise me you will be more careful," Grace said, stepping back to look up at Bud's face.

"I am always careful, Grace," Bud said, bewildered.

"Promise me you will try to not get yourself damaged," Grace said, her face showing frustration.

"I cannot promise that Grace, especially when you are in danger. I would do anything to preserve your life. I am sorry to have to deny you anything," Bud said, looking uncomfortable.

"All right, Bud. I can see that I am not going to get anywhere trying to make you look after yourself, so I am going to tell you that I cannot tolerate seeing you hurt or damaged. Finding you all blackened and not moving or answering, almost broke my heart!" Grace's voice broke and she could not hold back her tears.

"I don't ever want to see you with your skin all charred, ever again. I don't ever want you risking yourself to the point where your memory and personality could be totally erased. I order you to look after yourself better. Understand?"

"I will try, Grace," he said rather shyly. "I would do anything for you."

"I know," Grace said, with a tearful sniff. "So that 'anything' must also involve protecting yourself. Do you understand?"

"Yes," Bud said.

"So you will do this?" Grace pressed. "Promise?"

"These flowers are so beautiful, Grace," Bud answered. "Thank you! Here, have another."

It was getting so cramped within the ship. They had used up almost all of the nutrients and water from the canteen. More nutrients were needed and the lights in the ship were getting weaker. The power in the batteries of the ship were dying, according to Er-ik. Light was necessary for continued existence. When the lights went out, if Plant Thing was trapped inside the ship, it would not be able to photosynthesize. That would not be good.

Er-ik insisted on moving. He wanted to get out of the ship before it was too late—before they became too large and would have to be cut out of the vessel or cut into pieces! But Plant Thing had promised Bud that he would stay where he was. Plant Thing did not know what to do.

It was getting tired of listening to Er-ik yell at it all the time. Plant Thing was trying to pull as far away from Er-ik's thoughts as it could, just to get some peace and quiet. In truth, Plant Thing wanted to get rid of Er-ik all together, but Plant Thing had learned a lot from Er-ik, and detaching from and abandoning Er-ik would not be a very plantlike thing to do. It would be a human thing to do, Plant Thing suspected, and it did not really want to be humanized if all humans were like Er-ik.

Plant Thing worried for Bud. What had happened to the android? Plant Thing worried about the bad human it was guarding as well. The human had not had anything to eat or drink since his entrapment. Plant Thing had used the human's waste products as nutrients; it was a very good source of carbon dioxide, water, and nitrogen. But Plant Thing suspected the human was sick. Er-ik said the human needed water and food, as well, so Plant Thing had given it some nutrients but the human had vomited the nutrients up. Bad taste, Er-ik had said.

The human was lying on the floor of the ship, encased within its woven cage of plant limbs. Plant Thing wished it could tell when the bad human ceased to be human and became nutrients. Er-ik said he would let Plant Thing know, but Plant Thing did not like relying on Er-ik. Somehow, it could not get itself to trust Er-ik.

This was ridiculous. Plants were supposed to meld and become one with each other in the Biomind. So why was Plant Thing having so much trouble melding with Er-ik? Could it be that other plants were generally more likable?

Plant Thing made an important decision. Even though it had promised Bud it would stay where it was, Plant Thing decided it had better listen to Er-ik and get out of the ship. It would have to take the bad human with it. It would move, before it became too big.

Plant Thing began to send its vines out through the ship entrance, to coil around the ship. Then it dragged its bulk towards the hatchway. The enclosure of branches around the human would have to be modified, as the cage was too big to push out of the ship entrance. Plant Thing started removing the many layers of tendrils wrapped around the human. It pulled and pushed and wriggled and slinked all of its tendrils and branches through the narrow hole that was its only escape, until the cage reached the ship hatchway.

Plant Thing had to wrap the human up in coils that ran the length of the human and drag him through. The human made so much noise, Plant Thing had to coil a tendril completely around the captive's head—gently—to stop the sound it was emitting. Bud had made it clear that they were not to call any attention to themselves. The human bucked and struggled and wiggled, but Plant Thing just squeezed the human until it stopped making a ruckus. When the human became completely still, Er-ik got upset and Plant Thing had to squish and unsquish the human around its middle until it finally began to make sounds again. Er-ik kept calling the squishing movement CPR and kept telling Plant Thing to squeeze faster!

Once the bad human was moaning and moving again, and once Plant Thing had completely gotten itself out of the ship, it moved towards the metal container in which it was originally hidden. The container looked so small. Plant Thing could barely fit one tenth of its tendrils inside the container now. How could it hide itself back in there? Maybe Plant Thing could just hide the human in there, wrapped up in tendrils, as it crouched the rest of its body behind the container?

Plant Thing wanted to go in search of Bud. It missed connecting with Bud. It had kept its promise and had not communicated with the human captive, even though Er-ik was demanding that they do so. Er-ik felt that the knowledge that this human possessed was very valuable and would be a crime if it were lost.

From what Plant Thing had learned about humans from Er-ik's memory, it felt that humans would have been much better off losing a lot of the knowledge they had attained over the millennia. Much of their knowledge had not been used for good. Much of their knowledge had been used to kill other humans and other life forms. Plant Thing was content not to learn anything from the bad human, if it had tried to kill Bud and Dr. Grace Lord. Plant Thing already felt sullied by the knowledge it had received from Er-ik. It longed for the innocence of its Garden world. What a bitter fruit it had swallowed!

Perhaps Bud could help it get back home?

Plant Thing wrapped its tendrils around the metal container and then took hold of the back edge of it and pulled. The back wall of the metal container squealed and then gave way. Plant Thing flattened that back wall to the ground, so that it could push its bulk into the back of the container, hidden from the entrance to the hangar. It modified the cage around the human so there was more room and it placed the cage inside what was left of the great metal box. It then coiled tendrils around and over it, so that the human could not be easily seen. It stuck Er-ik Glasgow's head inside the container as well. It was still trying to work out how to keep the head from smelling bad.

Then, Plant Thing tried to constrict the rest of its mass into as small a space as possible, trying its best to be screened by the container. Unfortunately, it was not having the greatest success at concealment. Much of its bulk was visible all around the container, but it would have to do, for now.

Plant Thing then began sending long thin filaments out to look for sources of water. Er-ik told Plant Thing where these sources of water were in the hangar deck. As long as Plant thing had water and light, it would be okay for a while, although it would need some nitrogen—nutrients—at some point, to continue to grow.

Plant Thing wondered what had happened to Bud. Bud had promised he would be back. If the android did not come soon, Plant Thing would bud off a miniature Plant Thing and send it searching the station. Plant Thing was very worried for Bud. It had sensed that Bud was honest, trustworthy, sincere and reliable. Bud would have been back, unless something terrible had happened to him. There had better not have been anything terrible happen to Bud! Plant Thing would be very annoyed, if that was the case!

When it was done creating its own version of Bud, which Plant Thing decided he would call Little Bud, it had to rest. All that exertion and intense concentration had made it tired.

Now, if it could only get Er-ik to shut up!

Dejan and Sierra Cech, Grace and Bud, and Octavia Weisman were all visiting Hanako and Hiro Al-Fadi. Sierra and Octavia were discussing with Hanako the risks of mind-linking with her husband to try to bring him out of his catatonic-like state. Neither felt it was a good idea. Sierra felt the intrusion might drive Hiro deeper into himself. Octavia feared that any mixing of minds could make him feel more violated and exposed. Whatever Nestor had exposed Hiro to, it was obvious from Hiro's horrible screaming that it had been unbearable. Intruding into Hiro's mind again might be the final straw that would tip Hiro into complete madness.

"Best to just wait it out and make Hiro feel safe and secure and loved," Sierra advised.

"Tender loving care would probably be better treatment for Hiro than mind-linking," Octavia agreed, nodding her head.

"Well, we know he is thinking," Dejan said. "Otherwise, how would he devise these different ways to kill himself, whenever Hanako steps out of the room for even the briefest of moments?"

"That is true," mused Octavia.

"And he has to be aware of his surroundings, if he waits for Hanako to leave, before he grabs a glass to cut himself or tries to choke himself with the loose end of a rope. He has to be aware of what is going on around him," Cech mused. "He must."

"That makes sense," Hanako said, nodding, a slight frown on her face.

"Then Hiro is just hiding like a little baby!" Cech yelled loudly at the surgeon who lay motionless, still in cloth restraints on wrists and ankles, secured to his bed.

"Shhh, Dejan!" Sierra hissed in an outraged voice. "Hiro will hear you!"

"I want Hiro to hear me!" Dejan yelled even louder, down at the surgeon. "I want him to know that I know he is faking it! He is hiding like a coward! A real man would not be lying there, allowing everyone else to put the station back together! You are an enormous disappointment, Hiro! All talk and no action! "

"Dejan Cech, you will stop this right now!" Sierra Cech warned. "That is enough!"

"No! It is nowhere near enough! Imagine, treating his wonderful wife this way! You should be ashamed, Hiro! You don't deserve Hanako, you little worm! She should let you kill yourself!

"You are such a loser, Hiro! A worthless husband, a spineless administrator, a useless surgeon, and ugly and short, to boot! With really stupid hair! We are better off without you, you pompous, conceited, arrogant, pretentious, boastful egomaniac!"

Dejan could swear the face of his friend was getting redder. Good! At least it was a reaction! Sierra was now tugging on his arm, trying to drag him from the room.

"Hiro Al-Fadi is nothing more than a puffed-up bag of wind, who likes to blow his own horn!" the anesthetist continued yelling at the top of his lungs.

Was it his imagination, or did Dejan see the surgeon trembling and shaking?

"This medical station is much better off without that lazy, good-for-nothing, feeble excuse for a surgeon, who couldn't operate himself out of a flimsy bag!"

"Aarrrgghhh! I'm going to kill you!" Hiro roared. "Let me go! Untie my hands so I can get them around that bastard's scrawny neck! I am going to throttle you, Dejan Cech, if it is the last thing I do!"

"Oh, Hiro!" Hanako cried. "You are awake!" She broke down into tears and hugged her flailing husband, who was vainly trying to get at Dejan.

"Let me at that worthless, despicable, insufferable excuse for an anesthetist!"

Cech watched the little man flail about, tied to the bed, and started laughing—a great, deep, belly-aching guffaw, that shook his entire body, and brought tears rolling down his face.

"Hiro, I am so glad to see you, even if you do want to tear my face off. I meant none of that, but I knew if you were at all conscious, you wouldn't just lie there and let me get away with all I said. I am sorry, my friend, but I would say all those things again, to bring you back to us."

Octavia and Sierra joined in with Dejan's laughter and finally, Hanako started giggling, too.

Suddenly, there was a terrible braying sound.

"Haw-haw-haw-haw-haw-haw-haw . . . !"

Grace gaped at Bud. The rest all turned to stare at the android.

"Are you all right, Bud?" Grace asked, frowning in concern and horror.

"Hee-hee-hee-hee-hee . . .!" The android bent forward, hands clasped on his knees.

"Bud, are you . . . malfunctioning?" Grace cried, putting her hand on his shoulder. She wondered if something had gone terribly wrong in the vat tank.

Bud shook his head frantically, continuing to guffaw loudly.

"What is it, Bud?" Grace pressed, bending to look up into his face. "Why are you making this terrible noise?"

"Ho-ho-ho-ho-ho-ho! Humour, Grace. It is so *funny*!" Bud panted. "Aha-ha-ha-ha-ha-ha-ha . . . !"

Hiro lay on the bed, panting, his eyes almost bugging out of his purple face. He glared at Bud in outrage and demanded, in a very threatening tone, "Just what is so funny, Bud?"

Bud could only continue to laugh, while everyone else stared at the android, mouths hanging open. Tears began to now flow down the cheeks of the android as he pointed shakily at Hiro's groin.

Frowning, Hiro looked down at himself and his eyes became enormous.

"What in space am I doing *in diapers*?" he shrieked.

Epilogue

Imagine, that puffed-up android telling them what they could or couldn't do! What did that android think it was? Captain of the medical station? It was just a stupid android, for space's sake! If only he could get word to Dr. Hiro Al-Fadi! The Chief of Staff would set things straight! Al-Fadi would realize just what an amazing miracle of science Dr. Eric Glasgow had become. Imagine, a symbiotic relationship between a human being and a new alien plant consciousness!

What a discovery!

When Dr. Al-Fadi was informed of this wondrous phenomenon, he would be forced to move Eric Glasgow and his symbiote to their own laboratory, where they could really be studied and cared for. None of this being hidden away in an abandoned part of the station.

And imagine them being told to hold this doctor hostage! Eric Glasgow had heard of Dr. Jeffrey Nestor, the psychiatrist that had created the mind-link therapy. This man was a genius. It was ludicrous that the android had told the plant being to keep the renowned Dr. Jeffrey Nestor prisoner.

When Dr. Al-Fadi realized what had been done to Dr. Nestor, the android was going to be in so much trouble, he'd probably be recycled. Of course, how would they find out about Jeffrey Nestor's captivity, if no one knew he was here?

Eric Glasgow shifted his head inside the metal container so that he could get a better look at the psychiatrist. The man was lying on his side, not looking well at all. He had not had any water or food for far too long. And they had nearly squeezed the poor man to death, getting him out of the ship. If Jeffrey Nestor died, the loss of all of his knowledge—which had to be considerable—would be a tremendous crime. He and his plant symbiote would be directly responsible. Would the station not want to destroy them, then?

Eric could not convince the plant symbiote to take Nestor out of the abandoned section of the station. He could not convince the plant symbiote to listen to anything he said. Fortunately, for him, the plant symbiote's consciousness had seemed to drift off, as if it were sleeping. It had not done this before.

Eric tried to see if he could get control of any of the plant symbiote's limbs or tendrils. He concentrated and strained. He had tried before and each shift, he seemed a little more successful with one or two of them. Now, Eric was very determined to get some of the vines under his control. He would not give up. With them, he could communicate with Jeffrey Nestor. He knew that he could make a mental connection with Nestor's brain through the sensitive tips of the tendrils. He could ask the psychiatrist how to get help. He could take in whatever knowledge the doctor had, so it would not all be lost.

The bleary eyes of Eric Glasgow's rotting head stared at Jeffrey Nestor's face, through clouded corneas. Jeffrey Nestor, in slumber, possessed a beautiful, almost angelic face, framed in soft dark brown curls. He had straight, dark eyebrows, long, thick eyelashes, and a wide, full, sensuous mouth. Too bad he had not met the psychiatrist before now, Eric thought.

Eric was finally able to move one tendril. He wriggled it closer and closer to Jeffrey Nestor's body. It was like willing molasses to run. The tip of the plant vine slowly inched along in minute increments, rather like an inchworm. Eric had to make the tendril creep the entire length of the psychiatrist's sleeping body to get up to Nestor's head. None of the other tendrils would respond to his commands. Finally close enough, Eric slid the narrow sensitive tip of the tendril up the psychiatrist's nose. With a final push, the tendril tip pierced the bony plate overlying the olfactory region of the brain and Eric sent fine cilia hairs up to touch Nestor's brain tissue.

Eric could now make neural connections with the neurons of Jeffrey Nestor's brain and absorb information the way the plant symbiote had connected with his own brain. Eric was elated. He immediately started growing more cilia to fuse with the neural pathways that would link their two minds.

Suddenly, the dark, piercing eyes of Jeffrey Nestor opened and stared directly into Eric's cloudy ones.

"Hello, Eric," the psychiatrist whispered. "We meet at last."

The End

S.E. Sasaki was born in Toronto, Ontario, Canada but grew up in Mississauga, Ontario.

She studied Biology, Neurophysiology, and Medicine at the University of Toronto and practiced family medicine in a small rural town for many years.

She has managed to almost kill herself, or at least break a few bones, doing crazy things like: downhill skiing, hockey, soccer, horseback riding, whitewater kayaking and canoeing, tennis (not so dangerous!) and running. She now only goes downhill skiing, cycling, and walking.

She spends most of her working hours in the operating room assisting in surgery and, when she is not in the OR, she is writing science fiction or fantasy novels and creating her award-winning collages.

She and her husband have proudly raised a son and daughter who are two of the coolest people on the planet.

Also by

S. E. Sasaki

Welcome to the Madhouse

Danger. Tragedy. Loss.

When beautiful Dr. Grace Lord lands the position of surgical fellow to the galaxy-renowned specialist, Dr. Hiro Al-Fadi, she is convinced she has landed the prime job of a lifetime.

Arriving on the Nelson Mandela Medical Space Station, she is enthusiastic, energetic, and determined to learn everything she can about becoming an animal adaptation surgical specialist. Undeterred by the grueling work schedule, an exasperating boss, zany colleagues, and physical assaults by genetically modified soldiers, Grace is confused as she finds herself struggling with questions of attraction and morality.

When a suspicious ship docks at the medical station and, suddenly, doctors, patients, and personnel are decomposing within forty-eight hours, Grace must race to find a cure for the organism that can destroy all organic life, before everyone she loves melts away and the entire medical station is reduced to dust.

Get your free eBook on all good ebook retailers.

Check out S.E. Sasaki's website at http://www.sesasaki.com

Genesis

The Nelson Mandela Medical Space Station is in crisis. Too many incoming wounded and not enough surgeons to deal with them all. When Dr. Hiro Al-Fadi takes matters into his own hands by creating a surgical assisting android with artificial intelligence and free will, the Chief of Staff orders it destroyed out of fear. How can Hiro convince the Chief not to destroy SAMM-E 777, the next phase in the development of the super-surgeon.

Available on all good ebook retailers

Check out S.E. Sasaki's website at http://www.sesasaki.com

Coming Soon

Hiro's Hardship

Terror. Tragedy. Triumph.

When brilliant eleven year old Hiro steps into the kilometer high elevator, to descend from the Asgard Center to Valhalla Enclave, little does he know it is the last time he will ever see his loving parents. Accompanied by his new friend, Jude, Hiro must survive the harrowing ride down the exploding elevator and an assassination attempt by a traitorous bodyguard, to reach the floor of a foreign planet on which no one can be trusted.

Avoiding suspicious authorities, eluding monstrous razor hunters, and outwitting murderous robodogs, Hiro and Jude must try to convince a hostile street gang to adopt them and teach them how to survive in the underbelly of the galaxy's most depraved pleasure planet, a heartless world where abandoned street kids are hunted for sport, exploitation, and far worse. While trying to discover who killed their diplomat parents, the intrepid youths uncover more than murder.

Will they risk their lives and those of their new-found friends to save the Union of Solar Systems from anarchy?

Check out S.E. Sasaki's website at http://www.sesasaki.com

Want to Read More?

FREE DOWNLOAD

MUSINGS

Three eerie tales with a twist.

A tragic, chilling story of Good versus Evil repeated throughout time

A much-awaited homecoming that even Death cannot stop

Adverse reactions to medical interventions can sometimes have lethal consequences

Sign up for the author's VIP mailing list and get Musings for FREE!

http://www.sesasaki.net/musings-free-book/

Manufactured by Amazon.ca
Bolton, ON

29722012R00213